BLOOD OATH

Warrior's Path Book 1

MALCOLM ARCHIBALD

For Cathy

❧ I ❧
PLEDGING

1

DRUMMOSSIE MOOR, SCOTLAND, APRIL 16TH 1746

Sleet slashed into the face of Hughie MacKim, stinging his eyes and forcing him to bow his head as he ran. Reared in the hills, he ignored the rough heather that scraped against his bare feet and calves, leapt across the overflowing burns and splashed through the patches of bog. High above, a pair of questing oystercatchers piped as they flew arrow-straight, beneath the ominous dark clouds.

"Ewan! Wait for me!" Hughie shouted as his brother stretched his lead.

"No!" Ewan, five years older and six inches taller, shook his head. "You heard the tacksman as well as I did. If I don't join the clan today, he'll evict our parents and burn the roof above their heads."

"I can't keep up."

"You're too young, Hughie. You should have stayed at home."

"But I want to fight as well. I want to be a man." Hughie lifted his head when he heard the deep rumble ahead. "Can you hear that noise?"

"Yes. I don't know what it is. It's not thunder," Ewan said.

Hughie could see flashes reflected on the brooding clouds, followed by that heavy crashing and an acrid smell that he did not recognise. He shivered, feeling that something was very wrong, and ran on, trying to stretch his legs to match his brother's stride.

"That's gunfire." Ewan's Gaelic words seeming to echo in the damp air. "I know it is. They've started the battle without me. I have to go." Ewan stopped and held Hughie by the shoulders. "You're only ten years old. You're too young to fight. Go home!" Ewan looked behind him as gunfire crashed out again. "I have to go." Giving Hughie's shoulders a final squeeze, Ewan turned, checked the dirk which was his only weapon, and ran toward the gunfire.

"Ewan!" Hughie raised his voice to a high-pitched scream, "Don't leave me, Ewan!" But Ewan only ran faster. Nearly sobbing, Hughie followed towards the sound of the guns with Ewan fast disappearing across the damp brown heather. Cresting a small rise, Hughie stopped as the whole extent of Drummossie Moor unfolded before him.

"Ewan," he said. "Oh, Ewan, where are you?"

Half a mile in front of Hughie, Prince Charles Edward Stuart had arrayed his Jacobite army in tartan-clad regiments, each under a flapping clan banner. Opposite, across a stretch of the sleet-swept moor and arrayed in disciplined blocks of scarlet and black, the Hanoverian army of King George II waited. Between the regimental blocks, black-snouted cannon spouted flame, smoke and hate toward the Jacobites, while on the flanks, Campbell militia and troops of cavalry waited to pounce. From where he stood, Hughie could see that the government army was much larger than the Jacobites' force, whose few cannon soon gave up what was an unequal contest.

Undecided what to do, Jamie watched for a few moments as the Hanoverian cannon pounded the Jacobites, tearing great holes in the clan regiments who stood in growing frustration, swaying under the punishment. After a while, one section of the Jacobites streamed forward, covering the boggy moorland in great bounds. Even at that distance, Jamie could see that there

4

were only a few hundred men in the attack, against eight or nine thousand disciplined professional soldiers.

The Hanoverians responded with volley after volley of musketry which ripped into the advancing Jacobites. Hughie saw men fall in droves, with the cannon altering from roundshot to grapeshot that scythed into the attackers, mowing them down.

"No!" Hughie shook his head, holding out a hand as if he could stop the slaughter. For an instant, powder-smoke obscured much of his view, but the swirling wind shifted away the white curtain, so Hughie saw hundreds of Jacobites lying still or writhing in agony on the bloody heather.

"Ewan! Ewan, take care," Hughie said. "Please take care."

Fascinated despite his anxiety, Hughie watched as the ragged remains of the Jacobite charge crashed into the Hanoverian ranks. Sunlight flashed on the steel blades of broadsword and bayonet as the two sides clashed, then the front ranks of the redcoats splintered and the Jacobites thrust through the gaps. For a moment, Jamie thought that the few hundred tartan-clad men could rout the entire Hanoverian force, but then the second redcoat line met the ragged charge with volleys of musketry.

Scores of Jacobites died there, with the remainder falling on the bayonets of the second Hanoverian line. With the attack failing in bloody slaughter, a battered Highland handful withdrew, and the Hanoverians marched forward.

"Ewan." Hughie whispered the word. Amidst the confusion and powder smoke, he could not make out individuals. All he could see was a mess of tartan-clad bodies amidst swirls of grey-white smoke, and the advancing infantry butchering anyone they thought was still alive. In front of the redcoats, the Jacobites were in slow retreat, some firing muskets at the Hanoverian infantry and the cavalry that harassed their flanks, slashing at the writhing wounded.

"Ewan. I must find Ewan." The defeat of the Jacobites meant nothing to Hughie; in common with the majority of men who wore the tartan, he did not care which king placed a crown on his head. Hughie only followed his brother, as Ewan had obeyed his chief on peril of eviction. One king was much like another and Hughie already knew that none would spare him as much as a glance, however wet the day or wild the weather.

As the armies passed, Hughie lay amidst the heather, too small to be noticed. He saw the remnants of the Fraser clan regiment run past him, but as Ewan was not there, Hughie knew that he must still be on the field. Hughie lay for what seemed a long time, listening to the moans from the wounded and high laughter from the victorious Hanoverians. Peering through the heather fronds, he saw red-coated soldiers moving among the Jacobite casualties, robbing the dead and bayonetting the wounded.

"Ewan," Hughie said. "Please, God, don't let the redcoats kill Ewan."

Unable to lie still any longer, Hughie rose and, moving in a half-crouch, returned to the scene of the battle.

Trying to avert his eyes from the terrible sights of mutilated men, Hughie searched for the Fraser clan. They had been in the very centre of the front line, so would have been among the Jacobites who broke the Hanoverian ranks. Recognising some of the casualties, Hughie found a trail of twisted bodies leading towards the old Hanoverian front line. He shuddered at the sight of one of the wounded men who lay trying to hold his intestines in place. Unable to help, Hughie could not face the desperate plea in the man's eyes.

"Ewan," Hughie called softly, through the agonised moans of broken men. "Ewan." He slipped in a pool of congealing blood, held back his nausea and continued to search. The dead lay thick in front of the Hanoverian cannon, men with heads or limbs missing, men with their insides torn out, men so disfigured that Hughie could barely recognise them as human. He paddled through the blood-polluted mud, not bothering to hide his tears as the sleet still sliced into his face.

Ewan lay in the middle of a pile of bodies, one hand

outstretched, the other holding his dirk. He was moaning softly, fighting for every breath.

"Ewan!" Hughie bent over him, his heart racing. "I'll help you."

It took all Hughie's strength and courage even to touch the bloodied bodies that partly concealed Ewan. One by one, he pushed or dragged them aside, men he had known as neighbours or friends, now shattered things with splintered bones and pain-ravaged features. At last, Hughie reached Ewan and felt a spark of hope as his brother looked up.

"Can you walk?" Hughie asked.

"I don't know." Ewan tried to rise, gasped and shook his head. "No! No! My leg's hurt," he said. "You'll have to help me."

Hughie looked at Ewan's legs, shuddered and looked away. Either a musket ball or a piece of grapeshot had shattered Ewan's left shin so the bone thrust through a mass of congealed blood and muscle. "We'll get you home." Hughie swallowed nausea that rose in his throat. "Mother will fix that." Bending over, he placed a supporting arm around Ewan's shoulder. "Come on, Ewan, you can't stay here. The redcoats will find you." Hughie knew what the redcoats were like; they were the demons that haunted nightmares, monsters that laughed as they spitted children on the points of bayonets and maltreated women of any age or condition.

Ewan screamed as Hughie tried to lift him, with his weight pulling both boys down to the heather. He yelled again as his shattered leg dragged on the ground.

"No, I can't stand," Ewan sobbed, shaking his head frantically. "Leave me here. Run home and get help."

"But that will take hours." Hughie fought his growing panic. "There must be somebody here." He heard the drift of voices and looked up.

The men emerged from a bank of mist. Clad in Hanoverian scarlet, they were tall, with the mitre caps of grenadiers making them even taller. They spoke English, a language that neither Hughie nor Ewan understood.

"Keep quiet," Ewan hissed. "Lie down and pretend you are dead."

Raised on stories of the brutality of redcoats, Hughie slid to the ground, terribly aware of the thundering of his heart. He heard Ewan whimpering beside him, followed by footsteps thudding on the ground and closed his eyes tightly, feigning death.

The voices came closer, harsh, arrogant and unpleasantly guttural. Hughie could not restrain his gasp as a hard hand closed on his shoulder and hoisted him to his feet. He opened his eyes, staring into the bloodshot eyes of a Hanoverian soldier. The man's breath stank of tobacco and alcohol.

Two other soldiers crowded around, laughing, poking at Hughie with calloused fingers, speaking about him with words he did not understand. A fourth man, even larger than the others, stood a little apart with his mitre hat pulled forward over his face, shadowing his features. Gunpowder had stained the buff facings of their scarlet coats; one had blood spattered over his face and hands; all were mud-stained.

"Leave me alone!" Hughie tried to push the soldiers away. They laughed all the harder, surrounded him and shoved him from one to the other, enjoying the fun of tormenting a child.

"Leave him!" Ewan shouted. "If I had both legs I would show you the way to Hell." Lifting his dirk, he slashed sideways in impotent rage.

While the first soldier retained his hold on Hughie, the others retreated from Ewan's desperate lunges until they realised he was too severely wounded to stand. After that, they returned to their jeers, taunting Ewan.

"Leave him! He's hurt!" Hughie kicked out, catching the man who held him on the leg. Without hesitation, the soldier retaliated with a savage backhanded slap that stunned Hughie into silence.

Drawing their seventeen-inch long bayonets, the soldiers

circled Ewan, stabbing at him. When one pinioned Ewan's hand to the ground, another kicked away the dirk, laughing. Hughie could only watch as three soldiers surrounded Ewan and began to kick at his shattered leg. Ewan screamed, writhing.

"Leave him," Hughie pleaded. "Please leave him alone. He's hurt!"

Tiring of their sport, the Grenadier with the shaded face lit a length of fuse and held it high. He said something that made the other soldiers laugh, and pressed the spluttering fuse to the edge of Ewan's *philabeg*, his short kilt. Stepping back, the Grenadier grunted as Ewan's kilt began to smoulder. When he saw Hughie watching, he pushed his hat even lower over his face. His uniform was different from the others, with a white lace cord over his right shoulder marking him as a corporal. He laughed as the flames spread across Ewan's kilt, causing the wounded boy to squirm and cry out.

"Ewan!" Yelling, Hughie began to struggle again, much to the delight of the soldiers. They held him tight as Ewan writhed, screaming when the flames took hold.

"Ewan! You're burning him! Put the flames out. Please put the fire out!" Frantic in his agony for his brother, Hughie turned and twisted in the soldiers' grasp, kicking out at them, trying to push them away. However, a ten-year-old boy cannot defeat three trained Grenadiers. The fourth thrust his halberd – a seven-foot-long pole surmounted by a bladed, spiked head – into the small of Ewan's back, pinning him down as the flames spread over Ewan's writhing body. Ewan's skin blackened and blistered as Hughie recoiled from the nauseous smell.

Hughie never knew how long it took Ewan to die. He was sick long before the end, retching and gasping as his brother burned slowly in front of his eyes. When it was finally over, and the blackened, twisted, smoking thing that had been Ewan lay in peace on the damp heather, Hughie looked at the soldiers who held him. "I'm going to kill you," he said through his tears. "I am going to kill all of you, somehow."

The four soldiers laughed louder, unable to understand his Gaelic but recognising his words as a threat. Hughie looked at each face in turn, stamping them on his memory. As they were Grenadiers, they were the elite of the army, the tallest, broadest and most aggressive. The man who held him was dark-haired, with his nose broken and twisted to the side. The man who had thrust his bayonet through Ewan's hand had a seemingly permanent sneer lifting the left corner of his mouth. His companion was gaunt-faced, with nervous eyes that darted from side to side and a quick, short laugh. The fourth, the corporal with the hidden face who had set fire to Ewan, was the largest, yet quietest of them all.

"What will we do with this?" Broken-nose lifted Hughie high, so the boy kicked and squirmed.

"Throw it on the fire," the sneering man said.

"Cut its belly open, Hayes," the nervous man suggested and laughed high-pitched. "Go on, gut him like a pig!"

Hayes. Hugh caught the name through the torrent of unfamiliar words. *The man holding me is called Hayes.*

"What do you say, corporal?" Broken-nose Hayes shook Hughie and lifted him even higher.

Already strained by his gyrations, Hughie's shirt ripped further. Before the corporal could reply, Hughie slipped out of the remaining rags and fell to the ground. He landed with a soft thump, rolled and was on his feet and running before Hayes could react.

Hughie heard somebody call out, "After him, Ligonier's!" and the sound of heavy feet behind him. *Hayes and Ligonier's.* He repeated the names as he jinked through the dead bodies and clumps of heather. *Hayes and Ligonier's. One of the Grenadiers is called Hayes, and Ligonier's must be the name of the regiment.*

Light on his feet and running for his life, Hughie jumped from shrub to shrub across the boggy ground. Older, heavier and burdened with muskets, the Grenadiers blundered in Hughie's wake. After a few moments, the footsteps following Hughie slowed to a halt, but he continued for another five minutes before he dared to stop. Resting against a tree, gasping, with the breath burning his throat and lungs, he looked fearfully behind him.

Hughie saw Hayes staring at him, eyes poisonous. When the Grenadier slowly lifted his musket to his shoulder, Hughie gave a little whimper and ran on, sobbing, with his feet blundering over the rough ground. His world had changed forever, and the images of his brother's terrible death dominated his mind.

GLEN CAILLEACH, SCOTTISH
HIGHLANDS, APRIL 1746

"I'm going to kill them, Mother," Hughie said.

"Yes, you are," Mary MacKim agreed. "You will kill them when you are ready. At present, you're only ten years old, and they are full men and trained soldiers. I've lost one son. I don't wish to lose another so soon." She leaned closer to him. "You must avenge your brother, Hugh, but not until you are older."

"I'll join the army." Hughie fought the tears that threatened to unman him once more. "I'll be a trained soldier, too."

"Not yet," Mary MacKim said. "You're far too young. By the time you are old enough, you'll see that I am right. When the time is right, Hughie, you will learn how to fight the way the redcoats fight, and you will find the monsters who murdered Ewan."

Hughie knew he could not argue with his mother. He shook his head. "I did not know what they were saying. I want to learn to speak English."

"Then that is what you shall do, Hugh Beg MacKim. You will learn English and the ways of the red soldiers. I will find you a tutor who will teach you to read, write and even think in English as they do, and who will also teach you French, the language of the educated class. I put the duty of learning upon you, Hugh. To die in battle is honourable and proper. To be murdered when lying wounded is not. Your life must be to find these brutes of red soldiers, Hugh, and kill them."

Shocked by the sights he had seen and the sounds he had heard, Hughie looked up into the unrelenting eyes of his mother. "Yes, Mother."

"You must promise me, Hugh." Mary MacKim produced a Bible. Ancient, leather- covered and brass-bound, it had been in the family for generations, with the names of two score MacKims neatly inscribed in the fly-leaf. "You must swear on the Holy Book that you will avenge your brother."

For a moment, Hughie stared at his mother, and then he placed both hands on the Bible. "I promise you, Mother." The leather was cool to his touch, worn smooth by the fingers of Hughie's ancestors. "I swear on the Bible that I will avenge Ewan, my brother."

As he spoke, Hughie felt a thrill run through him. His words were not merely rhetorical. He had sworn by the family Bible, so generations of his people were witnesses to his oath. In Hugh's mind, his father and grandfather and all his relatives back through the centuries were watching him and would continue to watch him until he had fulfilled his oath. If he broke his word, they would know and disapprove.

Mary MacKim took the Bible from Hughie, opened the Book, placed her hand inside and said: "If you fail in your task, may your children and your children's children, and their children's children, follow your path until we have cleansed the debt." She handed the Bible over. "Swear it, Hugh Beg MacKim. Swear your oath."

Holding the Bible, Hugh said, "If I fail in my duty, I will pass over the task to my children, and their children, until the debt is cleansed." *But that will not happen*, he told himself. *I have sworn a blood oath.*

"Good." Mary MacKim closed the Book with a nod of satisfaction. "Now we can prepare you for the task ahead."

❀

HUGHIE LIVED IN THE CLACHAN OF ACHTRIACHAN, SET APART from the main Glen Cailleach, with a small burn running a few paces below and the summer shielings high in the hills beyond. Above them, the guardian hill of An Cailleach, The Witch, brooded over Achtriachan. Hughie was beside the rowan tree at the door of his cottage as the soldiers came to the glen, and watched the smoke curl as they fired the clachans one by one.

"They'll come here soon," Hughie said.

"They will," Mary agreed.

"Will we fight them?" Hughie lifted a flail, the only weapon Achtriachan had.

"We will not. We will not fight the soldiers their way." Mary took the flail from him. "Fetch the Bible, Hughie. We'll bury it deep."

They dug a hole beneath the rowan tree, placed the Bible within a small oaken chest and patted the earth back down as the redcoats marched to Achtriachan. The few other inhabitants of the clachan had already run into the hills.

"Come, Hughie, into the heather." Lifting her skirt, Mary strode away, not even deigning to look over her shoulder as the soldiers advanced to burn her home. "We'll watch from Clach nan Bodach."

Clach nan Bodach, the Rock of the Old Man, was a prominent Standing Stone that stood some two hundred feet above Achtriachan.

"Down there." Mary indicated a slight hollow in front of the stone. "We can see them, and they can't see us."

Together with Mary, Hugh watched as the soldiers burned their clachan and stole their livestock. He saw the blue smoke coiling skywards as the soldiers set fire to their thatch, and heard the redcoats' alien, guttural voices.

"Watch and learn." Mary seemed unmoved by the destruction of all she owned.

"Watch how they move and listen to how they talk, watch how they hold their muskets and how they march. Learn, Hugh, for they are our enemies, the enemies of our blood and the more you learn about them, the better it will be."

The rough laughter of the soldiers polluted the glen as they drove away the livestock and destroyed everything they could not steal, leaving behind smoking ruins, trampled crops and a naked woman swinging by her neck from a tree.

"Mhairi MacPherson," Mary said. "Her tongue was always longer than her brain. She would tell the redcoats what she thought of them. Take heed, Hughie. Keep your council with the English-speakers. Tell them what they want to hear and hide your thoughts from them. Let them dwell in their simplicity."

A small party of soldiers swaggered towards Mary MacKim and Hughie, led by a man wearing a philabeg below his scarlet tunic.

"That is a Campbell, one of Lord Loudon's men." Mary MacKim did not hide the contempt in her voice. "We can excuse the English-speakers, as they are brought up in ignorance, but when one of our own turns against us, they are worse than the devil." She pushed Hughie away and stood up. "Run and hide, Hughie."

"Hey, you!" Loudon's Highlander addressed Mary. "What are you doing?"

"I am watching you." Mary held the man's gaze.

"Where is your home?" The man was about thirty, with an open, freckled face and blue eyes.

"Over there." Mary indicated the burning clachan behind her. "You have seen fit to burn the home of a widow woman."

"The home of a traitorous bitch," the Loudon Highlander said. "Where are the rest of your cattle? I know this glen has more. Glen Cailleach always had cattle."

Mary MacKim hesitated for a moment. "We have no more

cattle."

"I can hang you for a traitor," the Loudon man ran his hand down Mary's face, curling his fingers around her throat as the redcoats behind him watched, chewing tobacco and spitting into the heather. "Or use you. You are a handsome enough woman, except for the smell." He said something in English that set his companions to laughter.

Hiding in the heather, Hughie fought the desire to rise and attack the Hanoverians. His mother had chosen to face them; she knew what she was doing. He saw the English-speaking soldiers crowd around his mother, still laughing loudly. Hating to see these arrogant strangers with their grasping ways in his glen, Hughie closed his eyes, trying to force the image of Ewan from his mind.

"We have cattle in the high shieling," Mary MacKim said at last.

"Take us, woman," the Loudon man said and spoke in English for the benefit of his companions.

Hughie shook his head, knowing there were no cattle at the high shielings, the summer pasture. He followed at a distance as his mother strode up the flank of An Cailleach with the Loudon man and his companions trailing behind her.

"How far are your shielings?" the Loudon man asked, after a quarter of an hour.

"A fair step." Mary did not reduce her speed. She led them around the flank of An Cailleach and continued, threading through a patch of peat bog that had the English-speaking soldiers swearing as they floundered and sank knee-deep in mud. "Tell your soldiers to walk where I walk," Mary said. "This bog is deep."

Once over the bog, Mary increased her pace, winding her way across the shoulder of a scree-scarred mountain, past the tumbled ruins of a hill fort and onto a pass between two hills. By that time, only one of the English-speaking soldiers had kept pace with her. The other two lagged far behind, struggling over the unfamiliar terrain. To Mary's right, the hills rose steeply into grey mist. To her left, the slope fell away, nearly perpendicular, towards a churning burn, before rising again.

"How much further?" the Loudon Highlander asked.

"Over the pass," Mary said. Stooping, she lifted a fist-sized stone from the ground. "We always pick a stone here. It's a tradition." Without hesitation, she folded the stone in a handkerchief, poised, and swung it hard against the Loudon man's forehead. Too surprised to retaliate, he fell at once, and Mary pushed him over the edge of the precipice. Gasping, the nearest soldier grabbed at Mary, missed by a yard and shouted something as she lifted her skirt and scrambled up the slope.

Astonished that his mother could act in such a manner, Hugh could only watch as the soldier clumsily swung his musket up to his shoulder to aim, but by that time Mary was sixty yards away and moving fast. The shot sounded flat, with the wind flicking away the smoke from the muzzle of the musket. Staring up into the mist-streaked hill, the soldier loaded his musket, muttering as he rammed home the ball, and began to climb after Mary.

Waiting on the skyline, Mary ensured the soldier could see her before running down the far side of the ridge and back toward Glen Cailleach. She whistled once, as she had when her boys were young.

"Mother!" Hughie ran to join her. "You killed that man."

"Yes. Let's get you back to the glen," Mary said.

"How about the other soldiers? They saw what you did."

"With the mist coming down, they'll be lost in the hills. They won't find their way back to the glen." Mary showed no concern as she added, "They'll probably die out here."

Hughie shook his head, struggling to come to terms with his mother's callous attitude. He stared down the slope where the Loudon Highlander had fallen. "You killed that man."

"Men or women who turn against their own deserve nothing else," Mary said. "Come on, Hughie. We've got a house to rebuild." She faced Hughie. "That's one for Ewan."

❦ II ❦

LEARNING

GLEN CAILLEACH, SCOTLAND,
1757

Thirty-one-year-old Simon Fraser of Lovat, son of 'the Old Fox' and un-blooded veteran of the 1745 Rising, rode into Glen Cailleach with his back straight and his head held high, as befitted the chief of a clan, albeit one without a square inch of land to his name.

"Gather the men," he said quietly to the tacksman who hurried to greet him. "I wish to speak to them."

Fraser's word was passed around from clachan to clachan and man to man until eventually, it reached Mary MacKim.

"Your time has come, Hugh," Mary said.

"Yes, Mother."

"Fraser himself has summonsed the men," Mary said. "That can only mean one thing. He is leading the clan to war."

Hugh nodded. There was no question of refusing the summons. He would follow the chief, as his brother had done, and his father, and his grandfather's father's father. He was a MacKim, a man of a sept of the Frasers; there was no more to be said. It did not matter who they were fighting; it only mattered that their chief required their broadswords.

The men of the glen hurried to the old gathering place at

Clach Mor, the ancient Standing Stone that legend attributed to the druids but which had thrust toward the damp sky for aeons before any druid's foot had trodden the land. From youths of fifteen to grey-bearded men who had faced Red John of the Battles on the field of Sheriffmuir, they gathered, fully aware that they may never return to their homes again.

"Men." Fraser looked around at them without dismounting from his horse. "King George is engaged in a just war against the King of France. I am raising a regiment to support his cause and I expect all the young men aged between eighteen and thirty to join. You will accept the King's Shilling at Inverness. God save the King."

"God save the king," a few of the men repeated. Lachlan MacPherson, a man of the same age as MacKim, pressed his mouth tightly shut.

"I'm not fighting for King George," he whispered. "Not ever."

"Three cheers for the king!" somebody else cried, and a handful of the men joined in.

Simon Fraser raised his hat in response. "I praise your loyalty," he said, without a trace of irony. "Now, you have your opportunity to prove it."

"Three cheers for the chief!" the same voice sounded, and the men cheered, louder than before.

Nodding once, Fraser wheeled his horse and rode away. He had said all that was necessary for him to say. Few of the men cared about King George or his quarrel with the King of France; they would join the regiment and follow their chief wherever he led, and whichever king he decided to support.

"Be a man, Hugh," Mary MacKim said. "Remember you are a MacKim and remember the blood oath you have sworn."

"Yes, Mother." MacKim glanced at the Bible, which they had dug up as soon as the last redcoat retreated from the glen.

"You are bound by your word." Mary MacKim had aged in

the years since her older son had died. Her dark eyes, now deep-set between a network of furrows, seemed to bore into MacKim. "You have learned English, and you know how these people live, talk and think. Now you must hunt and kill the men who murdered your brother."

"Yes, Mother." Revenge had dominated MacKim's life for the past eleven years and not a day had passed when his mother had not reminded him of the oath he had taken. At the age of twenty-one, MacKim was wiry rather than muscular, no taller than average height, but intense and better educated than most of his peers.

"Now go, Hugh." Mary gave him a gentle push in the back. "Go and do your duty."

Lifting his small bundle of belongings, MacKim stepped out of the cottage with its heather-thatched roof and the familiar scent of peat smoke. He did not know when, if ever, he would see it again. When he looked around, his mother stood at the door, with one hand lifted in farewell. She was alone now, yet MacKim knew she would never be lonely in the glen. The people would look after her, as they always looked after their own. Turning away, he began the trudge toward Inverness with his road and his destiny before him.

WITH HIS BRIGHT RED SASH OVER HIS LEFT SHOULDER AND THE white lace cord on his right shoulder, it was evident that the tall sergeant was a soldier of distinction. Although he must have been approaching middle age, he walked with a youthful spring as he inspected the curious line of recruits, shaking his head as if unable to believe what he saw.

"I am Sergeant Dingwall." He spoke in clipped Gaelic. "You will address me as Sergeant, or as Sergeant Dingwall." He stopped directly in front of MacKim. "You may think of me as your father if you ever knew that unfortunate man, and you will treat me as God for I have the power to have you shot, to flog you to bloody ribbons or even to make your life pleasant." Dingwall's smile could have frightened the Brigade of Guards. "Welcome to the 63rd Foot, Fraser's Highlanders."

MacKim watched Sergeant Dingwall and listened to every word. He was determined to be the best soldier he could be.

As Dingwall hefted his halberd, MacKim shuddered, remembering the Grenadier corporal pinioning Ewan with a similar weapon. The sergeant stepped to the red-haired youth beside MacKim and thrust the halberd at his breast. "Stand straight, my fine fellow, or I will tie you to a tree until you learn how to stand."

The man flushed scarlet and pulled himself erect.

"That's better," Dingwall said. "Now you look something like a man, if nothing like a soldier, even a first day, shambling recruit soldier. What's your name?"

"Neil Cumming, sir."

"Sergeant," Dingwall said, softly.

"Sorry, Sergeant." Cumming looked along the line of recruits for support. MacKim avoided his gaze.

Nodding slowly, Dingwall took hold of Cumming's nose and pulled him forward. "I ordered you to call me Sergeant, Cumming, and you called me sir. You will say sir only to officers who have His Majesty's commission. Now, as from this day, you are my eyes and ears in the company, Cumming. You will tell me what is happening and if anybody breaks the law, my law, you will inform me, or I will sit you astride the wooden horse and have you dragged over stony ground until you beg me to shoot you. Do you understand?"

"Yes, Sergeant."

Pushing Cumming back to his place, Sergeant Dingwall continued in a roar that MacKim thought people could hear twenty miles away in Glen Cailleach. "You are the most useless bunch of bare-arsed farmers I have ever seen in my life. My job," he said, "is to turn you into soldiers somehow, although only the good Lord above knows how." He shook his head again, sighing deeply at the burden that higher authority had passed down to him. "Your job," Dingwall continued, "is to obey every order I utter, instantly and cheerfully."

With the unfamiliar long red coat over his new waistcoat, and the kilt hugging his hips, MacKim was supremely uncomfortable, already hating the bonnet he had cocked above his left eye. The square-toed, iron-studded shoes pinched his toes, the straps of the knapsack cut into his shoulders, and the musket was long and cumbersome. Also, the broadsword was burdensome on his left hip and the bayonet awkward in front. Used to dressing lightly from spring to autumn, MacKim felt constrained by the unfamiliar layers of clothes and carrying such an array of weapons.

"This is your musket." Sergeant Dingwall held the weapon up to ensure the recruits saw it. "We know it as Bess, or Brown Bess."

MacKim nodded to show he was listening.

"Bess weighs fourteen pounds and fires a one-ounce leaden ball that can kill at fifty yards and wound at up to a hundred. It has a larger bore and is more reliable than the French equivalent and in the hands of a trained infantryman, can fire three times in a minute."

MacKim remembered the sound of musketry at Drummossie Moor that men now called Culloden. He had already seen the result of three volleys a minute on a mass of advancing men. A thousand muskets in the hands of trained men would create devastation.

"Bess is a flintlock musket," Dingwall continued, "so-called because she uses a flint to create a spark. The spark ignites gunpowder, which explodes inside your musket, propelling the lead ball in the direction of the enemy. Keep your flints sharp – the sharper the flint, the brighter the spark and so the less chance of a misfire."

MacKim listened. He wanted to learn everything.

"To load Bess, you need this." Dingwall held up a small, paper-wrapped packet. "This is a cartridge that contains a charge of powder and a lead ball. You will rip open the paper, either with your fingers or your teeth and pour some of the powder into the pan in the firing mechanism, here." He indicated the position at the lock of the musket.

MacKim nodded.

"The rest of the powder goes down the barrel. Then you fold the paper and stuff it into the barrel, with the lead ball on top. Do you understand, MacKim?"

"Yes, Sergeant." MacKim started when Dingwall shouted his name.

"Good man. Show me." Dingwall indicated that MacKim should stand in front of the other recruits. "Here is a cartridge." He passed over the paper package and stepped back.

Ignoring the bitter taste of the black powder, MacKim ripped the paper open with his teeth and followed the sergeant's instructions.

"Good." Dingwall nodded. "Now you use the ramrod, that's the long metal rod under the barrel of your musket, to force the ball and wad down the barrel."

Taking MacKim's musket, Dingwall demonstrated slowly. "When that's done, you aim at the advancing enemy and pull the trigger. You will notice the recoil as Bess ejects the ball to about a hundred yards on a good day and a lot less if it rains, which occasionally happens in Scotland."

The recruits gave a nervous laugh at the sergeant's attempt at humour.

"Now, you fire it, MacKim. Prove to me how clever you are."

"Yes, Sergeant." MacKim brought the musket to his shoulder. "What shall I fire at?"

They stood in the open countryside outside Inverness, with the grey-green hills of the Highlands in the distance and the river Ness surging blue at their backs, lapping at a group of small islands.

"You see that island?" Dingwall pointed to the nearest of the Ness Islands, from which trees grew to overhang the river.

"Yes, Sergeant."

"Try to hit a tree."

The musket was heavier than MacKim had expected. Lifting it to his shoulder, he closed his left eye, pointed the barrel at the nearest tree and pressed the trigger. From the corner of his eye, he saw the hammer come down. The resulting spurt of smoke in the pan took him by surprise and then musket seemed to leap back, hammering into his shoulder, so he staggered backwards.

Dingwall watched, smiling. "There. You see? It's not quite as easy as you think. A good soldier can fire and load three times in a minute. A very good soldier can do it four times. You recruits..." Dingwall shook his head. "Well, we'll see." He peered closely at MacKim. "Most of you will likely fall before you fire your second shot."

Some of the men laughed at that, as Dingwall had intended. He paced the line again, stopping at a tall man with a badly scarred face on MacKim's immediate right. "God, but you're ugly! I've never seen an uglier recruit, and I've seen plenty."

The man stared ahead without responding to Dingwall's jibe. The sergeant moved on, hectoring.

"We are Fraser's Highlanders." Dingwall paced the triple line, looking into every face. "We are a British infantry regiment; we fight for King George."

The men in the ranks shifted slightly. They already knew who they were.

"In King George's army, a battalion of infantry is divided into tactical units known as platoons. Whatever your previous allegiances, whoever your previous family might have been, in future, your platoon is your family. Each man will be closer than a brother. Depend on him, and he will depend on you. Let him down, and he may die, and so may you."

Dingwall stopped six inches in front of MacKim. "Look around at your neighbours. Get to know their faces. You will live in their company, march in their company, fight in their company and probably die in their company."

Red-haired Cumming on MacKim's left glanced at him and away again. He was pale-faced and pale-eyed, with the hands and shoulders of a labourer. To MacKim's right was the man with the disfigured face.

"Bid your neighbour good-day," Dingwall ordered.

The scarred man favoured MacKim with a wink. "James Chisholm."

"Hugh MacKim."

The names seemed to hang in the air for a long time, and then Sergeant Dingwall shouted again.

"That's enough! I told you to look around, not indulge in social tittle-tattle! Where do you think you are? The Duke of Gordon's wedding? Good God! You're meant to be soldiers, not women at a ball!"

MacKim faced his front immediately.

"We will drill until you hate me, we will drill until your feet bleed, we will drill until my voice fills your dreams, and we will drill until you obey the commands instinctively and without thought. You are soldiers. Soldiers do not need to think. Soldiers only need to obey orders, to march and to fight. To fight in battle depends on being able to form and manoeuvre in rigid, close-order lines and columns. You have to learn to obey orders, so you keep your place in the ranks whatever happens, even although your comrades are dead or dying."

MacKim shifted his gaze to left and right, wondering how much trust he could put in his neighbours. Cumming on his left fidgeted, breathing hard as he strove to remain still. Chisholm on his right stood as if carved from the same granite as An Cailleach.

"At Fontenoy, each half-company and each platoon fired volley after volley at the French. The British regiments remained firm, but our allies were not as well disciplined and refused to advance into the French musketry. The French saw our army was vulnerable and sent forward their Irish brigade, six battalions of fine soldiers, who came in on our right flank with the bayonet."

MacKim imagined the picture, transforming his memories of Culloden Moor to Europe and replacing the slaughter of the clans with two equally matched armies of professional soldiers.

"We drove them off," Dingwall continued as if he had been there. 'The Scottish regiments, the 43rd Highlanders, Royal Scots and Royal North British Fusiliers, marched with the rest of the British Army, equals in battle, and then we chased off the French cavalry as well. All because of disciplined firepower, good drill and guts. In a minute I'll begin to teach you."

Rain began, a slow, dreary drizzle that swept down from the hills to soak the recruits. Already they had been standing in ranks for hours, and MacKim guessed the day was far from over. He had not expected soldiering to be so monotonous.

"Some of you may wonder why we have bagpipers in this day of vast armies and artillery." Dingwall took a step back. "We have pipers to let the enemy know that the Highlanders are coming... we have pipers to let them know how long they have to live."

FOR THE NEXT FEW WEEKS, A PROCESSION OF SERGEANTS AND officers hammered the recruits. As well as the complicated procedures for loading, presenting and firing the Brown Bess muskets, there was training with the 17-inch triangular bayonets. Remembering the bloody blades plunging into the helpless Highland wounded at Culloden, MacKim handled the weapon with some trepidation. They practised live firing until they became used to the vicious recoil that bruised shoulders and rattled teeth. As the government fixed the annual allowance of ball ammunition used in training to a meagre four balls per man per year, Colonel Fraser ordered the target butts to be placed against a grassy bank, so the regimental pioneers could dig out the lead and re-cast it into serviceable ammunition.

The recruits fired individually, with Sergeant Dingwall snarling at every fumbling mistake, then they fired by files of three, and finally by ranks and by platoons, with the recruits gradually getting used to the powder smoke that obscured their vision and stung their eyes every time they squeezed the trigger. They fired at a mark, trotted over to it to check their marksmanship, reported back to Dingwall and endured his verbal assault. Once they had mastered the most straightforward techniques, Dingwall had them firing obliquely, then uphill and downhill. MacKim found he was a moderate marksman, while the scarred Chisholm was good.

"You've fired a musket before, Ugly!" Dingwall said.

"Yes, Sergeant," Chisholm agreed.

"I'll wager you were a Jacobite rebel!" Dingwall pressed his face close to Chisholm. "Were you? Did you fire at King George's army at Culloden? Is that where you got your scars, Ugly?"

"No, Sergeant." Chisholm snapped to attention with his musket at his side and his ruined face expressionless.

"No?" Dingwall grunted. "I wonder, Ugly, I really wonder." He took two steps back. "If you did, or if you did not, it does not matter now. You are a Fraser Highlander, and before I finish with you, you will all be the best marksmen in King George's British Army!"

Always in the background, officers hovered, watching, occasionally giving comments or sharp orders. They lived in a different world from MacKim, a world of authority and privilege, of carriages and soft clothes. He watched them with interest, knowing he could never join their circle and having no aspirations to do so. Three thoughts dominated his mind; become a good soldier; learn the skills, find the men who murdered his brother. He repeated the name in his head, day after day, *Hayes of*

Ligonier's. He knew that Dingwall was watching him when he volunteered for every extra duty; he did not care.

"Be careful, MacKim," Chisholm warned. "If you are too keen, they'll make you a corporal." His smile twisted his face into something even more hideous. "Keep your head down and become anonymous."

MacKim grunted. "I want to learn all I can."

"Soldiers that stand out from the rest become marked men," Chisholm said. "Either by sergeants like Dingwall, or the enemy." His grin only enhanced his scar. "Not that there's much difference."

"How do you know? You're only a recruit like us. Or was Dingwall correct and were you in the Jacobite army?"

Chisholm hesitated a moment, touching his face with his eyes suddenly dark. "I was in the old 43rd, the Black Watch at Fontenoy." When he relapsed into silence, MacKim left him to his memories.

The recruits learned how to march in column and deploy to fight in line. They learned how the front rank men knelt to fire and stood to load.

"This is a dangerous time," Sergeant Dingwall told them as he marched along the length of the line. "I have seen careless rear-rank men shooting the front-rank men as they sprang up. That will not happen in Fraser's Highlanders." He fixed MacKim with a terrible glare. "Will it, MacKim?"

"No, Sergeant," MacKim said.

"Why not, MacKim?"

"Because you will train us better, Sergeant."

Dingwall grunted. "That's correct, boy, that's correct." He moved on. "I have seen cartridge boxes blow up and burn careless soldiers. I've seen soldiers poke out their comrade's eyes when fixing bayonets, I have seen soldiers firing off their ramrods because they forgot to remove the damned things when they loaded. None of these unfortunate events will occur in Fraser's Highlanders."

The recruits listened and slowly learned the manoeuvres that they would use on the battlefields of Europe, where discipline and order were everything and armies moved on the word of command, "like chessmen on a board controlled by the general in command," as Chisholm said.

"We are not individuals," Cumming said, as he lay exhausted in their tents at the end of another long day. "We are only things to be ordered about at the whim of the sergeant."

"That's right." Chisholm blew smoke from the stubby clay pipe he had thrust between his teeth. "They will break you, rob you of your individuality and recreate you in the image they desire. Every second of our lives is regulated and controlled, every action we take, everything we eat, do and wear. All we have are our thoughts and our souls." He glanced across to MacKim. "They will try to brutalise you to take over your soul as well, MacKim. Don't let them do that. Always keep a little something for yourself, or you will end up like Sergeant Dingwall, with nothing except the army. Strive to keep hold of your thoughts. Don't let the army control your mind. Learn to soldier by all means, but retain a wee bit of yourself."

MacKim nodded. "I won't let them have my mind or soul."

"Easy to say, MacKim." Chisholm lay back within his clouding blue tobacco smoke. "A lot harder to do."

"I won't lose sight of myself," MacKim said. *I am not here to be a soldier for the rest of my life. I have a purpose. I have an oath to fulfil, somehow.* Yet he knew that the clan chief and colonel controlled his life, as the chiefs had controlled the lives of his brother and his ancestors for centuries. The chief commanded, and the men obeyed; it had always been that way, and the army was no different. Clansmen and soldiers followed orders. If they stepped outside of the system, they would be executed or outlawed to become homeless wanderers who belonged nowhere. It was essential to obey, to follow orders, to fit in with one's peers and allow the clan chief or the officers to make the decisions. When the chiefs and the officers were the same men, things were even more natural. There was no need to consider or even to think.

MacKim lay back on his cot, folded his hands behind his head and was asleep in seconds. Sergeant Dingwall's broad face and harsh voice filled his dreams, together with the ever-present vision of his brother slowly roasting and the mocking laughter of the redcoats. He woke with a start. *I'm a redcoat now, and I'm going to find you, Hayes of Ligonier's.*

❧ 4 ❧

HALIFAX, NOVA SCOTIA, 1758

"How many men are here?" MacKim looked around the assembly in the half-frozen harbour. "There must be every soldier in King George's army and half the fleet."

"We've got soldiers in Europe, too," Cumming sounded proud. "The British Army is stronger than it has ever been, and Fraser's is part of it."

Ignoring Cumming, Chisholm smoothed a hand over the stock of his musket. "I've heard there are more than twelve thousand men here, MacKim, and over forty ships." He grunted. "We have thirteen companies in Fraser's alone."

"That's enough to conquer the whole country," MacKim said.

"I think that's the idea." Chisholm thrust his pipe between his lips. "So here we are at Halifax, Nova Scotia, preparing to attack the French in Canada." He looked at MacKim. "I've been a soldier long enough to know that nothing will go according to plan, Hugh."

"Won't it?" MacKim watched as a squad of Royal Scots, the First Regiment of Foot, filed past.

"What are you doing, Hugh?" Chisholm asked. "You study every man that passes, all the time."

MacKim shook his head. "Nothing."

"That's not true. I've been in the army long enough to know men. What are you up to?"

"Nothing." MacKim clamped shut his mouth. *I must tell nobody what I am doing.*

"As you wish." Chisholm leaned back, his brown eyes thoughtful. "One thing I have learned, and that is not to interfere with another man's business. Another thing is that a loner cannot survive in the ranks. Everybody needs the support of his companions, and that includes you."

MacKim replied with a grunt.

"There are no secrets in a regiment, Hugh. Sooner or later, the lads find out everything."

"There's nothing to find out, James." MacKim forced a smile and tried to change the subject. "Tell me about your time in the army."

"I was in the 43rd," Chisholm said. "Right from the start. They're the 42nd now."

Cumming came closer, smiling ingratiatingly.

MacKim tested the edge of his bayonet and began to shave the stubble from his chin. "You told me you were at Fontenoy."

"I was." Chisholm's face again darkened with the memory of that bloody battle.

"We might be fighting the French soon. What was it like?"

Chisholm was silent for a few moments. "It was like nothing you can ever imagine, Hugh. The noise was deafening, with the cannon and musketry and screams of men and horses. There were tens of thousands of men all engaged in killing each other, yet I only saw small pieces. That was enough."

MacKim waited, guessing that Chisholm had more to say.

"Powder smoke; acres of powder smoke," Chisholm said. "You can only see a few yards in front of you. You obey orders and trust to your officers and the men on either side of you. You ignore the wounded because you can't help them anyway."

He shook his head. "I will never forget some of the sights I saw that day, Hugh. I hope to God that I am never in a major battle again. They say we may go to Hell when we die, Hugh. I've already been there."

MacKim nodded. He had seen his own version of Hell.

"I got this at Fontenoy." Chisholm touched his ravaged face. "The man next to me had a misfire and rather than draw his charge, he stuffed more powder on top, and the damned musket blew up. It blew his head off and turned me into a monster."

"You're not a monster," MacKim said.

Chisholm's face twisted into a smile. "No? I tried life outside the army when that war finished. Nobody wanted to know me. My wife turned her back on me, men I had known all my life threatened to shoot me if I went near their families." He shrugged. "Only the army accepted me. So this is my home until the French or disease kills me."

MacKim shook his head. "I am sure you'll find some woman."

"I doubt it." Chisholm stuffed more tobacco into his pipe. "You'll be all right, Hugh. You're a handsome enough young man. I expect King Geordie will disband Fraser's once this war is over and you'll be free to find a girl." He lit up, puffing slowly. "But that doesn't interest you, does it? You've never once looked at a woman, although there are some handsome fillies here. Yet you watch every man. What are you looking for, Hugh?"

MacKim took a deep breath. "Ligonier's Foot."

"Ligonier's?" Chisholm looked confused. "There's no such regiment, Hugh."

"What?" MacKim had no other links to the men who murdered Ewan. "Were they disbanded?"

"No, not at all," Chisholm said. "They have a different name, that's all. You must know that regiments are named after their colonels and change their name when a different colonel takes command. What was Ligonier's Regiment of Foot is now Webb's Regiment."

"Webb's!" MacKim started. "They're in Halifax."

"Yes. Now tell me why you have the interest?'"

Dingwall interrupted their conversation before MacKim could reply. "Come on, you lazy buggers! General Wolfe wants us to play in boats!" The sergeant glowered at them. "You're chatting like idle women there. Soldiers! I've seen children at play who looked more like soldiers."

As NCOs' sergeants translated officers' orders into foul-mouthed rants, the men of every regiment filed into boats, standing in rigid lines as mocking seamen rowed them out to ships, trained them how to embark, and rowed them back again.

"What's all this?" Cumming asked as they splashed ashore. "We've done this already."

"Pikestaff is making sure we know how to disembark onto a beach," Chisholm said.

"Who the devil is Pikestaff?'

"General Wolfe," Chisholm said. "That's the fellow over there." Scanning a knot of senior officers who stood on a slight eminence observing everything, Chisholm indicated a tall, thin man. "Just look at him. He's as slender as the staff of a pike and as unyielding. He can only be Pikestaff."

Although MacKim knew that General Wolfe had been with the British Army at Culloden, he knew little else about him.

"I heard that he's a good officer," Cumming said.

"We'll see." Chisholm reserved judgement. "He seems to be thorough so far." He nudged MacKim. "You were looking for Webb's. There they are."

After years of brooding, MacKim shook at the possibility that his brother's murderers could be within sight. Shifting his position slightly, he saw the boats that held Webb's regiment two hundred yards away. At this distance, the men were faceless, expressionless wooden soldiers, each man looking exactly like his neighbour.

If you are there, Hayes, I am after you. If you are still alive, I am going to kill you. MacKim felt the desire for revenge burning so fiercely, he was not surprised that Chisholm put a steadying hand on his arm.

"What ails you, MacKim? What is it about that regiment? Man, you're trembling!"

"It must be the cold." MacKim was aware that Cumming and some others were also staring at him. He forced an unconvincing smile. "I'm all right. I'm just fed up with this training. I want to get at these French rascals."

"What was that?" Lieutenant Cameron was perhaps a year younger than MacKim, a fresh-faced man from the banks of Loch Linnhe. "You want to get these French rascals do you, MacKim?"

"Yes, sir."

"Well, you'll get your chance sooner rather than later, my good man, I promise you." Cameron said. "In the meantime, do your duty, and all will be well."

"Yes, sir," MacKim said. It was unusual for an officer to address a private soldier directly, which was why the men would follow wherever Cameron led. When they disembarked on the beach, MacKim watched Webb's Foot marching away.

I won't forget you. Again, MacKim shook with hatred.

"Come on, MacKim. Whatever your business with Webb's, it will have to wait." Chisholm pushed him away. "Dingwall's watching."

❧❧❧

ON THE 26TH MAY 1758, THE ARMY FINALLY BEGAN THE arduous process of boarding the transports that would take them to war.

The leading regiment sang a song that MacKim had never heard before:

'Our troops they now can plainly see
May Britain guard in Germany;

Hanoverians, Hessians, Prussians,
Are paid t'oppose the French and Russians;
Nor scruple they with truth to say
They're fighting for Americay.'

"What's all that about?" MacKim asked.

"It's the truth,"Chisholm said. "Great Britain is paying foreign armies to fight the French in Europe, while we are over here. There are all sorts of armies marching all over the place, and all a blind, because we don't want land in Europe. We don't care if some foreign potentate or other moves a frontier fortress a few miles or not. We're after taking control of this continent of America from the French."

"How do you know these things?" MacKim asked.

"Experience, MacKim, and because I don't have distractions." Chisholm touched his scarred face. "When you look like me, you can't think about women or the future. All I have is the regiment and why we fight," he pointed to the waiting ships, "or why we sail."

"Thank goodness it's only a short voyage to Louisbourg," MacKim said. "Île Royale is not that far away, and then we'll capture Louisbourg from Johnny Frenchman."

Chisholm bit on a plug of tobacco. "You may not think it so simple when you see Louisbourg," he said. "The French have made it the strongest fortress in North America, with thousands of infantry waiting behind thick stone walls. It's the nearest thing to a European fort on this side of the Atlantic."

MacKim nodded absently. Rather than contemplating the impending struggle for Louisbourg, he was thinking about Hayes and Webb's Regiment. Surely, at some point, he would have the opportunity to serve alongside Webb's. He knew that Hayes and his companions had been in the Grenadier Company, which concentrated his search to a hundred men at most. It should not be too hard to find them, if indeed they were still alive in the army after twelve years. All he had to do was survive the French bullets and cannonballs.

THE FOG THAT HUNG THICK AND DAMP ON THE HARBOUR OF Louisburg that morning of the 2nd June 1758 did little to dull the thunder of the surf on the shore. Ships' masts thrust through the grey-white mist, with lights dimly glimmering and the resonant clang of bells marking the passage of time.

"By the mark, five!" A seaman cast the lead to test the depth of water under the ship's hull. What MacKim could see of Louisbourg was not prepossessing; massive grey walls squatting above the fog-smeared, ice-dappled harbour with the white flag of Bourbon France hanging limply above. With Louisbourg's walls augmented with a deep ditch and bastions, the fortifications closed off a small peninsula.

"It will be a hard nut to crack," Chisholm said. "We'll have to land a fair distance away or their artillery will blow us away."

"We won't be landing anywhere in this weather," Corporal Gunn said.

Chisholm puffed at his pipe. "The corporal's right. Settle down, lads, and live a day or so longer."

MacKim examined the surrounding ships, although he knew his chances of glimpsing Hayes or his companions were slight.

"You all right, Sawnie?" a grinning seaman asked. "Had you better not stay below and let us men do the work?"

"I prefer the fresh air," MacKim answered truthfully.

The seaman laughed. "You got the wrong job, Sawnie. You should have joined the Navy."

"Maybe next time," MacKim said and moved as a red-faced petty officer bellowed at him to get below where he belonged and stop cluttering up the deck.

The boisterous weather continued all that week, with the surf booming as a backdrop.

"That's another day to live," Chisholm said every morning.

"That's another day for the French to strengthen their defences," Sergeant Dingwall said. "And another day closer to winter."

MacKim smiled. "It's early June, Sergeant! Winter is months away yet."

"General Amherst wishes to capture Quebec and Montreal this campaigning season," Dingwall unbent to explain. "He'll have to take Louisbourg first, to secure our rear and ensure the French ships can't use it as a base to intercept our supplies. The longer we take to capture Louisbourg, the less time we have to sail up the St Lawrence to Quebec."

MacKim nodded. He did not care if the French held Louisbourg or Quebec or all of North America. In his opinion, it was a cold, stark place anyway.

"Up on deck!" Lieutenant Cameron ordered. "Musket drill, lads!"

Cold though it was, MacKim was always happier up on deck than trapped in the stuffy atmosphere down below. He took his place between Chisholm and Cumming.

"Something's happening," Chisholm said.

One of the Royal Navy frigates had detached from the fleet to approach the shore at Gabarus Bay. When the French responded with a rolling bombardment, the frigate adjusted her sails, steering from side to side to avoid the cannonballs that raised tall fountains of water around her.

MacKim took a deep breath. "That's the first time I've seen guns fired in war." He thought it best not mention his youthful experiences at Culloden.

"You'll hear plenty more," Chisholm said. "The Frenchies won't give up Canada easily."

As MacKim watched, the frigate fired her starboard broadside, sixteen cannon crashing out in an ear-pounding display of naval power.

"That'll show the French we mean business." MacKim tried

to peer through the thick banks of smoke to see what results the broadside had had against the stone walls of Louisbourg.

"Maybe," Chisholm said. "I think Admiral Boscawen is just keeping his men busy. Seamen get bored sitting at anchor, nurse-maiding thousands of grousing soldiers."

Standing on MacKim's left, Cumming shook his head. "No. I think we're going to attack today. We'll beat them. Everybody says that the French can't fight."

Chisholm grunted. "If everybody says that, then everybody is wrong. The French are bonny fighters, Cumming. We won't win this war in only a few weeks."

"The French can't fight," Cumming insisted.

"Oh, they can." Chisholm's scarred face twitched. "You'll be a different man at the end of it, Cumming. A long war makes a good soldier."

The firing ended as the frigate steered away. A drift of wind momentarily cleared the mist and smoke, revealing the walls of Louisburg seemingly untouched, with the white Bourbon flag proud above.

MacKim stared at the fortress as the reality of his situation hit him. Although he had to find four men who may or may not be in the ranks of Webb's Regiment, he also had to survive this campaign. Glancing sideways, he saw Chisholm standing like a piece of carved granite. He would need to emulate veterans such as Chisholm. He had a lot to learn.

LOUISBOURG, 8TH JUNE 1758

They filed into the flat-bottomed boats, so tightly packed that MacKim could scarcely breathe. The tension was palpable as men looked to their front, aware that after months of training, they were finally going to war. Fraser's Highlanders, more than a thousand untried men, would soon be facing veteran French battalions waiting behind entrenchments and stone walls. The raw young lads from the Highland glens would have to prove their worth to King George, or the stigma of the Jacobite Rising would continue.

"Keep your head down, MacKim. Don't try to be a hero," Chisholm advised. "A good soldier is a live soldier."

The British landing force fought sea-sickness and apprehension as they looked over to Louisbourg, where the black-mouthed muzzles of cannon waited in silent menace.

"The Frenchies can't fail to see us," Cumming said. "They'll hammer the boats long before we get ashore."

"Look around," Chisholm said. "We're in three divisions, Lawrence on the left, Wolfe in the centre and Whitmore on the right, so the French defences are spread thin. Even the French can't be everywhere and won't know where to concentrate their fire."

"I see the officers are sitting comfortably." Cumming jerked his head towards the stern, where young Ensign MacDonnell and Lieutenant Murray sat side by side, with Sergeant Dingwall one rank in front.

Chisholm grunted. "Don't they always get the best of everything? That bastard Dingwall is with them, I see." He tapped the lock of his musket. "If I get him in front of me, I might forget that he's on our side."

MacKim was pressed even closer to Cumming as more men jammed into the boat. "I'm not sure he is on our side. I think he's a Frenchman in disguise, planted here to make us suffer all the more." He grunted as a rogue wave exploded against the bow, splashing cold water onto the first three ranks inside.

"Where are we?" Private Cattanach asked plaintively.

"Freshwater Cove, near Gabarus Bay," Lieutenant Murray replied from the stern. "We're only a few miles from Louisbourg, my man." He spread his arms to indicate the fleet. "Now look to your front and do your duty. We have Admiral Boscawen and half the Royal Navy with us, so this is the day we teach the French a lesson."

Catching MacKim's eye, Chisholm winked before resuming his expressionless demeanour. MacKim tried to concentrate on Murray's words as he stared at the shore, where the French waited with artillery and massed muskets.

"The enemy has a chain of defensive posts all along this coast," Lieutenant Murray said. "He also has thrown up some defensive works to protect the most likely places for us to land, and armed them with artillery." Although he spoke casually, it was evident that Murray was warning the men that the landing would not be easy.

MacKim glanced at Chisholm, who winked.

"Keep your head down, MacKim."

A Navy longboat pulled beside the barge, and an agile seaman attached a line to the bow. "We'll soon have you ashore, ladies. Oh, I do like your skirts!" Blowing a kiss, he leapt back to his

44

boat and a moment later, a dozen seamen bent to their oars to tow the Highlanders to shore. MacKim swallowed hard to rid his throat of a sudden lump as his legs began to shake from either fear or excitement, or both. Taking a deep breath, he exhaled slowly, trying to calm his nerves.

"Here we go," Chisholm said as the battery on the heights opened up. MacKim saw the gush of greasy white smoke an instant before he heard the roar of the cannon. "The French don't like us very much."

"They can't know that their man Dingwall is on board." MacKim could not help ducking as the French canister shot whistled above him. The knowledge that some faceless Frenchman was trying to kill him was disturbing, yet also strangely exhilarating. For the first time, MacKim felt like a real soldier.

As the British crept closer to shore, the French fire became more accurate. Cannonballs crashed into the crowded boats, killing, wounding and maiming. MacKim saw a shot smash into one vessel, raising a thin curtain of blood and pieces of flesh and bone, while screams sounded across the water. Another boat was sinking, with men struggling to swim as their heavy equipment dragged them down. MacKim stared, unable to help as a huge-eyed corporal raised his hands in a frantic appeal for assistance. Pieces of equipment and fragments of wood bobbed on the surface, and then they surged past, with the seamen digging deep at their oars.

Grapeshot slammed into the bulwark of MacKim's boat, spreading an arc of vicious wood splinters. A young private yelped and stared at his arm, from which a length of wood protruded, soon discoloured by pumping blood. The French fired again, the deeper boom of a twenty-four-pounder accompanied by the usual blast of white smoke. Scores of musket balls spattered onto the landing flotilla.

"Jesus save us!" Cumming shouted.

"It's getting hot," Chisholm said. He raised his voice. "Steady the 63rd!"

"We're the 78th now," Dingwall growled. "They've changed our number."

"So we are," Chisholm said. "Steady the 78th!"

"Silence in the boat!" Lieutenant Murray roared. "You are soldiers! Keep silent!"

Case shot churned the water to creamy froth as the oarsmen ducked their heads and towed the boats ashore. MacKim watched one stocky seaman with a tarred pigtail that extended nearly to his waist. He bent and pulled in a constant rhythm, ignoring the musket balls that pattered only a few feet away.

If he can do that, I can stand still. Be a man, Hugh Beg MacKim.

Behind them, the warships replied to the French guns, heeling under the weight of their broadsides, so that at any given moment there might be a hundred cannonballs crossing each other above the heads of the landing barges. Besides the High-landers, boats held the Grenadier companies of various regi-ments and the American Rangers, men that intrigued MacKim by their green uniforms and casual, confident attitudes, although he had never spoken to any of them. Ahead of them, the French continued to fire, with the muzzle-flashes now the only thing to be seen. As a vast blanket of powder-smoke thickened across the surface of the water, MacKim's vision was limited to the barge he was in and a few square yards of water, with the occasional glimpse of another boat as gusts of wind temporarily eased a gap in the smoke.

"Back!" Bellowed through a speaking- trumpet, the words came faintly over the hammer of the cannon. "Return to the ships! We're losing too many men!" Accompanying the words was the rattle of a drum sounding the retreat.

"They've repelled us; God damn them!" Chisholm muttered. "The damned Frenchies have forced us back!"

"That's the fortunes of war, my good man," Lieutenant Murray said. "Calm yourself. There will be other times."

The landing force faltered as some boats continued to steer for the land while others obediently turned back to the fleet.

"Look!" Wrestling his left arm free, Chisholm pointed ahead. "The Light Infantry has got ashore."

Peering through the smoke, MacKim saw the kilts and red jackets of the 78th Light Company, together with the green uniforms of the Rangers, crowding onto a tiny pebble beach. A succession of muzzle flares showed that the French were resisting.

"That's Cormorandiere Cove," Murray was poring over a map until a wave soaked him and washed the map overboard. He looked up, laughing. "And that's all we'll know about that until this business is complete!"

"There goes Pikestaff," Chisholm said.

Using the powder smoke as cover, General Wolfe stood in the stern of his boat, tall, angular and erect as he steered for Cormorandiere Cove

MacKim had a momentary glimpse of a roundshot screaming from Louisbourg before it took the head clean off one soldier, cut the man at the tiller in two, crushed Lieutenant Murray into bloody pulp and smashed into the boat. Ensign MacDonnell stared, open-mouthed, at the mess that had been his superior officer. With the helmsman dead, the barge began to veer to one side, leaving it broadside on to the French. Musketry began to target such an inviting target. Fortunately, the range was so long that most shots fell short, although sufficient cracked onto the boat to make life distinctly uncomfortable.

The noise of cannon and musketry was deafening, while the smoke stung MacKim's eyes and dried his mouth. He no longer tried to speak, but Chisholm put his mouth to MacKim's ear and shouted.

"We're taking in water."

Until that moment, MacKim had been too preoccupied with events to realise that something had holed the boat. Now, he became aware of water lapping over his feet and up to his ankles.

Ensign MacDonnell shouted something, with the batter of cannon masking the words. Sergeant Dingwall spoke in the ensign's ear and raised his voice to a roar. "The French have holed our boat! Search for the damage and tell me where it is!"

MacKim stared at the planking beneath his feet. Unable to even crouch because of the press of bodies, he could do no more.

"Over here!" The voice came from behind MacKim.

"Take your plaid off," Dingwall took command. "Plug the leak!"

Men shrugged off their tartan plaids and tramped them into the hole, through which the water was bubbling.

"Now, bail!" Dingwall shouted. "Use your bonnets or your hands. Bail out the water, lads!"

For the first time, MacKim appreciated Dingwall. After months of training, the men responded to the sergeant's commands without thought. Although their efforts did not seem to diminish the level of water within the boat, they remained afloat, still slowly moving towards the contested coast.

When more musket balls pattered around the boat, Dingwall crumpled, with one hand to his throat.

"They've killed the sergeant," Cumming said.

"No," Chisholm shook his head, "look again."

Dingwall struggled upright, gasping. "A spent ball," he croaked. "I'll be all right in a few hours." Gasping, he ripped open the top of his uniform, revealing the pink and white mess of an old burn mark that spread right across his chest. "Are there any more wounds? I can't feel. I'm numb!"

MacKim looked. "Only an old scar," he said.

"Aye, that was a long time ago. Is there anything new?"

"No, Sergeant."

"Look!" Chisholm pointed over the side, where the rope that should connect them to the longboat bobbed in the water. The barge was adrift, an even easier target for the guns of Louisbourg.

"Oh, God, help us!" Ensign MacDonnell shrieked.

Glancing at the ensign, Dingwall fastened his jacket and took charge. "Hail that frigate!" His voice was hoarse. "Does anybody here speak English?" He glanced at the ensign hopefully, and looked away, shaking his head. "The officer's out of things."

"I do!" MacKim shouted.

"Get up here, MacKim!" Dingwall waved him closer. "The officer is useless just now, and I've no voice left."

Willing hands helped MacKim squeeze to the stern.

"Here." Dingwall lifted a speaking trumpet from the deck and handed it to MacKim. "Shout out to that frigate," he indicated the nearest Royal Naval ship. "Say 'ahoy there, we need help'."

"Too late." MacKim pointed to the two small boats that the frigate had launched. "They've already seen us."

Four men rowed each boat, ignoring the French fire as they steered beside the stricken barge. A very youthful midshipman stood in the stern, grinning. "In you come, Sawnies! We'll take you ashore."

"We've to board the boats," MacKim told Dingwall.

"I know! I heard him!" Dingwall spat out a mouthful of blood and tried to speak louder. "Come on, lads! Into the longboats!" He put a hand on MacKim's shoulder. "Not you yet, MacKim." He dropped his voice as the Highlanders transferred to the long-boats, with grinning sailors helping their kilted passengers.

"Come on, ladies," one of the sailors shouted. "Mind your petticoats now."

About to retaliate, MacKim closed his mouth, recognising the words as banter rather than anything more serious. "What is it, Sergeant?"

"I didn't know you spoke English, MacKim."

"Yes, Sergeant."

"How did you manage that?"

MacKim grunted. "I thought it might be useful sometime, so I learned."

"I see." Dingwall helped the shaken ensign onto a longboat

and watched as he sat in the stern. "I'll keep my eye on you, MacKim. Rankers who speak English are not common in Fraser's Highlanders."

MacKim said nothing. He did not like the idea of Sergeant Dingwall singling him out.

When the Highlanders removed their plaids from the shot holes, water surged in.

"Get off, you scoundrels!" Dingwall shoved the Highlanders into the longboats. "We're sinking!"

MacKim ducked as the French fired again, with roundshot crashing into the hull of the nearby frigate. Tall fountains of water rose around them, to hover a second and then slowly patter downward.

"On we go, ladies!" Ignoring the plunging roundshot, the seamen pulled mightily for the shore.

"We're well behind the rest now," Dingwall said. "We'll miss the ball."

"Come on, lads!" the midshipman, all of fifteen years old, piped up. "Get these ladies ashore!"

"Aye, aye, sir!" The seamen put all their muscle into trying to catch up.

"Don't you fret, girls," a gap-toothed seaman shouted. "We'll soon have you on land, all safe and sound!"

"There's heavy surf ahead." The midshipman in charge of MacKim's boat looked to MacKim to translate. "It will be a rough landing."

MacKim could hear the hollow crash of the surf and see great silver-white breakers splintering on the coast. The midshipman narrowed his eyes as he steered them through the long rollers. "Hold onto your petticoats, girls!"

MacKim did not translate as the Highlanders grabbed the gunwales.

"What a way to start a campaign," Chisholm said, as they tipped to the left, then the right. The boat rocked so violently that MacKim thought they would capsize until they roared onto the beach with the gravel crunching under their keel and the seamen lifting their oars at the final moment. MacKim was so intent on the landing that he hardly heard the constant hammer of the Royal Navy guns, responding to the defensive fire from the French.

"Out, lads!" Dingwall croaked. "Come on, sir, we have to go now." Once again, he helped the young ensign.

As the Highlanders scrambled ashore, the midshipman doffed his hat. "Best of luck, Sawnies! Sorry we couldn't land you any closer, but Louisbourg is that way!" Waving a cheery farewell, he had his men row back out to sea.

Watching the boats disappear, MacKim felt a sudden sense of abandonment. He and his small detachment of untried soldiers were in French North America, with no clear idea where the enemy, or the remainder of the British Army, might be.

Standing to attention beside the ensign, Dingwall produced a splendid salute. "What are your orders, sir?"

"My orders?" MacDonnell could not have been more than seventeen, a young boy out of his depth.

"Yes, sir. With Lieutenant Murray gone, you're in charge now." Dingwall's voice was slowly returning. He pointed to the men who stood in small clumps, staring around them at their pebble beach and the rising ground that dominated the beach. "Do you want us to join the rest of the army, sir? We're a bit away from them."

MacDonnell picked at the lieutenant's blood that was spattered on his uniform. "Where are we, Sergeant?"

"We're somewhere to the west of Louisbourg, sir." Dingwall coughed and spat up blood. "The rest of the army is that way." He pointed towards the town. "I believe that the Light Bobs landed, with General Wolfe."

"We'd better get to the general, then." MacDonnell was shaking so hard he could hardly speak. "You lead the way, Sergeant."

"We're lucky there's not a French piquet here," Chisholm

said. "Check your flints, boys, make sure they're still dry, and that goes for the powder in your pans, too."

Dingwall nodded. "Do as Chisholm says," he croaked. "Follow me."

Climbing up the range of scrubby heights that backed onto the beach, they had only advanced a hundred yards when they found a barrier blocking their path. MacKim stared at the long, deep construction of cut and sharpened logs, thorns and brushwood. "What the devil is that?"

"It's known as an *abattis*," Chisholm said. "That's the polite term. We also call it a right bastard."

Dingwall hawked and spat blood before speaking. "Thank God there's no Frenchies guarding it or we'd all be dead by now."

MacDonnell looked as if he was about to break into tears. "We'll have to go back."

"No, sir," Dingwall said. "There's nowhere for us to go. We have to press on."

Chisholm's voice was too low for the ensign to hear. "That's a savage barrier to our progress, MacKim." He raised his voice slightly. "Our axemen will have to cut through, if the ensign gives the order."

Dingwall threw another salute. "Sir, shall I order the axemen to cut our way through?"

MacDonnell nodded as if he had just witnessed salvation. "Oh, yes please, Sergeant. Do that."

The axemen rushed forward. Among the brawniest of the company, they swung their axes with enthusiasm, hacking a slow path through the tangle.

"Ugly, you and MacKim stand piquet at the top of the rise. Watch for Frenchies."

Aware of the increased hammer of his heart as he scrambled up the ridge, MacKim glanced at Chisholm and felt reassurance at the sight of that twisted, ruined face.

"Keep six feet apart," Chisholm said. "If we're closer, one ball can hit both of us, yet we need to be able to support each other, and for God's sake, don't stand on the skyline."

From up here, the abattis stretched away into the distance, a barrier between them and the rest of the British force but also a protection from French scouts. MacKim hardly noticed the hammer of artillery as the Royal Navy exchanged fire with Louisbourg; it was already part of life.

"Thank God the French haven't got piquets to defend the abattis," Chisholm repeated. "Imagine having to hack our way through that under fire! The French commander should be ashamed of himself, leaving this flank unguarded."

MacKim nodded. So far, his introduction to war had not been as he expected. No glorious charge against a brave enemy, no noble officers waving swords as the regiment's colours flapped in the wind, only gunfire, a damaged boat and this lonely shore.

"We're through, Sergeant." The leading axeman wiped sweat from his forehead.

"Report to the officer," Dingwall commanded and waited for the ensign's word before he led the men through the gap. Once the 78th had formed a defensive line on the far side of the abattis, Dingwall signalled for Chisholm and MacKim to join them.

"Take the rearguard, you two."

Again, there were no Frenchmen as the 78th climbed the ridge and advanced towards Louisbourg, muskets ready and throats dry.

"MacKim," Dingwall waved across the straggling column, "come here." His hard, suspicious eyes glowered at MacKim. "You speak English then, so you'll think you're better than us mere mortals."

"I don't think that, Sergeant." MacKim expected a trap.

Dingwall grunted. "Tell me then, if you're so clever, why we are here?"

"Why, to capture Louisbourg, of course," MacKim said.

"Aye, and why do we wish to capture Louisbourg?"

"Because it's French," MacKim said.

"It is that." Dingwall's voice was recovering although it would be some time until he regained his roar. "You see, Louisbourg's at the northernmost point of Île-Royale, or Cape Breton Island, if you prefer, and the French fortress here is above a harbour, where our navy is."

MacKim glanced over his shoulder, seeing the British fleet dominating the large harbour, the flare of their broadsides intermittent behind banks of powder smoke.

Dingwall fingered his throat. "Whoever has this fort and harbour, can control the entrance of the St Lawrence River, and whoever controls the river controls Canada."

MacKim frowned, taking in these concepts. He had never considered strategy before. "Why is that, Sergeant?" *More importantly, why are you telling me?*

"The St Lawrence river flows by Quebec and Montreal, Canada's two major cities. Ships bring supplies to both. If the French hold Louisbourg, they can deny us access to the river, so their grip on the country is secure. If we hold Louisbourg, we can deny the French supplies and bring in our army to capture Quebec."

"We'd better capture Louisbourg then," MacKim said.

"Aye, we'd better." Dingwall's eyes were never still as he surveyed the surrounding country. "Not only will we be striking a blow against France, we'll also show King George that his Highlanders are loyal."

MacKim pointed ahead, where the coast curved into a deep bay, marked by the silver-white of splintering surf. Hundreds of red-coated men crowded onto the beach, while the popping of musketry told its own story. "Is that not the main force, Sergeant?"

"Some of them at least. Others did not make it." Dingwall indicated the capsized boats in the breakers. He waved the men on and spoke to the ensign. "With your permission, sir, we will join these others."

"Oh, yes." MacDonnell still looked shocked. "Carry on, Sergeant."

"Urquhart, Cattanach, out on the flank and watch for Frenchies. The rest, follow the ensign and me." The 78th marched on, faster now that they knew they were joining the main landing party.

Men were still splashing ashore from the madly rocking boats; Highlanders in kilts, Grenadiers in tall mitre hats and with distinctive ornamental wings protruding from their shoulders, and the long, lean Rangers with weathered faces and a variety of headgear above their green uniforms. Officers and sergeants shouted in near apoplexy as they tried to instil some order into the mixed units.

Dingwall waved his hand. "Come on, lads!" He marched his small force toward the bulk of the 78th.

❧ 6 ❧

LOUISBOURG, JUNE 1758

"I thought we had lost you, MacDonnell," Captain Simon Fraser addressed the ensign. "I am glad you brought your men here. Well done."

Ensign MacDonnell gave a small smile. "Thank you, sir."

"You men, join your colleagues," Captain Fraser said.

"No appreciation for the sergeant, then," MacKim observed.

"Did you expect there to be?" Chisholm shook his head. "Don't worry about that, Hugh. It will never change. The men get the hard knocks, the officers gain the glory." He nodded to the left, where a knot of senior officers had gathered together. "There's Brigadier Wolfe himself, our own Pikestaff."

Close to, Wolfe was tall and thin, with a weak chin. MacKim grunted. "He doesn't look like much."

"Wolfe is a bloody man," Chisholm warned. "He'll go for the French throat, that I know." He pointed to a series of stone-and-earth fortifications that overlooked the beach. "We'll see in a few moments."

"Are the French up there?"

"They're watching everything we do," Chisholm said. "They're probably wondering what we are – soldiers in kilts and soldiers dressed in green. They won't have seen anything like it before."

MacKim forced a smile, although he felt very uncomfortable standing with French soldiers watching him.

"Lachie MacLachlan of Fraser's was first on shore." Chisholm sounded as relaxed as if he was in an Inverness tavern. "Pikestaff gave him a guinea, I heard."

MacKim grunted. "That's something."

"That's a lot more than Colonel Fraser gave Dingwall." Chisholm ducked as the French battery eventually opened up, spraying the beach with grapeshot. Two Grenadiers fell, one to lie still, the other kicking and twisting on the pebbles. Sparing them only a glance, Chisholm continued, "We'll show the king that we're the best soldiers in the army."

MacKim picked himself up from the beach. He did not remember having dived down. Chisholm winked at him.

"You'll get used to it, MacKim. The first few times are always bad. Then it gets worse, but you learn when to duck and when not to." He grinned. "They say you never hear the shot that hits you, so that might help."

"It doesn't help in the slightest."

MacKim was surprised how leisurely this business of war seemed to be. He had expected an immediate advance on Louisbourg, with a bloody assault, the thrill of drums and pipes, and bayonets flashing in the sun. Instead, the officers seemed more concerned with getting the men in proper ranks as the French continued a desultory fire that knocked down a man here and there without impeding the landing. The weather was more disrupting as it deteriorated during the day, capsizing boats and making each seaman sweat. However, the invading force was finally all on the beach.

"The Frenchies lost their opportunity there," Chisholm spoke around the stem of his pipe. "If they had even sent one regiment to oppose us, they could have caused serious damage."

"Let's pray they remain so indolent," MacKim said.

With Wolfe in charge of the Brigade and Brigadier General Lawrence landing to the left of Wolfe's force, the British dressed their line, the drums sounded the advance, eager ensigns held the Colours aloft, and the invasion force moved upwards toward the French.

Here we go, into battle at last. MacKim tried to moisten his suddenly dry throat. *Dear God, let me survive this day.*

Dingwall looked over his platoon. "Stay in formation, you scoundrels of the 78th. I want no stragglers and nobody bounding forward. Remember that you are soldiers, not warriors."

"I still preferred us as the 63rd," Chisholm said. "We were higher up the army list."

"They can give us any number they like, Ugly," Dingwall had the sergeant's ability to hear even the smallest sound from the ranks, "but they can't alter what we are. We are Fraser's Highlanders."

MacKim looked around at the kilted Gaels that surrounded him. For a moment, he was back at Drummossie Moor, with the piles of shattered bodies as laughing, red-coated soldiers paddled in Highland blood. He might be fighting in one of King George's regiments, but he would never forget that day. He would never forget his oath.

Concentrate on today. Win this battle. Gain experience. Survive.

Straightening his back, MacKim faced his front and prayed as they marched towards the waiting French outposts. The crackle of musketry and spurts of white smoke seemed muted, strangely unwarlike, as if events were happening to somebody else, and not him, and then MacKim ducked as something whined past his head.

"You're nearly a real soldier now, Hugh," Chisholm said, out of the corner of his mouth.

"When will I be a real soldier?"

"When you've tasted the enemy's powder smoke," Chisholm said. "Now keep in step and ignore the noise."

The spatter of musketry continued, and then MacKim saw a score of white-uniformed figures scrambling out of the closest earthwork. *Frenchmen! I can see the enemy!* MacKim readied his musket, only to see the French retreating before the British closed.

"Hold your fire!" Colonel Fraser ordered.

"Steady, MacKim!" Dingwall warned, as a couple of men began to surge in front. "Stay in formation!"

The British trampled over the first outpost and marched on to the next, with the French again withdrawing when the British closed.

"I thought the French were good fighters," MacKim said. "All they do is fire and run."

"They know that Fraser's Highlanders are coming," Urquhart said.

"Follow them. Don't allow them to regroup," Colonel Fraser ordered. "Ensigns, fire by platoon if you see a target."

"We'll take Louisbourg in one day," MacKim said. "The Frenchies aren't going to fight!"

Looking along the length of the British advance, he saw the mitre hats of the Grenadiers standing tall, wondered if Hayes was among them and watched in fascination as a musket ball burrowed into the ground in front of him. *Spent ball*, he told himself. *If the Frenchman were a yard further forward, it would have hit me. The margin between life and death is less than the span of an arm.*

"Pikestaff's doing his job," Chisholm said. Wolfe's angular form was prominent, leading from the front as the British pursued the French, exchanging fire whenever they could.

"This is rough country." Wolfe's voice was high and surprisingly clear over the sporadic spatter of musketry.

Cumming glanced at MacKim and shook his head. "I thought the general had served in Scotland."

"He did," Chisholm said dryly.

"He should know that this is hardly rough country, then,"

Cumming said, and added, "Maybe he's got soft with fighting in Europe."

"Not our Pikestaff." Chisholm said. "There's Louisbourg now."

MacKim had one glimpse of long grey walls before the French artillery opened up and white powder-smoke obscured his view. The cannonballs fell short of the British advance, ploughing into the hard ground or raising miniature volcanoes of dust and stones.

"Halt, 78th!" Colonel Fraser ordered.

On the word of command, the army stopped, with French infantrymen scurrying away to the shelter of Louisbourg's guns. When it became apparent that the British were coming no closer, the French artillery ceased fire. The smoke drifted away, giving the men a clear sight of the fortress they had come to capture.

"So that's Louisbourg," Chisholm said. "It looks a tough place."

Sergeant Dingwall nodded. "It's the lock that secures French North America, lads, and we have to be the key. There are two miles of perimeter walls, with four massive gates, seven bastions and five guardhouses."

"Bugger that!" Cumming said softly.

MacKim looked along the length of stone walls. Even from this distance, he could see the startlingly bright red tunics of French artillerymen standing by the guns.

"It's well defended," Chisholm said.

"A hundred cannon, they say, and over three and a half thousand French soldiers shipped over specially to keep us out." Dingwall was keen to show off his knowledge. "They have five warships in the harbour, too, bristling with cannon to repel our navy."

"They'll need more than five ships to defeat the Royal Navy," Chisholm murmured.

"There are more than three thousand of us," MacKim said. "Can we not just go and attack them?"

"On you go, son." Dingwall said. "You evidently know more about attacking a fortress than all the generals and admirals in the army of King George." He shook his head. "Let me educate you, MacKim." Dingwall pointed to the distant stone battlements. "Once the gunner puts in his thirteen pounds of gunpowder, the French cannon can fire its ball for a mile and a half. Now, imagine the power of that shot, and think of its effect on a file of infantry."

MacKim nodded, suddenly sober. He realised how little he knew about being a soldier. A year's drill and one day's skirmishing was not sufficient.

"Now that you are listening," Dingwall said, "I'll give you the good news. Most of the fort's cannon point seaward, toward the harbour. The French did not expect us to land in the face of their infantry and the high surf."

The invaders stood in disciplined ranks, glowering at the enemy fortification. MacKim searched the length of the stone walls.

"How big is Louisbourg, Sergeant? Is it just a fort?"

Dingwall settled down behind a rock. "It's not much more than a walled town," he said. "A very well defended walled town. You can see the fortifications. As well as the cannon, bastions and half bastions, Louisbourg has a ditch and a *glacis* – that's the sloping banks we'll have to climb if we assault the place."

Cumming's eyes did not stray from Louisbourg's walls. "Can we take it, Sergeant?"

"Yes," Dingwall said. "We can take it."

"If it's a town," Cumming sounded interested, "there will be women there as well as men."

"Some," Dingwall said. "Maybe a few hundred, but mostly merchants' wives or officers' wives."

"If there are wives," Cumming said, "there will be daughters as well."

Dingwall grunted. "Maybe so, Cumming, but we have to get in first, and that won't be easy."

※

WHILE THE FRENCH ARTILLERY REINFORCED DINGWALL'S words that taking Louisbourg would not be easy, the British Army settled down for a formal European-style siege. Wolfe found a suitable spot to land his guns three miles from Louisbourg and ordered them dragged to the British positions.

"We've no oxen or horses to pull the artillery," Cumming pointed out.

"We don't need them," Chisholm said. "We've got plenty other beasts of burden, Cumming."

"Where?" Cumming looked around until he realised that Chisholm was pointing directly at him.

"You, Cumming," Chisholm said. "You and me and all the other rankers in Geordie's army."

"Come on, you, men!" Dingwall's voice had nearly recovered. "We've got work to do."

Sweating, cursing and toiling with the others, MacKim helped to pull the guns around to the landward wall of Louisbourg.

"How come they aren't helping?" Cumming pointed to a group of Rangers, who stood a hundred yards from the toiling men, searching inland.

"They're the Colonial scouts, Cumming," Chisholm said. "They're guarding the flanks and watching for French or Canadian skirmishers. The Canadians will find a team of men hauling a naval gun a perfect target." He pointed to the Rangers. "You'll thank God for those lads. I've heard nothing but good of them."

"We can guard ourselves," Cumming said. "I thought we were soldiers, not oxen."

"Whoever said you were a soldier?" Dingwall kicked

Cumming's leg. "Soldiers obey orders without question, while you complain about everything!"

"I heard that the Colonials are poor soldiers," Cumming said. "They're badly disciplined and cowardly."

Chisholm grunted. "I suspect that one campaign in their company will make you alter your opinion, Cumming."

"How high are these walls?" MacKim wiped sweat from his forehead and jerked a thumb towards Louisbourg's fortifications.

"Thirty feet at a guess," Dingwall said, "and probably just as thick."

"We'll never get through them." Cumming shook his head. "We're wasting our time. The French must be laughing at us, with their artillery behind stone walls thirty bloody feet thick."

"They're sweating as much as we are," Dingwall said. "The French have two fronts to worry about and have to weaken their seaward defences by moving some guns to counter us."

Hauling heavy pieces of artillery across the unbroken country was as hard work as fighting. It took time and effort, while all the time, the British were digging in outside the walls of Louisbourg. During the landing, the British had taken about seventy French prisoners, who cheerfully said the garrison consisted of five battalions: Bourgogne, Artois, Royal Marine, Cambise, and Voluntaires Estrainger, plus about 700 Canadian Volunteers.

"Quite a strong garrison then." MacKim sat outside his tent after a hard shift with the artillery, shaving with his bayonet.

"It's a bit weaker than it was before we landed." Chisholm bit on a hunk of tobacco. "We also captured three twenty-four-pounders, seven nine-pounders, fourteen swivels and two mortars. Not a bad start." He grinned. "We're chipping away at them bit by bit. The beauty of it is, as long as we're here, the French can't get any reinforcements or supplies. Every day that passes, the French will be slightly weaker. Every time they fire a gun, they lessen their ammunition and every day they have less food."

"We don't have time to starve them out," Cumming said.

"We may as well go home now."

On the 12th June, with fog again rolling in from the sea, General Wolfe led twelve hundred men around the magnificent harbour. "Not us, MacKim," Dingwall said. "We're making entrenchments to defend the guns."

"I'd like to volunteer, Sergeant," MacKim said.

"Then you're a fool." Dingwall glowered at him. "As soon as you joined the army, you made an appointment with death. He's waiting, somewhere, in some shape or form. Why invite yourself into his parlour? Your time will come." Dingwall shook his head. "Soldiers seldom die of old age."

MacKim watched Wolfe's force march away and later heard the stories, wishing he had been there. He did not care about the glory, but having seen the Grenadiers close up, he had been awed by their professionalism and knew he had to improve his fighting skills if he hoped to kill Hayes.

"We were first to Lighthouse Point," MacLaughlin of the 78th's Grenadier company boasted. "We went in with the bayonet before they even knew we were there." In common with all the Grenadiers, MacLaughlin was taller than average, a robust man with a ready grin and forearms that would put a small man's thighs to shame. "Some of the lads drew their swords," MacLaughlin said. "Chop, slice and the Frenchies were no more."

"Poor buggers," Chisholm said. "They're soldiers, just like us."

"They're the enemy." MacLaughlin's laughter died as quickly as it had started.

"MacLaughlin's correct," Dingwall said. "They're the enemy. We are here to destroy them."

Nodding, MacKim closed his mouth. He was a soldier now. His occupation was killing the enemy. He could not think of them as people. They had to be faceless, outside the orbit of humanity. He had to consider the French as the epitome of evil, at least until after King George had won his war.

7

LOUISBOURG, JULY 1758

"Our artillerymen will set up guns here," Chisholm said, as they stood on recently captured Lighthouse Point. "It's an excellent spot to batter the French."

"It's a strange angle to hit the town," MacKim said.

"We won't target the town. See the artillery battery on that island down there?" Chisholm pointed to the wind-ruffled blue of the harbour. "Their guns defend the harbour. From up here, our guns can silence the French battery, and that will allow our ships to move closer, maybe cut out the French vessels. A siege is like chess, each move calculated to cancel out the enemy's pieces and move closer to capturing his king."

"It's very cold-blooded," MacKim said.

"War is cold-blooded. Move and counter move, with careful planning as important as courage." Chisholm sighed. "The old days of a crazed charge with swords are gone, MacKim. We learned that on Culloden Moor. Now we have to fight by manoeuvre. Disciplined bravery and firepower win battles, not a few moments' recklessness. Courage counts for nothing before massed musketry."

On June 19th, with all the guns in position, the batteries on Lighthouse Point opened fire on the island.

"How many guns have we?" MacKim asked.

"Seventy," Chisholm knew all the answers, "including cannons and mortars. Not all on Lighthouse Point, of course."

After a few moments, the powder smoke hid everything from view, and the constant thunder of the guns prevented any conversation. Only when the guns fell silent and an offshore wind blew away the smoke, did MacKim see that the guns had marginally damaged Louisbourg's wall and holed the roofs of some of the more visible buildings. It seemed little result for such a great effort.

"What happens next?"

"We have to make a breach in the walls," Chisholm explained. "When we've done that, we'll ask the French to surrender. If the French commander thinks he can't hold off an attack, he will surrender, and we'll take possession."

"And if he thinks he can hold out?"

"Then he'll refuse to surrender, and we'll capture Louisbourg by assault." Chisholm sucked on an empty pipe. "That's a horrible, bloody business. Once we're in, if we carry the breach, the French might fight street by street. If we take the town, the lads will run wild. There will be pillage and rapine on a scale you can't imagine, Hugh. Men you know as quiet and orderly, will become drunken brutes."

"Why?"

"You will understand if you experience the battle for a breach. Once you've seen your friends burned alive, spitted on swords, shredded by artillery and left as screaming wrecks on the ground, you will understand why men go berserk after they capture a town. Pray that the French surrender and spare everybody such horrors."

"We're pushing them back to their walls," MacKim said. "They must surrender soon."

"Never underestimate Johnny Frenchman," Chisholm said. "The French will retaliate, they're too good soldiers just to sit back and leave us in peace."

Chisholm was correct. Night after night, small parties of Frenchmen slipped from Louisbourg to harass the British entrenchments. The British doubled their piquets and sent patrols to roam in front of their lines, so the ground around Louisbourg became the scene of skirmishes as units of French, Canadians and British clashed.

"MACKIM," DINGWALL KICKED MACKIM AWAKE AN HOUR before reveille, "you haven't been on a scouting piquet yet."

MacKim blinked up at him, his mind dazed from sleep. "No, Sergeant."

"It's time you advanced your military education then. Ugly, Cattanach, Urquhart, Cumming, you come too."

"Where are we going, Sergeant?"

"Out towards the French. Keep silent and do as I tell you," Dingwall said. "If I say stop, you stop. If I say fire, you fire. If I say run, you take to your heels and run as if Old Hornie was prodding his tail into your lazy arse!"

"Yes, Sergeant." MacKim reached for the fragment of bread he had saved from last night. He seemed to be permanently hungry out here.

"Keep your head down, Hugh," Chisholm murmured. "You're not here for glory."

"Keep quiet," Dingwall whispered. "The French will also have piquets out."

Gripping his musket so tightly that his knuckles were white, MacKim followed Dingwall into the night-dark bush. With his kilt swishing against his bare knees and the air cool on his face, he tested each step for twigs, loose pebbles or anything else that could alert a wary Frenchman.

They moved forward slowly, hearing the rumble of artillery and the query of a nervous sentry. Once a bird called, the sound melancholic in the dark, and the distant hush of the sea was a reminder of where they were.

"Stop." Dingwall put a hand on MacKim's shoulder. "Somebody's ahead."

The Highlanders halted. MacKim wondered if they all felt as nervous as he did. Urquhart's laboured breathing suggested that he was not as confident as he looked, while Cumming was muttering under his breath. Nodding, MacKim met Chisholm's eye and winked. Chisholm responded with a grin.

"Ugly, MacKim, come with me, I hear Frenchies. Corporal Gunn, look after the rest until I return."

Gunn was a keen man in his thirties with a long face and a bitter tongue. "Yes, Sergeant!'

MacKim moved forward again, even slower than before, licking dry lips as the voices came to him, soft on the breeze and speaking French. The smell was next, tobacco and rum.

"Follow in my footsteps," Dingwall murmured. He eased them over a ridge and stopped, with his left hand held high.

"Dear God." MacKim felt the breath stop in his throat.

The French waited in three seemingly endless rows. A shift of wind allowed moonlight to filter through the clouds, shining on white uniforms and a plethora of faces. MacKim thought they looked even younger than the 78th, youths with pinched faces and immature moustaches, carrying muskets that seemed too long for them. Despite their proximity to the British lines, some were openly talking, and one man sipped at a bottle.

Is this the enemy of which we are so nervous? They don't look as ferocious as I thought

Wordless, Dingwall motioned for MacKim and Chisholm to withdraw. Only when they were back with the rest of the piquet did Dingwall speak.

"I estimate about four hundred men," he said quietly.

"I'd guess double that," Chisholm said. "How about you, MacKim? You're an educated man."

"I didn't count them," MacKim admitted. "I've never seen so many Frenchmen together before."

"Never lose an opportunity," Dingwall said. "Learn all you can about the enemy before you fight them. Intelligence is half the battle. Now, we have to report this to the colonel. Follow me, lads."

COLONEL FRASER LISTENED TO DINGWALL'S REPORT, NODDING. "Between four hundred and a thousand Frenchmen, you say?"

"Yes, sir."

"What were they doing, Sergeant?"

"I'd say they were preparing a major raid on our positions, sir."

"How long before they come?"

"Not long, sir. They seemed nearly ready to advance."

Colonel Fraser nodded again. "No time to alert General Wolfe, then. We will have to move without the support of other regiments."

MacKim guessed that Colonel Fraser welcomed the 78th acting alone. Ever since the Jacobite Risings of 1715 and 1745, the other people of Great Britain had viewed Highlanders with great suspicion. Colonel Fraser's father had been the Lord Lovat who the government had beheaded for his part in the Forty-five, so the colonel was eager to prove his loyalty to the Hanoverian crown.

The 78th marched out within ten minutes, each man with his Brown Bess at his shoulder, his powder and ball in their pouches and his broadsword at his waist.

Chisholm touched MacKim's arm. "This could end in a real battle, Hugh. Look to your front and do your duty."

MacKim tried to analyse his feelings; he was undoubtedly nervous, but he also felt some excitement, even exhilaration. He had joined the army to become a soldier, and here was his first real test. *Once I am trained and experienced, I'll be able to match Hayes, even although he is a Grenadier.*

"Load your flintlocks," Colonel Fraser ordered. MacKim worked with the routine precision that had been drilled into him, ramming powder and shot down the long barrel of his musket.

"March," Colonel Fraser ordered. "Sergeant Dingwall, you saw this French battalion. Join me in front."

At one time, MacKim had envisioned marching to battle behind the scream of the battle-pipes, with great silk banners above and all the glory and panoply of war. Instead, he was engaged in this almost furtive advance in the half-darkness with whispered orders and no clear idea of what they might face.

"How far are they now?" Colonel Fraser asked as they advanced into the darkness.

"About three hundred yards, sir," Dingwall reported.

"Make ready your muskets," Fraser commanded, with junior officers and NCOs passing the orders down the ranks. Remaining in column, the 78th halted, and then continued, moving closer to the enemy. The French had not moved. They stood in their lines, awaiting orders from their officers, or waiting to ambush any unwary British force.

The wind had risen, passing fitful clouds over the moon so one moment the French were visible, the next they were in darkness.

The 78th took up positions as they had been trained, forming a long line in as much silence as they could, two hundred yards from the enemy. Still in line, they moved forward, step by step. MacKim felt the ground rough under his feet, heard the rustle of kilts and the scrape of boots on loose stones and wondered how the French could not detect them.

Is this some elaborate ruse? Are the French leading us into a trap so that a thousand Canadians will open fire on us? I feel sick.

A hundred yards, fifty; the French were now in killing range, two lines of unsuspecting soldiers, young men from the back streets of Paris who had come to Canada in the hopes of a better life, soon to feel the weight of a British infantry volley.

"Present."

Hundreds of muskets rose to hundreds of scarlet-clad shoulders.

"Fire," Colonel Fraser ordered, so softly that MacKim hardly heard him.

There was no point in aiming. The Brown Bess was notoriously inaccurate, and British soldiers were trained to fire at the mass of the enemy. The 78th fired by company, vast blasts of sound as white smoke jetted out and bright muzzle flares split the night. MacKim followed orders, barely aware of the men on either side as he lifted his musket and pressed the trigger.

Taken by surprise, the French lines staggered as hundreds of musket balls crashed into them.

"Now, 78th! Out claymores and charge! *Charge*!"

It was an order that MacKim had never expected to hear. The last time the Frasers had charged with swords had been at Culloden. Here, Colonel Fraser's tactics had followed the example used by the Marquis of Montrose a century and more before, during his year of victories over the Covenanting armies. After their musketry had unsettled the enemy, the 78th launched a screaming charge with naked swords.

When used correctly, the Highland charge was nearly irresistible. Seeing the kilted Highlanders pounding toward them, yelling their Gaelic slogans and with broadswords raised high, the already-shaken French infantry panicked and broke. Within seconds, the 78th were among them, slashing with the swords, decapitating, slicing off limbs, hacking into defenceless bodies. MacKim charged with the rest, feeling his sword light in his hand. He saw a young Frenchman lifting his musket, bravely standing to face the Fraser's charge. MacKim raised his sword high, as his father had done at Sheriffmuir, as his great grandfather had done at Killiecrankie and Dunkeld. The Frenchman took a step backwards, his face suddenly white; his mouth dropped open as he turned to run.

MacKim swung his sword. The blade sliced into the Frenchman's shoulder, taking the arm off cleanly. The Frenchman carried on running with bright blood spurting. After a dozen steps, he halted, stared at his shoulder and screamed once. MacKim stopped in horror at what he had done.

"Oh, God in heaven!"

"Aye, MacKim, you're a soldier now." Dingwall pushed him onward. "Don't stop, lad! The more of them we kill, the less of them there are to kill us."

As the Frasers' charge continued, many of the French dropped their weapons and surrendered, although the majority escaped into the dark.

"Come on, 78th! We can take the city ourselves!" Waving his sword in the air, Cumming ran towards the outlying defences of Louisbourg. "Advance the Fraser Highlanders!"

For a moment, MacKim believed Cumming was correct. In the elation of temporary victory, it seemed as if the Frasers could capture Louisbourg without help. The roar of the great French cannon broke the dream as grapeshot and cannonballs hammered down, churning up the ground around them.

"Enough!" Colonel Fraser yelled. "Halt and reform! Drummer! Sound the recall!"

Most of the Highlanders obeyed the order, but a few ran on until they realised they could not break through the outer defences and scale the thirty foot high walls without ladders, especially in the teeth of an alerted French garrison.

"Get back now, Hugh." Chisholm grabbed hold of MacKim's sleeve. "You can't capture Louisbourg on your own."

MacKim took a deep breath to calm his racing heart. The frenzy of battle had temporarily taken control of him. Now, he looked around at the dead, dying and prisoners.

"MacKim!" Dingwall's roar proved he had recovered entirely

from the effects of the spent musket ball on his throat. "Get back to the ranks!"

Fraser's Highlanders withdrew in good order, laughing as they shepherded their prisoners.

"These French lads look very young," MacKim said. "Some are little more than boys."

"So much the better for us," Chisholm said. "If all the French soldiers are like them, this campaign will be easy." When he replaced his broadsword in its scabbard, MacKim noted that the blade was clean. Chisholm, the veteran, had not killed any of the enemy.

"I HEAR THAT SOME IRISH FELLOW, LIEUTENANT COLONEL O'Donnel, led these French lads," Chisholm said. "They were going to sortie against us."

"They'll have to be quick to catch the 78th," Cumming said, looking up from sharpening the flints of his musket.

"They were just boys," MacKim said. "The French must have better than that."

"They have," Chisholm said. "I met them at Fontenoy."

"Were you at Fontenoy, Chisholm?" Urquhart asked. "I didn't know that."

MacKim joined in the general laughter. Chisholm was fond of bringing up his Fontenoy experiences at every opportunity.

"Somebody killed O'Donnel with the bayonet," Chisholm said. "But old Sergeant MacLeodwas wounded. Some Frenchie shot him on the nose." Drill Sergeant Donald MacLeod was one of the characters of the regiment. Nobody knew how old he was, but some claimed he had fought at Killiecrankie in 1689, while others said he had advised the Marquis of Montrose back in 1644.

"So there are Irishmen on the French side," MacKim said. "Loyalty appears to be a flexible concept."

"You swore an oath to the king when you joined the regiment," Dingwall said. "Keep your oath, boy, and nobody can think ill of you." He leaned closer to MacKim. "Break your oath, and you're a traitorous dog who deserves hanging."

I have taken two oaths in my life, and one is far more important than the other.

The action against O'Donnel's force brought the British a few yards closer to Louisbourg, gaining them high ground opposite to the Dauphin Gate. Within hours, General Wolfe had men and horses dragging up the artillery to further pound Louisbourg's walls and town.

"We're winning," Cumming gloated.

"I've said before that siege warfare is like chess," Chisholm said. "We make a move; they make a move. We cancelled the last French move, so they'll try something else."

Once again, Chisholm was proved correct, as a French raid on July 9th took the British by surprise. MacKim and the 78th heard the shouting and sporadic firing as the raiding party burst into the entrenchment and used picks and crowbars to reduce a long section of the siege works, pushing back the British efforts by some days. The French withdrew, ushering nearly thirty Grenadiers from the 45th and 22nd Foot back to Louisbourg as prisoners.

"They didn't attack the 78th." MacKim was not sure if he was pleased or disappointed.

"They know better,"' Chisholm said, as Dingwall sharpened his bayonet with a stone.

"They've given us work to do," Dingwall said. "We'll have to rebuild the siege lines. That will take time we can't afford."

Increasing their piquets, the British cursed, spat on their hands and repaired the damage. Every few days, the British guns crept closer to Louisbourg, naval 24- and 32-pounders that hurled their iron shot against Louisbourg's walls and the buildings inside. But every day they spent outside the walls was more time the French had gained.

MacKim watched the dust rise from another artillery strike on Louisbourg. "I wouldn't like to be on the other side of these cannon."

"We're creeping closer to the Dauphin Gate," Chisholm said. "That must be the general's objective."

Day by day, the bombardment continued, with British cannonballs and mortars hammering at Louisbourg and the shipping in the harbour. Day by day, the British reduced the defending walls, silencing cannon after French cannon. Day by day, the British extended their lines, digging trenches, putting in gabions, inching closer to the walls of Louisbourg.

"Are you volunteering again to go on piquet, MacKim?" Chisholm asked.

"I am," MacKim said.

"You won't be happy until you get your fool head blown off or a Frenchy bayonet in your gut."

"I won't get either," MacKim said.

"Why are you so keen?"

"I want to be the best soldier I can be." MacKim tested the lock of his musket, ensured the flint was sharp, dabbed candle-grease on the inside of his scabbard to ensure his bayonet drew smoothly and joined the piquet.

He did not tell anybody, not even Chisholm, why he had joined the army. That was his affair alone. Every time on piquet duty increased his experience, every minor skirmish with the French hardened him to death and killing, and every day he learned more about the British formations. By the third week of July, MacKim knew exactly where Webb's 48th Foot was positioned, and he could tell by the tall mitre hats which section of line the Grenadiers usually guarded.

One day, soon, he promised himself. *I'm coming for you, Hayes.*

On the 21st July, a mortar shell from Lighthouse Point landed on the 64-gun French vessel *Le Célèbre*.

"Look at that!" Chisholm nudged MacKim. They watched as the wind caught the flames, doing Britain's work by increasing the fire, which quickly spread to two nearby French vessels, *Le Capricieux* and *L'Entreprenant*.

"That's half the French fleet ablaze,"Chisholm spoke around the stem of his pipe. "Without these ships to defend the harbour, the Frenchies will be hard-pressed, and our navy lads will be cock-a-hoop." They watched as *L'Entreprenant*, the most powerful French ship, slowly sank.

"Even although she's French," Chisholm said, "it's sad to see such a beautiful ship go down." He thumbed tobacco into the bowl of his pipe. "You never mention much about beauty, Hugh."

"No," MacKim shook his head. "I don't think about it much."

"No?" Chisholm applied a light to his tobacco and puffed out blue smoke. "Not even a beautiful woman?"

"I've never met one I liked," MacKim said, truthfully. "I only know soldier's wives and camp followers."

"You don't have to like a woman to bed her," Chisholm said. "You don't look at the mantelpiece when you're stoking the fire."

MacKim looked away. "Maybe someday."

"It's not natural, a young man like you not chasing women." Chisholm took the pipe from his mouth.

"I've other things to think about," MacKim said.

"I know. You think about the Grenadier Company of Webb's Foot," Chisholm said. "I've seen you watching them, and I've heard you asking for them. What's the attraction, Hugh? Is your father there? Your brother? Or somebody else?"

"Somebody else." MacKim felt as if he were under interrogation.

"A good friend?"" Chisholm's eyes were sharp above his ravaged face.

"No." MacKim shook his head. "No friend at all."

"Oh?" Chisholm seemed slightly relieved. "You are looking for somebody who is not a friend but who is important to you. Does this mysterious Grenadier have a name?"

Looking away, MacKim took out his bayonet and began to sharpen it. "I'll tell you sometime."

"Yes," Chisholm said. "Tell me when you feel you can trust me."

"It's not that." MacKim searched for words. "I do trust you."

Chisholm gave a slow smile. "Even with a face like mine? A face like the devil's brother?"

"I don't care about your face," MacKim said.

"I know you don't," Chisholm said softly, "and do you think I'd care about your reason? We've fought side by side, Hugh. You can trust me with your secret."

"Someday," MacKim said. *Maybe.*

❧

HEATED SHOT WAS ONE OF THE MOST FEARED WEAPONS IN ANY arsenal. On the 23rd July 1758, a red hot cannonball landed on the King's Bastion in Louisbourg and started a fire. MacKim watched the flames grow and a column of smoke spiral skyward.

"That place is said to be the largest building in North America." Chisholm puffed on his pipe. "Its destruction will dishearten the Frenchies." He glanced over to MacKim. "Whether the French surrender or not, when we occupy Louisbourg, the lads will go a bit wild."

"Will they?" MacKim could not see how such an occasion would affect him.

"There'll be hundreds of men reeling drunk in the streets," Chisholm said. "All the regiments mixed together." He paused, puffing slowly. "Including us, and Webb's 48th Foot, I shouldn't wonder."

MacKim took a deep breath to quieten his suddenly racing heart. "I shouldn't wonder," he agreed.

Chisholm eyed him for a long moment before leaning back to enjoy his pipe. "Aye," he said. "I shouldn't wonder at all. Us and Webb's 48th."

BY THE 25TH OF JULY, THE FRENCH HAD ONLY TWO VESSELS remaining in the harbour, and the fog returned, slithering in above the water to cover every ship and each secret cove and beach.

"It's a night for the lads," Chisholm sucked on his pipe. "Mark my words, Hugh, my boy, there will be movement tonight. Keep a sharp lookout, now. It had to happen when we were on piquet duty."

Staring into the rolling white blanket, MacKim gripped his musket. Somewhere in that fog, French soldiers were peering out, imagining the very same things as he was. They might be creeping towards him now, muskets in hand, hoping to kill and maim British soldiers. Because he expected trouble, MacKim was not surprised by the echoing of voices distorted by the mist, the clatter of steel on steel, the sudden crack of pistol and musket.

"What's happening?"

"Sounds like a raiding party." Chisholm lifted his musket, checking the rag he had laid over the pan to keep his powder dry. "I can't tell where in this muck."

The glow was next, ruddy through the night as it rose from beyond Louisbourg.

"It's coming from the harbour," MacKim said. "The Navy is busy."

MacKim was correct. Using the fog as cover, Admiral Boscawen sent six hundred seamen in two divisions of small boats to attack the two remaining French ships.

"I wish we could go and watch." MacKim waved a hand in front of his face in a vain attempt to clear away some of the fog.

"If we do, Dingwall will have us at the halberds in a minute," Chisholm said, "and quite rightly. If the French come and there's no piquet, they could take the army in the flank, with God only knows what results."

The firing lasted some time, interspersed with wild cheering and a growing glow of flames. It was not until next morning that MacKim learned the Navy had captured the French warship *Bienfaisant* outright and set fire to *Prudent*.

"That means the Frenchies have no ships left in Louisbourg harbour," MacKim pointed out.

"They can't hold out for long now," Chisholm said. "You wait. They could come out fighting, or they could surrender. By removing their ships, we've taken an important piece off their chessboard," he jabbed his pipe in the direction of Louisbourg, "and we've also made a breach in the walls."

"That beach is our key," Dingwall said. "Sharpen your bayonets, lads, and get ready. Unless the French surrender, we'll be storming the town before they have time to shore up the wall and bring in artillery to blast us when we attack." He grinned. 'Remember, we've knocked out all their artillery on the walls. If Amherst knows his stuff, he'll call on the French to lower the flag."

Chisholm looked at MacKim. "Here we are, Hugh. It's death or glory now, unless the French do the sensible thing." He thrust out his hand. "Good luck, my boy."

"Good luck, James." MacKim took Chisholm's hand. They looked at each other for a second before letting go. "If I fall," Chisholm said, "take my things." He hesitated for a moment. "I've no family."

"The same goes for me," MacKim said. "I have a mother back in Glen Cailleach, but she won't want my few pennies."

They said no more. MacKim knew he had made another oath; he had bound himself to Chisholm.

8

LOUISBOURG, JULY 1758

"They're surrendering!" Chisholm pointed to the battered walls of Louisbourg. The French flag was fluttering down over the shattered houses.

"About time!" Sergeant Dingwall puffed at a black pipe. "I didn't want to go through a storming. That would be a bloody business." He shook his head. "The French governor, Drucor, virtually demanded that we accord him the Honours of War, so they keep their standards and weapons." He shook his head. "Amherst gave him his marching orders."

"Why was that?" MacKim asked.

"The French lost their honour after what they did to our lads at Fort William Henry." Dingwall blew out a long ribbon of tobacco smoke. "You'll remember the French captured the fort, then allowed the Canadians and Indians to torture, murder and scalp our boys. I'm glad that Amherst turned him down. We'll have the Frenchie's flags and weapons as souvenirs."

MacKim watched the white Bourbon flag finally vanish from above the battered skyline of Louisbourg. He would not have to help storm the place. His first campaign as a soldier was over, and he had not received so much as a scratch.

I'm a soldier now, he told himself. *Yet I am not one inch further forward in fulfilling my oath. I have never seen Hayes or the other Grenadiers who murdered Ewan.*

At eight in the morning of 27th July 1758, the Grenadier companies of the Royal Scots, Amherst's and Hopson's Regiment marched to the open gate known as Porte Dauphine. With the bands playing and the Grenadiers marching at attention, MacKim thought it seemed more like a parade than an occupation, except for the backdrop. Although the wind had blown away the powder smoke, there was no mistaking the acrid reek of fire-damaged buildings, the dozen or so still burning buildings and the depression that sat on the faces of the defeated garrison.

At noon that day, the French drew up on the esplanade, with the rigours of the siege rending the white uniforms less splendid than they should have been.

"It's all very formal," MacKim said. "I thought we would be scaling the walls with fire and sword and fighting our way in through streets awash with blood."

"Oh, very poetic," Chisholm said.

The two sides, British and French, faced each other in ordered ranks across the cobbled ground of the esplanade. At a signal that MacKim did not see, four of the five French regiments laid down their colours and arms and then marched out of the fortress and down to the ships, to be carried away as prisoners. There was no cheering from the British, and no jubilation at having captured what was said to be the strongest fortress in North America.

"What the devil?" Chisholm said, as the men of the fifth French regiment, the *Cambis*, smashed their muskets on the ground and set fire to their regimental colours. Having made their protest, they marched away to captivity.

"Cheeky buggers!" Chisholm shook his head. He smiled. "We've taken thousands of prisoners, and the strongest fortress in the Americas. Nobody can blame the Frasers for disloyalty now, Hugh. We proved ourselves in this campaign."

"Did you hear what some of the Frenchies were saying?"

Urquhart was a freckle-faced youngster with wide, clear eyes. "They said they would have surrendered sooner except they were scared of Frasers. They thought the Rangers and the Highlanders would have scalped them and then cut their throats."

"They must think we are all savages," MacKim said.

"Aye, maybe so," Urquhart said. "And maybe the enemy are the savages. Corporal Gunn was after telling me that some of the French officers were German, and as soon as they surrendered, they broke open the military chests and stole the gold."

"Thieving buggers," Chisholm said, with another smile. "I wanted to do that."

"Corporal Gunn said we've not to be too hard on them," Urquhart said. "He said the Frenchies claimed we fought like lions."

"Roar!" Chisholm responded, looking at the ranks of the 78th. "Some lions. More like tabby cats."

As Brigadier General Whitmore became governor of Louisbourg and with the French garrison safely out of the way, the British had liberty to explore the town that had defied them for so many weeks. As Chisholm had said, with the restraints of discipline loosened, men crowded into the taverns.

"Stay close," Chisholm advised. "Some of the French civilians might seek revenge on stray British soldiers. Don't go wandering around alone."

MacKim nodded. "I'm a soldier, James, not a child."

"I know that," Chisholm said. "Come on then. We'll see if the artillery's left a grog shop standing."

The architecture of Louisbourg would have been more in place in France than on the shores of the Americas, with shutters, flared roofs, dormer windows and a profusion of carved fleur-de-lis. Apart from that, the place was all stone and austerity, with no public spaces.

"It's a bit stark," MacKim said.

"It's a military fort," Chisholm reminded him.

There were no flowers; the French had used every patch of

earth to grow vegetables or herbs. Any animal was there to work; there were no pets. "The civilians were subsidiary to the military," MacKim said. "What a strange way of living."

"We'll be in there soon." Chisholm nodded to the very heart of Louisbourg, the King's Bastion Barracks, a vast building by North American standards if bearing the scars of British artillery. "The French governor's quarters are in there, as well as a chapel and barracks for hundreds of men." He shook his head. "If we had taken this place by storm, MacKim, we could have looted it from Monday to Christmas. As it is," he screwed up his face, "we get our pay and live another day."

"'A lot of our army won't be getting any more pay again,'" MacKim said. "Nearly two hundred men are dead and over three hundred and fifty wounded."

"Aye," Chisholm said. "The king and generals will say that's a cheap price to pay to capture the strongest fortress in North America."

"The wives and mothers won't agree." Cattanach showed a side that MacKim had not expected.

"They don't count." Chisholm touched his scarred face. "Ordinary soldiers may be the pawns in the King's game of chess, but women are not even dust. Not even Pikestaff has any time for them." He glanced at MacKim. "Nor has MacKim, I think."

MacKim grunted. "Someday," he said. "When I'm ready."

"You're strange, you are," Cumming began to sneer, until MacKim put a hand on his bayonet.

"Come on, Hugh!" Chisholm nudged MacKim. "Never mind him. We're off to taste the delights of Louisbourg."

"You're strange," Cumming repeated. "I'll not be turning my back on you, MacKim."

The taverns were roaring with British infantry and Colonial Rangers, while others roamed the streets, celebrating the victory or, as MacKim cynically thought, celebrating their relief at still being alive. Not a drinking man, MacKim allowed

Chisholm to steer him into a small tavern where a group of seamen were arguing with a pair of artillerymen, while a Ranger watched from a distance, smoking a long-stemmed pipe.

"In we go, MacKim." Ignoring the men who stared at his malformed face, Chisholm ordered rum for them both, squeezed onto an already crowded bench, stretched out his legs and sighed. "Here we are, then. We have one victory under our belts and the door to Canada in our hands."

MacKim tasted the rum and looked around. Knots of men of all regiments filled the small room, with each group seeming in competition to boast the loudest. MacKim ran his gaze from man to man, searching for the buff facings of Webb's 48th. He saw three of that regiment, but none had the broad shoulders of Grenadiers. The only Grenadiers he saw carried the motto *Nec aspra terrent* – difficulties be damned – on their mitre caps, the motto of the 43rd foot.

"What's next?" MacKim asked.

"Up the St Lawrence to Quebec," Chisholm said. "We've made a start, nothing more. We were lucky that the Frenchies surrendered. I heard the Royal Highlanders had it hard at Ticonderoga. They lost hundreds of men when General Montgomery threw them in a frontal attack."

MacKim nodded. "Highlanders always go forward with great bravery, and often get slaughtered."

"One day we'll learn to temper our courage with caution." Chisholm immediately caught MacKim's drift. He looked up and smiled. "Halloa, there. That's worth looking at."

The woman was tall, dark-haired and wore a dress cut deliberately low to show the cleavage of her breasts to best advantage. She stopped inside the doorway and ran her gaze around every man in the room before approaching the table where MacKim sat.

"You have an interesting face." Her voice was low, nearly husky. "May I sit here?"

MacKim's voice dried up until he realised that the woman was addressing Chisholm.

"I have an interesting face? I have a face that looks like a lion chewed it and spat it out again." It was the first time MacKim had heard Chisholm speaking in English.

"It is a face that speaks of experience and battle."

MacKim made way as the woman squeezed onto the crowded bench. Rewarding him with a smile, she took hold of Chisholm's arm. 'I'm Michelle." She spoke with the most delightful accent MacKim had ever heard, part French, part North American.

"I'm James Chisholm, and my companion is Hugh MacKim."

Michelle threw another brief smile at MacKim before returning her attention to Chisholm. "Tell me about yourself, James."

"There's not much to tell, Michelle, except I am the ugliest man in the army. I got myself wounded at Fontenoy, you see."

Michelle widened her eyes. "I've heard of that battle," she said, with every breath exhaling a whiff of perfume. "You are an old soldier then, a veteran."

Realising he was one man too many in the present company, MacKim rose from the table. "Good luck, James," he said, lifting a hand in farewell as he slipped out of the tavern to breathe fresh Atlantic air, albeit still tinged with smoke. *So James Chisholm speaks English, too. That man is full of surprises and secrets.*

Soldiers crowded the streets, some already the worse for drink, others enthusiastically attempting to reach that state. A few were singing, others challenging the residents of the town to a fight, while a lucky half-dozen paraded the women who clung to their arms.

When the group of burly veterans reeled from a corner tavern, the face jolted MacKim back to his childhood. The years had not been kind to the Grenadier, deepening the lines that seamed his features. The dark hair was thinner and greyer than MacKim remembered, the face broader but still leering, while the broken, twisted nose was red-tinged with drink. Even so, MacKim recognised him at once. *Hayes*. MacKim felt his stomach churning with a mixture of hatred and fear as memories of that day, twelve years ago, resurfaced.

The Grenadier was singing an obscene song, with the coarse words spewing from his mouth as he swayed into the street.

MacKim's fist curled around his bayonet. A scrutiny of Hayes' three companions told him they were strangers. They had not been with Hayes at Drummossie.

"You're doing it again, Hugh." Chisholm's voice sounded in MacKim's ear.

MacKim started. "What? Where did you spring from? I left you with Michelle!"

"Michelle's a whore," Chisholm said. "She's probably riddled with every kind of pox you can imagine." He shook his head. "A woman who looks for the ugliest man is to be trusted as much as a woman who seeks out the richest. Michelle was hiding something, as are you. You're doing it again."

MacKim immediately became defensive. "Doing what again?"

"Watching people." Chisholm pulled MacKim away. "Come on, Hugh, and we'll find some rum and maybe a real woman for you, not some poxed-up jezebel."

MacKim jerked himself free of Chisholm's grasp. "Sorry, James. I'll have to leave you to drink alone."

"Cumming was right; you're a strange man, Hugh. What's the matter? You look as if you've seen a ghost."

"Maybe I have." MacKim watched the Grenadiers roll along the street, shouting, abusing everybody they passed and kicking at doors just for the sport of it.

"Ah." Chisholm began to stuff tobacco in the bowl of his pipe. "You've found your Webb's Grenadier, have you?"

"He's one of these four." MacKim nodded to the Grenadiers.

"Who is he, Hugh?" Chisholm asked quietly. "You've been looking for him for months. Who is he?"

"Nobody. He's not important." MacKim wished that Chisholm would leave him in peace so he could follow Hayes.

"That's not true. I've seen you examine every lobster that passes," Chisholm said. "You look at them and then shake your head. When you saw these Grenadiers, you looked as if you'd seen your dead granny. Which one is it?"

"The one in the middle," MacKim said.

Chisholm grunted. "What's he done to you?"

MacKim stepped away. "I can't tell you."

"As I said before, boy, there are no secrets in the regiment. We've fought together, you and I, we've faced the French and survived Sergeant Dingwall. Tell me."

MacKim took a deep breath. "It's something I have to put right myself."

"Good." Chisholm smiled. "You put it right yourself, and I'll come along with you to make sure nobody else interferes." He nodded. "You'll have noticed that there are four of them, four Grenadiers, each one bigger and uglier than you are and undoubtedly more experienced in fighting as well. God in heaven, Hugh, they're nearly as ugly as me!"

"It's not your fight." MacKim ignored Chisholm's attempt at humour.

"Why is it yours?" Chisholm smiled again. "I'm going to keep asking you until I find out, and dog your footsteps whatever you say."

"He murdered my brother," MacKim said sharply. He had not intended to tell anybody, but once the words were out, he continued, telling Chisholm the whole story of Drummossie Moor.

"Aye," Chisholm said when MacKim finished. "What do you want to do about it?"

"I'm going to kill him," MacKim said at once.

"You'll swing if you're caught."

"I know."

Chisholm nodded. "Our concern is to separate your man from his companions."

"No." MacKim shook his head. "It's not *our* concern. It's my fight and my concern. You should not get involved, or you could swing, too."

Chisholm ignored the interruption. "It's unlikely your man Hayes will recognise you after all this time, Hugh. You were only a boy then." There was no humour in his grin. "Damn it, man, you're still only a boy! Do you think you can handle him?"

"Yes." Hugh touched his bayonet again.

"All right, if you think so." Chisholm nodded. "Come on then, Hugh. Follow my lead and keep in the shadows so nobody can identify you later."

Manoeuvring around a carousing group of Rangers, Chisholm raised his voice. "Hey! Grenadiers!"

Two of the Grenadiers turned around, one swaying on his feet. "What do you want?" Alcohol slurred the speaker's voice.

"There is a woman back there." Chisholm gestured with his thumb. "She's looking for a Grenadier. She says men in skirts aren't good enough for her."

All four Grenadiers lurched around. Hayes leered at them, his nose looking more twisted than ever. "What sort of woman?"

"A good-looking woman," Chisholm said. "She said that I'm too ugly for her."

The youngest of the Grenadiers laughed. "There's no wonder at that. It must be me she wants."

"This way, then," Chisholm ducked into the shadows and stalked away. The Grenadiers followed at once, with two of them supporting each other and the youngest man the most eager. Waiting his moment, MacKim thrust his foot forward and tripped Hayes.

The Grenadier staggered and fell face-first on the ground. Looking around, MacKim stooped and helped him slowly to his feet. The other Grenadiers were already thirty yards away, reeling drunkenly behind Chisholm.

MacKim nodded. He had Hayes to himself, but with this part of the town filled with revelling soldiers, he had to find somewhere quieter.

"Where's everybody gone?" Hayes' breath stunk of rum and tobacco. He peered suspiciously at MacKim.

"They're off to find women," MacKim reminded.

"Where's mine?"

"Over here. This way." MacKim put an arm around the man's shoulders as if to support him. Hayes was broad, with muscles as hard as granite, yet touching him made MacKim's skin crawl. "Over there." He nodded vaguely to a section of the town that British artillery had turned into a rubble-strewn mess.

"I can't see her."

"What's your name, my friend?" MacKim had a sudden fear he had the wrong man.

Hayes drew himself erect. "Private Edmund Hayes," he said, "a Grenadier of Webb's Regiment of Foot."

"I'm Hector MacDonald," MacKim lied. "We've met before, Hayes." He guided the Grenadier to the darkest part of a ruined building. "Sit down here."

"Where's the woman?" Hayes slumped onto an irregular square of masonry.

MacKim checked to ensure they were alone. The voices of drunken soldiers rose in the distance. "There isn't one." He leaned closer as Hayes began a foul-mouthed protest. "Don't you recognise me, Edmund Hayes?"

"What?" Hayes peered closer. "No."

"Think back." Leaning forward, MacKim removed the bayonet from Hayes' belt and threw it far into the ruins. "Think a long way back. Think back to April 1746 and the field of Culloden, when you were with Ligonier's."

"We won the battle," Hayes said. "We crushed the rebel dogs."

"You did," MacKim agreed. "You mowed down the Jacobites

before they got close. You shattered them with grapeshot and cannonballs and riddled them with massed musketry."

"Yes." Hayes smiled as if at a pleasant memory.

"And afterwards...?" MacKim allowed the words to hang in the air. "Can you remember what happened after the battle?"

"Yes." Hayes' smile did not falter. "We bayoneted the scoundrels. We killed the Scotch rebels." He gave a little laugh.

"That's right." MacKim realised that Hayes was too drunk to know what he was admitting. "But you did not bayonet them all, did you? Can you remember one young boy with a shattered leg? Can you remember what you did to him?"

Hayes giggled. "We put a torch up his arse."

"That's right." MacKim fought the nausea that burned the back of his throat. "You burned him alive, slowly."

Hayes laughed again, swaying on his lump of masonry.

"Who else was with you?" MacKim had to force the words from his throat when his first instinct was to plunge his bayonet into Hayes' chest. "There were four of you." MacKim knew he would never forget the faces, but if he matched them with names, his quest would be a lot easier.

"Yes, there were four of us," Hayes said. "Have you anything to drink? And where is this woman you promised?"

"I've nothing to drink," MacKim said. "Who were your friends?"

Hayes smiled, swayed and seemed to sober up. "There was Corporal Bland. He was the fellow who set a torch to that rebel dog's skirt."

Bland. "It's a kilt, not a skirt," MacKim corrected softly.

"He got made sergeant after the battle," Hayes said. "Scarred Sergeant Bland." He smiled, shaking his head in memory. "He often told people how he had set a rebel on fire after Culloden."

"I wager he had many a jolly rant." MacKim tried to control his anger. "Where is the good sergeant now?"

"Dead, I fear," Hayes said.

MacKim felt a stab of disappointment. Of them all, he had

most wished to kill the corporal who had burned his brother alive. "How did he die?"

"We left him down with fever in the Low Countries," Hayes said. "He never came back. Fever is the worst enemy of the soldier."

"How about the other two?" MacKim fought to restrain his temper. He gripped his bayonet so hard that his fist shook.

"Hitchins and Osborne? They're still going around. Hitchins got promoted to corporal, but lost his stripes and gained a hundred lashes for having a crooked queue on parade."

I hope the drummer laid it on with a will, MacKim thought. *So, Bland is dead, but the others are still alive and still in uniform. Hitchins and Osborne. I will remember those names. Hitchins and Osborne.*

"Do you remember the even younger boy who was at Culloden?" MacKim kept his voice soft. "Do you remember a ten-year-old child?"

"We held him so he could watch the other one dying," Hayes laughed again. "He was gibbering in Erse, pleading for the boy's life, no doubt. We gave no quarter to rebel dogs. The Duke said 'no quarter', and we obeyed."

"That's right," MacKim said. "The Duke said 'no quarter'. That lad had nightmares for years." He paused, fighting the memory. "That was me, Hayes."

Hayes looked up, suddenly comprehension in his dazed eyes. "*You?*"

"Me." MacKim had dreamed of this moment for twelve years, but now it had arrived, he was not sure what to do. He had thought that his military training and experience would help, but fighting Frenchmen in honest battle was utterly different from killing a man in cold blood. *This man laughed as his friends murdered Ewan, and I gave my oath on the Bible.*

"You Sawnie bastard!" Drunk as he was, Hayes was a Grenadier, one of the prime soldiers in the army. Without another word, he threw himself forward. Grabbing at MacKim's throat, Hayes bore him back by sheer weight until MacKim lay on the ground with the older man on top. Hayes' mouth was open, showing irregular, brown-stained teeth as he snarled his hatred in MacKim's face.

"I'll kill you, Sawnie bastard. I'll squeeze out your breath, rebel dog!"

It was instinct more than anything made MacKim twist his head to one side and bite deep into Hayes' thumb. Hayes yelled and jerked his hand free, nearly loosening two of MacKim's teeth in the process. Following up his advantage, MacKim shoved Hayes away and rolled to his feet. He sized up the opposition. Hayes was older and less agile, but stronger and a vastly more experienced brawler.

Snarling, Hayes lifted a jagged chunk of masonry and swung at MacKim, who stepped smartly aside. Again they grappled, with Hayes pushing MacKim back down, and clamping his arms around MacKim's body.

"I'll kill you, Sawnie!" Hayes promised. "I'll kick you to death and burn you like we burned your brother."

The words broke the last of MacKim's reserve. The memory of Ewan's screams returned in all their horror. Knowing he was no match for Hayes' strength, MacKim used his agility to wriggle free and push himself upright before Hayes was on his feet. Without a pause, MacKim swung his nailed shoe hard into Hayes' groin. When the Grenadier doubled up, gasping, MacKim grabbed Hayes' head and hauled him down, smashing his face against the masonry again and again, sobbing with a combination of effort, fear and hatred as the Grenadier's yells muted to moans and then to silence.

"You murdered my brother!" MacKim crashed Hayes' face against the stone. "You murdered my brother!"

"You can stop now," Chisholm's voice sounded.

MacKim looked up. Chisholm sat on a stone block, calmly smoking his clay pipe.

"How long have you been there?"

"Long enough," Chisholm said. "Your man's dead now. You don't have to waste any more effort on him."

Panting, MacKim dropped Hayes' broken body. All his anger had dissipated. He looked at his tunic, now spattered with droplets of Hayes' blood and fragments of his bone.

"We'd better hide him," Chisholm said. "We'll scrape a hole and throw him in." He considered for a moment. "Take his clothes off, Hugh."

"Why?"

"If somebody finds him in uniform, people will know what he was and ask questions. If he's naked, whoever finds him might take him for a Frenchie. We can burn his uniform."

MacKim nodded. "Have you done this sort of thing before?"

"Not exactly. Come on. Search his pockets first."

Having taken Hayes' few shillings, they stripped him naked, dragged him to a depression and pushed him in, piling stones on top until they could no longer see the corpse. Chisholm looked down dispassionately. "With any luck, by the time somebody finds him, the body will be too decomposed for anybody to recognise him."

With a dozen fires still smouldering in the aftermath of the siege, it was not hard to find the largest. MacKim and Chisholm fed in Hayes' uniform, piece by piece. As MacKim watched the flames slowly devour the scarlet serge, the memories of his brother were strong inside his head. He could feel Ewan standing close by him, with their mother watching, slowly nodding her head in approval.

Now I am a murderer. I sought out that man and killed him. How do I feel about that? Nothing. I feel nothing. Four men murdered my brother. One, the worst, died of fever. I have killed another. I have two more to kill before his spirit will be at rest.

That night, MacKim begged a scrap of paper and a pen from the stores and wrote down four names. *Bland; Hayes; Osborne; Hitchins,* and added the date *16th April 1746.* He looked at them for a long moment, before he scored out Bland's name and added, *died of fever*. Then he scored out Hayes' name and added the date alongside, *28th July 1758*.

Two more, he told himself, *two more and I will have redeemed my oath, and I'll be free to live the life that I wish to live. Two more and then I can return to Scotland.*

To do what? I have no land, no money and no skills. MacKim sighed as he contemplated his future, then he shrugged, placed the paper in his pocket and walked away. There was no point in thinking of his future until he had fulfilled his oath, and he might not live that long.

❧

"WELL, HUGH." CHISHOLM SUCKED AT HIS EMPTY PIPE. "WE captured Louisbourg, but the French might yet win the war."

"Why is that?"

"They held Louisbourg long enough, so we don't have time to capture Quebec this year. That gives the French all winter to strengthen their defences." Chisholm sighed. "Next campaigning season will be a lot harder than this one, I reckon."

MacKim nodded, disguising the sudden leap of his heart. *Anything can happen in an entire winter. I might find Hitchins and Osborne.* "Well, James, that might not be a bad thing."

Chisholm threw him a level look. "Cumming's right about you, Hugh. You are a strange man."

❧ 9 ❧

LOUISBOURG, AUGUST 1758

The woman stood alone on the battlements, staring out to sea with the wind ruffling her long brown hair. MacKim looked up, seeing her silhouetted against the rising sun as he marched his beat, musket in hand. *What the devil is she doing here? A blasted woman can only mean trouble.*

"Halloa." MacKim stopped at her side, grounding his musket. "You're up early." He forced himself to sound pleasant.

When the woman turned around, MacKim saw she was about twenty-five, with a comfortably round face. "I didn't know that there would be a soldier here." She was North American by her accent, possibly from one of the New England colonies.

"I'm on piquet duty," MacKim said. "In case the French come back." He touched the lock of his musket.

"Do you think they will come back?" The woman neither sounded nor looked nervous in the company of a soldier.

"No," MacKim shook his head. "Not with the Royal Navy in command of the sea and our garrison holding the town." He looked out toward the harbour, where the low sun highlighted the masts of the ships. "They look pretty from here, don't they?" *I'm encouraging her, blast it!*

The woman turned around again to face the harbour. "The sun makes anything look beautiful, even men-of-war."

They stood side by side in companionable silence as the sun rose higher. "It's very peaceful." MacKim wondered why he did not continue with his piquet, as duty demanded.

"Strange that it should appear peaceful when we're in the middle of a war and this place was the scene of so much death and suffering." The woman spoke without moving her head.

"Perhaps the knowledge of war enhances the feeling of peace." MacKim suddenly felt very old and wise.

"That's a deep thought for a soldier," the woman said. "Most of the British soldiers I've met spoke only of drink, fighting and ... and women."

"Perhaps that's because soldiers' lives centre on fighting and their only escape is drinking." MacKim did not mention women. He paused for a moment, hoping that Corporal Gunn was not watching him neglect his duty.

"And women?" The woman asked, still staring out to sea.

"I don't know much about women," MacKim said.

The woman turned her head, a small smile creasing the corner of her mouth. "I don't think I've ever heard any man admit that, let alone a man in a scarlet tunic."

"What men say, and what they think, are not always the same." MacKim sighed. "I apologise, I sound like a book."

"You sound like a philosopher." The woman had turned fully round to speak to him. She was taller than he had at first thought, nearly as tall as a man, with serene grey eyes and a complexion too tanned to be fashionable. She frowned as she scrutinised MacKim as carefully as he studied her. "You're a Highlander, I see."

"I am." MacKim glanced down at his kilt.

"I've never spoken to a Highlander before. I thought they were savages who only spoke Erse. Are they all like you?"

"Highlanders are just like everybody else," MacKim said. "We come in all sorts of guises, tall, short, ugly or handsome and many do only speak Gaelic, although most have learned at least some English."

The woman's laugh was unexpected on the stark battlements of Louisbourg. "So I hear, Private Philosopher." She stepped towards him. "May I join in your perambulations along the parapet?"

"You are most welcome, madam." MacKim gave a little bow, although he had no idea how to act in these unusual circumstances. He found this woman more interesting than any other he had ever met. "If you see a large, dark-visaged man with a permanent frown, I would ask you to hide, for that will be Sergeant Dingwall, and he may not take kindly to me conversing with a lady while on piquet. If you see a younger and slighter version, that is Corporal Gunn, another man best avoided."

The woman laughed again. "I promise not to get you into trouble, but I am no lady."

MacKim felt the colour rushing to his cheeks. His previous experience with women had been limited to the girls at home before he took the King's Shilling, and a couple of brief encounters with prostitutes in Inverness and Ireland. "I think you are undoubtedly a lady." He suddenly felt tongue-tied as all his words deserted him. The woman matched him step for step as he paced the ramparts, enjoying the warmth of the morning sun on his face while he wondered what to say.

"Why, thank you, sir." The woman swept into a curtsey so deep that MacKim was sure she was mocking him. "With such courtesy, I cannot continue to call you Private Philosopher. What name do you bear, Highlander? Is it Alexander, like so many of your countrymen? Should I call you Sawney?"

"No. I am Hugh MacKim." MacKim found he was fascinated by her slow drawl.

"Oh?" The woman seemed to be waiting for more, but MacKim could not think of anything to say. "And does the suddenly silent Private Hugh MacKim wish to know my name?"

"Oh, yes, of course." MacKim felt his face turning an even

deeper shade of crimson. "What is your name, my lady of the ramparts?"

"Priscilla Wooler." The woman smiled again. "You see, Mr MacKim, I can be as laconic as you, if not as philosophical."

"You may be as laconic, yet you are far fairer in looks." MacKim blurted out the words, and immediately wished he had remained silent.

Priscilla looked sideways at him, smiled and looked away. They reached the end of MacKim's beat, turned and paced back in silence as MacKim desperately scraped his mind for something to say. The words that had come so easily only a few minutes before had gone absent without leave, while Priscilla Wooler seemed content to walk with her eyes roving over the sea and her mouth closed.

"I am not good company," MacKim said at last.

"On the contrary, Private MacKim," Priscilla said. "You are the best kind of company. You do not attempt to interfere with my train of thought, yet you are with me." She placed a light hand on his arm. "Most men would tell me how wonderful they are, while most soldiers would bore me with tales of their heroism as they captured a French battery or raided a Mohawk village single-handed, or some such moonshine."

"I have done neither," MacKim said. *I could tell you how I bashed a man's head in a few days ago,* he thought, *but I doubt you would be impressed, and I do wish to impress you. Why? I will probably never see this woman again.*

"Nor have I," Priscilla said solemnly.

MacKim did not stop his smile. "I am glad to hear that."

The sound of bells came to them from the ships below, a reminder that time was always passing. "The guard will be changing soon," MacKim said. "Then you will have somebody else to not talk to."

Priscilla sighed. "I had best be elsewhere," she said. "I have no wish to get you into trouble with the ferocious Sergeant Dingwall."

"Wait." Suddenly, MacKim had no desire for this woman to go away. His words returned in a rush. "I have so much to ask you."

But Priscilla shook her head. "There is no time, Private MacKim. There is never enough time." Turning away, she smiled over her shoulder and walked away, so gracefully that she seemed to glide across the scarred slabs.

MacKim watched her go, and wondered at the blankness she left behind on the ramparts of the fort and inside his head. *There is so much I wished to ask you*, he repeated to himself. *Who are you? From where do you hail? Why are you here in this place of war?*

"MacKim!" Sergeant Dingwall's roar shattered his sudden desolation. "March at attention, damn your hide!"

MacKim straightened his back. Life was back to normal after his few moments of distraction.

That night, for the first time in many years, MacKim did not dream of his brother lying a twisted, blackened thing on the bloody field of Culloden. Priscilla's smile took Ewan's place, and the supple way she moved as she walked away remained in his mind long after he fell asleep.

LOUISBOURG, AUTUMN 1758

The song rose from the assembled regiments in Louisbourg as Fraser's Highlanders filed into the transports that would carry them to New York.

'Come, each death-doing dog who dares venture
        his neck,
Come follow the hero that goes to Quebec
And ye that love fighting shall soon have enough
Wolfe commands us, my boys, we shall give them
        hot stuff.'

MacKim smiled. After the siege, he could consider himself as a veteran, although he knew the fighting had been mild in comparison with the great battles fought in Europe. "Who wrote that little ditty?"

"A fellow named Ned Botwood, a Grenadier sergeant from the 47th." Chisholm negotiated the entry-port into the transport, with the seamen making the expected good-humoured sallies to the kilt-wearing Highlanders.

"Come on, ladies, mind your skirts now!"

"Don't these English ever learn?" Cumming asked. "They all repeat the same stupid insults."

"They lack imagination," MacKim said. "Each one thinks he is original when he copies the jokes of the others. It amuses them to ridicule anybody who's not English."

"Maybe we're fighting for the wrong side," Cattanach said.

"Colonel Fraser, the chief, chooses who we fight for," MacKim said. "All we have to do is prove our loyalty to King George."

"Why?" Cumming said. "He's done nothing for me."

"He's paid you for months," Sergeant Dingwall said. "You mind your mouth, Cumming! Any more of that seditious talk and it'll be two hundred at the halberds for you!"

Chisholm said nothing as he tramped the scrubbed deck and thumped down the wooden companionway to the cramped accommodation below. MacKim followed, bowing his head to avoid the low beams, already choking in the thick air that combined the stench of the scuppers with the stink of scores of men crammed together with inadequate fresh air and no facilities for washing or basic hygiene.

"Here we are again." Chisholm found a square of deck space and crouched down. "Let's hope it's a short voyage to wherever we are bound."

"Troopships are hell-on-earth," MacKim agreed.

"We're lucky we're in a cool climate," Chisholm said. "It's ten times worse sailing in a transport to the Indies, so I've heard. Foul water, insects and every disease known to man running rampant below deck."

MacKim touched the folded paper he kept close to his breast. He had Osborne and Hitchins to score off, yet with the 78th being shipped away, his chances of meeting them again were slender. Only if Fraser's happened to be based close to Webb's would the opportunity arise again.

"You'll be happier now, MacKim," Chisholm said. "Now your brother's been avenged."

That was the first time Chisholm had referred to the incident with Hayes.

"Yes," MacKim said.

"But you're not, are you?"

"I don't know what you mean," MacKim said.

"You've had your revenge. Do you feel better for it?"

MacKim analysed his feelings. "No."

"No," Chisholm repeated. "You can put that episode behind you now, Hugh. It's finished."

"It's not finished." MacKim looked up. "There are two murderers left alive."

"You won't feel any better if you kill them, too," Chisholm said.

"It's not about me feeling better," MacKim said. "I took a blood oath."

Chisholm was silent for a few moments. "You must have been very young."

"I was ten years old."

Chisholm winced. "That's too young."

"Age does not matter. Ewan was my brother." MacKim leaned against the wooden bulkhead. "I took a blood oath to avenge him. It is my duty."

WHILE MOST OF FRASER'S HIGHLANDERS REMAINED BELOW decks as the ship left Louisbourg, MacKim climbed into the open air. Ignoring the taunts of the sailors, he stood at the bulwark and watched the walls of the fortress gradually disappear. Hoping to see Priscilla standing on the battlements, he only saw the splurge of scarlet uniforms as the sentries marched their beats.

Suddenly, MacKim felt lonely and strangely homesick. He had come to Louisbourg as a Johnny Raw, a recruit with no knowledge of war. He thought that he was leaving as a veteran, an old soldier who had seen battle and death. He knew that the siege had changed him; he was a murderer as well as a man, and now he had met a woman who would haunt him for the rest of his life. MacKim wished he had not become unaccountably tongue-tied in Priscilla's company, so he knew where she was from and why she was in the battered ruins of a captured French fortress.

The wind whistled through the rigging as MacKim watched Louisbourg sink gradually away. *Priscilla Wooler*. He repeated the name as he stood on deck; *Priscilla Wooler*. Somewhere in the world, Priscilla Wooler would have a home and perhaps a small memory of the Highland soldier with whom she had spent a few short minutes on a lonely post in Canada. *Priscilla Wooler*.

MacKim knew that he now had a new quest that was in no way connected to avenging the murder of his brother. As soon as he had achieved one objective, he would concentrate on the other. *Priscilla Wooler*. At that moment, the name sounded more desirable than anything MacKim had ever heard in his life. He now had a reason for living. He had to complete his oath as a matter of urgency, and then search for Priscilla, wherever she happened to be.

Ignoring a sudden squall that threw salt-spray into his face, MacKim remained at the bulwark, watching the heaving seas that separated him from Louisbourg and Priscilla. Although he could never have articulated his feelings, he was falling in love.

I'm sailing away from the two things that matter most to me, killing Osborne and Hitchins of Webb's Regiment, and finding Priscilla Wooler. Two opposed objectives, neither of which is it in my power to obtain. Swearing, MacKim thumped his fist onto the solid oak of the rail, again, and again, and again.

BOSTON WAS COLD. THE SNOW WAS DEEPER THAN MACKIM had ever seen, and the wind cut cruelly into him. The men of the

78th Highlanders looked around them. Most had never been in a city so large before and gaped at the busy streets, crowded with people, horses and carriages. Louisbourg had been a village in comparison, and the men of the 78th joined the other British soldiers in roaring into the taverns and inns. Pleased that the British were gradually reducing the French threat, the Bostonians extended generous hospitality to the redcoats, with the women in particular fascinated by the kilted Highlanders.

"You look bemused, MacKim." Chisholm had his bonnet pulled low over his face in an attempt to disguise his scars.

"I've never seen so many people before," MacKim stepped back as a coach and four whizzed past, with the yellow wheels turning so quickly they appeared as a blur, "except soldiers."

Chisholm chuckled. "Wait until you serve on the continent," he said. "There are towns and cities everywhere, and villages in between. And people! Tens of thousands of people! London, too." He shook his head. "Now, Hugh, London is a country in itself."

MacKim did not like to admit how uncomfortable he felt in the presence of so many strangers. "I'll wait."

"You should go out and see the sights of Boston," Chisholm said. "Take Cumming with you. The change might wipe the sourness off that rascal's face."

"How about you?"

Chisholm indicated his burn. "This face scares people. It gets me into bother. Civilians stare at me and some men laugh, so I flatten them, and there's all sorts of trouble."

"I didn't realise they would be like that."

"You're used to me and used to wounds now. Civilians live sheltered lives." Chisholm sat down. "Sometimes, I wish I had died rather than live with the face of a monster."

"You're no monster," MacKim said.

"I look like one."

"Come on, James. I'll buy a bottle of rum, and we'll drink the night away together."

"Would you not prefer to see the sights of Boston?" Chisholm pointed to Cattanach as he reeled out of a tavern with a woman on each arm. "Rum, women and song. You and Cumming could learn a lot."

"No." MacKim shook his head as Urquhart slid drunkenly down the wall of a house with his kilt ruffling to waist height. A group of women began to giggle at what Urquhart unwittingly revealed, until one pretended to be shocked and hustled the others away. "No, Cumming can get into trouble without any help from me."

Chisholm patted MacKim on the shoulder. "You're a good man, Hugh, and an unusual one, not chasing after the girls."

"You're not chasing after them, either."

Chisholm touched his face. "I told you, Hugh. I have a reason."

MacKim frowned. "You have an excuse, not a reason."

"What's your excuse, Hugh? Or your reason?"

MacKim had another swallow of rum. The taste was growing on him, as was the sensation of not caring what he said. "You're a good man, James. The best."

"That's the drink talking."

"No, I mean it. You stood by me with Hayes and didn't ask any questions." MacKim did not care that he was grinning foolishly.

"You never laugh at my face." Chisholm was also smiling. "Most men do when they think I'm not listening. Dingwall calls me 'Ugly' and others smirk, or copy him."

MacKim tried to imagine the internal pain of living with the hideous scars Chisholm had to bear, day after day for the rest of his life. "I don't notice," he said.

Chisholm grunted and passed across the bottle of rum. "You should be with Cumming and Urquhart and the rest."

"I don't like the town," MacKim said. "I don't like crowds of people."

"Nor do I."

Wandering to the waterfront, they sat in silence for a long time, alternately drinking and passing across the rum. When the level in the bottle had dropped considerably, Chisholm sighed.

"So you have two more men to find," Chisholm said at last.

"Two more. Osborne and Hitchins."

"I'll help you." Chisholm gave a bleak smile. "You don't laugh at me."

"Thank you." MacKim watched as Chisholm drained the last of the rum. 'You don't laugh at me, either.'

❦

"PRIVATE HUGH MACKIM! WHERE IS PRIVATE HUGH MacKim?" Sergeant Dingwall roared out the name.

Struggling from the room above the inn where he was quartered, MacKim came to attention. "Sergeant."

"What have you been doing, MacKim?" Dingwall glowered at him.

"Nothing, Sergeant. I was about to go on piquet duty."

"You're not paid to do nothing, MacKim; you're paid to be a soldier." Dingwall walked around MacKim, making slight adjustments to his clothing and equipment. "Well, Lieutenant Hugh Cameron wants to see you now."

"Why, Sergeant?"

Dingwall leant closer. "How the devil should I know? Maybe he's found out about all your sins and omissions, MacKim! Report to him!"

Lieutenant Cameron was young, with dancing eyes and a small, healing scar across his cheekbone. MacKim knew him as an active officer during the siege of Louisbourg. "You are Hugh MacKim?"

"Yes, sir." MacKim kept as erect as he could.

"Your sergeant told me about you," Lieutenant Cameron said. "He informs me that you are intelligent, quick on your feet and always eager to fight the French."

MacKim said nothing. It was not a private's place to speak to an officer unless asked a direct question.

"Sergeant Dingwall has recommended you for the Light Company," Lieutenant Cameron said. "As you should know by now, the Light Bobs are employed upon all martial services, are always first to contact the foe and are exposed to more fatigue than all the army."

"Yes, sir," MacKim said.

"Might you be interested?" Cameron was still smiling as he walked around MacKim, seemingly inspecting him from every angle.

MacKim guessed that if he refused, the lieutenant's opinion of him would drop considerably and Dingwall would make his life a misery. "Yes, sir."

"I wanted to see you first. You fought in a couple of skirmishes around Louisbourg, I heard, and acquitted yourself quite well." He nodded. "And we share the same first name. All right, MacKim, as from tomorrow you are to be trained as a Light Infantryman."

"Yes, sir." MacKim took a deep breath. "Sir, may I ask who else will be in the Lights?"

"What?" Cameron looked surprised that a mere private had dared to ask a question. "Sergeant Dingwall suggested that you, Private Cumming and Private Chisholm should be selected."

"Thank you, sir." MacKim had grown used to Chisholm's reassuring presence.

"Report to Lieutenant Gregorson tomorrow." Turning, the lieutenant walked away.

MacKim saluted Cameron's back. He knew that his life was about to change, for the Lights, like the Grenadiers, were considered the elite of the infantry. Sergeant Dingwall must have been impressed with something that he did.

"OUT HERE, YOU WILL MEET THE NATIVE TRIBES." Gregorson's faded green uniform only highlighted his hard, weather-bronzed face; MacKim had never experienced his casual manner of speech in an officer before. "These are the men the French call savages, and we know as Indians."

MacKim listened. Men from half the British regiments then in North America stood in ranks, with coats that varied from the brilliant scarlet of recruits to the patched and faded pink of veterans. Highlanders stood beside men of Anstruther's, Royal Americans next to Webb's, Bragg's or Kennedy's. Knowing it was a futile exercise, MacKim scanned the faces for Osborne or Hitchins. Neither man was there; tall and bulky Grenadiers did not suddenly become wiry Lights.

"These natives are neither savage nor Indian. They are probably the best warriors in the world at scouting and hunting, with hearing more acute than any dog. Their art of war consists of ambushing and surprising their enemies and in preventing their enemies from ambushing and surprising them." Gregorson paused for a moment. "If you wish to ask any questions, please do so. Your life may depend on how much you know about your enemy."

MacKim started. He had not expected an officer to invite questions from the men. By the time he recovered, Gregorson was speaking again. "The natives do not fight in rigid lines and columns, giving and receiving volleys of musketry as we do. That does not make them cowards."

MacKim nodded. He had been brought up on tales of the old clan wars of cattle raids and ambush in the heather and wooded slopes of the Highlands. He could perfectly understand the native way of war.

"There are many tribes out here, and most prefer the French to the British." Gregorson stepped onto a small knoll, the better to address the gathered men. "The reason for that is obvious. There are fewer French settlers than British, and they have assimilated far better. The French hunt with the Indians, intermarry with the Indians and allow the Indians to continue the life they have always known. On the other hand we, the British, come over here by the thousand and the ten thousand, take the Indians' land and push them out."

MacKim could understand the Indians' grievances. He would not like it if some alien people came into the Highlands, took over the land and displaced the indigenous inhabitants.

Gregorson continued. "The native people around our colonies live in tribes, the Huron, Algonquian, Abenaki, Mohegan, Seneca and many more, all of whom dislike the British who have stolen their lands. Others, such as the Missisaugas, Ottowas, Potowatomis, Iowas, Delawares and the Foxes from the far west fight because they desire French gold, or for muskets, powder and rum. They trust the French more than they do the British, which means that as long as the French control Canada, we are surrounded by potential hostiles."

Gregorson looked around his audience of trainee Light Infantrymen. "Are there any questions so far?"

Glancing around at his neighbours, MacKim raised his voice. "How do they fight, sir? What sort of ambushes do they mount?"

Gregorson seemed glad to elaborate. "Their muskets are as good as ours and their forest skills infinitely better than the average British soldier. Only the Rangers come close, although the 60th Royal Americans might do well, given time."

MacKim noted that most of the trainees were listening intently.

"The Indians surround their enemies, fire and when pressed, withdraw. They will not stand to receive a charge by the bayonet but will retreat, regroup and surround you again, usually selecting a small party. They've no concept of glorious last stands. Indians fight when they think they will win and retreat when they think they will lose."

MacKim nodded. The Indian way of war was pragmatic and eminently sensible.

Gregorson fixed his gaze on MacKim. "The Indians are

warriors rather than soldiers. If they shoot an opponent, they will jump on him, crush his skull with the butt of their musket or a war club, and scalp him. Alternatively, they will throw their tomahawk at him or close and cut out his heart." He paused. "If you think of them as merciless, you are right. They have no more mercy towards an enemy than a charge of grapeshot. In European warfare, there are rules about the treatment of civilians and prisoners-of-war. Out here, these rules do not apply. The Indians can cook and eat their prisoners, or torture them in ways worse than anything you can imagine. If their prisoner is lucky, the Indians will only enslave him." Gregorson smiled. "Two units of our army have more chance than anybody else of being captured by these formidable warriors. One is the Rangers, the colonial-born men who scout in front of our army. The other is you, the Light Infantry." Gregorson's pause was significant.

MacKim said nothing. Being a Light Infantryman seemed to add hazards to the already perilous life of a soldier. Yet the training would make him a better fighting man, better able to take vengeance on the men who had murdered Ewan. He braced himself, knowing that his war was about to take on a new twist.

"Anybody who is scared at the thought of facing these tribesmen in their forests, take one step back."

When three men withdrew a pace, MacKim remained static, refusing to admit his fear.

Gregorson did not appear impressed. "I see. We have only three honest men among us, for I tell you that anybody who is not scared of facing the tribes is a fool. It is the fear that makes you cautious and caution that may keep you alive a little bit longer. What I am about to teach you will make you better soldiers, more able to meet the Indians, and kill them, but you still need the help that fear gives you."

MacKim nodded. He understood. North American frontiersmen were different from Europeans, despite their shared heritage. Here, with the French and Indians always ready to strike, people seemed to be less prone to false images. Pragmatism was more important than image.

Then followed the most intensive, yet interesting, training that MacKim had so far endured, as a mixture of officers and sergeants, British, European and American colonial, taught the Light Infantry recruits the skills of forest warfare.

Firing and aiming was emphasised, fast loading and firing from standing, kneeling and lying positions, with Gregorson handing out small prizes for the best shots, and leading hunting expeditions to give live practice.

The Rangers were experts. MacKim had seen them outside Louisbourg, and now they taught the Lights how to march over all kinds of terrain, how to pitch and fold tents and carry equipment efficiently and quickly. One Swiss instructor, Colonel Henry Bouquet, on temporary loan from the 60th Royal Americans, was keen on fitness. First, he had the Lights marching, and then he set running competitions with small prizes for the winner.

With the weakest athletes weeded out, Bouquet trained the rest to run in extended order, then to wheel in formation so they could attack the flanks of the enemy. Rather than the traditional military drums, Bouquet used a bugler to give signals for the Lights to disperse or rally, with the day not complete until the men followed a course of jumping over logs and ditches. Brought up in rough terrain, the Highlanders found that they excelled in these exercises, rivalled only by those back-wood Colonials who had joined the British army.

Next was swimming, where the Highlanders were not so good. Striving to learn, MacKim pushed himself as hard as he could.

"I wanted to be a Grenadier," MacKim panted to Chisholm, as they lay side by side beside a fast-flowing river. "Not a Light Bob."

Chisholm shook his head. "You're not tall enough. The

Grannies are all big, brawny men, chosen for their experience and aggression."

"You're tall enough," MacKim pointed out, "and you're a veteran. Did you never think of being a Grenadier?"

"Yes, I was a Grenadier for a couple of years. I found them an arrogant, big-headed bunch," Chisholm said. "You would not like them." He was silent for a while, watching the ripples of the river. "What's your plan, Hugh?"

"I'm trying to be the best soldier I can be," MacKim replied.

"Aye," Chisholm raised an eyebrow. "Are you pushing for promotion? Corporal? Sergeant?"

"I hadn't thought about it," MacKim said. He wondered how Priscilla would view him as a corporal, smiled and dismissed the thought. *I must not think of pleasure until I've fulfilled my oath.*

"Well, don't even consider promotion," Chisholm said. "I was a corporal once. You're happier as a private soldier, responsible only for yourself and surrounded by your colleagues. The little extra money you'll make as a corporal is more than compensated by the worries in looking after a bunch of drunken scoundrels such as these." Chisholm jerked a thumb at the hopeful Light Infantry as they sprawled naked along the river bank, enjoying the last of the autumn sunshine. Being British soldiers, some had managed to find rum and were tippling happily.

Once Bouquet was satisfied that everybody was a proficient swimmer, he moved them on to the next stage of training.

"If you are out in the forests, you'll find rivers and lakes. You will have to cross them, either by swimming or by canoe."

MacKim found the light native canoes hard to handle but very manoeuvrable once he had some experience. He was intrigued by the alternative method of river crossing, where the men made rafts, placed their clothes and weapons on top and pushed them through the water. When the temperature dropped, serious-faced Rangers showed them how to use snow-shoes, while Bouquet instructed them in bridge-building.

Veterans of Louisbourg, they were already skilled in making fascines and digging entrenchments.

Only when the recruits had thoroughly learned the basics did the instructors teach them the elements of skirmishing. "I don't want to hear of brave men making themselves targets for the sake of glory," Gregorson said. "A dead soldier is no good to the King. On the command 'tree all', or whenever you are attacked, find a tree to shelter behind. Make yourself as small a target as possible. You win battles by killing more of the enemy than they kill of you."

MacKim learned how to shelter, look for dead ground, to avoid the skyline and how to wait in patient ambush.

"Patience is the friend of the Light Infantry," a succession of sergeants told them. "A hurrying man makes noise, noise attracts the Indians, and then you are tied to the torture pole with your scalp decorating some warrior's belt. Learn patience or die."

It was well into winter, with snow blowing in a biting wind, before Gregorson considered them to be fully trained and released them back to their regiments.

"I wonder what the future holds," Cumming said.

"War, battles, disease and suffering," Chisholm said. "That's the lot of the soldier. And no thanks from the civilians we guard or from King George."

MacKim grinned. He felt fitter and leaner than he had ever done in his life. Now, all he had to do was find Osborne and Hitchins, and life beckoned him with promise.

Priscilla, he thought. *The future holds Priscilla.*

❧ II ❧

NEW ENGLAND, WINTER
1758-1759

Boston was busy. Although a major port, it struggled to cope with a rising number of poor, plus a steady increase in the number of soldiers' wives who looked for accommodation when the regiments were up-country. Men and women from Great Britain and Ireland, spending their first winter in the New World, were shocked at the severity of the weather. They huddled up against the cold, searched for accommodation and hoped for a short war as, all that winter, the towns of the eastern seaboard of North America saw an increase in the number of ships preparing for next year's campaigning season.

"The weather is too bad to sail now," Cumming said, as a north-easterly wind howled into the harbour.

"It's worse further north." Chisholm took the pipe from his mouth. "Louisbourg harbour is choked by ice, blown from the Gulf of St Lawrence. Our ships can't get out, yet I heard that a French fleet of sixteen ships sailed right up to Quebec."

"How can they get up and we can't?" Cumming asked. "I thought our navy was meant to be the best."

"The Frenchies know the St Lawrence river," Chisholm said. "We don't. Now Quebec will have months of provisions, so we might have to assault it rather than having a siege as we did at Louisbourg." He puffed out foul smoke. "God help us."

"We'll take it," Cumming said. "We took Louisbourg, and we'll capture Quebec."

"I hope you're right, Cumming, I hope you're right."

Rumours abounded, with British prisoners informing the French that a sixty-thousand-strong British army would advance the following year, while the French captured a document sent from General Amherst to London containing all the details of the forthcoming campaign. In Quebec, the French commander, the Marquis de Montcalm strengthened the defences.

While generals and politicians worried over national policy and high strategy, the ordinary foot soldiers, the men who did the fighting, suffering and dying, struggled to survive day by day.

"'Right, you men.'" Recently promoted from Lieutenant, Captain Hugh Cameron viewed the Light Infantrymen. "You Light Bobs will now be the flank company that will operate either on the left of the line or in front, in skirmishing order." He walked with a devil-may-care air, his eyes dancing as he surveyed his men. "I doubt what I say is official, and it certainly will never be entered in any regimental order book, but we're going to break every military rule." He paused. "You men won't be held accountable, as you are following my orders."

MacKim and Chisholm glanced at each other, wondering what was coming next as Cameron rubbed his hands together.

"Cut the skirts off your long coats, cut your hair short, brown the barrels of your muskets, wear short leggings and throw away the pointless hair dressings you carry; bring in more meal instead. I want soldiers fit to fight the French, not powdered flunkeys."

MacKim did not hide his smile. Following the intensive training in the woods, such orders made perfect sense to him. Warfare out here was not the same as in Europe so there was no need for the formality.

Captain Cameron waited until his Lights settled down. "We

are going up-country lads, to Fort Stanwix, deep in the colony of
New York and on the route from Lake Ontario to the Hudson
River. You'll need all your training out there."

MacKim hid his pleasure. It would be a relief to get away
from the city, despite the undoubted threat from the Indians up-
country.

"Fort Stanwix," Chisholm said with a grin. "That sounds suit-
ably wild."

"I won't find Osborne or Hitchins there," MacKim voiced his
only regret.

"Don't let revenge ruin your life," Chisholm advised. "You are
too young to be so bitter. Soldiers live for today because
yesterday is gone and there might never be a tomorrow." He
looked sideways at MacKim. "I mean that, Hugh. If you are
intent on going after these Grenadiers, then you know I'll stick
by you. I understand your anger, but my advice would be to get
drunk, find a willing woman and forget things for a while."

"I've only ever met one woman that I especially like."
MacKim cursed his loose tongue the minute he spoke.

"Oh?" Chisholm's smile was as innocent as a striking viper.
"You haven't mentioned that before. Who was she?"

"Just a woman."

"Did she have a name, this 'just a woman'?"

"Yes." MacKim looked away. "Priscilla."

Chisholm waited for more. MacKim kept his mouth shut.

"Well, next time, my boy, don't you worry about *liking* them.
You're a soldier. You may die tomorrow, so live for today. The
next time you meet a woman, enjoy her. She may be your last."

"You don't do that," MacKim pointed out.

"No," Chisholm said. "No, you're right. I don't do that."

FORT STANWIX WAS IMPRESSIVE FOR ITS SITUATION OUT IN THE
wilds, a roughly star-shaped building not far from the Mohawk

River, with white frost on the ramparts of its uncompleted timber walls. An outer ditch provided extra protection, while the interior boasted a rectangle of rough wooden buildings that overlooked a small parade ground. Four companies of the 78th squeezed behind its walls, some complaining about the Spartan accommodation after the fleshpots of Boston.

"We're here for the remainder of the winter, boys." Captain Cameron sounded cheerful. "Get settled in. Most of the lads will be helping complete the building and fortification work. Light Infantry, you'll be patrolling outside in case the Canadians or Indians attack."

"It's always the bloody Lights that gets the patrolling," Cumming said.

"That's because we're the best," Chisholm told him. "Would you trust the Grenadiers with a patrol? With the noise they make, they may as well be bringing the pipes and drums with them!"

A group of Rangers watched as the Light Infantry filed out of Fort Stanwix, each man looking around at the looming forest.

"Everything here seems much bigger than in Scotland," MacKim said. "I'm not sure if it's daunting or exciting."

"It's different from campaigning in Europe," Chisholm said. "Why, when we were marching toward Fontenoy, our foraging parties could wave to the French doing the same thing."

"When I was at Fontenoy," Cumming murmured, "I wasn't such an ugly bastard as I am now."

"You wouldn't have lasted at Fontenoy." MacKim held Chisholm back. "You got the ugly bastard part right though, Cumming. You're certainly all of that."

Cumming touched his bayonet. "You be careful, MacKim. Someday you'll be alone without your big friend to look after you."

One of the Rangers had been an interested spectator. "If you make any more noise, the Indians won't have any trouble finding you." He stepped forward, a long, lean and laconic man, with his face walnut brown and a feather decorating his tricorne hat. "You'll need a guide."

"Local knowledge is always useful." Captain Cameron gave his usual smile. He indicated his Lights. "You Rangers are welcome."

The Ranger nodded. "I saw you boys at Louisbourg, didn't I?"

"We were there," Cameron agreed.

"I wasn't sure if you were the same regiment. There are two regiments of Highlanders, aren't there? Montgomery's and Fraser's."

"We're Fraser's," Cameron said.

The Ranger loped alongside, looking at each face in turn. "Have you much experience in the forest?"

"Not yet," Cameron said. "Although most of the men have been extensively trained."

"That's a start. The Rangers will go in advance in case the Indians come. Single file is best, with a space between each man so a musket ball cannot pass through one man and kill the next."

MacKim thought this forest felt different from the one in which he had trained. There was the same snow falling and lying in the clearings, the same grey-green light filtering between the trees, but there was also an aura of menace. The threat lay all around, as it had in the disputed land between the British lines and the walls of Louisbourg. Predatory Indians haunted these forests.

"Listen, Captain; you have ten men in your patrol. There are three of us Rangers, and we're better versed in this kind of warfare."

Some British officers would have objected to a mere colonial speaking in such a manner, but Cameron nodded. "Carry on, Ranger."

"We could split up, and one Ranger could guide a small number of men. That way, each man has a better chance to learn."

"Do that," Cameron said.

"We'll go with you," Gunn said to the Ranger. "I'm Corporal Gunn, this is MacKim, and the big fellow is Chisholm."

"I'm Jacob Wooler." The Ranger did not comment on Chisholm's scarred face.

Wooler? MacKim followed the Ranger into the forest. The cold was more intense than anything he had felt before, making breathing painful. About to question the Ranger, MacKim bit back the words. He was sensible enough to know that there might be Indians on the prowl, so that any noise could bring instant retribution.

Wooler was Priscilla's name. This man may be related to her, possibly her brother? MacKim pushed the thought to the back of his mind. He must concentrate on his surroundings, for every experienced man had hammered home that the Indians were dangerous, very skilled foes. MacKim watched Wooler as he walked slowly and cautiously, checking each step, his head moving all the time to survey his surroundings. While a Light Infantryman fought differently from the men in line, a Ranger was another step ahead, scouts for the main army, a screen to protect the redcoats from the guerrilla tactics of the Indians and Canadians.

They stopped on the edge of a small clearing, with Wooler pointing to the ground. MacKim saw the imprint of a snowshoe.

"Not one of ours," Wooler said quietly. "Indian sign. That footprint is about three hours old: see how the edges are blurred? That's because sunlight has partly melted it."

"Three hours?" Gunn spoke quietly, looking around at the dark trees. "He'll be long gone now."

"Maybe. Maybe not. The Indian could be watching us right now."

MacKim pulled back the hammer of his musket. The thought that one of those ferocious forest warriors might be aiming at him was not pleasant.

Wooler stood up. "One footprint means nothing except the Indians have been here. Shall we carry on, Corporal Gunn?"

Gunn looked around. In MacKim's opinion he was probably

too quiet to be a corporal. "Yes. We need to learn about the area."

That patrol was uneventful, with Wooler guiding them through the woods, pointing out the local features.

"You carry a rifle, Wooler," MacKim said. "Is that not a bit long in the barrel for forest fighting?"

"Yes." Wooler opened the front of his jacket, revealing two double-barrelled pistols. "I use the rifle when we are in ambush and these," he tapped the pistol butts, "if we meet the Indians."

"Have you fought them often?"

"Our lives are a constant battle."

About to ask if Wooler knew Priscilla, MacKim closed his mouth. He was not ready yet to disclose his feelings towards that woman.

"You're learning fast," Wooler praised his apprentices when they returned to the fort. He gave a twisted smile. "You've the makings of Rangers in you." Even as he spoke, Wooler watched the woods.

"King and country, was it?" Wooler faced MacKim directly.

"King and country?" MacKim did not understand.

"Did you don the scarlet coat for King and country?"

"Oh." MacKim considered. "No. That was not why I took the King's Shilling."

Wooler nodded. His eyes were steady as he scrutinised MacKim. "You must have badly needed a job, then."

"No." MacKim shook his head. He tried to turn the conversation. "Why did you join the Rangers? Are you keen on fighting for the King?"

Wooler seemed to consider the question before replying. "I can't say I've ever met the man. No, no, I'm not fighting for King George."

"Why are you fighting then?"

There was another long pause before Wooler replied. "We live right on the edges of settlement. Whenever King George argues with King Louis, the French send the Indians to attack us."

"Is that bad?"

"It's worse than bad," Wooler said. "The French and Indians want to eradicate us. Over in Europe, losing a war means moving a border a few miles, or some town or province gaining or losing a king. Here, losing would mean extermination. The Indians are the enemies of our blood."

"Us?" MacKim noted the term *enemies of our blood*. "Do you mean the settlers?"

"I mean, my wife and me."

So you are married then. Are you married to Priscilla? MacKim nodded. "Would you not be better at home looking after your good lady?"

"She's in the fort," Wooler said. "That's probably the safest place to be unless the French capture it." He frowned. "Please the Lord there's no repetition of Fort William Henry."

"Please the Lord, indeed."

MacKim did not pursue that conversation. The British army seethed with anger at the memory of Fort William Henry, and the Colonials must share that emotion. MacKim thought of Priscilla under the scalping knife of a fierce Indian brave, shuddered and looked away.

"You are not here to defend your family," Wooler said. "You are not a staunch king's man, so why join the army?"

"One reason was that my clan chief ordered it."

Wooler grunted. "What's a clan chief?"

"It's a bit like the chief of a tribe," MacKim said.

Wooler looked at him sideways. "Your clan chief ordered you to join the army and fight in another continent. Did you do something wrong? Did you offend him?"

"No. The chief was raising a regiment for the king and called for volunteers." MacKim decided to keep his other reason to himself.

"How many volunteered?" Wooler sounded genuinely interested.

"About fifteen hundred, mostly from the clan lands."

Wooler whistled. "You must think a lot of your chief."

MacKim screwed up his face. What did he think of his chief, a man he had never spoken to but who demanded his followers fight to help restore him to lands on which MacKim could only ever be a tenant? Although MacKim had never questioned the chief before, now Wooler's words made him wonder. He could not forget his brother, called into the clan regiment aged sixteen and killed without being able to strike a single blow. "It's what we always do. It's what we've always done."

The Ranger frowned, evidently struggling to understand. "Why could you not tell him to fight his own battles?"

"He's the chief," MacKim said.

"What would have happened if you had not joined his private army?"

"If he regained his lands, he might have had my mother evicted." MacKim said. "And our name would have been blackened."

Wooler grunted. "Your clan chief is not a pleasant man. In your own way, you are also fighting for your family then."

"In a way," MacKim said cautiously.

"I'm glad we don't have that sort of thing," Wooler said. "No landlords, no chiefs, no evictions. We make our own decisions, farm our own land and look after our own families." He gave that twisted grin again. "That's why we came out to the frontier, and why our forefathers left Great Britain for the Americas." Producing a short pipe, he stuffed tobacco in the bowl. "We call it freedom, and damn the French and Indians."

MacKim nodded. "I can't imagine that."

All his life he had been surrounded by the people, both in Glen Cailleach and then in the regiment. In Fraser's Highlanders, he knew a hundred people, friends and cousins and all looked to the chief, and now the colonel of the regiment, for leadership and guidance. MacKim made no decisions; he followed orders and moved with the rest. His Light Infantry training had stirred some new ideas of individuality that Wooler was now expanding with his talk of freedom on the frontier. MacKim shifted uncomfortably; being all alone on the edge of civilisation was an unsettling concept that scared him as much as it excited him.

"I can't imagine somebody telling me what to do all the time," Wooler said. "Would you not like to be free to decide your own life?"

MacKim stepped back a little. "I don't know," he said. The idea was so strange he shoved it aside. "I know I prefer the wilderness to big cities. How do you know what to do?"

Wooler laughed. "We don't, much of the time," he said. "We just try and see if it works."

MacKim considered that for a moment. "I don't know if I could do that." Yet even as he spoke, he wondered at a life where men could make their own decisions rather than obey orders from others. *I have my oath to fulfil. I cannot think of freedom, as Wooler calls it.*

"It's precarious at times," Wooler went on. "It's worthwhile, though. I have fifty acres of my own land that I own and which I broke from the forest. My wife rules the house, and I rule my land." His eyes crinkled at the thought of his wife.

"Does she have a name, this wife of yours?" *Please, God, don't make it Priscilla. Let me keep that woman inside my heart.*

MacKim's hope died when Wooler said: "Priscilla."

MacKim's growing liking for the Ranger took a severe dent. "Priscilla?" He tried to sound both surprised and pleased. "I am sure I met your wife in Louisbourg."

Wooler's smile broadened. "You'll be the Highlander she spoke to on the battlements. I know all about you!"

For some reason, MacKim felt a thrill of painful pleasure that Priscilla had mentioned him. "You are a lucky man to have such a wife."

"With that, I cannot argue," Wooler said. "Come and bid her good-day."

Oh, my Lord. What can I say to her?

Priscilla started when she saw her husband and MacKim together. "Jacob! This is the Highland soldier I told you about!" She curtseyed to MacKim. "You find us in difficult circumstances, sir. I am afraid I cannot offer you the hospitality I would like to."

"Your company is hospitality enough." The words sounded stilted as MacKim gave his first-ever bow. "Your gallant husband has been guiding us through the woods and telling me about your life on the frontier."

"Oh, Jacob!" Priscilla shook her head. "Jacob could talk the legs of an ass and still have sufficient words left over to write the Bible!"

When Wooler smiled over to his wife, MacKim realised that Priscilla's relationship with Wooler was different to anything he had encountered in the regiment. Soldiers' wives seemed to belong to the regiment as much as the men did, so if their husband died of disease or in battle, they could find another man within a few weeks or even days. MacKim guessed that out on the frontier, men and women were in less abundance, and they depended on each other. Priscilla and Jacob seemed as close as brother and sister.

"I'll have to return to the regiment," MacKim said. "Thank you, Wooler, and it was good to meet you again, Mrs Wooler."

"You too, MacKim." Jacob had his arm linked with Priscilla.

Turning quickly, MacKim marched away. *Damn, damn, damn! I want that woman, yet I like her husband as well. She is happy with him. Would Priscilla leave Wooler for me? Would she leave her fifty acres of land for the life of a soldier's wife?*

"You're pensive." Chisholm was trying to clean his kilt. "What's in your mind, MacKim?"

"Women."

Chisholm stopped what he was doing. "All of them, or one in particular?"

"One in particular."

"Ah." Chisholm returned to brushing off the worst of the dirt. "That would be Wooler's wife, then."

"How the devil did you know that?"

"A blind man with one leg could see the way you looked at her, Hugh." Chisholm sighed. "Forget her. She's not for you."

"I love her."

"Even if you do," Chisholm said, "she's picked her man. Do you want her to live like this?" He indicated the crowded quarters, with soldiers squeezed into every space and a foul-mouthed soldier's wife exchanging crude jokes with a circle of men. "Could you bring her into this?"

MacKim shook his head. "No."

"Exactly. No." Chisholm lay on his cot. "Did I ever tell you that I was married once?"

"Were you?" MacKim tried to tear his thoughts from Priscilla.

"Once. When I was a corporal." Chisholm shook his head. "I thought she was for life. She followed me for two years, cooking, cleaning, mending and then," he touched his face, "this happened, and she left without a word, or a gesture. She vanished overnight, and I never saw her again. I heard that she took up with a handsome young private in another regiment. That's another reason for not pursuing Priscilla, Hugh. Our lives are not our own. They belong to the regiment, the army and ultimately to the king."

"Our lives are not our own." MacKim repeated the words. "I wonder what we would do if our lives ever were our own. What would you do, James? If you suddenly had the freedom to live your life as you wished?"

Cumming and Urquhart had gathered around, listening to the conversation.

"I'd find a place where nobody could see me, and I'd live out my life alone," Chisholm said. "Or I'd shoot myself if suicide was not a sin."

"Why?" MacKim was shocked at the answer.

"Need you ask?" Chisholm lifted his mutilated face. "Need you really ask, damn you?"

MacKim closed his mouth. He had never seen Chisholm angry before.

"I'd open a brothel," Cumming said. "In Boston. I'd have to sample the girls first, one a night, every night."

"You!" Harriette Mackenzie, the wife of Corporal Gunn, gave a screech of laughter. "You wouldn't know what to do with a woman. You silly little boy!"

"I'd buy an inn," Urquhart said. "That would do me. I want an inn in Inverness."

Others joined in, with their desires ranging from lands and estates to a simple yearning for home. MacKim listened and said nothing. He knew he would have no freedom until he had fulfilled his oath, and at present, he could not see that happening. Taking out his list, he reread the two remaining names. *Osborne and Hitchins.*

"What's that?" Cumming made a snatch for MacKim's note. "What do you have there?" He peered at the paper. "What's this, MacKim?"

"Give it here," Harriette said. "You can't read, Cumming!" She read out the names. "Osborne. Hitchins. Who are they, MacKim?"

"They're none of your damned business." MacKim grabbed the list back and stuffed it inside his tunic.

The rattle of drums sent the men to bed, with Harriette withdrawing to the corner she shared with Corporal Gunn. When she hung up the ragged blanket that was all the privacy afforded to her in that place of men, MacKim thought of Priscilla again.

I've only met her twice. She is married. I can't have a future with her. Despite MacKim's conscious thoughts, the image of Priscilla's serene eyes returned. *I could add Wooler to my list. If I got rid of him, I could have Priscilla.* The thought was shocking, yet guiltily appealing. *One musket ball is all I need. Nobody will know, and the Indians will get the blame.* MacKim closed his eyes. *No! Wooler is a decent man and Priscilla is happy with him. I will not ruin her happiness for the sake of my own. Anyway, I'd be a murderer.* He shook his head. *I'm already a murderer. One more would not matter. No!*

"No?" Chisholm sat up. "No what, MacKim?"

"Did I say no?" MacKim jerked himself awake. "I must have been talking in my sleep."

"Well, learn to keep your mouth shut!" Cumming snarled from the far corner of the room. "We're trying to get some sleep."

Now that the idea had entered MacKim's head, it was hard for him to dismiss it. He envisioned a score of scenarios where he could shoot Wooler without any blame being attached to him. *I must have that woman. I want her for myself, and nobody and nothing will stop me. I must kill Wooler the next chance I get.*

❧ 12 ❧

FORT STANWIX, WINTER
1758-1759

Jacob Wooler lifted his hand, stopping the scouting party at once. MacKim slid behind the bole of a tree, lifting his musket. He listened to the silence in the snowy forest, wondering what had alarmed Wooler. He scanned the trees, looking for scuff marks or anything that might signify the presence of a human.

It was less than a movement, more of a flutter, like the wings of a butterfly, except that there were no butterflies in the New York backcountry in winter. Dropping slowly to his knees, MacKim lifted his musket, waiting. He saw a downward drift of snow from a bough, a twig twitching without apparent cause, heard a slight skiff and knew somebody was out there. Taking a deep breath to still the increasing hammer of his heart, MacKim saw Wooler give a nearly imperceptible nod towards a leftward-leaning tree.

It was the eyes that gave the Indian away. Although his body shape merged perfectly with his surroundings, his eyes were mobile, darting from side to side as he watched the British scouting party. MacKim altered his stance slightly, moving as the Rangers had taught him.

The shot came a second later, with the crash of the musket

echoing in the forest. Wooler fired almost immediately, followed by Chisholm. MacKim held his fire, not wishing to waste a shot and have to reload in the presence of hostile Indians.

Wooler crossed to the leaning tree in seconds, sliding to the ground to reload as the Highlanders moved in support. By now, the Light Infantry knew how to act in the forest, covering each other, jinking from tree to tree, keeping in close contact.

Wooler held up his left hand with four fingers erect. There were four Indians then; a hunting or scouting party rather than a war party.

The musket sounded again, a puff of smoke betraying the shooter as the ball hissed through the air a yard from MacKim's head, to thump into the bole of a tree behind him. He reacted instinctively, aiming and firing at the smoke and dropping onto the snow to reload without waiting to check his marksmanship. Ramming home his charge, he replaced the ram-rod and eased to the shelter of a tree before standing again. He followed the rest of the patrol, cursing as the hem of his ice-frozen kilt snapped against his bare thighs, breaking the skin.

"They're running!" Sergeant Dingwall had come along to get experience in the forest. His towering figure was out of place with the lither Light Bobs, and his movements too clumsy.

"Don't follow!" Wooler hissed. "Tree all! They might be leading us into a trap."

The Highlanders stopped at once, each man seeking cover. Once again, they were silent in a quiet world, with snow falling, large white flakes ghosting down in a scene that would have been beautiful if there was not so much danger. The snow fell harder, forming a veil through which MacKim peered, more in hope than expectation. Within three minutes, the snow had blurred all their snowshoe prints. Within ten minutes, there was only whiteness covering the ground. A flight of birds rustled over-head, and then the silence returned.

"I don't like this." Wooler spoke quietly. "These Indians were Abenaki, a dangerous bunch, yet they retreated at once. They could have shot one or more of us with ease. So what were they doing here?"

"Hunting?" Dingwall ventured.

"We passed the tracks of three deer," Wooler said. "The Abenaki crossed them without hesitation. They were not hunting." He glanced over his shoulder. "Best get back to the fort."

"Are you scared of four savages?" Dingwall asked.

"I'd be scared of one Abenaki," Wooler said. "And so would you be if you knew them better. These are not your civilised French soldiers who obey all the rules of war. These are men from beyond the confines of your world."

"We go on," Dingwall said. "I'm not retreating from shadows, or because of four savages."

"You're a fool, Sergeant," Wooler said. "'It's my job to guide and advise you."

"I heard your advice, but it's my job to make the decisions," Dingwall reminded him. "Keep apart and alert and we'll see what these Abenaki were after."

"The Ranger may be right, Sergeant." MacKim dared Dingwall's displeasure.

"You lead, MacKim," Dingwall said, "since you know better than I do."

Cursing that he had opened his mouth, MacKim loped to the front, knowing that Chisholm would watch over him. Even wearing snowshoes, every step sunk in virgin snow, while every touch on a tree sent a fistful of snow down MacKim's back. Expecting to hear the report of a musket and feel the tearing agony of a lead ball through his body, MacKim wondered how Priscilla would react to his death, pushed aside the thought and moved on, with his nerves screaming for him to take care. He stopped suddenly, aware that something was wrong. The sound did not belong.

He heard it again, a slight *something* he could not define. Raising his musket to his shoulder, he swung slowly around, searching the forest ahead, looking for shadows, footprints, or the flash of sunlight on metal as the snow flurry eased and stopped. MacKim saw only snow-covered boughs and the white-smeared trunks of trees.

"Over there!' Wooler mouthed the words, pointing to a small bush twenty yards to the left. As MacKim looked, he saw a hint of movement, with a patch bare of snow beneath the branches. He remained still, watching, ignoring the cold that bit into him. Movement was deadly in the forest.

Sliding from tree to tree, Wooler inched closer to the bush. The woman erupted from it in the opposite direction, jinking and weaving between the trees with her skirt not long enough to hamper her movements. Seeing that she outpaced Wooler, MacKim followed. He had always been proud of his speed, but the woman was as fast as he was. The crash of a gun took both by surprise. MacKim dropped at once, lying prone in the snow with his musket ready and his eyes darting from side to side, probing the woods for tell-tale powder smoke. *Who fired? Who was he aiming at?* The woman was close by, lying between two trees with her arms covering her face and the soles of her feet pointing toward MacKim.

Who are you and why are you running? Are you leading me into an ambush?

MacKim saw the face first, peering from a network of branches. The forehead was painted black, with red vertical streaks down each side of intense, predatory eyes. An Indian, probably one of the Abenaki that Wooler had mentioned. MacKim felt his heart begin to hammer. He had never seen an Indian so close before, and all the scare stories welled up inside him. *This man could kill me with musket or tomahawk and scalp me in a second.*

No! I am a trained soldier, with my colleagues nearby. One enemy warrior will not scare me.

The Abenaki moved, flicking snow from an overhanging branch as he ran toward the woman. Sunlight glinted from the tomahawk in his right hand, while the musket in his left was of a

French pattern, longer than MacKim's Brown Bess. Waiting until the Indian was so close he could not miss, MacKim fired, hearing a second musket crash from his right side. One of the shots hit the Indian high in the chest, knocking him back against the bole of a tree. The impact knocked a shower of snow onto the Abenaki as the woman rose at once, grabbed the warrior's knife and ran again, straight into Wooler's waiting arms.

"What have we here?" Dingwall shouted.

Lying on his back, MacKim reloaded his musket, watching for the remaining three Abenakis. "That Indian was chasing her."

Wooler was struggling with the woman, holding the wrist of her knife hand as she tried to slash at him, her eyes wide.

MacKim hurried up. "It's all right. We won't hurt you." Leaning his musket against a tree, he wrapped both arms around the woman, struggling to hold her as she wriggled, kicked and threw her head backwards in an attempt to smash his teeth.

"She's a savage." Dingwall drew his bayonet. "We should kill her."

"No!" MacKim roared over his shoulder. Memories of the aftermath of Culloden came to him once more. "She did not attack us. She was running away from that man." He pointed to the Abenaki, lying prone against the tree with his wound red and livid.

"So?" Dingwall growled. "Stand aside, private, or I'll have you at the halberds."

"Your man MacKim is correct." Wooler bent back the woman's wrist and removed her knife. "The Abenaki are one of the main allies of the French, from further north and east of here. That brave is carrying a French musket." Taking the woman from MacKim, Wooler pinioned her to the ground. "I don't know what this firebrand is."

MacKim lifted the woman's knife and thrust it into his belt. "It's all right," he said quietly to her. "We won't hurt you."

"You men keep watch," Wooler said. "There are at least three more Abenaki. They'll be watching us now."

"I'll cut her throat." Dingwall ignored Wooler's advice as the patrol fanned out, each man facing outwards.

"If she's an enemy of the Abenaki, she could be friendly to us," MacKim said. "Killing an unarmed woman is just murder."

Chisholm spoke over his shoulder. "What does Wooler advise? He knows conditions here better than all of us put together."

"I don't trust the Abenaki as far as I can spit," Wooler said. "I'm inclined to follow the sergeant's words."

"She's our prisoner," MacKim said. "You said yourself you don't know if she's Abenaki or not."

Wooler tied the woman's wrists with a piece of twine, checking the knot to ensure it was secure. "You're right, MacKim. We could take her back to the fort for questioning, if the sergeant agrees. She's not saying much just now."

"Aye, we could do that, but how about the other three?" Dingwall asked. "We can hunt them down and kill them."

"With Abenaki Indians," Wooler said, "if they leave you alone, then you leave them alone. They're not bothering us now, so we move before they gather a war party and hunt us down."

"MacKim, watch the rear," Dingwall ordered.

Throwing the woman over his shoulder like a sack of corn, Wooler led them back to Fort Stanwix.

❧

PEOPLE PACKED THE INTERIOR OF THE FORT WHEN THE PATROL brought back their captive. Some of the civilians scowled at her, with a few suggesting that they kill her out of hand. Wooler dumped the woman unceremoniously on the ground.

"Shoot her," Cumming said.

"She's a prisoner," Chisholm said. "We don't murder prisoners, especially not women."

"She'd murder you," a lean, sour-faced local woman said. "The women are the worst when it comes to torture." She began to describe in some detail what Indian women did to their captives, until Wooler pushed her away.

"None of that, Mrs Van Tyne. Go and attend to your business."

Harriette Mackenzie grunted. "Mrs Van Tyne is right. We should cut its throat. We've no space for savages inside the fort. She's probably here to spy on us."

"What's this?" Captain Cameron bustled up. "Who's the Indian lady?"

"We don't know, Captain," Wooler said. "We found her in the woods, being chased by a party of Abenaki."

"I see. Can the lady talk?" Extending a hand, Cameron helped the woman to her feet. Tossing back the hair that covered her eyes, she glowered at him.

Cameron smiled. "She could do with a good wash. Don't Abenaki Indians believe in cleanliness?"

"I've never seen such a dirty Indian woman," Wooler agreed. "She's said nothing so far." He pointed to the guardroom. "I was thinking maybe we could place her in there and ask who she is. Private MacKim thinks that she might be friendly to us if she's hostile to the Abenaki."

"Private MacKim has too much to say for himself, sir!" Dingwall growled. "With your permission, I can do something about that."

"Good thinking, Wooler." Cameron ignored Dingwall. "Mac-Kim, you try and communicate. Let me know what you find out." He hesitated a little. "Don't be too rough on her. I don't hold with any of this scalping business."

"I'll make sure she doesn't escape, sir." Dingwall grabbed the woman by the neck. "Come on, you! I know how to deal with murdering savages."

About to interfere, MacKim closed his mouth. He did not know if the woman had another knife secreted about her person.

He watched as Dingwall hustled her into one of the small cells in the guardroom, throwing her against the far wall.

"Right, my dirty one. Let's see what's under that costume of yours. God, you stink worse than a cesspit!" Dingwall looked over his shoulder. "Fetch a bucket of water, MacKim and a hard brush. I'll scrub the filth of this creature before I introduce her to a man."

"Yes, Sergeant." When MacKim saw the fear in the woman's eyes, he wondered if she understood Dingwall's words, or if his intentions were as transparent to her as they were to him. Orders were orders, so MacKim found a bucket, filled it with water and returned with the softest-bristled brush he could find.

The woman crouched in the corner, still with her hands tied behind her back while Dingwall loomed over her.

"Strip her clothes off, MacKim, and leave. There's no need for you to watch unless you need lessons on how to handle a woman."

The woman's terrified eyes fixed on MacKim. Although she was wordless, he knew she was pleading for his help. MacKim shivered; Ewan had that same expression when the Grenadiers had tortured him. "I'll stay, Sergeant, with your permission. There's no knowing what these devils can do." MacKim hesitated a little. "Or what diseases they have."

"I've had them all, lad," Dingwall said. "Strip the bitch."

"I heard that these Indian women carry something horrible." MacKim could not escape the woman's fear. "Something that even our best surgeons can't cure. Something that rots men away," he gestured to his groin, "terribly painfully. You know what I mean, Sergeant."

Dingwall winced. "Where did you hear that?"

"That Ranger fellow, Wooler, told me. 'Keep clear of the savage women,' he said." MacKim affected a shudder. "He told me details, Sergeant, but if I repeat them, I'll be sick."

"Right." Dingwall's savage backhanded slap knocked the

MALCOLM ARCHIBALD

woman to the ground. "Dirty bitch. You hold her while I get her chained up."

Strangely, the woman did not resist as Dingwall chained her to the wall. "There now, my filthy, you stay here until we find somebody that understands your gibberish, and we'll find out all about you." He nodded to MacKim. "Guard her, MacKim, if you know so much about her, and see if you can make her talk. I'll have you relieved in a few hours." Dingwall slammed the cell door behind him.

MacKim took a deep breath. "I know you don't understand me, my lady, but I apologise for the sergeant."

The woman spoke for the first time. "*Il est un cochon.*" ("He is a pig.")

"You speak French?" MacKim did not hide his surprise. He repeated the phrase in halting French. "*Tu parles Français?*"

"I speak some French." The woman looked at her chains, sighed, rattled them and sighed again. "That pig was going to rape me."

"Yes." MacKim's French was minimal, while the woman's accent was different from anything he had heard before. He struggled to understand her.

"Why did you stop him?"

"Did you want him to rape you?"

"No."

"That's why I stopped him."

The woman leaned against the wall. "You speak French as well."

"Only a little," MacKim said. "You'll have to speak slowly."

"What's your name?"

"Hugh MacKim. What's yours?"

"Tayanita," the woman said. She was slender and much more composed now that Dingwall was out of the cell. She was also even dirtier than MacKim had thought.

"Were the Abenaki chasing you?" MacKim sat on the floor

on the opposite side of the cell, making sure that his musket and bayonet were well out of Tayanita's reach.

"Yes." Tayanita tried to slide her left hand free of the manacles.

"Why?"

"One of them owns me," Tayanita said. "I am his slave."

"I did not know Indians kept slaves."

Tayanita rattled her chains again. "These are tight."

"If I loosen them, will you promise not to attack me?"

Tayanita smiled. "Are you afraid of me? Is that why you wear a skirt and not trousers? Do the other soldiers make you wear a skirt because you are afraid of a woman?"

"I'll leave your manacles as they are for now," MacKim decided. "A prisoner should not try to antagonise her guard, you see."

"I have run from one slave owner to another," Tayanita said.

"I am no slave owner," MacKim said. "How were you a slave? I am not sure how your culture does things."

Tayanita sighed. "I was in a Seneca village, and the Abenaki raided and took me as a slave. That man you killed was my owner."

"I see. You are a Seneca then."

"No. My people are further west. The Seneca captured me when I was young, and adopted me."

MacKim shook his head. "I am a bit confused."

"Someday I'll return to my own people," Tayanita said.

MacKim nodded. "I hope so," he said. *Someday I might return home, too.* At that second, Glen Cailleach seemed very far away. He thought of his mother, surely an old woman now, and the mist sliding across the slopes, the lowing of the cattle and the music of the burns.

"Will you loosen these?" Despite her dirt, Tayanita had a pleasant smile.

Sighing, MacKim stepped closer. "Your culture and ours

differ." He wondered if he could mention her pungent smell
without insulting her.

"Yes." Tayanita moved her hands around when MacKim loosened the manacles. She smiled again, showing teeth that were
surprisingly even and white. "Your people smell strange."

"We think that you stink," MacKim told her, more bluntly
than he had intended. "Don't you wash?"

"No." Tayanita shook her head.

"Why not?"

Leaning against the log-built wall, Tayanita gave a slow smile.
"Would you like to make love with me, Hugh MacKim?"

"I would not," MacKim answered without thinking

"Why is that?" Tayanita wriggled slightly. "Am I not young
and attractive?"

MacKim frowned. He had not expected his conversation
with his prisoner to be so provocative. Tayanita was undoubtedly
in control of the situation, despite her chains. "I hadn't noticed."

"Notice." Tayanita suggested, smiling again. "You see? Now,
would you not like to make love with me? That other man
wanted to."

"He didn't, though."

"You stopped him. Why do you think I am unclean?"

MacKim smiled, suddenly understanding. "You stay dirty to
protect yourself from men."

"I'm safe from you."

"Yes." MacKim thought of Priscilla. *She knew she was safe from
me as well. Am I abnormal? Should women be afraid of me? Do I want
them to be afraid of me?*

"You can wash." MacKim pushed across the bucket. "I won't
look." He turned his back, hearing furtive rustlings as he stared
at the solid walls of the cell.

"Thank you, Hugh MacKim."

When MacKim faced her again, Tayanita was clean of face,
although her clothes were as filthy as before. Her smile was even
more pleasant now.

"I'll take the water away," MacKim said. "You must be cold. I'll see if I can find a blanket for you." *Why am I running around after a bloody prisoner?*

"Attention!" Sergeant Dingwall rammed the door open before MacKim could move "Here she is, sir, with MacKim on guard."

Captain Cameron entered the cell and doffed his hat to Tayanita. "Good evening, madam." He glanced at MacKim. "There's no need for the chains, she's only a young woman." He frowned "Has she given you any trouble, MacKim?"

"Not a whisper, sir."

"Release her from these damned manacles then," Cameron ordered. "I don't like even to see men in chains, let alone women."

"Yes, sir." MacKim freed Tayanita from the manacles. She looked up, rubbing at her wrists and glowering at Dingwall.

Cameron nodded. "Isn't that better, miss? You don't understand me, do you? Has she said anything, MacKim?"

"She doesn't seem to speak English, sir, although she knows some French."

"'Does she, by Jove?" Cameron sounded pleased. He began to speak in French that was too rapid for MacKim to follow. Evidently, it was too fast for Tayanita as well, judging by her look of bemusement.

"*Non!*" Tayanita said. "Speak slowly."

"I am sorry, madam." Cameron moderated his speed, asking questions to which Tayanita gave halting answers.

After a few moments, Cameron grunted. "She says that the French have sent Indian war parties to this area, but no artillery that she knows of." He looked at Dingwall. "What do you think of that, Sergeant?"

"We can hold off a few savages, sir."

"I'd like to think so, Sergeant." Cameron glanced at MacKim. "That'll be all, MacKim. Dismissed."

MACKIM DID NOT ACTIVELY DISLIKE NIGHT-TIME PIQUET duty, even out here in Fort Stanwix with the menacing forest almost within musket range. He paced slowly, with his feet thudding on the frost-ingrained planks, wondered what animal was howling in the dark, shivered, cradled his musket in his arms and moved on. He thought of that other fortress where he had met Priscilla. It was maddening to know she was only a hundred yards away, warm and snug in her husband's arms while he was out here in the cold.

I could have shot Wooler in the forest, MacKim thought. *I could have ended this agony and claimed Priscilla for myself.* He sighed and stamped his feet to restore some warmth. After six weeks at Fort Stanwix, he was familiar with his surroundings. That animal howled again, closer to the fort. MacKim peered into the dark. Perhaps the defenders should put torches out there; a dozen or so lamps a hundred yards out would make it easier for the sentries to see if any enemy was approaching. MacKim sighed; standing sentinel was undoubtedly one of the most tedious duties for a soldier, but it allowed him to be alone, and to think.

"Corporal Gunn!" That was Urquhart's voice, further along the parapet. "I heard something."

MacKim listened harder, hearing only the natural sounds of night, a bird calling and the soft sough of the breeze shaking the trees.

"I heard it again!" Urquhart added. "It's a man!"

MacKim saw something flicker through the dark and heard a sickening thump and a gasp. Urquhart crumpled down, staring at the tomahawk that protruded from his chest.

"Stand to!" Corporal Gunn roared. "Indians!" Raising his musket, he fired at one of the dark shapes that swarmed up the walls of the fort. "Stand to!"

MacKim moved closer, knelt, fired and stood again, slotting his bayonet in place rather than taking the time to reload. A drummer beat his mad tattoo to rouse the men while Lieutenant Douglas, the officer of the watch, buckled on his broadsword as he ran to the wall. Behind him, lights flared as men tumbled out of bed, grabbing clothes and muskets in their mad dash to answer the call to arms.

The Indians set up the first war-whoop that MacKim had ever heard, a high-pitched scream that raised the hackles on the back of his neck. Only instinct made MacKim roar the old MacKim motto, *Je suis prest* – I am ready – that he and Ewan used to shout when they played at war as children in Glen Cailleach.

The Indians were over the ramparts and inside the fort, firing their muskets and hacking with their tomahawks as the 78th responded with bayonets and musket butts. Only the sentinels carried loaded muskets and, once fired, they had no time to reload.

"With me, 78th!" Douglas slashed at the invaders with his broadsword. "Drive the painted devils out!"

"Ensign MacDonnell! Take Sergeant Dingwall and a score of men to guard the women and children." Captain Cameron sounded as calm as if he were on the parade ground. "Keep them secure."

To MacKim, all these actions and words were in the background as he advanced against the invaders. He saw the Indians as individuals, appearing and disappearing as they flitted from shadow to shadow, with the light gradually increasing as men lit lanterns.

One Indian brave reared from the shadows, tomahawk raised. MacKim moved to the on-guard position, parried the tomahawk swing with the barrel of his musket and lunged forward. He had a fractional image of the warrior, with his face hideously painted half red, half yellow, and then he was gone, darting away into what remained of the dark. MacKim whirled around, searching for any of the enemy.

"With you, MacKim!" Chisholm emerged from the barracks, bare-chested, with his kilt awry but his bayonet already fixed to his musket.

"Can you see any Indians?" MacKim blinked in the increasing light. "They've all disappeared."

An outburst of firing on the west wall indicated where the Indians had gone. "With me, boys!" Lieutenant Douglas flourished his broadsword. "We'll teach the devils not to meddle with Fraser's!"

"Lanterns!" Cameron ordered. "Bring more lanterns! Smoke them out, boys!"

Clearing the Indians out of the fort was a confused, untidy affair as the defenders poked into every corner and probed every shadow. By that time, some of the civilians were outside their quarters, with women holding their children close. Harriette Mackenzie gripped a cudgel and was swearing that she would brain any Indian she came across.

"They struck and ran." Captain Cameron mounted the ramparts with a lantern man at his side. "Who saw them first?"

"Private Urquhart, sir," Corporal Gunn said. "He raised the alert, and the Indians killed him with a hatchet."

"Thank God for Urquhart," Cameron said.

"They would be raiding to kill some of us and retreat." Douglas sheathed his sword. "They were probing our defences for the French."

"No, sir." Wooler had a pistol in his hand. "They were after a specific objective." He nodded towards the cells. "That woman we brought it. They wanted her back."

MacKim raised his eyebrows, saying nothing.

"All that for a woman?" Douglas said. "Was she the chief's wife, perhaps?"

"Maybe." Wooler shook his head. "I'd reckon that the Abenaki were annoyed to lose one of their own and hoped to either get her back, or kill her."

"So that woman's trouble then," Douglas said.

"In my experience," Cameron said with a smile, "every woman is trouble."

"Maybe we'd better let her go," Douglas suggested. "If we hand her back to the Abenaki, they might not attack us."

"If we hand her back to the Abenaki, they'd probably burn her alive for running away," Wooler said.

Cameron nodded. "We can't have that. She stays where she is."

WHEN THE SCOUTING PATROL ENTERED THE WOODS THE NEXT day, the Abenaki were waiting for them, firing from cover and launching a screaming attack that sent the patrol lurching back with two men wounded.

"We'll have two patrols tomorrow," Captain Cameron decided. "We'll have the usual scouting piquet of twelve Lights and two Rangers, followed by one of twenty-four men. The Abenaki will attack the first patrol, which will withdraw by stages, and the second patrol will meet the Abenaki head-on." Cameron paused for a moment. "I'll have another fifty men in reserve, ready to sally out, take the Abenaki in flank and destroy them."

"That's a good plan," Chisholm said to MacKim. "Lure them on and play them with their own tactics, deception and ambush."

The garrison spent the remainder of that day preparing for the expedition, ensuring every musket was in good condition, with sharp flints and dry powder.

"You're going out again with Jacob." Priscilla appeared at MacKim's elbow.

"That's right." MacKim tried to hide his feelings for her.

"I worry when he goes out in the forest." Priscilla's smile was strained.

"He's a good man." MacKim tested the edge of his bayonet before sliding it back in its scabbard. "He's probably the best woodsman I've ever met."

"Hugh." Priscilla sat on the stub of a log with her skirt folded neatly under her. "I need your help."

MacKim looked up. It was painful even looking at this woman, knowing that she belonged to somebody else. "It would be an honour to help you, Mrs Wooler, if I possibly can."

"It's Priscilla, if you please, as you well know, Private Polite. Could you look after Jacob for me?"

MacKim felt something lurch inside him. "Look after him? I can't think of any man who less needed somebody to look after him, Priscilla. I am only a private soldier, the lowest rank possible, with no experience of this type of warfare."

"I know what you are, Hugh. Could you guard Jacob's back when he's out there? I'm not asking you to follow him or go against your duty. Please, try and look out for him." Priscilla hesitated. "I've had visions these past few weeks, where Jacob is on the ground, and an Indian is above him, about to strike him with a tomahawk."

"That's only a dream," MacKim said. "A nightmare."

"It feels like a premonition," Priscilla said. "Please, Hugh. Would you?"

I want this woman. Oh, God, I need her. MacKim began to clean the barrel of his musket. "I would do anything for you, Priscilla," he said quietly, with the words tearing at him. "If it is humanly possible, I will look after Jacob." He looked up, meeting her eyes for the first time. "I promise you." MacKim took a deep breath. "I swear that I will do all I can to look after him."

That's another oath I've taken and the hardest one yet to keep. Only a few days ago, I was pondering if I could shoot Wooler. Now I have promised Priscilla, the woman I love, to look after him. If he dies when I am nearby, I will always wonder if I let that happen.

"Thank you, Hugh." Leaning forward, Priscilla kissed his forehead. The touch of her lips seemed to burn like red hot iron. When MacKim looked up, Priscilla was walking away, with her hips swaying in a rhythm he found both disturbing and fascinating. He watched her until she entered the building that held the families.

"Nice view, MacKim?" Cumming shouted across to him. "I see you watching that woman's arse."

I hope to God Priscilla did not hear that. "What woman, Cumming?"

"Wooler's wife." Cumming kicked at MacKim's boots. "The sergeant wants you, anyway."

"Which sergeant? There are many."

"Our sergeant, MacKim. Sergeant Dingwall."

"What does he want?" MacKim refused to let Cumming hurry him.

"How should I know? Go and ask him, and you'd better be quick, or it'll be the halberds for you, boy!"

Deliberately banging his shoulder against Cumming on his way past, MacKim found Dingwall sitting in his quarters with a glass of rum in his hand.

"I've detailed you and Chisholm to go with the scouting piquet tomorrow, MacKim." Dingwall lifted his rum and lowered his voice. "I can't think of a better man to lead the piquet than you, MacKim."

Not sure if Dingwall was complimenting him or not, MacKim nodded. "Yes, Sergeant. Will you be with us?"

"Not me." Dingwall swallowed more rum. "The scouts are Rangers and Lights. I'm in the reserve company, so if you lads fall into difficulties, I'll be there to support you, MacKim, don't worry." He passed over the bottle. "I've been watching you since the old training days in Scotland, MacKim. You're a natural soldier."

"Thank you, Sergeant." MacKim took a swig of the rum: such munificence from Sergeant Dingwall was rare.

"I've put your name forward to Captain Cameron for promotion." Dingwall quickly reclaimed the bottle. "The next vacancy and you could be a corporal." He poured himself more rum. "Now, get back to where you belong, you rogue."

"Yes, Sergeant."

Full of conflicting emotions, MacKim returned to barracks. "We're to be in the scouting party tomorrow, and Dingwall says I'm a natural soldier," he told Chisholm. "He's recommended me for promotion to corporal."

Chisholm exhaled smoke from his pipe. "Best stay a private, son. No responsibility and no worries. You're too young to be a corporal, God, man; you've still got crib marks on your arse!"

"Too late now," MacKim said. "I can't deny I'm a little pleased, although I'm not sure what a natural soldier is!"

"A natural soldier?" Chisholm contemplated the ceiling for a moment. "A natural soldier digs himself a little hollow to sleep in every night on the march, as we were trained with the Lights. He aims and fires with care, as we were trained with the Lights. He does not show how scared he is. Well, nobody shows their fear." He smiled across to MacKim. "Except Cumming."

"I'm not scared," Cumming shouted across, with others either agreeing or saying nothing. Nobody admitted to being afraid.

"What else does a natural soldier do?" Cattanach asked.

"He runs forward with care, zig-zagging from cover to cover."

"As we were trained to do in the Lights," Cumming said.

Chisholm grinned. "Quite so, Cumming. He can sleep anywhere, at any time."

"We all do that," a prematurely greying man named Sinclair said. "We're so bloody tired all the time."

"A perfect soldier eats anything and everything," Chisholm continued, "ignores the cold or the heat and, most importantly, he obeys orders and doesn't think too much."

"That's you then, MacKim; you can't think," Cattanach said.

Corporal Gunn growled from across the room. "Aye, eat all you can, sleep when you can, keep out of the sergeant's way, never get promoted as the French marksmen shoot the officers and NCOs first, avoid the lieutenants and don't worry about higher-ranked officers."

"Why not?" Cumming asked.

"Because you're only a private soldier, Cumming and they are far too dignified and self-important to notice beetles such as you," Gunn said. "I missed one thing out. Do as Corporal Gunn tells you!"

"Or as I tell you," Harriette added, to a general, if uneasy laugh.

A natural soldier, MacKim repeated to himself. *I am the least natural soldier in this regiment. I don't belong here at all.*

🐝 13 🐝

FORT STANWIX, WINTER
1758-1759

"They're out there," Wooler spoke quietly. "I can feel them."

MacKim took a deep breath. He trusted the instincts of this serious-faced man. "We'll still have to go," he said.

"Aye, MacKim. We'll still have to go." Wooler checked the flint of his rifle. "Let's hope our supports aren't far behind. We're like the forlorn hope in your European wars."

"I've never been in a European war," MacKim said. "Chisholm here has."

Chisholm nodded. "It's a different kind of fighting."

"All right." Wooler took a last long look at the forest. "Pray to God that we get through this day."

For one betraying moment, MacKim thought of Priscilla, and then he pushed her image away. If Priscilla knew how much he loved her, she would not have put her faith in him to guard her husband.

"Snowshoes, boys, and may God be with us," Wooler said again.

Their footsteps sounded hollow as they crossed the bridge over the newly deepened ditch and stepped onto the open ground between the fort and the forest. MacKim felt his heart thump then, for men in the open were very vulnerable to Abenaki musket-men.

Only a few yards into the trees, Wooler raised an arm, calling a halt. The patrol stopped at once, with MacKim's breathing ragged with tension. He felt his hands sweating on the stock of his musket as he listened to the stressful silence.

"They're out here," Wooler said. It was the first time that MacKim heard genuine fear in his voice.

"What do you want to do, Jacob?" MacKim knelt in the shelter of a bush with the butt of his musket grounded three inches in front of his knees.

"The deeper in we go, the more chance there is they'll come behind us," Wooler said. "I think we should spring their ambush when we still have a chance to retreat."

"Captain Cameron has two bodies of men waiting to support us," MacKim reminded.

"With all respect to Captain Cameron, he's not out here with the Abenaki."

MacKim raised his eyebrows. Only last night, his colleagues had been talking about the unquestioning obedience of a natural soldier. Now, here was Wooler, a Ranger with the lowest possible rank, deliberately contemplating breaking the orders of a King's officer. It was a form of freedom totally against anything MacKim had ever known.

"Do you want to die tied to an Abenaki torture pole?" Wooler's eyes were never still as he probed his surroundings.

"I'd prefer not to," MacKim replied.

"Nor I," Chisholm said quietly.

"I can't see a damned one of them," Wooler said. "There's not a sound out there, and that's the worrying thing. It's like a void in nature, no bird call. Nothing."

"Our supports have not left the fort yet," Chisholm murmured.

"All right. We'll advance another hundred paces and assess

the situation." Wooler barely brushed snow from the branches as he moved cautiously forward. MacKim followed, with Chisholm at his back and the rest a few steps behind.

"There!" Wooler lifted his rifle and fired, with the crack of the shot deafening in the dark. "I see you!" He reloaded hastily as MacKim and Chisholm covered him, not firing until they saw a target.

"I can't see a blessed thing!" MacKim peered into the shrouded trees. The drift of powder-smoke slowly dissipated. There was no sound except the nervous breathing of the piquet.

"They're there all right." Wooler finished loading. "Come on, back we go."

"I see one!" Cumming fired into the trees. "There's more!"

"Hugh." Chisholm placed his hand on MacKim's shoulder. "If the Indians are there, why are they not firing back?"

MacKim had not fired yet. "What do you mean, James?"

"There are no Indians, Hugh. Not here, anyway."

"What do we do, James?" MacKim accepted Chisholm's assessment. "Obey orders, or return with the rest?"

Chisholm grunted. "We return with the rest, Hugh, and say we saw Indians. Do you want to get Wooler into trouble, or accuse him of cowardice?"

"No." MacKim thought of his oath to Priscilla. "Come on, Chisholm." He fired blindly into the trees, loaded quickly and waited for Chisholm to fire and load.

Leading the second wave, Captain Cameron looked frustrated as the scouting patrol retreated and his whole plan collapsed.

"They were waiting for us," Wooler reported.

"Hundreds of them, sir," Cumming added. "The painted devils were everywhere. We were lucky to get away."

"Damn it." Cameron looked at his men. "Back to the fort then."

"It's that bloody woman's fault." The murmur grew among

both soldiers and settlers. Some cast dark looks at the cells where Tayanita languished.

"Things might get ugly here," Chisholm said. "We should have left that Indian woman alone."

MacKim grunted. "If we had left her, the Abenaki might have killed her."

"Better have one Indian woman killed than lose more of our men," Chisholm said. "I've heard some of the lads say they want to break into her cell and hand her over to the Abenaki."

"Will they do that?"

Chisholm raised his eyebrows. "I don't know, Hugh. I could not see that happening in any other campaign I've been on, but things are different out here. We saw that with your friend Wooler."

"I've never known a ranker make decisions like that before," MacKim agreed.

"It's a dangerous precedent that may spread," Chisholm said. "Once discipline collapses, the enemy has the advantage, yet I wouldn't like to think of a woman tied to a torture pole." He looked over his shoulder, where a group of children exploded from the living quarters of the fort. "I'd like it less if the French and Indians captured this fort and scalped the women and children because of our single prisoner."

For one shocking moment, MacKim thought of Priscilla in the hands of the Abenaki. The idea made him shudder. *There must be another way.*

"Tayanita!" MacKim eased the cell door open. "*C'est moi.* It's me."

Tayanita looked up from the rustling straw of her bed. "Hugh MacKim?"

"*Allons. Se dépêcher.* Come on. Hurry!"

"Where are you taking me?"

"Out of here! Make haste, woman!" Reaching down, MacKim took hold of Tayanita's arm and nearly dragged her out of the cell. "Keep quiet!"

"You're the one making all the noise!"

With a blustering wind and flurries of snow driving the sentries to seek shelter, MacKim eased Tayanita onto the parapet where he was supposed to be on sentry duty. "The main gate's too well guarded. You'll have to go down the wall. Here..." He handed her a bundle of food and clothing, with a knife on top. "It's only army issue bread, or what they call bread."

MacKim glanced along the length of the parapet. Cattanach was to his left, looking the other way as he huddled into his plaid against the weather.

"Why are you doing this?"

"Because you need to be free," MacKim said. "Go on! Get back to your people."

For a moment, Tayanita's gaze met his. "You are a good man, Hugh MacKim."

"I am not." MacKim thought of the man he had killed and the men he planned to kill in the future. "I am not a good man, Tayanita. Now go."

"We'll meet again, Hugh, somewhere."

"For God's sake, woman!" Hugh looked along the parapet, where Cattanach was now moving, stamping his feet on the timber walkway. "Go when you can!" He leaned closer. "Be careful, Tayanita."

And then Tayanita was gone. MacKim saw her drop to the ground, roll into the ditch, pick up the clothing and food he had given her, scramble up the far side and run for the trees. Cattanach sounded a challenge; there was the roar of a musket, the flash from the muzzle and the swift return of darkness.

"What's that?" Corporal Gunn's voice echoed in the night.

"Nothing, Corporal," Cattanach said. "I thought I saw somebody."

Gunn swung a lantern over the parapet, sending yellow light

dancing on the hard-packed snow. "There's nobody there now. MacKim, did you see anybody?"

"No, Corporal," MacKim said.

"Sorry, Corporal," Cattanach said.

"No harm done, son. Better fire at nothing than have a hundred Indians in the fort. Reload and get off duty. You too, MacKim, your time's up."

Returning to his quarters, MacKim slid into his cot. He felt Chisholm's eyes on him as he pulled the blankets over his head. *What have I done? I've helped a prisoner escape. I am now liable for the triangle or even the rope. Was it worth it?*

Yes, it was worth it. That woman Tayanita was a victim of her enemies. We should never have locked her up.

"What was the musketry?" Chisholm asked.

"Cattanach thought he saw somebody."

"Did he see anybody?" Chisholm propped himself on one elbow.

"He might have." MacKim suddenly felt drained. All he wanted to do was sleep. He had joined the army to find his brother's killers and the last few months he had not advanced that cause the width of a fingernail.

"You're hiding something," Chisholm said. "Tell me tomorrow." Rolling on his side, he was asleep in seconds, leaving MacKim to wrestle with his thoughts.

If I do nothing else in my life, MacKim told himself, *I have helped one person in need. It's not much, for I'm undoubtedly destined for the fires of Hell for the life I lead. I have also failed in my duty and broken my word to King George.*

Sleep did not come easily as MacKim lay there in the stuffy room, with his breath freezing on the blankets and his companions snoring or shifting in fitful sleep.

Taking his much-crumpled sheet of paper from its hiding place in the waist of his kilt, MacKim read the names. *Bland. Hitchins. Osborne. Hayes.* He still had two men to find. He still had two men to kill. Tayanita had called him a good man. Good men did not spend years hunting down and murdering people. Good men did not find other men's wives attractive. Good men did not spend half their time in the fort waiting and hoping for even a glimpse of another man's wife.

Lying on his back, MacKim stared at the ceiling. Sometimes duty was hard. It controlled his life so he could not make decisions for himself. He wondered what it would be like, living in such a place as North America, where men and women decided their own fate, unless they were scalped, murdered or enslaved. He sighed. It did not matter what he thought; he was promise-bound to hunt his brother's killers, and until he had fulfilled his oath, he had no other future.

❧ III ❧

FIGHTING

❧ 14 ❧

LOUISBOURG, JUNE 1759

"Someday," Chisholm said as the drumming woke him up, "someday soon, I will take these drummers and beat them to death with their own drum sticks."

"I can think of something else to do with the drum-sticks," Cumming said. "I would stick them so far up their arses they would knock out their teeth."

"Rise up!" Dingwall's roar shook the tents. "The sun's burning your bloody eyes from their sockets! Come and do your duty, you lazy scoundrels!"

"Come, children," Chisholm said. "Papa wants us."

"Papa can bloody want," Cumming said, sighed and peered out from his thin blanket. "Can a man not get any peace in this world?"

The drummers paced relentlessly outside the tents, drum-sticks hammering on the drumskins. MacKim thrust his face outside the tent, about to shout at them until he realised the drummers were up first every morning and had some of the worst and most unpopular duties to perform, from carrying the wounded from the battlefield to wielding the cat-o'-nine-tails. In the bright morning, the sun shone from the red-painted upper and lower hoops across the light buff front of the drums. For a second, MacKim saw the King's cypher, crown and the LXXVIII of the regiment as the drummers beat out the 'General', waking the men from their slumber to face the rigours of another day.

It was five in the morning, with the long Canadian winter lingering in the bite of the wind and the snell-scent of the sea a reminder that they were back in Louisbourg.

"It's our morning, lads," Chisholm said. "We're sailing soon." For days, the Highlanders had spoken of nothing except the forthcoming expedition to expel the French from Quebec. "Admiral Saunders is taking nearly three hundred ships up the St Lawrence River. It is a feat that nobody has ever done before."

"The French regularly sail up the river," MacKim reminded him.

"Yes, one ship or a small flotilla at a time, and with pilots to guide them," Chisholm replied. "Saunders is sailing into the heart of French territory without a single pilot, and the Fraser Highlanders will be in the van."

Cumming spat with the wind. "Saunders isn't the first. We tried this before," he said, "back in 1711."

"What happened?" MacKim asked the expected question.

"The fleet was wrecked on the rocks and shoals," Cumming said. "Eight ships sunk, over eight hundred men drowned."

"How do you know that?" MacKim asked.

"I can't remember. Somebody must have told me."

"If this weather does not ease," Chisholm puffed on his stubby black pipe, "nobody will be going anywhere. The harbour is so full of ice that the boats can hardly row ashore."

"I've had enough of winter," Cumming said. "It's time for spring, surely." He sipped at the grog in his water bottle. "I heard that an officer in one of the English regiments shot himself today. I suppose he was saving the French the trouble."

"Or he was in dread of the Indians," Chisholm said.

"I've seen enough Indians to last me forever," MacKim said.

"We never did find out how that Indian squaw woman

escaped," Cumming said. "You were on sentinel that night, weren't you, MacKim?"

"I was," MacKim admitted. "Cattanach saw somebody outside the fort that might have been her."

"We should have hanged her," Cumming said.

"Parade!" Dingwall's voice sounded. "Come on, you unwashed rascals, you refuse of the prisons, you hell-bound scoundrels! Out you come!"

The fleet filled Louisbourg harbour, an impressive display of Great Britain's maritime strength, with the Union Jack flapping and cracking from hundreds of masts as busy seamen ushered the army on board. MacKim watched the bustle, filed into his boat and knew he was a tiny part of history.

"We have eight and a half thousand men," Chisholm said. "Montcalm has twelve thousand to defend Quebec, so they say, and many of them are locals who know the land far better than we do. We'll have a tougher fight than we had to capture Louisbourg."

"The Canadians and their Indians are savages," Cumming said. "We saw that at Fort Stanwix."

"You're not wrong, for once, Cumming," MacKim agreed. "They torture people, scalp them and take pleasure in burning folk slowly. For God's own sake, don't let them take you alive."

"Aye," Chisholm gestured towards the enormous mass of Canada that lay to the west, "God only knows what's out there."

MacKim nodded. "Jacob Wooler told me that we're not real soldiers until we've fought the Indians. He thinks that our European wars are just for show."

Cattanach grunted. "Well, maybe we've never fought the Indians before, but maybe they're saying the same thing about us. Maybe they're saying that they're not real warriors until they've met Fraser's Highlanders."

Chisholm laughed. "That's the spirit, Cattanach. We're Fraser's Highlanders and bugger the rest."

They filed on board the ship, ignoring the standard ribald

remarks from the sailors about their kilts and packing the upper deck as soon as they had stowed their kit.

"Which regiments are coming with us?" MacKim squeezed against the rail to watch the Navy ferry the army across the iced harbour.

As Chisholm reeled off the names and numbers, MacKim recognised a roll-call of heroism and honour.

"Amherst's 15th Foot, Bragg's 28th, Otway's 35th, Lascelle's and the other regulars as well as the Louisbourg Grenadiers, artillery and the Rangers."

"Webb's is not coming then?" MacKim fought his stab of disappointment.

"Hugh!" Chisholm stubbed tobacco into the bowl of his pipe. "Are you still looking for those two Grenadiers?"

"Yes, Hitchins and Osborne," MacKim said.

"Over there, then. Look." Chisholm pointed astern. A small flotilla of boats was nosing through the ice, each one packed with regulars standing shoulder to shoulder. "That's Webb's."

"Webb's? Are you sure?" MacKim did not hide his agitation as he stared at the men, searching for familiar faces.

"I'm sure," Chisholm said.

MacKim felt the cold anger return, sliding up his spine. He would concentrate on doing his duty, learning all he could and surviving to fight another day, yet he would search for an opportunity to fulfil his oath. *Then what?*

For a moment, the leading boat of the regiment was broadside on, allowing MacKim to see the soldiers. Each man wore the distinctive mitre hat of the Grenadiers, and each man seemed enormous, with broad shoulders and experience etched into every line of their faces. MacKim took a deep breath, wondering how he could ever deal with men such as these. He had been fortunate with Hayes; the man had been too drunk to know what was happening. Such luck would not come again.

I'll find a way, he told himself. *I have to find a way.*

Chisholm touched his shoulder. "You're not alone, Hugh."

Yes, I am. It's my oath and my duty. You can walk away, James. I can't.

❧

THEY SAILED IN CONVOY, THE CLUMSY TRANSPORTS IN THE centre with their enormous spread of sails and the busy naval ships snapping at the flanks, chivvying the laggards and sending signals back and forth. MacKim had nearly forgotten the sound of wind in the rigging and the creaking of wood, the hard patter of the seamen's calloused bare feet on deck and the crisp orders of the officers. Even as a passenger, he could appreciate the magnitude of this operation, with hundreds of vessels moving under the direction of a single brain as Rear-Admiral Charles Saunders manoeuvred the fleet from Louisbourg to the St. Lawrence.

The swell of the sea forced some of the soldiers to cram the rails in terrible seasickness that had petty officers screaming in anger.

"Keep it off my deck! By Christ, I'll see the backbone of any man who soils my deck with his spew!"

"I don't think they like us on their boat," MacKim said.

"I don't like us on their boat, either." Cumming ran to the rail.

Unaffected by seasickness, MacKim stared across the fleet, searching for the vessel on which Webb's Regiment sailed. *If Priscilla knew how long I spent thinking about murder, she would recoil from me in horror. Even Tayanita would not want to know me.*

On 8th June 1759, Fraser's Highlanders sighted the snow-streaked heights of Newfoundland, and the following day the fleet entered the Gulf of St Lawrence, to faint cheers from the soldiers. Three days later, as they sighted land in the Bay of Gaspe, a gale roared from the north.

"Get these sails furled!" Ship's officers screamed orders that sent seamen scurrying aloft to shorten sail as ferocious waves

161

hammered at the hulls, inducing fresh seasickness from the soldiers. When the storm abated, the fleet continued, keeping within sight of the southern shore.

"That storm was only a foretaste of what's to come," Cumming said. "The St. Lawrence is said to be the most dangerous river in the world."

"We're with the best seamen in the world," Chisholm said. "Stop your moaning, Cumming. If the Frenchies can do it, our Navy boys can do it with both hands tied behind their back."

"The French will lure us onto rocks for sure," Cumming said.

"Saunders isn't stupid," Corporal Gunn said. "Stop moaning, Cumming."

"We're deep in French territory." Chisholm's face twisted into a smile. "Where are the French? Should they not be out to get us, Cumming?" His smile expanded to a laugh. "Look at the Navy. Do you think that any Frenchman living would dare attack us?"

"It's not the French we have to worry about," Corporal Gunn said seriously. "It's the river itself. Nobody has ever taken a fleet up here." He motioned to the fires that flared along the banks of the river. "They're watch-fires, warning the French upriver that we're coming. They'll know exactly where we are."

"There are more than fires." MacKim pointed to the small groups of armed militia and settlers that stared at the British fleet. Some men aimed muskets, and one militiaman fired his rifle, with the ball falling far short. "Even if the French navy won't face us, the locals don't like us much."

"Ignore them," Chisholm advised. "Look aloft! What the devil is Admiral Saunders up to?"

Every ship in the fleet had hoisted a French flag, with officers waving triumphantly to the watchful men on the riverbank. The militia lowered their weapons, while some of them lifting their hands in acknowledgement.

"The Canadians think we're French!" MacKim said. "They're coming out to see us." There was movement on the shore as a small fleet of open canoes paddled out towards the British, with men who had been hostile now waving in welcome at these supposed friends.

"Wave!" A narrow-faced naval lieutenant ordered. "Look as if you're pleased to see the scoundrels! You lobsters! Get off the damned deck! Don't let these French rascals see British redcoats!"

Just as the seamen hustled the 78th below decks, one smiling Canadian boarded the ship. He looked around, saw the last of the kilted Highlanders, stared in astonishment at his mistake and turned to flee.

"Grab that man!'" the thin-faced lieutenant ordered. A burly petty officer ran across the deck and wrapped powerful arms around the Canadian.

"You're with us now, François!"

Another seaman clapped a firm hand over the Canadian's mouth to prevent him from shouting out. Up aloft, the French ensign fluttered down, with the Union Jack raised in its place.

"That was artful," Chisholm approved. "The Navy knows all the dodges."

"I don't understand." Cattanach looked puzzled.

"Saunders will use these Canadians as pilots," Chisholm said. "A neat little trick, perhaps unethical but one that may save hundreds of lives and help remove France from North America."

The captured Canadian was not happy. Speaking in French with a strong colonial accent, he began to shout as soon as his captors gave him room. "Oh, some of you will return to Britain," he warned, "but you'll have a dismal tale to tell. Canada will be the grave of your whole army, and we'll decorate the walls of Quebec with British scalps."

"What's he saying?" Cumming asked and MacKim gave a rough translation.

"Throw the bastard overboard." Cumming fingered his hair nervously.

"We need him," Chisholm said. "Besides, it's only words. The more they rant and rave, the more we know that they are afraid of us."

"I don't know about them being afraid of us," Cattanach voiced the apprehension that many of the soldiers felt, "I am afraid of them. I don't want to be captured and scalped by the savages."

MacKim kept silent although he agreed with Cattanach. The Indians had already proved themselves redoubtable enemies. The deeper the British moved into their territory, the more dangerous they would be. He noticed more than one of the Highlanders touch his hair fearfully.

"Aye, every hour takes us further from civilisation, boys," Corporal Gunn said.

"May God help us all." Somebody began to sing a psalm. Others joined in, so the ancient words surrounded the ship as they glided into the land of the enemy.

When Admiral Saunders placed his reluctant pilots on board the leading warships, the fleet continued, with the weather-battered sails and Union flags a bold provocation to the French and Canadians.

MacKim nodded. "We ambushed them," he said. "We can't complain about the French tactics when we do the same to them."

Over the next few days, MacKim sensed the nervousness of the seamen as they sailed deeper into Canada along a river that dwarfed any he had seen before.

"This is a huge country."

"We're still only knocking at the gates," Chisholm said.

"It feels as if it's swallowing us up." MacKim indicated the land that seemed to go on forever. "We're lost in this immensity."

Chisholm puffed on his pipe. "Aye. Scotland looks small now, doesn't it? And our wee affairs look petty out here."

On the 18th June, the fleet anchored off the Isle of Bic, with the thin-faced lieutenant warning the men to beware of lurking

French and Indians, "and make sure these pilots don't try to swim ashore. We need them for the next stage when the river gets hazardous."

"Indians!" Cumming yelled, pointing to a sudden splashing close to the ship. On his word, the thin-faced lieutenant ran to the side.

"Those are seals, you blasted lubber!" Without hesitation, he clipped Cumming across the head. "I ought to have you triced up and flogged, damn you." Still glowering, the lieutenant stalked away.

"These are seals," Cattanach repeated, solemn-faced as Cumming rubbed his head. "Be more careful next time, Cumming, you blasted lubber."

The resulting laughter was as much nervous as genuine.

"The lads aren't happy," Chisholm said as the fleet anchored at the Île Verte. "We're better at fighting than waiting to fight."

"Why are we stopping now?" Cattanach asked. "The slower we move, the more time the French have to strengthen their defences. Don't Pikestaff and Saunders realise that?"

"The tides are strong here." A tobacco-chewing seaman coiled a line with effortless skill. "Trust old Saunders. He knows what he's doing."

"As I said before, the Royal Navy is the best in the world," Chisholm said. "They'll get us to Quebec, and then the real trouble will start. Rest all you can, Hugh, this campaign will be a lot harder than the last. The French will defend Quebec to the death."

"Let them come!" Cumming was suddenly defiant. "We'll meet them!" He was quieter on Saturday 23rd June at the Île aux Coudres, where Indians fired at a British landing party. The 78th lined the rail, listening to the distant popping of musketry and trying to visualise what was happening.

"Here we go," Chisholm said, "that's the first shot. There will be many more before this campaign is done."

Corporal Gunn sucked on an empty pipe. "I think you're

right, Chisholm. Harriette was not long after telling me that she dreamed of a river of empty coffins sailing upstream, and when they returned, they were all full."

When the Highlanders heard Harriette's dream, the Roman Catholics among them crossed themselves, and the others looked solemn, for all the soldiers knew that Harriette Mackenzie possessed second sight. MacKim raised his eyebrows to Chisholm, saying nothing. He knew that before this campaign was over, there would be at least two deaths, for he may never have another opportunity to kill Hitchins and Osborne.

🌿 15 🌿

CANADA, SUMMER 1759

"I heard that Pikestaff is putting the Grenadier companies together when we land." Chisholm was usually first with the gossip. "He wants a striking force of the best men to use as a hammer for Quebec."

MacKim nodded. "So the Grenadiers of the 78th will be fighting beside Webb's?"

"That's right." Chisholm was cleaning his uniform. "I thought you might be interested. If you get friendly with one of our Grenadiers, you might hear where he's going. Then you'll be able to track Webb's if you're still intending fulfilling your damn fool oath."

Until I kill these two murderers, my life is not my own. "I will not break my word." MacKim stood up and pushed through the crowded deck toward Dingwall.

"Sergeant Dingwall," he asked, "what are the chances of me transferring to the Grenadiers?"

Dingwall scanned MacKim from the top of his head to his boots. "You want to join the Grannies, do you? How tall are you, MacKim?"

"Five foot seven, Sergeant." MacKim pulled himself erect to try and add inches to his height.

"Come back when you're three inches taller and five years older and you might have a chance," Dingwall said. "The Grenadiers are the tallest and oldest men in the regiment, not the smallest. You stick with the Light Bobs, boy, where you belong."

"You're a fool, Hugh," Chisholm told him amicably, passing over his water bottle. "You'd not like the Grenadiers at all. They're big men with big mouths. Here, try this grog. Harriette is friendly with one of the sailors."

I'll have to find another way.

۞

IN THE EVENING OF THE 27TH JUNE, AFTER A HISTORIC AND nearly incident-free passage up the St Lawrence, the fleet arrived at the Île D'Orléans, only a few miles downstream of Quebec. Île D'Orléans was a long island that effectively split the St Lawrence in two, with several small Canadian settlements among the trees. Almost at once, as MacKim and the 78th checked their muskets, General Wolfe sent a few boatloads of Rangers ashore to take and hold a landing place.

"Good lads, the Rangers," Chisholm approved. "And with a mind of their own."

"Brave, too, with so few of them landing in the dim when there could be Canadians and Indians around." MacKim thought of the debacle at Fort Stanwix. "I wonder if Wooler is among them." He ran a hand up the barrel of his musket, fighting his increasing nervousness.

"The French could attack at any time!" Captain Cameron's voice rang around the transports. "Light Company, into the first boats, disembark and find a defensive position! The other companies will follow."

Once again, MacKim followed the rest into the small boats, where they stood shoulder to shoulder as nonchalant seamen rowed them ashore. The Île D'Orléans reminded him of the

Black Isle north of Inverness, a place of low ridges, mixed forests and farmland, where threads of mist drifted through the tree-tops.

"I wonder how many French are watching us now."

"It's not the French I'm concerned about," Chisholm said. 'They're decent enough fellows once the actual fighting is over. It's the Canadians and Indians. We didn't meet many at Louisbourg, while at Fort Stanwix, the Indians were not defending their territory. I wager they'll be fiends incarnate out here."

To MacKim, the island looked more forbidding than the forest around Fort Stanwix. The thought of lurking Canadians and Indians increased his apprehension as he came ashore.

"I heard that Quebec was to be easy after Louisbourg," Cattanach said. "I heard that the Frenchies depend on the river to defend them, rather than fortifications."

"I hope you're right," Chisholm said.

"So do I." Gunn tested the ground with his boots. "I can't forget my wife's dreams, though."

"Lights! Advance three hundred paces and form a defensive perimeter!" Captain Cameron strode in front, clearing the shrubs with swings of his broadsword. MacKim was on his heels, for once not caring about the noise he made. Any Indian or Canadian would have to be deaf and blind not to notice the presence of the British fleet, with commands ringing out from officers and sergeants.

"The wind's getting up," Cumming said, as they crested a ridge and took positions behind trees and rocks. "I think we're in for the devil of a blow."

Cumming was correct. The wind rose from the east, hammering at the ships anchored in the river. From his position on the ridge, MacKim watched as the storm blasted ship after ship towards the shore, capsizing some of the smaller vessels and damaging others. He flinched as a transport lost her topmast, which descended in a flurry of cables and spars.

"The Frenchies were right; the river and the weather fight for them." MacKim said. "If they had a gun battery on this island, they could cause havoc while our ships are struggling."

"We'll never take Quebec," Cumming said.

"You three are on piquet duty tonight." Sergeant Dingwall stood four-square on the ridge, seemingly impervious to wind and rain. "You're probably the best we have, God help us." He glowered at them for a moment. "Don't go wandering off alone, for any reason."

"He cares, bless him," Chisholm said, when the sergeant marched away.

"No, he doesn't," Cumming said. "He's only concerned that the savages don't get past us to lift his scalp."

❦

Standing in front of the regimental position, MacKim shivered. He loosened the bayonet in his scabbard. *Whatever happens, they won't take me alive. I'll stab myself to death rather than be tortured like Ewan was.*

Cumming was first to see the distant glow up-river. "The Frenchies are up to something."

"Where?" MacKim searched the night-dark interior of the island.

"On the water," Cumming said. "Fireships. They're sending fireships into our fleet!"

The glow increased as ship after French ship set themselves alight, with over a hundred radeaux – small fire-rafts – adding to the scene. MacKim heard men shouting in the British camp, with some voices raised high. A group of soldiers ran from their outpost towards the Highlanders, until Lieutenant Douglas roared at them to take hold of themselves. Other soldiers backed away as the fiery fleet floated downriver.

"What do we do?" MacKim stared upriver.

"We stand tight, boy, we stand tight." Checking the piquets,

Dingwall planted his huge legs apart. "We're the 78th, not some regiment of ploughboys!"

"We'll be trapped here!" Cumming stared at the approaching inferno.

Chisholm nodded. "It's certainly spectacular,' he said, 'but they've set the ships on fire too early."

MacKim watched, appalled, as the blazing French vessels bore down on the British fleet anchored in the Basin, the semi-circular stretch of water between the Île D'Orléans and Quebec. After the recent storm, the British ships were vulnerable, with many sporting damaged rigging and others ashore or stranded in shoal water.

"Look!" Chisholm pointed downward as there was some movement among the British ships. "First, the French chess-master moved his flaming bishops, and now Admiral Saunders has countered with his pawns."

With the flames reflected on the dark waters and the sound of exploding gunpowder acting as a backdrop, Saunders had sent out dozens of small boats, each one manned by a handful of sailors. Ignoring the leaping orange flames and choking smoke, the British seamen closed with the fireships, threw grappling hooks or attached boat hooks, and steered the blazing vessels to the shore.

"Brave men," Chisholm said. "If these things exploded, the seamen would be blown to nothing."

MacKim watched in fascination as the grounded fireships burned themselves out in spectacular, if impotent fury. The flames reflected on the plume of blue smoke that ascended to the dark sky, then slowly died away.

"Pawns beat bishop that time and the second round to Admiral Saunders," Chisholm said. "Wasn't it kind of old Sergeant Dingwall to give us such a splendid view of all the fun?" He thrust the end of his pipe into his mouth. "That's another tale to tell your grandchildren, MacKim. Haven't I always said that British seamen are the best in the world?"

"Kind old Sergeant Dingwall is watching you, Chisholm! Smoking on duty! And you too, MacKim and Cumming! Your duty is to make sure no Indians skulk up on us, not watch the show the French put on for your entertainment."

"Yes, Sergeant," MacKim said. The interior of the island appeared dark and uninteresting after the spectacle on the river, but the danger was just as real.

☙❧

"THE FRENCHIES ARE NOT HAPPY," CHISHOLM SAID. "LISTEN to the church bells."

"I can't hear any church bells." Cumming took off his bonnet to hear better.

"Nor can I," Chisholm said. "The French have been ringing the damned things like crazed men ever since we arrived here, and now they've gone silent. I'll wager they are keeping them as a signal when we attack the town."

MacKim grunted. He had taken to smoking a pipe, favouring a long-stemmed version with a small bowl. Now, he used the stem to point to the north bank of the river, where Quebec loomed defiantly above the water, like a mediaeval castle in this vast, brooding land. "I don't fancy crossing the St Lawrence under fire. It was bad enough at Louisbourg."

"Pikestaff will think of a way," Chisholm said. "We'll follow our Pikestaff through the gates of Hell and beard Auld Hornie in his den."

Cumming kicked at the stump of a tree. This southern shore of the river was heavily wooded, with the notorious St Lawrence current sweeping the coves and beaches. "We're all going to die here. I can feel it in my bones. Last night, I dreamed of a thousand coffins floating down the river with a piper playing a lament."

"Did the coffins all float away?" MacKim asked.

"They floated downstream, heading back to Scotland."

"That's them gone, then," MacKim said, "and we're still here so they can't have been our coffins."

"Was that not Harriette's vision?" Chisholm asked. "Did you borrow it?"

"Hers was different," Cumming said, sulkily.

Chisholm slapped Cumming on the shoulder. "Be of good heart, Cumming, we're the 78th and Pikestaff Wolfe is leading us. We beat the Frenchies at Louisbourg, and we'll beat them here, too, coffins or no coffins!"

"They beat us at Ticonderoga, though," Cumming reminded them, "and at the Monongahela River, aye and Fontenoy, as you well know, Ugly!"

"They did that." MacKim refused to allow Cumming to get him down. "So all the more reason for us to defeat them here."

"What was that, MacKim?" Sergeant Dingwall had appeared in time to hear MacKim's final few words.

"I said that we would defeat the French at Quebec to make up for our reverses at Ticonderoga and Monongahela, Sergeant."

"Monsieur Montcalm may have something to say about that," Dingwall said. "Now get yourselves ready, lads. I heard a whisper that General Wolfe has plans up his sleeve, so that means we'll be busy."

In the afternoon of 29th June, MacKim filed aboard another boat to cross the St Lawrence.

"Where are we off to this time? I'll be growing fins and gills if I'm on the water much more."

"We're off to capture Point Levis on the south shore of the river," Captain Cameron explained cheerfully. "We'll land near Beaumont and dispose of any French that stand in our path." He gave a small smile. "As a great man once said, 'Trust in God and keep your powder dry'."

"Who said that?" Cumming asked.

"Oliver Cromwell," Chisholm said. "If he were out here, he would have added not to go wandering alone in the woods."

Captain Cameron's frown stopped all other conversation in

the boat. "We have to take this position on Point Levis," Cameron said. "If the French retain it, they can build a battery that could prevent our ships from coming further upriver." He ran his gaze over the men. "I am relying on you to do your duty and enhance the good name of Fraser's Highlanders."

With Cameron sitting at attention in the stern, the seamen pushed into the current. A flight of birds whirred close overhead, with the sound so similar to a passing roundshot that MacKim instinctively ducked. When he straightened up, a little shame-faced, he realised that only Dingwall, Chisholm and Captain Cameron had not flinched.

"Every bullet has its billet, Hugh," Chisholm sounded calm. "If it's for you, it won't go past you, whether you duck or not."

MacKim gave a small smile. *I still have a lot to learn.*

"If Montcalm knew his business, he would already have artillery on Point Levis," Dingwall said. "These French are not as good as they think they are."

"Let's hope you're right, Sergeant." Gunn checked the flint of his musket for at least the fourth time. "Please the Lord that you are right."

As well as Fraser's Highlanders, Wolfe sent Amherst's Regiment and a couple of companies of Rangers. The Rangers looked tanned, intense, self-reliant and above all, nonchalant, as if doing battle with an unknown number of the enemy was all in a day's work to them. MacKim saw Wooler amongst them, with a feather in his hat and a pipe in his mouth.

I see you, Wooler. I am honour bound to protect you, which is a distraction I don't need. I want your wife, Jacob.

The British force rowed across the south channel of the St Lawrence, from St Laurent on the Île D'Orléans to the picturesque little settlement of Beaumont, nearly directly opposite.

"Ready your muskets," Captain Cameron ordered, "and as soon as we touch land, run ashore, keeping formation!" He gave his characteristically cheerful smile. "We're the best, lads, let's prove that to the world!"

Musket ready, MacKim vaulted from the boat onto a quiet shore. He looked around. "Where are they? Don't they want to defend their land?"

"Don't complain," Chisholm said, "just savour being alive."

That night, they camped without tents, each man crowding as close as he could to smoky fires built of damp wood. Behind them, they could hear the flow of the St Lawrence, a reminder that only the Navy allowed them space to manoeuvre or withdraw.

"Double piquets," Captain Cameron ordered. "Don't stray from each other and if you see an Indian or a Canadian, fire at once."

"Fire at once, he says. Don't you worry, Captain, sir," Cattanach said. "If I as much as smell the sweat of an Indian, I'll fire."

"'You'll get used to them." Wooler had attached himself to the 78th once more. "They're just a part of life out here." He gave his easy grin. "No death and glory actions in this world, boys, it's fight to survive, not to fly the flag, however pretty."

They were up before dawn, preparing for the march as Captain Cameron gave crisp orders. "Light Infantry, you and the Rangers go in front in open formation. The rest, form columns and march for Point Levis."

Chisholm winked at MacKim. "This is the real thing, Hugh. Our wee patrols at Fort Stanwix were piss water compared to this."

"If the Indians take me, James," MacKim said, "shoot me, will you?"

"Aye, and you do the same for me, Hugh, if they take me." They shook hands, stamped their nailed shoes, checked their flints were sharp and the powder in the pans was dry and looked ahead.

Leaving the security of the river with the reassuring presence of the Royal Navy, they advanced into the forest. Operating with the Rangers, while the central column of redcoats trudged behind, MacKim and Chisholm moved from tree to tree, trying to be as quiet as possible as they scanned the undergrowth for any sight of the enemy.

The first mile was uneventful, with only a startled deer to break the rhythm of the advance. MacKim relaxed a little, telling himself that things were not as bad as he had anticipated. *I'm a veteran now. I've fought at Louisbourg and around Fort Stanwix. There's nothing new here, nothing I haven't seen before.*

The brief muzzle flare and spurt of smoke brought him back to reality. MacKim ducked behind the trunk of a tree and quickly aimed where the smoke had been. He did not see any sign of the enemy, only a slight shiver of the undergrowth. Powder smoke drifted through the leaves.

"Mohawk, I think," the Ranger beside MacKim said laconically. "There will be more."

They moved on, with more shots from the trees, more invisible enemy and the occasional grunt or yell as a man was hit. MacKim felt his apprehension rise with every step. He heard the intermittent spatter of muskets, saw the Rangers fire and move, yet he did not see any of the enemy. *Show yourselves, you painted devils! Fight like men, rather than skulking like cowards!*

Only when they reached a small clearing did MacKim catch sight of an Indian. Frustrated at his inability to help in the stubborn, tree-by-tree advance, he had stepped slightly forward of the Rangers and pushed into the trees. He knew he was putting himself in terrible danger, but was determined to be the best soldier he could.

My oath can wait. I have colleagues here who depend on me as much as Ewan ever did.

The man stood behind a tree, so focussed on watching for the advancing redcoats in front that he neglected to look to his flank. He was tall, taller than MacKim by half a head, naked except for a loin-cloth, and painted in red and black. As the

Indian levelled his long French musket, MacKim aimed, and squeezed the trigger. Although the Brown Bess was notoriously inaccurate, MacKim's shot took the Indian square in the chest. The man spun, stared down at himself in disbelief and crumpled to the ground.

"Good shot," Wooler said, as MacKim hastily reloaded. "We'll make a Ranger of you yet. Not many redcoats could outshoot a Mohawk."

Feeling happier now he had done something to justify himself, MacKim stepped to the Mohawk he had killed, noticed there were two human scalps at the man's belt and moved on. MacKim did not feel the same repugnance for scalp-gathering as some other regulars did; after witnessing the butchery after Culloden, he knew that British soldiers were every bit as capable of atrocities as any native of North America.

"Halt!" The call came from Brigadier Monckton, in charge of the entire force, with officers and NCOs passing the order down the column. Men peered warily into the surrounding forest, hoping not to see the enemy; hoping that the screen of Rangers and Light Infantry was sufficient protection.

"What's happening?" Cumming asked.

"It looks like a council of war," Lieutenant Fletcher of the Rangers replied. MacKim always found Ranger officers willing to pass information onto the men. "The Brigadier has called the senior officers to him to debate what to do." He gave a slow smile. "While they jaw, boys, we'll watch for the enemy."

"What do we do if we see anything, sir?" Cattanach asked.

"Why, Cattanach, you shoot it, and kill it dead."

Sheltering behind a tree, MacKim watched his front, aware of every rustle and the dart of unfamiliar birds. The longer they delayed, the more chance there was for the French to reinforce the Indians and Canadians. Sighting on a slight movement in the trees, he squeezed the trigger and immediately began to reload. He did not know if he had hit his mark or if it had been an Indian or some small animal. He heard sporadic firing around the perimeter as the Light Infantry and Rangers held off the enemy until Monckton eventually came to a decision and the advance continued. Behind MacKim, the cumbersome column crunched on.

Looking over his shoulder, MacKim could see Quebec, little over a mile away through the trees and across the St Lawrence.

"Somebody told you lies," MacKim said to Chisholm, as he peered across the Basin at the city they had come to capture. "The French don't just rely on the river and the weather to defend Quebec. Look at it!"

The shore beneath Quebec was thick with defences, with the ugly snouts of cannon protruding from earth-and-timber redoubts linked by lines of neat entrenchments.

"Crossing in little boats in the face of that much firepower will be suicide," Chisholm said soberly. "But so is gawping across the river when we're in the presence of the enemy." He pointed to the left flank. "There are the Indians." A group of bare-chested men flitted between the trees, well out of musket range.

Even from a distance, the Indians looked capable opponents, brawny men who held their weapons with the ease of long famil-iarity and who walked with long, gliding strides. No sooner had he raised his musket than they vanished, leaving only a single swaying branch to mark their passage.

"They're withdrawing," Wooler reported. "Don't rush forward, boys, it could be a trick."

Sullen, still fighting, the Canadians and tribesmen backed off as the British column reached their destination, with the Rangers and Lights spreading out to act as a protective screen. Even with his inexperienced eyes, MacKim could see the strategic position of Point Levis, a spit of land thrusting into the St Lawrence, with rising ground overlooking Quebec. "A battery here could make major mischief among the French."

"We have to hold it," an older Light Infantryman of Amherst's Foot said. "But that might not be easy. All Montcalm has to do is reinforce the Canadians, and they could harass us to death." He glowered at MacKim. "I'd have thought you Sawnies were on the French side. Did you not all fight against us in the late rebellion?"

"Some did," MacKim answered cautiously. "I was only a boy when the Jacobites rose."

"Bloody traitors." The Amherst Light spat on the ground. "Stabbing us in the back when we was already at war with the Frenchies."

Resisting his impulse to plunge a bayonet into the man's chest, MacKim forced what he hoped was a friendly smile. "I'm Hugh MacKim," he said.

"Are you now?" The man produced a plug of tobacco, bit off a chunk and put the remainder inside his tunic. "I don't give a tinker's damn."

"Do you have a name?" MacKim swallowed his pride.

The man seemed to consider for a long time before he replied. "Chaplin." He looked across at the French positions of Quebec. "I fought you bastards at Culloden."

MacKim controlled his surge of anger. "I didn't know Amherst's Foot was there."

"I was with another regiment." Chaplin's eyes were vicious as he faced MacKim. "We transferred."

"*We?*"

"Me and some others."

MacKim felt his heartbeat increase. He had already dealt with Hayes, while Bland was dead. Would he be fortunate enough to meet Osborne and Hitchins as well? Perhaps they had also transferred. His attempts at being civil stalled. "I suppose that soldiering is an honourable profession, despite the occasional murder of wounded men and civilians, like at Culloden."

Chaplin swore, a procession of foul language that MacKim found amusing. "Honourable profession? Who told you that? You skirt-wearing bastards believe anything, don't you? I joined the army because I was bloody starving. I was begging in the streets."

MacKim had already realised that the men of Lowland and English regiments were from a different stamp to the Highlanders.

Chaplin continued to talk, even as they took up positions in front of the main force. "Take Croker now. A recruiting sergeant dropped the King's Shilling in his tankard when he was drunk to the world. Or old Smithy; he was hauled before the beak for stealing and ordered to join the army or be transported. That bastard Hitchins was on the run from the law."

The name was burned into MacKim's mind. "Hitchins?"

"Aye, Hitchins." Chaplin spat brown tobacco juice onto the ground between MacKim's feet. "What's he to you?"

"I met a man of that name once," MacKim said. "I owe him something."

Chaplin chewed his tobacco. "You can keep it. The bugger deserted. He came to us from Webb's for some reason I don't understand, but hardly lasted a week before he slipped over the side of the ship and swam to the French. He was a thieving bastard anyway, a roaring, ranting, plundering Grenadier."

MacKim grunted as if somebody had punched him in the stomach. *I'll never see Hitchins now if he's deserted to the French.* "Oh, well," he said. "That's five shillings that I can keep."

"That's five shillings more than Hitchins is worth," Chaplin said. "The bastard joined the army as a thief and left with Smithy's grog. Hark! The French are firing at something."

MacKim readied his musket as artillery in Quebec opened fire.

"They're firing at shadows.' Chisholm was standing close by, listening. "They must think we're attacking them." He grinned. "The French are as nervous of us as we are of the Indians."

Cursing his luck that Hitchins had deserted, MacKim was restless that night. How could he pursue Hitchins if the man was with the French? Would he have to desert as well? MacKim groaned. *No. Leave Hitchins. Concentrate on Osborne; take one at a time.*

When he did eventually sleep, MacKim's dreams were interrupted by visions of that single Mohawk warrior he had killed. The image of the man lingered at the back of his mind, lying with his eyes wide open and the musket-wound oozing blood. MacKim struggled awake when Monckton ordered "stand to your arms," and the British scrambled to their defensive positions along the river bank.

Two deep and with hands gripping their muskets, they peered across the sun-dappled river, waiting for the French to launch a counter-attack. "It will be a change for us to be defending," Chisholm said. "See if they like a British volley as they row across the river."

"Here they come now." MacKim took a deep breath. Fighting like this, standing shoulder to shoulder with comrades he trusted, was far different to the secret war of the forests. Both needed a different kind of courage. MacKim licked his lips, savouring the breeze as French ships approached. His hands involuntarily tightened on his musket, imagining the coming battle. *Perhaps Hitchins was among the French?* That thought was engaging; he might have the opportunity to kill him legally. He heard roars from somewhere to his left, where Amherst's Grenadiers were challenging the enemy.

"Come on, you bastards! We're the death-dealing dogs of Amherst's Foot. Come over and die, Frenchmen!"

"Big-mouthed buggers." Cattanach spoke without rancour.

When the sharp order of an officer silenced the Grenadiers, the sound of the rushing river dominated everything again, together with the creaking of the French vessels.

"Where's the Navy when you need it?" Cumming breathed. "When can we fire?"

"You can fire when they're in range, Cumming! Until then, face your front and keep your mouth shut!" Corporal Gunn said.

The French vessels came closer, large, curious-looking craft with a single mast.

"They're gun vessels, wooden rafts with a cannon on top.

There are no infantry on them." Chisholm glanced behind him. "We're living targets here. The brigadier would be better to have us shelter behind these rocks." He indicated a ridge that ran parallel to the shore.

Brigadier Monckton did not agree. He maintained the line of scarlet along the river bank as the French vessels opened fire. MacKim saw one twenty-four-pound ball crash into a file of Fraser's, crushing two men into a bloody pulp. When another felled a sergeant and eight men of Amherst's Regiment, MacKim wondered if Chaplin was among the casualties. It was hard to stand there, trying not to duck or even wince, knowing that any shot could kill him, or turn him into a screaming wreck.

"Can we fire back?" MacKim asked out of the corner of his mouth.

"We're out of range. We just stand here and take it," Chisholm said. "We're the King's pawns, Hugh."

As the gunboats continued to fire, more British soldiers fell without having the chance to retaliate. Only when the Royal Navy ventured out, did the French gunboats withdraw, leaving fourteen British soldiers dead and many others injured.

"What a bloody waste of lives," MacKim said. Now he knew how the Jacobites had felt at Culloden. It was not comfortable.

"At least the Frenchies didn't fire canister," Chisholm said. "They could have wiped us out with canister."

"That's a small consolation," MacKim said.

I might have found Hitchins when he was with our army. I have no chance of finding him if he has deserted to the French. He could be inside Quebec, or some other French fortress, or he might be shipped back to France itself. I don't know. Damn and blast it to hell!

❧

AFTER THE ROYAL NAVY DROVE THE FRENCH GUNBOATS across the river, work began in earnest at Point Levis. Wolfe chivvied the brigadier, who badgered the regimental officers, who gave crisp orders to the sergeants, who in turn snarled at the men who did the actual work. MacKim found himself digging trenches and breastworks for the artillery that would soon pound at the walls of Quebec.

"Here we go again, Louisbourg all over again." Cattanach rested on his spade. "If I wanted to dig holes in the ground," he said, "I'd have joined Caulfeild's road builders and never left Scotland."

"You're talking, not digging, Cattanach! Get back to work. The brigadier wants redoubts in all the open places," Sergeant Dingwall spoke in his accustomed roar, "and *abattis* in those places where there are trees." He walked past them. "For those of you who are totally ignorant rather than merely bloody stupid, a redoubt is a small stronghold enclosed by earth."

"Why earth?" Cumming asked.

"Christ's blood, Cumming! I've taught you buggers all I know, and you still know nothing, and not much of that! Earth stops musket balls better than stone does," Dingwall said. "An abattis, as some of you remember from Louisbourg, is a barrier made from chopped-down trees with the ends sharpened into points."

"I hope they stop the Indians," Cumming said. "I don't like these fellows at all."

"That's all right, Cumming," Dingwall said. "They probably don't like you, either. Get to work, you idle bastard!"

When MacKim was not on piquet duty, felling trees, or swearing and hacking at the hard soil, he was hauling at the drag ropes of the heavy artillery that would batter at the walls of Quebec. All the time the British soldiers laboured, the French watched through telescopes.

"They must know us by name by now," Chisholm said, "the length of time they spend gazing at us."

"Is that tobacco?" Cumming picked up some of the leaves that Chisholm had used to stuff his pipe with.

"It could be, for all I know," Chisholm told him. "I smoke anything handy."

"You're not all there, Ugly," Cumming said. "That scar's damaged your brain."

"I'll damage your bloody brain, Cumming, if you don't get back to work! Come on, lads," Gunn led by example, "keep working! The sooner we get these guns in position, the sooner we can break the Frenchies' blasted telescopes."

Cumming swore. 'I'll give the French something to gaze at!" Turning his back on the river, he lifted his kilt and bent over. "There, you nosy French bastards! That's what I think of you and your spyglasses."

"You've probably brightened their day," MacKim said. "They'll be swarming over to see what else you've got to offer them."

"You've annoyed them, Cumming," Gunn said, as a cannon boomed from the French side of the river.

"Aye, that's what the monsoors thought of your arse, Cumming!" Chisholm exhaled foul smoke. "For what we are about to receive, may the Lord make us truly thankful."

The French ball crashed into the trees a good hundred yards from where they worked.

"Missed!" Cumming jeered.

"Get back to work," a saturnine marine sergeant shouted. "Hiding away from one French cannon. By the living Christ, I've seen virgin nuns with more manhood than the lot of you ladies combined!"

That first French shot was the precursor of others as the Quebec defenders sought to slow the work at Levis. Sometimes half a dozen French cannon fired together, at other times there was only a single, carefully aimed shot that screamed towards the British, occasionally killing or maiming an unlucky man.

"Never mind, lads," Chisholm said. 'Every time the French fire a shot, they deplete their magazine, and our Navy boys make sure they can't get any more. Even as targets, we're helping to win the war."

MacKim grunted, thinking of Hitchins over there in Quebec.

"Come on, boys! Get working! As soon as we get this battery finished, the sooner we can get over there and sort them out."

"You bloodthirsty little varmint," Chisholm said. "Did you not get enough at Louisbourg?"

MacKim looked away. He could feel Sergeant Dingwall's gaze on him.

"Are you still looking for promotion, son?" Dingwall crouched at MacKim's side. "I've got you earmarked for the corporal's white lace cord, MacKim, as long as you keep active. You keep fighting and sober, and I won't forget you, boy!"

"I'm not seeking promotion, Sergeant," MacKim said. "I just want this campaign finished."

"Don't you like Canada?" Dingwall expressed astonishment, yet his eyes were shrewd as they surveyed MacKim. "I've worked with men all my life, MacKim. I know when they're hiding something. What are you hiding, MacKim? What's behind all your eagerness and don't tell me it's a desire to defeat the French."

"I just want this campaign over, Sergeant," MacKim repeated.

"Do you now? Or do you like the killing part? Are you one of these men who like to kill?" Dingwall's gaze did not leave MacKim's face.

"No, Sergeant." MacKim shook his head.

"I'm watching you, MacKim." Dingwall stood up. "Don't forget that, lad. I'm watching you for good and ill." His smile was as sincere as a hunting cat. "Corporal MacKim. Do you think that rank suits you? Well, you're only a private. In future, Private MacKim, I'll tell the lads what to do. That's my duty. Your duty is to obey orders."

When Dingwall walked away, MacKim knew he had made a mistake. *Dingwall is after me now, and I'm not sure why.*

185

"There are two ways to attack Quebec." Chisholm addressed them as they sat around the campfire, with the flames combating their fear of Indians and showing up the stained white canvas of their ranked tents. "We could either land upstream or downstream of the town."

MacKim nodded; even he with his limited military experience could understand that a direct assault against the strong French positions would result in horrendous casualties.

"Downstream seems the easy option," Chisholm said. "We know we can't climb the cliffs of the Heights of Abraham. We thought we could land on the north shore of the St Lawrence at Beauport or nearby, cross the St Charles River and put the town under siege."

"What do you mean, *thought?*" Cumming asked. "That's the best option."

"I am sure that's what Pikestaff believed," Chisholm said. "That's why he sent the Navy there. They discovered a nasty sandbank at Beaumont. The warships won't get close."

"We don't need the warships," Cumming said. "We always land in rowing boats or barges."

"If you remember Louisbourg," Chisholm said, "the Navy provides artillery support. Without their guns, we would be landing unprotected under French artillery and musketry."

Cumming thought for a few moments. "It would be a massacre."

"I agree." Chisholm patted Cumming on the shoulder. "So that leaves the north shore above the town. Our Rangers patrols say there are no French artillery or outposts, probably because the Frenchies think our boats can't get that far."

"Why not?" Cumming was immediately truculent. "Are there more sandbanks?"

"Possibly," Chisholm said, "but that's not the main problem. To get above Quebec, our ships have to push through the narrows of the river, which the French have protected with batteries of artillery and more of these evil little gunboats."

"The Navy will be running the gauntlet, then," MacKim said.

"That's right," Chisholm agreed. "Even so, I expect that Pikestaff will send somebody to properly reconnoitre the north shore of the St Lawrence upriver of here." Leaning back, he thrust the stem of his pipe in his mouth. "And that's your lesson in strategy for the day, children. Now go away and leave Papa to meditate on life, love and alcohol."

From their position on Point Levis, Fraser's Highlanders had a grandstand view of the skirmishing in the St Lawrence Basin outside Quebec as the Royal Navy and the French battled for control. In terms of gun-power, the Royal Navy held the advantage, but the French were experts with shallow draught gunboats that could fire and retreat vanish into the shallows, while the agile native canoes landed small parties of warriors, or ambushed isolated boats in daylight or dark.

"The French use their Indians well," Chisholm approved. "I wish we had some of our own to meet them."

MacKim nodded. "They're a formidable people."

"We can be sure of one thing," Chisholm said. "We're crossing the river soon, and not just on a raid."

"According to the rumours I heard," Corporal Gunn said, "the Rangers have found a possible landing place three miles west of Quebec. If that's true, we'll be headed upriver."

"Not long now, then," Chisholm said.

"Not soon enough." *Every day we delay increases Hitchins' chance of escape. The quicker we get into Quebec, the more chance I have of finishing this business.*

EVEN WHILE HE VIEWED A LANDING UPSTREAM OF QUEBEC AS his best option, Wolfe tried to convince Montcalm his intention was to land downstream. His diversion centred on the Falls of Montmorency, on the north bank of the St Lawrence, to the east of the town.

"Something's happening." Chisholm nodded to the runner that panted into Monckton's camp at Point Levis. "That man's on important business."

Within half an hour, orders came for detachments of the Light Infantry to gather their kit and move.

"Where are we going, sir?" Gunn asked.

"I don't know yet, Corporal. We've to report to the general."

MacKim's heart began to pound at the prospect of the pending action.

I wonder what Priscilla is doing now? MacKim shook his head, pushing the image of Priscilla away as an impossible dream, and concentrated on his duty. *Priscilla is Jacob Wooler's wife. She is unobtainable.* Yet somewhere at the back of MacKim's mind was the hope that somehow he could capture Priscilla for himself. He had a brief, startling image of walking up Glen Cailleach with Priscilla at his side and his mother waiting with a smile on her face. He could smell the perfume of the peat-smoke and feel the soft rain on his face, with the gentle lowing of the dun cattle melodious above the whisper of the wind in the heather.

"We are going to land at the Falls of Montmorency." Wolfe's voice broke MacKim's reverie. "The siege of Quebec is proceeding satisfactorily. Do your duty, and all should go well. God save the King."

It was a very brief address, but coming from Pikestaff Wolfe, it was enough. Glen Cailleach vanished, and harsh reality dominated.

MacKim ensured he was ready for the coming attack. He sharpened the blade of the tomahawk that hung from his waist, checked he had his regulation number of musket balls, ensured his flint was sharp and his frizzen in the correct position to keep his priming powder dry.

"Ready, Hugh?" Chisholm selected a musket ball, rolled it down the barrel of his musket and rammed it home.

"Ready," MacKim said.

"Remember what we said last time, Hugh. Don't let the Indians take me."

"I won't forget. You do the same for me."

There was no need to shake hands. With Captain Benoni Danks' Rangers and the Light Infantry in the van, Wolfe's two thousand men left the camp to pursue their attack on New France.

As daylight faded, two British gunboats, *Porcupine* and *Boscawen*, began a bombardment of the French positions on the western side of Montmorency Falls. The gunboats' heavy 24- and 32-pounders hammered at the French entrenchments, knocking down the earthen walls, splintering the timber and causing casualties. After enduring a few murderous hours, the French withdrew, with the British cheering at the sight of white-uniformed men retreating from their defences.

All the length of the French defences, Wolfe had organised feints and deceptions to keep Montcalm guessing as to his real intentions. With Royal Naval ships sailing back and forth, firing and pretending to land parties of men, the French shifted their defenders from post to post.

"Pikestaff has got the Frenchies chasing their tails!" Chisholm said. "They don't know if it's Monday or Maggie's birthday."

"Right, men." Captain Cameron had to speak loudly against the hammer of artillery. "I know you'll do your duty. I know you'll fight for Fraser's and King George. May God protect you all." He boarded the leading boat and sat in the stern. MacKim was one of the first to follow, looking at the north bank of the river and wondering what lay ahead.

"Thank God for the Navy," Chisholm said, thrusting his stubby pipe into his mouth. He winked at MacKim. "Here we go again, Hugh."

"Aye, here we go again," MacKim agreed. *We're one step closer to defeating the French. I'm one step closer to avenging Ewan.*

Possibly because of Wolfe's feints and despite the wooded

slope behind the beach providing cover for a hundred Indians and Canadians, the British landed without opposition. MacKim hesitated for a moment, looking around for the enemy.

"Don't dawdle!" Cameron ordered. "Push inland!"

With his feet sliding on the long grass, MacKim moved quickly up the slope, listening to the thump of feet on the ground and the grunting breath of his colleagues.

"Where are the French?" MacKim held his musket ready.

"Not here," Chisholm said.

Behind the Light Infantry, the Grenadiers crashed ashore. Many were veterans who had seen the vast armies counter-march across Europe; to them, this affair was just another campaign in another war, albeit on a different continent.

"We're King George's death-dealing dogs!" one Grenadier roared. "Run and hide, you French. We'll find you wherever you go!"

Behind the flank companies were the line infantry of Braggs 28th and Lascelle's 47th Foot. These were the backbone of the army; the footsloggers who made up the bulk of the forces, the faceless, hard-used men who filled the red-coated ranks and occupied the nameless graves wherever King George waged his wars.

MacKim powered up the wooded slope, looking for the enemy, hoping, somehow, to find Hitchins. To the west, the Montmorency waterfall hammered down with stupendous force and sufficient noise to blanket the sound of a hundred Indians. Fortunately, the Canadians and French had withdrawn, so the Light Infantry and Rangers ascended unmolested. Above the Falls, the river surged between steep banks, dark with trees.

"Pikestaff is giving orders," Chisholm said, as the British halted to consolidate their position, dig entrenchments and haul up artillery.

"He's good at that." MacKim peered into the forest. General Wolfe lived in a world of manoeuvre, tactics and privilege.

MacKim lived in a world of mud, sweat and fear. The only place the two could meet was on the field of battle.

"Get these blasted guns up the slope!" Captain Cameron raved at the men at the traces. "I want artillery cover for my men!"

Lying behind a fallen tree, MacKim stared into the forest. "This forest doesn't look any different from the one at Fort Stanwix, or Point Levis."

Chisholm nodded. "One dark forest is much like another, wherever in the world you happen to be."

Now experienced in creating entrenchments, some of the Light Infantry hacked down trees for a temporary barricade while others fashioned redoubts or dug trenches.

"You're pensive again," Chisholm said as MacKim relapsed into silence.

"We're a bit insecure here," MacKim said, "with the Montmorency River and the St Lawrence behind us and thick forest in front. It's no place to be if the French attack."

"Pikestaff must agree with you," Chisholm said, as Danks' Rangers filtered through the Lights' defences to patrol three hundred yards further forward. Captain Benoni Danks paused for a moment to talk to Captain Cameron and then hurried after his men. MacKim watched him slide into the gloomy forest and disappear.

"Captain Danks tells me that the French have sent a couple of hundred Ottowa Indians to harass us," Captain Cameron explained to the Lights. "We're going to support the Rangers."

It was not the news that MacKim wished to hear. Even after his training, he knew that the Ottowas and Canadians were his superior in woodcraft.

"Orders are orders," Chisholm said with a wink, "one enemy is much like another."

"Come on, lads," Captain Cameron said quietly. "Don't let the Rangers down."

The forest was eerie, with the noise of the Falls echoing

through the trees. As MacKim moved forward, the rain began, light at first and then hurtling down onto the leaves, hiding any sounds the enemy might make. Distantly, behind the hammer of water, MacKim heard the chunk of axes as British working parties felled trees, and he saw the battered green tunics of Danks' Rangers a hundred yards deeper in the trees.

Without speaking, Chisholm nodded towards Danks' men and stepped cautiously in that direction. The shots seemed to come from nowhere, a ragged volley that sent MacKim to the shelter of the nearest tree. He saw two Rangers slump to the ground and heard another yelling in pain.

"Ambush!" MacKim shouted.

"Jesus! Already!" Chisholm raised his musket and fired at the powder-smoke. "Stand fast, MacKim."

Crouching behind his tree, MacKim peered out as the fear-some war-whoop of the Ottowas followed the shots. He watched in horror as a horde of warriors emerged from the trees, charging onto Danks' stunned Rangers. MacKim had a glimpse of near-naked warriors slicing with knives and chopping with toma-hawks, killing the wounded and scalping the dead.

"Help the Rangers!"

Aiming and firing in a single fluid movement, MacKim reloaded at once, hammering the butt of his musket on the ground as a faster alternative to using the ramrod. He did not know if he had hit his man, but saw another Ottowa passing a gap in the trees, fired again and flinched as a musket ball burrowed into the wood an inch from his head.

"Chisholm!"

"Still here!" Chisholm was also loading and firing, alternating between standing and kneeling so the Ottowas could not accurately mark his position.

"How many?" MacKim loaded without thought.

"Too many." Chisholm shifted to a neighbouring tree, peering ahead. "The Rangers are hard hit. There's another man down."

The Ranger was on his own, trying to load a long rifle when

two Ottowas exploded from the forest. One held a tomahawk in his right hand, the second what looked like a large wooden club. Unable to load in time, the Ranger swung his rifle, catching the second Ottowa, and fell as a musket ball smashed into his side.

Priscilla's words came to MacKim. *"Could you guard Jacob's back when he's out there? I'm not asking you to follow him or go against your duty. Please, try and look out for him. I've had visions these past few weeks, where Jacob is on the ground, and an Indian is above him, about to strike him with a tomahawk."*

"That's Wooler!" MacKim threw himself forward to the skirmish as the thoughts crowded into his mind. *I could leave him. I could let the Ottowas kill him, and Priscilla would be free for me. No! I gave my word. Wooler is a good man!*

"MacKim!" Chisholm shouted. "They'll kill you!" Swearing more obscenely than MacKim had ever heard before, Chisholm followed a few yards behind. "You'll get us both killed, you mad bastard!"

"Hold on, Wooler! I'm coming!" Fitting his bayonet as he ran, MacKim leapt over a moss-furred branch. "Hold on!"

Panic gripped the surviving Rangers as they fled towards the British lines, with some dropping their muskets and another man falling wounded. Wooler was on the ground, fighting frantically as the Ottowa warrior tried to split his skull with a tomahawk. Ignoring the others, MacKim lunged with his bayonet, catching the Ottowa high in the side of the chest. The man stiffened and turned around, his eyes wide. Dropping his hold on Wooler, the Ottowa grabbed at MacKim's musket with his left hand. Close to, MacKim could see he was a muscular man in his prime, with red war paint covering most of his face.

Cursing as he struggled to twist free his bayonet, MacKim saw the Ottowa raise his tomahawk again.

"Shoot him, Hugh! Fire, for God's own sake!"

Chisholm's words jolted sense into MacKim. Praying that his musket did not misfire, he pressed the trigger. There was a heart-stopping delay, a puff of smoke from the pan and then the musket recoiled in his arms. So close, the flare of the muzzle burned the Ottowa's flesh as the ball slammed into him. He jerked backwards, slid off the triangular blade of the bayonet, and fell.

"Come on, Hugh!" Chisholm grabbed MacKim's arm.

A dozen and more Ottowas were bounding towards them, knives and tomahawks raised as they screamed their war-cries.

"I can't leave Wooler," MacKim pointed to the Ranger.

"He's a dead man! Come on!" Chisholm was as close to panic as MacKim had ever known him.

"He's alive." MacKim took a deep breath. *My quest for revenge will fail. I will die here, killed by the Ottowas in a pointless skirmish in this faraway land, defending a man who is married to the woman I love.* Straddling the wounded Wooler, MacKim raised his musket. Blood dripped from the bayonet he presented at the Ottowas. "Come on then!"

"You're a bastard, MacKim." Chisholm stood beside him, swearing as he stood on guard.

"Get away, James! Get back while you can!"

The Ottowas slowed as they came closer, forming a wide semi-circle around the three soldiers. Remembering that Wooler carried two pistols, MacKim stooped, lifted one and passed it to Chisholm, thrusting the second through the waist of his kilt.

The Ottowas came again, advancing with tomahawks raised. Chisholm fired his pistol, wounding one man as MacKim presented his bayonet.

Dear God, please make it quick. Don't let them take me alive. Sorry, Ewan. I failed you.

"You're a good man, James." MacKim took a deep breath.

"We're a pair of bloody fools," Chisholm responded.

The roar of British voices interrupted them as a platoon of Grenadiers of Bragg's 28th Foot crashed through the forest. "Kill the savages!" somebody shouted.

"Come on, you death-dealing dogs! At them!"

The Grenadiers charged forward, plunging with bayonet and musket-butt.

A hard-faced corporal with a sneering mouth stopped beside MacKim. "Bloody Sawnies," he said. "Always causing trouble."

MacKim looked round ready to thank the Grenadier corporal, until he saw the man's face and his gratitude stopped before he said a word. The last time he had seen that man had been on the blood-sodden field at Drummossie when he thrust a bayonet through Ewan's hand.

CANADA, SUMMER 1759

"Thank you, Corporal," Chisholm said.

"So you bloody should." Corporal Osborne glanced at the wounded Wooler. "What are you up to, trying to get yourselves killed for a bloody Colonial?"

MacKim tried to hide the hatred that surged through him. "He's a friend of mine, Corporal." *I could bayonet Osborne now and blame the Ottowas.* He felt his musket twitch in his hand. *That would be another gone. I thought he was in Webb's, not Bragg's!*

Corporal Osborne spat on the ground. "Best get him back then, although my men have chased the savages back."

MacKim nodded, fighting temptation. *There are too many people here, and always the possibility that some Grenadier or even a Highlander will see me. Osborne will have to wait, but now I know where he is, I can find him easier.* "Yes, Corporal."

The Ottowas had not stayed to fight. As soon as the Grenadiers closed with the bayonet, they had melted into the trees, although hoarse yells and the occasional shot proved that the two sides were still in contact.

For a moment, Osborne stared directly into MacKim's face, frowning. "You remind me of somebody."

"I'm just myself." MacKim dropped his eyes. *Damn the man! I must have changed since I was ten years old. He can't know me – or does he see Ewan in my face?*

"Aye. I've seen you before somewhere." Osborne nodded slowly. "It will come to me."

Despite his experiences at Louisbourg and here outside Quebec, MacKim suddenly felt vulnerable. Osborne was a man in his late forties, a burly Grenadier and a veteran soldier who MacKim knew had aided in at least one murder. Another killing would probably not shake his conscience, if he had one.

"You have my thanks for your help," MacKim said. "Now, I will get this poor fellow back to our lines."

"It was a long time ago." Osborne continued to scrutinise MacKim's face. "Years ago, so you would be younger." He frowned with the effort of concentration. "Much younger."

"Excuse us, Corporal." Chisholm helped MacKim lift the wounded Wooler.

The Ranger moaned as they moved him. "No, leave me be. Please."

"We're taking you where you can be cared for." MacKim slipped an arm under Wooler's. "Come on, Wooler. Priscilla will want you to live."

Chisholm frowned. "Hugh..."

"Don't say any more, please, James." Hating himself, hating Wooler, MacKim allowed Chisholm to take Wooler's other arm and together, they carried him down the wooded slope with the sounds of conflict fading in the distance.

"That corporal," Chisholm said. "Do you know him?"

"Yes. I'll tell you later." MacKim glanced at Wooler, not sure how much the Ranger understood.

"He is dangerous," Chisholm said. "I've met his kind before in the Army. He likes to kill yet, he's not just a brute, he's intelligent as well. He's a predator."

Looking over his shoulder, MacKim saw that Osborne was still watching him, slowly nodding, as if working something out. *I'll have to get rid of Osborne somehow before he realises who I am.*

"WHO DO YOU HAVE THERE?" CAPTAIN CAMERON ASKED.

"A wounded Ranger," MacKim said. "His name's Wooler. He was our guide at Stanwix."

"Take him to his unit," Cameron gestured to a huddle of Rangers. "They'll look after him."

A shaken Rangers lieutenant stepped forward. "That's Jacob Wooler. I thought he was dead."

"He might still die." Chisholm indicated Wooler's wounds. "You'd better get him to hospital quickly, sir."

The officer nodded. "I saw him fall. Did you go back for him?"

"MacKim did," Chisholm said.

The officer was still shaking from the Ottowa attack. "Why?"

"I met him last winter," MacKim said. "He's a friend of mine."

"You saved him when his fellow Rangers ran away." The lieutenant stuffed tobacco into his pipe with trembling fingers. "Not many men would do that."

"It won't be worth it unless he gets to a surgeon soon," Chisholm said. "He's bleeding to death as we stand here talking."

"You're the sort of men we want in the Rangers." The lieutenant lit his pipe with trembling fingers, drew strongly and exhaled slowly. "What are your names?"

"I am Hugh MacKim," MacKim said, "and this is James Chisholm of the 78th Fraser's Highlanders."

"How would you like a transfer to the Rangers?" the officer said. "I'll speak to your Colonel once we get Wooler in hospital."

"And that's the last we'll hear about that," Chisholm said, as the lieutenant slouched away.

"MacKim." Wooler looked up as they deposited him into the hands of a surgeon's mate. "God bless you, Hugh."

"You'll be all right now," MacKim said. "You're in the best

possible hands. You get fit for that wife of yours." He watched as two men carried Wooler away.

"Poor bugger," Chisholm said. "He has no idea of the nightmare ahead of him."

"It's a lot better than the nightmare he would have if we'd left him to the Ottowas," MacKim said. "At least he'll keep his hair."

Wolfe had set up a field hospital at the Île D'Orléans, which meant a painful, if relatively short, journey by land and water for the wounded man, followed by an agonising visit to the surgeon, who would operate without anaesthetic except for a swallow or two of rum. After that, there was always the possibility of gangrene or fever in the foetid camp.

"God be with you, Wooler," MacKim said. He pushed aside his betraying thought of Priscilla. "God be with you, Jacob."

❦

As British artillery maintained an intermittent barrage on the city, the Canadians and Indians mounted pinprick raids on the British at Montmorency. Both sides were under siege in their own way, and little or no quarter was given to those captured by the Indians, or often to prisoners the British and Rangers grabbed.

It was then that Corporal Gunn took out a routine patrol out and did not return.

"The Indians have him," Dingwall said. "Poor bugger." He glanced at Harriette, who sucked on her pipe and nodded.

"Aye. Sandy will be missing me now."

MacKim had never thought about Corporal Gunn having a Christian name.

"He might come back," Harriette said. "I'll not believe Sandy is gone till I see his body, and that will come back to the regiment." Pressing tobacco into the bowl of her pipe, she lifted a candle and was soon puffing smoke into the room. "Until then, I don't want anybody to mention him again."

Nobody did. Soldiers were always aware of the possibility of death, but losing a man in battle or to disease was far different from a man being captured and tortured to death. MacKim found more purpose in soldiering after the disappearance of Gunn, while a new grimness entered the regiment.

"The Indians are vicious fighters." Once again, Chisholm browned the barrel of his musket, so it did not reflect light.

"I don't mind that so much as the scalping and torture," Cattanach said. "If they were a civilised enemy like the French, I could even admire their skill, but they are just barbarians."

"They're turning us into savages, too," Chisholm said. "I've heard that the Rangers and even some of our boys are looking for Canadian or Indian scalps now. Imagine British soldiers fighting like that."

Remembering the aftermath of Culloden, MacKim kept silent. He began to sharpen his tomahawk, knowing he would kill anything that came in his path, Indian, Canadian, French or rogue British murderers. He had changed even from the man who had fought at Louisbourg. Fighting out here on the fringes of European settlement had thinned some of the veneer of civilisation. Testing the edge of his tomahawk on the hairs of his arm, MacKim thought again of the sneering face of Corporal Osborne. Even while he was in the forest, MacKim hoped to come across Osborne, or even Hitchins. Fighting these two parallel wars had also altered him, although only Chisholm seemed aware of the extent of the changes.

"Ready, Hugh?"

"I'm ready." MacKim checked that the flint in his musket was sharp and he wore nothing that could rattle or catch the light. The days of pristine uniforms and powdered hair were long gone. Taking a deep breath, MacKim faced the forest once more. He knew that a soldier only had a certain amount of luck, and each time he stepped into the trees, he diminished his store a little. In time, he would reach the bottom and death would find him. That was a soldier's reality.

EVERY FEW DAYS, A PARTY OF INDIANS AND CANADIANS slipped across the river to raid the British lines, while the Light Infantry tried to stop them amongst the trees. With Danks' Rangers no longer an effective fighting force after the Ottowa ambush, there was more pressure on the Lights. They were now the eyes and ears of the British on the north side of the St Lawrence.

"Take it easy, now Hugh," Chisholm advised. "You're one soldier, a King's pawn. Don't try and do all the fighting on your own."

"Come on, James." Testing his bayonet was loose in its scabbard, MacKim stepped out.

They moved slowly from tree to tree, careful not to break any twigs, trying not to rustle the leaves. Behind them was the comparative security of the British camp; in front and all around was the forest, the natural home of the Indians, the adopted home of the Canadians, the battleground with which MacKim was becoming daily more familiar. Following the advice of the few remaining Rangers, the Light Infantry had built small timber stockades in prominent positions and manned them with piquets to keep watch over the river. Small parties patrolled between these posts, praying they would come home alive, hoping also for revenge on a foe they were beginning to loathe.

On their eighth night on scouting piquet, MacKim found the remains of what had once been a man, a British soldier. Stripped and scalped by either Indians or Canadians, his heart had been ripped out and placed at his side.

"Oh, God in heaven." Chisholm stared down at the body. "That's Corporal Gunn."

"Aye." MacKim knelt at the side of the man he had once known. "Rest in peace, Corporal. We'll give you a Christian burial."

"Savages," Chisholm said.

MacKim nodded. "Savages," he agreed. "Harriette will be upset."

"I think she expected nothing else," Chisholm said. "She's a real soldier's wife, that one."

Both men swooped for cover at the flat report of the musket. MacKim lay prone, trying to peer all around him. The ball had passed within a foot of his head, clipping off half a dozen leaves before thudding into the bole of a tree some ten feet away. MacKim could see the blue-grey ball protruding from the wood.

"That shot came from behind us," Chisholm said. "The savages are between us and the camp."

MacKim heard the controlled fear in Chisholm's voice. "Keep still." He lay flat with his heart pounding and every sound of the forest magnified. He could hear the roaring of the river nearby, the hiss of rain on the ground and the rustle of the leaves. He fancied he could even hear the patter of insects and the whisper of wind in the wings of fluttering birds. *Is this where I am to die, thousands of miles from home and with my task unfulfilled? No! I will not die here.*

MacKim moved his musket to his shoulder, preparing to fire at anybody he saw. Nothing happened. There was no reaction from the Indians. *How far are we from the British lines? About three hundred yards, if that. This war party is very bold to come so near. If they are between us and safety, then we are also between them and their home.*

"Come on, James. Let's hunt these savages."

"Hunt them?" Chisholm mouthed the words.

"We'll drive them back onto our posts. I've had enough of running from them."

Slowly rising to a crouch, MacKim took a cautious step toward the British redoubts. He could not see any signs of Canadians or Indians, only the dripping trees of the forest, the undergrowth and a distant flicker of a scarlet uniform.

The musket sounded again, with the jet of smoke white

against the forest green. MacKim had no time to react before he heard the ball zip past him. 'I can't see him,' he said.

"Nor can I." Chisholm had his musket at his shoulder as he swivelled, searching for the attacker.

"It must be a lone Canadian," MacKim said. "The Indians hunt in war parties."

Knowing that it would take only fifteen to twenty seconds to reload a musket, MacKim moved quickly, more intent on covering the ground than thinking of concealment.

"It's not an Indian." MacKim had another glimpse of the scarlet tunic. "It's a British soldier."

"He must think we're French." Before MacKim could stop him, Chisholm raised his voice. "Halloa! We're British!"

The man in the scarlet jacket, his face shaded by night and the undergrowth, lifted his musket again and fired.

"We're British, damn your hide!" Chisholm shouted.

"Stop that blasted noise!" A roar came from the nearest British stockade. "You'll alert every Frenchman in Canada. Get over here, you bloody idiot!"

"Ignore him." MacKim pulled Chisholm down low. "Get back into the trees. They can't see who we are."

"What?"

"Do you want to be flogged for making a noise? Follow me."

Stuck between the devil of the cat-o'-nine-tails and the deep sea of the Indians, MacKim and Chisholm eased away from the British stockades, deeper into the forest.

"Lie low for a while and then head back," MacKim whispered.

"Pray that fool has realised we're British." Despite the chill, Chisholm was sweating.

"I don't think he was a fool," MacKim said. "I think he knew who we were." He placed his hand over Chisholm's mouth to prevent him from speaking again.

A musket sounded somewhere far away as a nervous sentry fired into the trees. MacKim remained still. The rain pattered off the leaves, grew stronger as the wind gusted and then eased away.

"Come on, Chisholm. Let's get back." MacKim realised that something had changed. No longer was he following Chisholm's advice; now he was taking the lead.

A British soldier had fired at him. A single shot could be excused as nervousness in this environment. Two shots could not be put down as accidental. *Somewhere in the British camp at Montmorency is a man who has tried to kill me. It can only be Corporal Osborne. He must have worked out who I am. Life has got even more complicated.*

⚜

"MACKIM!" DINGWALL'S MASSIVE FORM FILLED THE ENTRANCE of the tent. "Captain Cameron wants you."

"Why?"

Dingwall put a massive arm around MacKim's shoulder. "When I asked him, MacKim, I said, 'Hugh Cameron, my old friend, why do you want to see Private MacKim?' 'Well, Sergeant Dingwall,' said the Captain, 'I want to borrow a sovereign.'" Dingwall pressed his face closer to MacKim. "How the devil should I know what he wants? Do you think I'm his drinking companion? Go and find out, damn you for a useless scoundrel!"

Captain Cameron eyed MacKim up and down as he reported. "Ah, MacKim, Sergeant Dingwall tells me that you have been prominent in recent operations. I recall you saved a Ranger from being killed by the Ottowas."

"Private Chisholm was there too, sir."

"Sergeant Dingwall brought you to my attention, Corporal MacKim."

"It's Private MacKim, sir."

"Are you arguing with me, Corporal?" Cameron may have been smiling.

"Of course not, sir."

"Put on your cord of rank as soon as you can, Corporal."

"So you got my man's cord," Harriette said, as MacKim walked across the camp. "I suppose you'll want to share my bed as well."

"I didn't ask for the corporal's cord," MacKim said, "and I certainly didn't want it this way. Corporal Gunn was a good man."

"Aye, he was a good man," Harriette said, "and now he's a dead man mouldering in his grave." She looked around the slowly gathering 78th. "I have to find another husband, or I'll be out of the regiment. Wolfey doesn't approve of wives coming along with the men, let alone unattached women."

"You'll be all right, Harriette," Chisholm said.

"Aye, I'll be all right." Harriette was suddenly bitter. "I've lost two husbands before. Sandy's just another one. Somebody will want an auld harridan like me." She raised her voice. "Well? Who wants me?"

MacKim watched as, one by one, the men walked away. Only then did Harriette allow her tears to appear.

"Come on, Harriette." MacKim put an arm around her shoulders. "You're safe with us. I'm not the marrying type and James..."

"James is too ugly for any woman to want," Chisholm said.

"Corporal MacKim!" Dingwall roared. "Come here! I don't want these Ottowas to get away with Gunn's death. We have retaliation to organise." He put his heavy arm around MacKim's shoulders once more. "Between you and me, Kimmy my lad, Gunn was a bit soft. He had no aggression in him at all. I've had my eye on you for some time, and I think you and I can carry this fight to the savages. Here's what I want you to do..."

❧ 17 ❧

OUTSIDE QUEBEC, JULY 1759

The Ottowas came without warning, running through the trees with tomahawks held high. Only when the British piquet turned did the Ottowas release their war-whoops, the sound high and chilling.

"Fight them!" MacKim stood in the middle of the piquet, as he and Dingwall had planned. "There is no retreat from here, my boys!" He wished fervently that Chisholm had been with him, but he was back in the camp with a fever.

Rather than run, the piquet slid behind the nearest trees, fired a volley and quickly fixed bayonets. MacKim swore. He had not expected the Ottowas to be in such numbers. "Form a circle, boys, guard the flanks." He raised his voice to a roar. "Now! Now, Grenadiers!"

Emerging from their positions fifty paces behind MacKim's piquet, the mixed Light Infantry and Grenadier patrol advanced at a run, with the Lights outstripping the more cumbersome Grenadiers by some yards. They met the Ottowas head-on, bayonet to knife, tomahawk to musket butt. The forest became the scene of a desperate struggle as men wrestled, panted, grunted and swore. MacKim lunged with his bayonet at a near-naked Ottowa and cursed as the warrior evaded his blade. Having expected a comfortable victory against a numerically smaller group of soldiers, the Ottowas began to withdraw.

"Chase them." Captain Cameron had led the ambush. "Teach them not to murder Highland corporals. Come on, Lights! Show the Grenadiers how to fight!"

"Stay together!" a scar-faced Grenadier sergeant roared, but by that time the Grenadiers had lost their discipline in the joy of getting to grips with their normally elusive enemy. As the Ottowas retreated, the Grenadiers thundered in pursuit. More experienced in forest fighting, the Lights retained their caution, keeping close together as they watched for a counter-ambush, firing when they had a glimpse of a target and reloading before moving on.

To his left and slightly ahead, MacKim saw Osborne lead a small group of Grenadiers towards a single Ottowa. The Ottowa was dodging between two trees when two of the Grenadiers took aim and fired. Either one of the men was an unusually good shot or very lucky, for the Ottowa crumpled, holding his left leg. Yelling in triumph, the Grenadiers powered forward. MacKim edged in that direction, keeping Osborne in view.

"Scalp the savage." Osborne produced a long knife from inside his tunic.

Two of the Grenadiers cheered while the last, a broken-nosed, near-middle-aged man, shook his head. "We're not savages," he said.

"We treat savages as they treat us." Osborne knelt beside the Ottowa. "I'll have this one's scalp."

For a moment, MacKim was a young boy again, watching the redcoat soldiers torturing his brother to death.

"Enough!" The memory forced MacKim forward. "You can't scalp that man. We're British soldiers, not savages!"

The Grenadiers stared at MacKim as the wounded Ottowa lifted his chin in defiance. Osborne began to laugh. "Yes, I *can* scalp this man," he said. "Watch me." Pressing the point of his knife into the Ottowa's skull, he carved a bloody circle, grinning, as the other Grenadiers watched in fascination.

"No!" MacKim tried to intervene, only for the Grenadiers to grab him. Each one was inches taller than MacKim and broader in the chest.

"Hold him tight, boys," Osborne said. "That's the Scotch bugger I told you about, the rebel boy we let go at Culloden." Taking a firm grip of the Ottowa's hair, Osborne wrenched it upwards. The sound was sickening as the Ottowa's scalp ripped from his head, followed by a gush of blood. The Ottowa grunted once, glaring at Osborne.

"Hold the Sawnie down." Osborne held up his bloody trophy, grinned and stuffed it under his belt. "I'll do him next."

"But he's British!" the broken-nosed Grenadier said. "It's bad enough scalping a savage. You can't do it to one of us."

"He's a Scotch rebel bastard," Osborne said. "I know him and his family. He's probably going to desert to the French. That's why he wants to help the savage."

"Sawnie bastard," the ugliest of the Grenadiers snarled, while even the broken-nosed man looking confused.

"Hold the rebel until I finish the savage off."

The musketry took MacKim by surprise. The ugliest Grenadier fell at once, bleeding from the mouth, while his companion took one glance at the body and fled toward the British lines. Broken-nose hesitated for only a moment longer before he, too, followed, leaving MacKim and Osborne with the wounded Ottowa.

Lifting his musket, MacKim dropped to one knee and peered into the trees. Only the drift of powder-smoke revealed from where the shots had come. There was no sign of the enemy.

"Now what are you going to do?" MacKim asked, as his hatred of Osborne conquered his fear of any lurking Indians. "All your friends have gone." He presented his bayonetted musket. "You're all alone now, Osborne."

Sheathing his knife, Osborne lifted his musket and stepped

toward MacKim. "I'm going to kill you slowly, you rebel bastard."

Closing his mouth, MacKim prepared to receive Osborne's attack. *I hope these blasted Ottowas leave us alone until I kill this man.*

Older, taller, heavier and more experienced, Osborne was a formidable opponent as he balanced on the balls of his feet, his eyes fixed on MacKim and his mouth twisted in a permanent sneer.

This man is dangerous, MacKim said to himself. *He is far more formidable than Hayes was.* Too intent on Osborne, MacKim barely noticed the Ottowa warriors who emerged from the undergrowth. They stood in a silent circle, watching as MacKim and Osborne faced each other.

MacKim feinted left, and then slashed right, catching Osborne on the outside of his arm, ripping his tunic and drawing blood.

"You little bastard!" Osborne lunged forward, heavy on the ground but irresistible if he made contact. He swore loudly as he noticed the Ottowas that surrounded them. "Christ, man, the Indians!"

"Aye, I see them." MacKim said. "I'll deal with them once I've killed you." His death was less important than the oath he had sworn. If the Ottowas killed him, he would only be dead. If he broke his sacred oath, he was condemning his soul to everlasting torment, and his name would be shunned by his family forever.

"Run!" Osborne yelled. Backing away, he turned on his heel and tried to force through the ring of Ottowas. They closed around him, sinewy hands clutching, bodies gleaming.

Save yourself, Hugh! The Ottowas have Osborne.

MacKim slashed at the nearest Ottowa, saw the man pull back, feinted left, grunted as the Ottowa moved instinctively to block him, slid right and dashed through the gap. Suddenly afraid, MacKim fled into the trees, heading for the intermittent crackle of musketry, stopping only when he was sure there was no pursuit. He stood still, trying to still the pounding of his heart as the breath rasped in his throat. *No, I won't run further. I must see what happens to Osborne. I must see him die, or kill him myself.*

The hands stretched from the undergrowth, grabbing at MacKim's legs before he relaxed. He slashed with his bayonet, swearing. "No! I have things to do!" MacKim's words were lost as the Ottowas surrounded him. Two snatched the musket from his hands, and then they were pushing him back the way he had come, prodding their knives into his back and legs, holding the edge of their tomahawks to his throat.

Three tribesmen held the madly struggling Osborne as the scalped but still living Ottowa pointed to him, speaking in a low, pain-racked voice.

"The man you scalped is pointing you out, Osborne," MacKim said. "They're going to kill you, sure as death." Despite his fear, he forced a grin. "It will be long and slow, as you deserve, you murdering bastard."

Held by two muscular Ottowas, Osborne was pale beneath his weathered face. He shook his head. "I didn't do that! It was the Scotchman!" He indicated MacKim with a lift of his chin. "It was him, not me."

"They don't understand a word you say." MacKim knew that everything he predicted for Osborne would also happen to him. "They'll kill you slowly, Osborne, you murdering bastard. You'll die screaming, and I'll enjoy every second."

The Ottowas were watching with interest. A tall, middle-aged warrior stepped forward. "You two are enemies." He spoke in French. "You were going to fight each other."

"We are, and we were." MacKim's French was not as fluent as the Ottowa's. He felt his heartbeat increase as he held the Ottowa's gaze, determined not to show his fear.

The middle-aged warrior gave an order, and the Ottowas stripped MacKim and Osborne naked before forming a ring around them.

"Fight." The spokesman pushed MacKim forward. "Fight your enemy."

MacKim eyed Osborne. The Grenadier was a head taller and much more muscular than he was, with a body seamed with scars. Osborne's sneer seemed more pronounced than ever. "What will happen to the victor?" MacKim asked.

"We will release him."

"What's he saying?" Osborne glanced over his shoulder at the watching tribesmen.

"We have to fight," MacKim said. "The Ottowas will let the victor go." *Or so they say.*

With the Ottowas watching in total silence and the occasional gunfire in the distance a reminder that the greater battle continued, MacKim circled. Knowing that the Grenadier was aggressive and experienced, he hoped that if he kept Osborne on the move for long enough, the older man should tire, allowing MacKim to move in and finish him off. On the other hand, if Osborne managed to close and grapple, MacKim knew he had little chance against the Grenadier's strength.

"I thought you were a death-dealing dog," MacKim taunted. "Or do you need your friends to support you? There were four of you to hold a ten-year-old and torture another boy to death. Now you are alone. You're a coward, Osborne, a ranting, bullying coward."

Osborne's sneer intensified. Crouched low, he moved forward, grabbing for MacKim with his long arms. MacKim avoided his attack with more ease than he had expected, landed a sharp punch to the side of Osborne's head and stepped away.

The Grenadier shook away the blow, turned, and swung a massive roundhouse punch that would have felled MacKim if he had not ducked.

"Run, Sawnie, run. When I catch you, I'll break your spine over my knee and leave you to die."

Feinting left, right and left again, MacKim landed another right-hander to Osborne's jaw, ducked from the now-expected turn and swung his left. Osborne grinned. "You can't hurt me, MacKim. You're a lightweight."

That was true. MacKim realised that his punches had no effect on the large Grenadier. Without a weapon, he had only his speed and agility and fighting within an enclosed space curtailed both of these.

"This is the second time you've tried to kill me, Osborne," MacKim taunted. "You failed last time, and you'll fail this time, too."

"What?" Osborne stepped back slightly. "If I had tried to kill you, rebel, you'd be dead."

"You tried to shoot me, remember?"

Osborne shook his head. "Not me, Sawnie!"

"So you're a liar as well as a cowardly bully?" MacKim ducked left, threw another punch and gasped when it bounced off Osborne's massively muscled shoulder. "You tried to shoot me in the back a few days ago."

"I said, not me, Sawney." Osborne's lips curled further. "You must have another enemy, somebody else who recognises you for the rebel dog you are!"

"There they are!" The Gaelic words came clearly through the trees as the 78th's Lights arrived. There was a spatter of musketry, with one shot hitting the Ottowa who held MacKim's musket. For a moment, there was chaos as the Lights erupted into the clearing and the retreating Ottowas grabbed at Osborne and dragged him away. Lifting his musket from the ground, MacKim aimed at the Ottowa spokesman.

"Shoot him, for the love of God, help me!" Osborne shrieked. "Don't let them get me!"

Bringing his musket to the present position, MacKim did not fire. The Ottowa spokesman met his gaze, expressionless. The last MacKim saw of Osborne was his terrified eyes, and then the leaves closed around him.

"MacKim!" Cattanach ran up to him. "Are you all right?"

"I am now," MacKim said. "I think you saved my life."

Hurriedly pulling on his uniform, he followed the Lights as they pursued the Ottowas as far as the Fords of the Montmorency, which the Indians crossed with ease. A platoon of Grenadiers thundered up, shouting as they lined the river. Some of the Lights knelt to fire at the Ottowas; others waded across the river onto the opposite bank until Sergeant Dingwall ordered them to return.

"Don't follow them over," Dingwall shouted. "We don't know how many savages are across the other side."

"How about their prisoner, Sergeant?" Cumming asked.

"We'll have to leave the poor fellow with them and hope they hand him to the French."

MacKim joined the others on the river bank. He peered to the French-controlled side of the river. "I could go over, Sergeant." *And shoot the bastard.*

"No, Corporal," Dingwall said. "I want you to form a defensive perimeter with the Lights and wait here. The savages might try to follow us as we return."

MacKim watched as the Grenadiers tramped away, boasting of their deeds and lying about the number of Indians they had killed. Most of the Lights also left, leaving a lonely platoon of the 78th to guard the ford.

Fast and forbidding, the river seemed like a spiritual as well as a physical barrier between the British and French territory. *Has Osborne escaped me? Will the Ottowas hand him over to the French?*

The screaming began a quarter of an hour later. High-pitched, it rose to a crescendo and died away to a bubbling squeal that raised the small hairs on the back of MacKim's neck.

"Oh, Jesus. That poor bugger." Cattanach crossed himself. "What are they doing to him?"

Nothing he does not deserve. MacKim felt Ewan at his side, and a host of his ancestors crowding around, nodding approval. There had been no mercy in the old clan wars, and MacKim felt little compassion for the man who helped murder his brother.

The screaming began again, a sound of hopeless agony that unsettled the Highlanders.

"We should ford the river, Corporal," Cattanach said. "We can find that Grenadier fellow and rescue him."

MacKim felt humanity battling through his desire for revenge. *Despite what Osborne did, I don't like to think of the Indians torturing him.* "I reckon that the sergeant was right, Cattanach. The Ottowas will be expecting us to come. I'm not leading anybody into an ambush."

"Can we at least fire at them?" Others echoed Cattanach's desperate plea.

MacKim pondered. "Our muskets have a maximum range of a hundred yards. The Ottowas will be well beyond that."

"We have to do something!" Cattanach said.

As the screaming began again, MacKim agreed, more to assuage his men than to help Osborne. "All right. We'll send a scouting patrol of three men. Stay close to the ford and don't expose yourself. I want one man to fire towards the noise and the others to watch for the Indians." He knew it was futile, yet he also knew it might help his men think they had not abandoned Osborne.

Why did he deny trying to shoot me? There was no need for that. Either Osborne is a natural liar, or he was telling the truth, and somebody else wanted to kill me. Who and why? I don't understand.

Cattanach led two men across the ford and into the gloom on the French side of the river. For the first time in his life, MacKim felt the burden of command; if the enemy killed these men, he was responsible. MacKim listened as the irregular crack of the Brown Bess punctuated the night, without interrupting the terrible sounds of torment. An hour before dawn, MacKim waded the ford and called back the piquet. They returned in silence, with their heads down as if ashamed that they could not alleviate Osborne's suffering.

"You tried, lads," MacKim said.

"We bloody failed." Cattanach replied. "Torturing Indian savages."

"You could do no more."

The piquet had no sooner returned when a lone Ottowa appeared through the trees on the opposite bank of the river. Wordless, he ran halfway across the ford, poised and threw something across to the 78th. The spatter of musketry from the sentinels did not touch him as he disappeared back into the trees.

"What did he throw?" Cumming asked.

"It's that Grenadier's head." Cattanach lifted it. "They've scalped him."

MacKim looked down into the staring eyes of Osborne. He could read the terror and agony of the Grenadier's final hours, yet felt neither pity nor remorse. *I hope Ewan watched you die, Osborne. That's Bland, Hayes and Osborne dead. Only Hitchins to go, and I am free of the duty laid on me.*

Once again, the image of Priscilla came to him. Once again, he shook it away. He had given his word there as well.

FRENCH CANADA, JULY 1759

On the evening of the 12th July 1759, the British completed their artillery batteries at Pointe-aux-Pères, directly opposite the city of Quebec.

"Watch how these boys work," Chisholm said. "This is the future, MacKim, long-range warfare."

MacKim grunted. "They'll always need us." All the same, he watched as artillerymen in blue uniforms checked their guns, looked over the earth-packed gabions and defences of sloping damp soil, measured the range to their target, spat on their hands, took a deep breath and prepared to fire. In Chisholm's chess-moves of siege and marching that was the warfare of the mid-eighteenth century, the guns were the queens. They provided the firepower to smash defences and capture the fortresses that guarded frontiers and marked borders.

"We're mere pawns compared to the artillery." Chisholm said. "If saints ever favour those who brought death and destruction from afar, Saint Barbara, the patron saint of gunners, will be looking down in pride as her men work."

Each cannon required a team of eight men under the stern gaze of a sergeant, with an officer in overall command of the six-gun battery. Once the officer inspected each gun for weaknesses, a sweating gunner rammed a charge of powder down the barrel, followed by a wad and then the huge thirty-two-pound cannonball itself. With the loading process completed, the officer thrust a quadrant into the mouth of the gun to calculate the best elevation. Firing across the St Lawrence, these cannon were at their extreme range, so the gunners adjusted the elevating screw beneath the belly of the beast, raising the business end of the barrel.

At nine in the evening, a rocket soared skyward, signalling the beginning of the bombardment and weeks of torment for the good people of Quebec.

Idle for once, MacKim leaned against a tree, puffing at his long-stemmed pipe as the closest artillery sergeant roared. Immediately, ventsmen pricked the cartridges through the vent on top of the cannon's barrel and poured in fine powder before stepping smartly back.

When he was sure all was correct, the sergeant lifted his head. "Fire!"

The word seemed to hang in the air for a moment before anybody moved. Beside the ventsman was a pole holding three strands of hemp impregnated with saltpetre, known as linstock or slow match. Setting the linstock alight, the ventsman thrust it into the prepared vent. The powder flashed, igniting the cartridge within the barrel of the gun, with the explosion pushing the cannon and carriage backwards. The muzzle flared, the cannonball roared out together with a thick gush of smoke, and when the cannon settled, the ventsman covered the vent to protect any residual powder from igniting as air gushed in.

MacKim could watch the passage of the shot as a black streak through the air. He knew that the men on the defences of Quebec were doing the same thing, ready to throw themselves to safety if the great iron ball should hurtle in their direction.

When he was sure it was safe, the spongeman soaked the fleece end of his sponge in a bucket of water and thrust it inside the barrel to douse any smouldering powder. The process was complete, and the cannon ready for the team to reload.

"The range is too great." Chisholm gave his opinion between puffs of his stubby pipe. "They're just wasting powder and shot."

After experiencing the siege of Louisbourg, MacKim was used to the spectacular sights of cannon fire at night, with the eye-blinding flashes and the reflection of the muzzle-flare on the clouding white smoke. Even so, he watched the opening bombardment with interest. "You are right, James," he said, when the opening volleys fell short, with the cannonballs falling into the river with mighty splashes.

"Aye. The gunners will have to elevate their pieces more." Chisholm coughed and wiped the back of his hand across his perspiring face.

"Are you sure you're fit for duty?"

"Fit enough," Chisholm said. "Captain Cameron was going to send me to the hospital on the Île D'Orléans until Harriette Mackenzie said she'd act as my nurse. She's a good woman, that. Gunny was lucky to have her."

MacKim nodded. "Be careful there, James, or she'll have you next."

"With a face like mine?" Chisholm grunted. "I can't see that happening."

The firing ceased for a while, while the artillerymen adjusted their aim, and then the guns started again, aiming at the Upper Town of Quebec.

"Should they not be firing at the batteries so we can storm the bloody place?" MacKim asked.

"I would think so." Chisholm exhaled blue smoke. "I don't agree with making war on civilians."

MacKim stuffed more tobacco into the bowl of his pipe as he watched the show. "Nor do I." He paused for a moment. "Except that out here, it is difficult to know who is a civilian and who is a soldier. Half the Canadians we fight are from the local farms. They are farmers one minute and shooting at us the next. Do we treat them as civilians or as soldiers? The tribesmen are the same. They are here for one campaign or even less, then go back to hunting for their families."

"Even so," Chisholm said, "war has rules. When kings quarrel, they send their professional soldiers to fight against other professional soldiers. Civilians should be left alone."

Once more, MacKim remembered the aftermath of Culloden when British soldiers raped and flogged women, and shot or hanged men merely for wearing traditional Highland clothes. "That does not always seem to be the case."

"It's wrong," Chisholm said.

"Aye. It's wrong," MacKim agreed. "The people at the top bend the rules to suit themselves, and the ordinary people suffer."

"We should remove the people at the top, then," Chisholm said.

"Have a revolution?" MacKim sucked at his pipe. "That would only replace one set of scoundrels with another – King James for King George, or suchlike."

Chisholm nodded. "That's true. So what's the solution?"

"Find somewhere to live where there are no people at the top, or create a society where everybody is equal, with no leaders, no kings to cause wars and no clan chiefs or anybody else to order young men to fight for causes about which they know nothing."

"A society with no leaders would be anarchy," Chisholm said. "Everybody would do whatever they wished."

"Not if there were laws agreed by all, a common parliament where everybody had their say."

"That's too radical." Chisholm shook his head. "What was your other idea?"

"Go somewhere where there are no kings or chiefs," MacKim said.

"Everywhere has kings or chiefs," Chisholm said. "France, Great Britain, Spain, Russia," he lifted his hand to indicate the greying scene around them. "Why, Hugh even here, hundreds of miles away from civilisation, King Louis and King George are fighting, while these tribes all have chiefs to order them what to do, just like Simon Fraser orders us."

"Even the territories of Geordie and Louis have frontiers," MacKim said. "We could go beyond the frontier."

"There are other kings, other chiefs," Chisholm said.

"Perhaps," MacKim said, 'but they would not be *my* chief, and they'd have to find me first." He frowned as reality bit again. *Before I even think of freedom, I have my family sacred oath to fulfil. I have to find Hitchins somehow. All the rest is just smoke.*

While the artillery roared continuously, the Navy brought bomb-ketches into the river opposite Quebec, whose thirteen-inch mortar bombs arced high above the walls before plummeting down to explode inside the city.

"I pity the poor buggers under that," Chisholm said, as the mortars fired carcasses, iron baskets full of combustible material that left a fiery trail through the sky and burned anything on which they landed. "War is a terrible thing for civilians."

"Aye," MacKim agreed. "It's all right, though, because we're civilised, remember? We fight with rules." He blew smoke into the air. "Now tell that to the French women and children whose houses are on fire."

"Here comes the reply," Chisholm said, when the French artillery opened up, firing at the British batteries. "It's Louisbourg all over again."

Daybreak brought no relaxation of the bombardment. The British artillery pounded Quebec, and although the barrage did no significant damage to the defences, it was demoralising to the population. When the governor opened the city gate, hundreds of civilians, mainly women and children, escaped into the surrounding fields.

"As I said," Chisholm sighed, "now we are making war on civilians, and not only men but on women and little ones as well. King George must be proud of us."

"What kings don't see, don't bother them," MacKim said. "And what they learn about, they ignore if it's to their benefit."

"I did not think that Pikestaff would deliberately fire on civilians," Cumming said. "Maybe he's looking for revenge because the Canadians and Indians tortured and scalped our men, like Gunny and that Grenadier."

"He may use these horrors as an excuse," MacKim spoke slowly, "but I think that everybody's favourite general is a natural bloody man." He waited for a lull in the bombardment before he continued. "During the Jacobite rising, Pikestaff was going to massacre the entire MacPherson clan."

"Oh?" Chisholm raised his eyebrows.

"Pikestaff planned to send a patrol to capture Cluny MacPherson, the MacPherson chief, in the hope that the clan would wipe out the patrol, giving him an excuse to kill all the men and exile the women and children." MacKim allowed his words to sink in before he continued. "I heard other tales about our glorious Pikestaff," he said. "Did you know that only four years ago, when he commanded the 20th Foot in Canterbury, he ordered that any man who left the ranks was to be immediately shot? He said that 'a soldier does not deserve to live who won't fight for his king and country'."

Chisholm shook his head. "Bastard."

"After the battle at Monongahela," Cumming reminded them, "the savages burned British prisoners alive and ate some of them."

"British soldiers can also do that," MacKim said curtly.

"I've never heard of British soldiers eating people," Cumming said.

"No," MacKim admitted. "You're right, Cumming. I've never heard of British soldiers eating people."

Cumming smiled; his point proved.

The pitiless day-and-night bombardment continued. When the carcasses caused fires, the gunners targeted the flames to spread them over a wider area. During the day, dark smoke blanketed the city; at night, flames reflected orange from the clouds above. Some-times a scream sounded, and often the rattle of military drums.

"Why don't they surrender?" Chisholm asked. "Why doesn't Montcalm surrender? It's cruel sore to subject women and chil-dren to such suffering."

"Let the bastards suffer," Cattanach said. "I'll never forget what they did to that poor Grenadier."

Chisholm took a deep breath. "This isn't war. I saw war in Europe. This campaign is much worse. It's positively mediaeval."

"The French officers don't seem to care what happens to their civilians," Chisholm said. "Cold-hearted bastards."

"That's how they got to be officers," Cumming said. "People don't matter to them, only victory and advancing their careers."

MacKim listened and said nothing. *I don't belong in the army. Nobody should live to inflict suffering on others.*

"I once believed that we, the British, were the most civilised and gentlemanly people in the world." Chisholm flapped a hand toward Quebec. "I no longer believe that."

"The officers still believe that," Cumming said, "and so do many of the men. They think we are better than anybody else, so they are justified in treating others as they wish. If other people accept the supposed superiority of the British, then the officers smile with gentlemanly condescension, but if anybody challenges that order of things, then they feel it acceptable to use cruelty or other measures to rectify things, at least in their opinion."

"Not all officers are like that," Chisholm protested. "Captain Cameron's a good man."

"No, not all are like that, but many are," Cumming said.

Even as the cannon pounded Quebec, the daily skirmishes around the Montmorency position continued. The Canadians and tribesmen regularly ambushed both Lights and working parties cutting fascines, with losses on both sides. Bearing the brunt of the struggle, the Lights sent a slow trickle of casualties to the hospital on Île D'Orléans.

"We say we are trying to conquer this Canada," Chisholm said. "Why, we only control the land on which we stand. Ten yards beyond our entrenchments, the French and Indians are complete masters."

As the weeks passed, MacKim honed the skills the Rangers had taught him by emulating the enemy, enhancing his ability to seek dead ground and increasing his patience so he could lie unmoving for hours waiting for a sight of the enemy. The sight of a scalped man no longer concerned him, and he kept a tally of the tribesmen and Canadians he shot. Every night, he opened his much-crumpled paper and read the one remaining name. *Hitchins,* he said to himself. *I have to kill Hitchins before I can find freedom.*

"You're turning into a soldier, Corporal." Sergeant Dingwall sounded grudgingly approving.

"I'm doing what I can to remain alive," MacKim said, truthfully.

Dingwall nodded. "What's driving you, MacKim?"

"I want to live," MacKim said.

"If you want a long life, then you should never have gone for a soldier," Dingwall said. "There's something else." He prodded MacKim's chest with a huge finger. "I'll find out, Corporal, don't you fret, I'll find out."

"During the Fontenoy campaign," Chisholm puffed at his pipe as Dingwall walked away, "things were much more civilised. Sentries and piquets were left alone, and we treated civilians with respect. We considered it murder to kill the enemy's sentries, and after a march, we would find a market for fresh food. If the Frenchies had men out for the same reason, we spoke to them or ignored them."

"Different continent, different war." MacKim was cleaning his teeth with a twig.

Chisholm removed his pipe. "With Osborne gone, you've only one to go, then."

"That's right," MacKim said. "Only one. I'm already tired of fighting and hunting and killing."

"You're a good soldier," Chisholm said. "Remember what I said. Live for the day and don't think about tomorrow."

"I'm not a natural soldier," MacKim said.

Chisholm touched his ruined face. "Nor am I," he said and MacKim swore there was a gleam of moisture in Chisholm's eyes. "A soldier wishes to live. I only hope to die." Before MacKim could respond, Chisholm walked away.

To keep the enemy at bay, the British constantly strengthened their camp at Montmorency. By August, there were eleven stockades, with supporting trenches and palisades to daunt the Indians. Sentries were doubled or tripled, and the patrols that ventured beyond the fortifications were never less than eight men strong. The officers issued passwords to ensure any men seen in the woods were returning patrols and not a French raiding party.

"Are we keeping the Canadians out, or are we showing how afraid we are of them?" Cumming asked.

"We're marking our territory," Chisholm said. "Within the palings, the palisades, is our land. Beyond the pale is the wild land of the enemy."

Behind the fortified walls, the tents formed regular canvas streets as the men attempted to live a normal life. Some of the local Canadians slipped in to sell small items of food, spruce beer or even rum, while Harriette joined the more audacious of the regimental wives in sailing across the St Lawrence. Harriette arrived in a Royal Naval longboat with a laugh and a smacking kiss for the petty officer in charge.

"Thank you, lover," she said, "and when I want a ferryman, you can be sure I'll think of you first!" She strode into the camp with her skirt snapping against her legs, and her head held high. "Where's that ugly scoundrel Chisholm?"

"You're wanted," MacKim said. "I'll leave you two alone."

"Hugh," Chisholm called, but MacKim was already walking

away. The enclosed camp of a military force was not the best place to seek privacy, so he made his way to the shore, where the sound of the rippling St Lawrence reminded him of the burn that ran through Glen Cailleach.

"Hugh." The voice was low, yet still cut through the raucous noises of off-duty soldiers. "Hugh, it's me."

MacKim looked up. "Priscilla?" He felt the smile spread involuntarily across his face. "What are you doing in a place like this?"

Dressed in a long green cloak that nearly brushed the ground, and with a tricorne hat thrust low over her head, Priscilla looked as attractive as MacKim remembered. She looked around her as a group of red-coated infantrymen jostled past, swearing mightily. "My husband sent me," she said.

"How is he?" MacKim had pushed the wounded Wooler to the back of his mind. "I had hoped to visit him in the field hospital, but I haven't had the opportunity."

"He's recovering slowly," Priscilla said. "He told me that you saved his life."

Of course I saved him. I gave you my oath. "He's a good man," MacKim said. He stepped beside Priscilla, and they matched each other stride for stride as they skirted the banks of the St Lawrence.

"He told me you risked your life to save his," Priscilla said. "The Indians would have killed and scalped him."

MacKim did not say anything to that. "It's good to see you again." He glanced over to her. "You are a brave woman to come into this camp alone."

"Why is that?"

"Some of the soldiers would not respect a woman," MacKim said. "And some of the soldier's women are worse than the men."

"I can look after myself."

"I don't doubt that," MacKim said, "but looking after your-self on the frontier and looking after yourself in a camp of thousands of rough men..." He shook his head. "Many of these men have not seen a proper lady for months."

Priscilla smiled. "I understand what you mean," she said. "Look." Opening her cloak, she revealed a heavy pistol and a long knife. "I have taken precautions. As I said, I can look after myself. We have rough men on the frontier as well."

A crackle of musketry made both pause, but the shouts of a sergeant informed them the platoon was only shooting at a mark.

"One gets nervous out here," MacKim excused himself.

"I am not surprised," Priscilla said. "You have no idea how much we hate the French and Indians on our frontier." She launched into a conversation about the depredations of the tribes along the borders of the New York colony. "Nowhere is safe," Priscilla said. "Any homestead, and sometimes even whole villages, are at risk from Indian attack. The French bribe them with brandy and guns, so they kill and scalp and burn. We need British troops to defend us."

"Your Rangers are pretty handy at Indian fighting," MacKim said.

"Our Rangers cannot capture forts or defeat French regulars," Priscilla said. She looked up at him, her eyes bright and intense. "Only the British Army can do that." She lowered her voice. "Men like you."

"I'm glad we're useful," MacKim said.

"I did not come here because you are useful," Priscilla said.

"I know. You came to thank me because I helped save your husband."

"Is there somewhere we can talk without a thousand soldiers watching us?" Priscilla asked.

"Only officers can find privacy within the palisade. We'll have to cope with the stares of the other ranks." MacKim grinned. "They're either intensely envious, or are wondering how a Highland private can attract such an obvious gentlewoman." MacKim realised he was so close to Priscilla that they were touching. He moved slightly further away. "Only you and I know that you are here about your husband."

Priscilla was silent for a few steps. "I am no gentlewoman," she said eventually. "And I hope you realise that I have a secondary reason for coming to see you."

It was MacKim's turn to be silent. "I have mixed feelings about that."

"So have I."

They walked between the rows of tents as MacKim wrestled with his emotions. He knew that he loved this woman, yet betraying the trust of her husband would be the worst thing he had ever done, much worse than killing Hayes, as well as damaging the sacred bond of marriage. And yet, as he looked at Priscilla, he felt an overwhelming desire to hold her close and kiss her.

I cannot. I cannot break Jacob's trust and ruin his life and hers. Once Priscilla's reputation is gone, she can never replace it. Once again, he had that image of walking down Glen Cailleach with Priscilla on his arm and his mother waiting for him, smiling.

"Where do we go from here?" They had reached the first of the defences, stark and sturdy to hold back the tribesmen of the forest. The private on sentinel duty nodded and returned to his study of the river, watching for Indian canoes. Priscilla looked up at him.

"We can go back, or we can head left," MacKim said. "Either way will take us on a circuit of the camp. We may have to move quickly if there is an alarm, or if an officer desires us to get out of his way."

"Your officers are very presumptuous, but that's not what I meant, Private Evasive, as you well know. Where do we, you and I, go from here?"

They walked left, passing along the inside of the defences, where nervous sentries spared them a glance before concentrating on the dangers that could erupt at any minute. Somewhere in the lines of tents, men were singing:

'Down, down with French dishes, up, up with
roast beef.

Here's liberty, loyalty, aye, and roast beef.'

The words made Priscilla smile. "It sounds as if I'm in
England, yet I'm talking to a Scotsman in French Canada."

"You are. Where can we go?" MacKim continued their
conversation. "You are married."

"I don't love him."

That revelation shook MacKim. He had thought Priscilla and
Wooler to be very close. "He is a good man."

"I know, but I don't love him."

MacKim took a deep breath. At that second, he thought he
would rather face an attack by Ottowas and Canadians than
wrestle with his emotions. *No, I would not. Don't lie to yourself.*
When he looked at Priscilla, she was waiting for his response
with her face tilted toward him and her eyes challenging.

"Perhaps not," MacKim said, "but he is still your husband,
legally and morally."

Priscilla looked away, sighing. "I know," she said softly. "I
can't hurt him. He was so happy to tell me that you saved his life,
and I was so happy to see him alive."

"He is your husband." MacKim had an impulse to lift this
woman off her feet, throw her over her shoulder and run off into
the forest. He knew he could not, and he would not wish
Priscilla to love a man who would betray his friends, break his
oath and murder British soldiers. "Oh, God, Priscilla. What can
we do?"

"We can do nothing," Priscilla said hopelessly. "We are
trapped." They walked on for a few more steps, with the evening
drawing on. A lone piper played deep in the camp, the sound a
reminder of Scotland yet somehow fitting in this wild land.

MacKim desperately tried to think of something to say. With
his comrades, he could talk about the war and soldiering. He did
not believe these subjects would appeal to Priscilla. "Do you

know what they say about pipers? They say that a man's as proud as a bubbly-jock – that's a turkey – who is half as proud as a piper."

"Oh?" Priscilla looked at him without understanding.

"I have no conversation," MacKim admitted. "I'm sorry."

"I can sometimes talk for hours," Priscilla said. "Tell me about yourself."

"There is little to tell," MacKim said. "I am now a corporal in Fraser's Highlanders."

"You speak English." Priscilla was desperate for something to say. "Until I met you, I thought Highlanders only spoke Gaelic."

"I speak both languages," MacKim said. He strove to sound interesting, knowing that soon he would be ordered to his tent. Free time was a precious commodity for a soldier. "And a little French. How did you get out here? It's a long way from Fort Stanwix."

"I came by wagon and on foot," Priscilla said. "Is that drums I hear?"

"Yes," MacKim touched her arm. "They're calling us to our tents. I must go."

"We need more time," Priscilla said, desperately. "We have so much to discuss."

Now that the drums had signalled an end to the conversation, MacKim found a hundred things he wanted to say. Only one came to his lips. "I love you, Priscilla."

"Oh!" She looked at him, open-mouthed. "I know," she said. "I feel the same."

The temptation was too much. Despite the persistent tapping of the drums, despite the hectoring of a dozen sergeants and the cold stares of a nearby officer, MacKim took Priscilla in his arms. He held her close, wishing he could hold her forever and kissed her once.

"You must go." Priscilla pushed him away. "You'll get into trouble."

"Take care," MacKim said. "Please take care of yourself."

"Go!" Priscilla gave him a little push. "Go quickly."

MacKim ran back to his tent, stopping twice to look over his shoulder. Priscilla waited, watching him in that place of brutal men. When he looked back for the third time, she still stood there, with one hand raised in farewell. Then a rush of infantrymen passed between them, and MacKim saw her no more.

❧ 19 ❧

FRENCH CANADA, JULY 1759

"I have a request, sir." MacKim stood at attention, acutely aware that it was unusual for a mere corporal to approach an officer directly. He hoped that Captain Cameron's leniency extended to such an imposition.

"What is it, MacKim?" Cameron waved a hand to calm down a nearby indignant sergeant.

"I wish to visit the hospital at the Île D'Orléans, sir." MacKim knew he could be flogged for approaching an officer, and his request might be taken as an opportunity to desert.

"Why?" Cameron was instantly suspicious.

"I have a friend there, sir. A Ranger named Wooler."

Cameron's frown cleared. "Oh, yes. I remember you brought him back from the forest."

"Yes, sir."

"Sergeant Dingwall!" Cameron had no sooner shouted than Dingwall appeared at his side, frowning at MacKim.

"Sir!"

"Corporal MacKim wishes to visit a man in the hospital. Can he be trusted?"

Dingwall eyed MacKim for a long moment before he replied. "Yes, sir."

"Then send him to the hospital, Sergeant." Nodding, Cameron turned on his heel and marched away.

"You heard Captain Cameron, MacKim. Go to the hospital, find out how many of our men are sick and report back to me." He lowered his voice. "And if I hear of you approaching an officer again without asking my permission, I'll have you at the halberds, and I'll see your backbone, by Christ, corporal or no corporal!"

"Yes, Sergeant." MacKim nodded. Although flogging was virtually unknown in Fraser's Highlanders, MacKim knew that Dingwall's was no idle threat. Such punishment was common in other British regiments, with sentences of hundreds of lashes reducing men to crippled wrecks. He was risking a lot to see a wounded Ranger, and for the hope of a few stolen moments with that man's wife.

MacKim found the hospital in a church at the tip of the Île D'Orléans, with scurrying wives, and women who called themselves wives, looking after the sick and wounded. After obeying Dingwall's orders to count the men of the 78th, MacKim found Wooler lying on a stained cot. The stench from infected wounds and men with diarrhoea or other complaints was sickening.

"Good afternoon, Ranger." MacKim knelt beside him. "How are you?"

"MacKim!" Wooler was pale and gaunt, with dark shadows under his eyes. "You saved my life."

"How are they treating you here?" MacKim noted the bloody rags that swathed Wooler's chest. "Should these not be changed?"

"Priscilla changed them yesterday," Wooler said. "Thank you for coming." He gripped MacKim's arm with hands so thin they were like claws.

"Are they looking after you well?" MacKim struggled for something to say.

"We have milk from cows captured from the French, plenty

of spruce beer to fight scurvy and Pricilla comes to see me." His smile stretched the taut skin over his cheekbones and jaw.

"You're a lucky man having such a devoted wife," MacKim said. "Now, let's get you more comfortable. I'll see if I can find some fresh bandages and clean bedding as well. Is there anything you want?"

"Water," Wooler said. "I'd like a drink of water and some fresh air."

"Fresh air is bad for you," MacKim said. "Sick people should be kept indoors."

"Please," Wooler said. "I need to breathe. I can't breathe properly in here."

"It's dangerous..."

"Please, Hugh, I want to breathe."

MacKim coughed in the foetid air and nodded. "Come on then, Jacob. Let me support you."

Rather than immediately kill Wooler off, draughts of fresh Canadian air seemed to revive him. He took a deep breath. "Thank you, Hugh." His eyes showed nothing but gratitude. "I was stifling in there."

"You wait here," MacKim said. "I'll find a new bandage for your wound."

The hospital was fortunate in that the Navy kept it supplied with medical supplies, so MacKim had little difficulty in finding bandages. When he returned, Priscilla was sitting beside Wooler. She looked up, smiling. "Jacob told me you were here, Hugh."

"I was getting him bandages." MacKim hoped that Wooler could not sense his feelings for Priscilla.

"That's not a job for a soldier." Priscilla stretched out a hand. "I'll take them. Come on, Hugh."

MacKim watched as Priscilla stripped Wooler's bandages. The wound was clean if slightly inflamed. "That's healing well."

"We're tough out on the frontier," Priscilla said. "We're used to wounds, cuts and broken bones. The ball went right through, which made things easier."

"Is she not the best of wives?" Wooler asked, as Priscilla washed the wound with clean water and expertly tied a bandage around it.

"You're a lucky man, Jacob," MacKim hated himself for wanting to hold Priscilla close.

"Once this war is over and the Indians are back in Canada," Wooler said, "you'll have to stay with us. Maybe leave the army and settle nearby?"

MacKim felt a lurch in his stomach. The thought of living near to Priscilla without being able to touch her was more than he could bear; it would be a form of exquisite torture. "Thank you. I would like that, if the army allows me to leave."

When the war was over? Wars last for many years, and I still have to account for Hitchins. Why is life so complicated?

"I am a fortunate man," Wooler said. "Having you two."

Oh yes, fortunate with a friend who is in love with your wife.

MacKim patted his shoulder. "Don't you hurry to recover, Jacob. If you are truly a fortunate man, the war will be over before you're fit to fight again."

Wooler smiled. "Do you think you can defeat the French without my help?"

"You've done your bit, Jacob. Once we've humbled the French, they won't be able to encourage the Indians to attack, and the frontier will be a much safer place."

"I hope so," Priscilla said. "Oh, I do hope so."

"You two!" An army surgeon appeared, frowning beneath an untidy wig. "What's that man doing out of the hospital?"

"He needed to breathe some clean air, sir." MacKim stood to attention.

"You should know that cold air could be fatal. Take that man back inside." The surgeon glowered at MacKim. "You Sawnies are worse than the blasted savages." He stormed away, stopped to sip at a bottle and stomped back inside the hospital. A few moments later, a couple of orderlies came to recapture Wooler.

"I'd better get back to the regiment," MacKim said. "I'm meant to be checking our sick and wounded."

Wooler lifted his left hand. "Thank you for coming, Hugh."

"I'll see Hugh on a boat, Jacob, and come back to you," Priscilla said.

More casualties congested the hospital as they left, a constant trickle of men with minor wounds or fevers of various kinds.

"They never stop coming," Priscilla said.

"Are you here all the time?" MacKim asked.

"I work here," Priscilla said. "A lot of the wives do. It justifies our existence and helps keep the men a bit more comfortable, if nothing else."

They stopped at a small copse of trees a few yards from the landing stage.

"Hugh," Priscilla slipped her hand into his. "Kiss me, Hugh."

No, I can't betray Jacob.

MacKim shook his head. "Priscilla." The temptation was too great. MacKim bent forward, with his lips brushing those of Priscilla. He moved away quickly. "There."

"That was hardly a kiss."

"It was a betrayal." MacKim stepped back as self-loathing battled with a desire to kiss Priscilla again, to hold her close and take her away forever. "I should not have done it."

"But you did do it," Priscilla said. "And we're going to do much more." Taking hold of MacKim's sleeve, she guided him away from the hospital.

"No." MacKim thought of Wooler, lying wounded as his wife lay with a man he considered a friend. *I'm a murderer, but I won't betray a friend.*

"Hugh." Priscilla stared at him. "I told you that I don't love him."

"He's still your husband," MacKim said roughly. Turning away, he strode toward the nearest boat.

"Hugh!" Priscilla followed after him, wading knee-deep into the water. "I don't care!"

"Priscilla." MacKim felt as if something was tearing his heart out. "We can't."

"I'll wait," Priscilla said. "I'll wait, Hugh."

MacKim saw her step deeper into the water as the seamen plied their oars. *Oh, God,* he prayed. *Please let Jacob die.*

❦ 20 ❦

FRENCH CANADA, JULY 1759

"What date is it?" Cumming asked as they slumped into their tent after a nerve-shredding night manning a stockade.

"God only knows," Chisholm said. "July the somethingth, I think."

"We're no closer to Quebec than we were a month ago," Cumming said. "All we're doing is chopping down trees and losing men to the savages."

"Aye, even the Navy can't breach the French defences," Chisholm said. "Maybe Pikestaff has lost this one."

"Winter comes early out here," Cumming reminded them. "Every day the French in Quebec hold out is a small victory for them. I don't fancy our chances if we have to overwinter here in the deep snow."

"It's only July," MacKim said. "Winter is months away." Yet within him, he felt a twinge of hope. If the regiment overwintered in Fort Stanwix, he might see Priscilla again. It was a faint hope, but enough to send a tingle through him.

Do I want to see her? How about Jacob? And what about my oath? Hitchins is still alive and within the walls of Quebec. I can't do anything as long as he is above ground, but even if I manage to kill Hitchins, Priscilla is married.

The competing thoughts plagued MacKim as he lay in his narrow cot within the crowded tent. What could he do?

I must fulfil my oath. I must avenge Ewan. After that, I can turn to other things. After that, I can concentrate on Priscilla.

"Corporal MacKim!" Chisholm was standing over him, shaking him awake. "It's reveille. Can't you hear the drums, man?"

Staggering into the pre-dawn dark, MacKim took his place at the head of his section. A thin drizzle smeared the camp, adding to the misery of the surrounding woodland and the knowledge that the British attack on Quebec had stalled.

"We're moving, Corporal," Chisholm murmured, out of the corner of his mouth. "Pikestaff himself is leading us."

The mention of Wolfe stimulated MacKim's interest. Wolfe would not be here for a mere raid.

Together with Otway's 35th Regiment and a company of Rangers, the 78th's Lights joined another five Light companies and two six-pounder cannon deep into the woods. "We're heading for the ford well upstream of the Falls," a laconic Ranger said. "Wolfey is getting impatient, I fear."

"Are we going to cross over?" Chisholm asked.

"As to that, only God and Pikestaff knows," the Ranger said. "And neither of them tells me anything."

MacKim grunted. "The quicker we take Quebec, the better pleased I will be."

"The quicker we take Quebec, the better pleased everybody will be," the Ranger said. "Except for the French."

Once again, MacKim watched and listened for the enemy, yet also heard the sounds behind him as the central column blundered slowly onward with infantrymen straining to drag the artillery.

"Bloody artillery," Cumming grumbled. "It takes dozens of

men to move the things in this woodland. They're just an attraction for the savages."

Wolfe seemed to agree for, soon after Cumming's words, an order came from above. "These blasted guns are slowing us down. Send them back!"

Lighter of burden and firepower, the column moved faster into the trees.

"Let's hope the Frenchies haven't any redoubts ahead," Cumming said. "We'll miss the guns then."

"It's alright, Cumming," MacKim said. "If we come across any, I'll send you up first. Your constant moaning will soon make the French flee."

About four in the morning, the first of the expected ambushes occurred. There was the usual crackle of musketry from unseen opponents, the sudden acrid sting of powder smoke and the wild war-whoops of the tribesmen.

"Steady, boys." Half seen in the dark, the closest Ranger eased into cover and readied his rifle.

The Indians launched themselves on the most forward Light Infantry piquet, with the Highlanders and Rangers quickly moving forward in a counter-attack. Before MacKim could lead his section to the spot, the affair was over, with one dead and one wounded Light Infantryman and an Indian left gasping on the ground. The Ranger slit the Indian's throat and scalped him.

"That's a fine trophy for my belt," he said casually, as the Lights watched dispassionately.

The column moved on cautiously, with the Lights and Rangers probing deeper into the woods, occasionally seeing the flitting forms of Indians or Canadians, firing when they could and ensuring they did not present a target or stray far from support.

Cattanach fired at an elusive shadow and stopped to reload. "Missed him. Why can't they stand and fight like men?"

"They are fighting as they have always fought," the Ranger said.

"They are cowards," Cattanach said.

"No." The Ranger shook his head. "I don't agree with standing in line to get shot at, either. I've got a family to get home to."

After a year in North America, MacKim agreed with the Ranger's sentiments. He could appreciate the bravery of men standing in line to exchange fire with the enemy, but why should they throw away their lives for a king who cared nothing for them?

The Lights moved on, step after step into the forest, until the roaring of the Falls was far behind them and the quieter murmur of the river in front.

"Here's the ford," the Ranger said. "Now it's up to Wolfey to do something to defeat the French."

At that minute, MacKim was not sure the general could do anything. The river ran swiftly across the ford with dawn sunlight casting dappled shadows on the water. On the surface, it seemed peaceful until MacKim looked to the other side, where formidable entrenchments and timber redoubts glowered at them, with the tricorne hats of French regulars visible above the parapets. Behind the defences, the ground rose steeply, hard to attack and easy to defend.

"Where are those guns when we need them?" Cumming whispered.

"Montcalm must have expected our attack," Chisholm said. "So far, the French have countered every move we have made."

MacKim checked to ensure that morning dew had not dampened his musket flint. "As you said before, James, war is like a game of chess, and we are the expendable pawns."

"I hope Wolfey does not expect us to charge over the ford onto the redoubts," the Ranger said.

"So do I." Fingering his bayonet, MacKim peered across the river. One tall Frenchman had climbed the parapet to scan the British side through a spyglass. "It will be a miniature Ticonderoga once more." The previous year, Montgomery's Highlanders had attacked the French at Fort Ticonderoga, only for the defenders to repulse them with great slaughter.

"I wish we had kept the guns," Cumming said.

"Hush. Here comes Pikestaff."

Slender and seemingly very fragile, Wolfe resembled his nickname as he stepped close to the water's edge, with his bodyguard of tall Grenadiers around him.

Immediately Wolfe appeared, the French opened fire, a rolling fusillade that raised fountains of water from the river, ripped bark from the trees and flicked half a dozen leaves from their branches.

"The Frenchies don't seem pleased to see our Pikestaff." Chisholm said.

Wolfe stepped back quickly as powder smoke temporarily concealed the French redoubt.

"Permission to fire back, sir?" Sergeant Dingwall pushed forward as Captain Cameron stepped toward them.

"Yes, fire away, Sergeant. Keep the devils' heads down."

The Ranger fired immediately, sending the Frenchman with the spyglass back with a bullet through his shoulder. "Got you, Jacques!"

Lying or kneeling under cover, the Light Infantry and Rangers fired, aiming each shot and grunting in satisfaction when they thought they had scored a hit. The French regulars replied with volley fire.

"How many French are there?" Cumming asked.

"A few hundred, perhaps," Chisholm said. "I wonder if Pikestaff wishes to draw out the entire French army for a general engagement?"

"Not here, I hope," MacKim said. "In these woods, the French Indians will have the advantage over our infantry. Maybe the general hopes to bring the army over the ford and march onto Quebec."

"Bring ten thousand men through the forest and over the river?" Cumming spat tobacco juice on the ground. "We could not drag up a couple of six-pounders! The Indians and Canadians would snipe us to pieces!"

Sighting on the tricorne hat of a French infantryman, MacKim fired across the river, grunted when he knew he missed and hastily reloaded. One Frenchmen more or less would make no difference to the outcome of this war. Kneeling behind an overhanging bough, he aimed again just his target stood up. For a second, MacKim looked directly at the Frenchman, or rather, at the man in the French uniform. The face had aged over the years but was unmistakable, still with those nervous, mobile eyes.

"Hitchins!" The shock made MacKim jerk the trigger so although he had a clear shot, the ball flew well wide. He swore, reloaded and swore again when he realised that Hitchins had vanished.

"I hope Pikestaff gives us the order to attack!" MacKim said. Suddenly, capturing Quebec was unimportant. As memories of that day at Drummossie flooded back, MacKim knew his oath superseded any political victories. He wanted to kill Hitchins far more than he cared about capturing Quebec.

"You fire-eater!" Captain Cameron said. "That's what we like to hear, keen men in the regiment!" The lieutenant looked closer. "Oh, I remember you, Corporal! You're the man who was concerned about his friend in the hospital! You're that MacKim fellow who shares my Christian name!"

"Yes, sir!" MacKim stiffened to attention.

"At ease, man! If you stand erect here, the Frenchies will pink you, sure as death, and they'll also know I'm an officer and shoot me, too!" Cameron laughed out loud, a strange thing to hear in the middle of a battle. "Now, do your duty and allow the general to make the decisions. Us lowly soldiers are here to obey orders, not to decide tactics."

"Yes, sir." MacKim fought his desire to salute. Glancing across the river, he could no longer see Hitchins. Thick powder smoke obscured the French redoubt as they fired another volley.

Now I know you are still alive, Hitchins, and I know where you are hiding. I'm coming for you, I'm going to get you and then I am free. Then I can pursue Priscilla instead. Except that she is married. Oh, God, what should I do?

MacKim heard the firing and war-whoops from his left a few moments before a rag-tag of Light Infantry appeared, running in panic. "All is lost!" one young ensign yelled, as he scurried into the 78th position. Wide-eyed, and lacking his hat, he approached Captain Cameron. "The savages are upon us."

"Calm yourself!" Cameron grabbed the youth by his shoulder and turned him around. "You're a British officer, not some schoolboy! Get back to your men where you belong!"

"The savages!" the ensign repeated.

Watching through narrowed eyes, the men of the 78th shook their collective heads.

"The poor wee bugger's lost his nerve," Chisholm said.

"Stand ready, 78th." Lieutenant Cameron was as calm as if he was on the parade ground in Inverness. "It seems as if the men on our left have collapsed. The Highlanders will prepare to receive an attack."

A couple of years previously, an attack by Indians on a column of British redcoats would have spread panic. The tactics were unexpected, the enemy unrelenting and the surprise total. Now the British were veterans. They knew what they were facing and had scores to settle with the tribesmen and Canadians. The 78th stamped their nailed shoes on the ground, checked their muskets and waited for the enemy.

"Tree all!" The command had the Lights sliding into cover.

A straggle of British infantry still scrambled from the left flank, some hatless, others having thrown away their muskets. One man screamed as an Indian crashed a tomahawk on his arm.

"Steady, the 78th!" Cameron shouted.

"There are hundreds of the buggers," Chisholm said, as the tribesmen followed the panicking redcoats, their near-naked bodies visible through the trees as they fired and moved, or threw the vicious tomahawks at those British soldiers they could see.

"Fire!" Cameron ordered.

The Light Infantry dodged behind trees and fired when they saw a target, supporting each other and loading as quickly as they could.

"The savages are attacking Otway's 35th," Chisholm said. "Now we'll see how good they are."

MacKim expected Otway's 35th Foot to either break under the Indian assault or form the traditional British line. Instead, they fixed bayonets and advanced, shouting challenges.

"Come on, Otway's! Show them the bayonet!"

The two sides clashed among the trees, with both British and Indian casualties. Not used to fighting an enemy who met them head-on, the tribesmen began to withdraw.

"After them, 78th! Don't let Otway's grab all the glory!"

MacKim plunged forward with the rest. He saw one tribesman, fired a snapshot and stopped to load while Chisholm remained to cover him.

"Don't stop, Corporal!" Captain Cameron had his broadsword in his hand. "Push them back!"

"Come on, my lads!" Fixing his bayonet, MacKim led his section forward, brushing aside branches as he pursued the elusive enemy. He did not see another Indian until they reached a ford further upstream.

"That was hot." Chisholm fired a parting shot at the enemy as they vanished into the forest beyond the ford.

"And costly," MacKim said. "We must have lost dozens of men."

"We chased them away, though. We've got the savages' measure now. There'll be no more Fort William Henry's, by God!" Chisholm indicated the panting men of the 35th. "Whoever thought that ordinary British infantry could best the savages in their own environment?"

"Who indeed?" MacKim gave an answer he hoped was appropriate as he stared across the river. *Come on, Pikestaff, send us over the river. Let loose the leash and I will find Hitchins.*

Rather than launching his army across the ford, General Wolfe withdrew. He had reconnoitred above and below Quebec and found both flanks of the city strongly held. His artillery was steadily pounding the city to rubble, and powerful foraging parties of British soldiers were terrorising the civilians, denuding the local French settlers of their food stocks. Yet General Montcalm, the French commander, retained his larger army and sat securely behind the defences of Quebec.

"As long as the French army is intact, Montcalm holds the king in this game of chess." Chisholm puffed on his pipe as they sat outside the British tents. "Wolfe has to checkmate the king, not dabble with the pawns, and every day brings us closer to winter. If we withdraw for the season, next year the French will have this place so heavily fortified that a skinny mouse won't be able to ascend the river. We have to capture Quebec soon, or the French will win this North American war."

MacKim nodded. "We have to take the town." He remembered the look on Hitchins' face, the mobile, scared eyes that hid underlying cruelty he would never forget. "We have to conquer Canada."

I don't give a two-penny damn if we conquer Canada, leave it to the French or hand it over to the Abenaki tribesmen, as long as I find Hitchins.

"We will," Chisholm said. "Just have patience."

MacKim glanced upwards. *If we don't take Quebec by the winter, I will desert to the French, hunt down Hitchins, kill him, and run. I'll take my chances in the forest with the Indians, make my way to the British colonies and decide what to do. Priscilla said she will wait for me.*

Once again, that vision entered his mind, walking up Glen Cailleach with Priscilla at his side and his mother waiting for him in the cosy clachan of Achtriachan under the shelter of An Cailleach.

FRENCH CANADA, JULY 1759

The fire blazed from end to end of the river, slowly approaching the ships of the British fleet. Yellow flames rose from an orange base, licking higher as they crept closer, with the reek of smoke sending the sentinels into racking coughs.

"That's not fireships," Cattanach said.

"They've set the river on fire," Cumming stared. "I've never seen anything like it before."

As the flames rose ever higher, the awed British had a better picture of what was happening.

"They're fire rafts," Chisholm said.

The French had built a hundred rafts, loaded them with timber and anything else that could burn, roped them together and floated them downriver.

"The Navy will tow them away like they did last time." Chisholm spoke with confidence.

MacKim nodded. "I hope you're right, James."

Cumming shook his head. "There's too many rafts for that to work We'll lose the ships, and be trapped here. Montcalm will send in his Indians and Canadians until we surrender. That's the end of our war, boys."

"You're a cheery bugger, Cumming, aren't you?" MacKim pushed him away. "Go and check the ammunition. Count the musket balls or weigh the powder – in fact, do anything as long as it's far away from me."

By the light of the flames, MacKim could see a score of small boats approaching the fire-rafts as the Navy attempted to counter the threat. He started at the explosion when a French booby-trap blew up, instantly killing a Royal Navy crew.

"Jesus! Poor buggers! What a way to go!" Chisholm crossed himself.

"At least it was quick," MacKim said.

Refusing to be intimidated by the danger, the seamen rowed out, grappled the fire-rafts and towed them away from the British ships. The sailor's voices drifted to MacKim above the terrible crackle of the flames.

"All's well," they shouted to one another.

"Bugger but it's hot, my boys!"

"Damn me, Jack," somebody yelled, "didst thee ever take hell in tow before?"

One by one, the seamen dealt with the fire rafts, braving the heat and the explosives to save the fleet and the entire expedition. The Army could only watch, pray and bless the Navy.

MacKim took a deep breath, coughed as the smoke entered his lungs and recovered. "Thank God for the Navy."

"Well now," Chisholm said, calmly, "Montcalm has used his knights to attack our bishops. I wonder how Wolfe will respond. Will he continue battering at the town with Saint Barbara's daughters, send in the pawns, use his nautical bishops again, or muster the castles? We have no mounted knights in this terrain."

"Surely the French have the castle." Cumming sounded confused. "What do you mean? I don't know what you mean."

"Our knights are cavalry, my young apprentice soldier," Chisholm said. "Our seamen with their doughty ships are the bishops, we are the pawns and the Grenadiers, our loud-mouthed heavy infantry, are the castles."

"I don't understand," Cumming said.

"Have you ever played chess?" MacKim asked.

"What's chess?" Cumming asked. "I used to play shinty."

"Chess is a board game, centuries-old,"Chisholm explained. "It came from India to Persia and spread across Europe."

"How do you know these things?" Cumming asked. 'You're only a private like us, yet you think you know everything."

"If I knew everything," Chisholm said, "I would not be here, ugly as the devil's arse, cowering behind an earthwork in the middle of a wilderness. I would be sitting on a velvet cushion in a grand house with a hundred servants pandering to my whims." He lay back, puffing on his pipe and sending reeking smoke around. "I would have a dozen naked women running after me, a score of horses from a long blood-line, a fine carriage and six and never again would I hear Sergeant Dingwall roaring at me to stand to attention."

Cumming grinned. "Could I come and visit?"

"You could come for as long as you liked, Cumming, and bring your family as well."

"How about Corporal MacKim? Could he come too?"

Chisholm eyed MacKim. "Not yet," he said slowly. "MacKim won't wish to come until he completes his duty. Then he can come, and welcome."

Cumming grinned over to MacKim. "You see, MacKim? Chisholm likes me better than you."

"I know he does," MacKim agreed at once. "He always tells me that. So, as Cumming asks, Chisholm, how are you so clever?"

"I am no cleverer than you lads are, or I would not be beside you. Knowing facts does not make one clever." For one moment, MacKim saw Chisholm's mask drop and the real man appeared beneath. He was shocked at the depth of sadness, amounting nearly to despair that he saw there. *What history do you have, James Chisholm? Why did a man with your knowledge join the army?*

On the 31ST July, the drummers' rapid staccato called the Light Infantry to muster.

"Come on, boys!" MacKim moved along the line, kicking at feet to wake the laggards, encouraging the reluctant, nodding to the keen. "We're moving again!"

"Where are we going?" Cumming asked.

"Wherever King George commands," MacKim said, happy to be doing something, anything, to further the siege.

Led by Lieutenant Colonel Howe, the Light Infantry marched from the safety of the camp at Montmorency and hurried along the bank of the river.

As they left, MacKim saw the pioneers and artillerymen dragging the camp's artillery toward the lip of the cliffs, aiming toward the entrenched French.

Don't kill Hitchins, MacKim said. *I want him. Leave him to me. I want to watch him die.*

"Sing, boys," Captain Cameron ordered. "Let the French know where we are. Let them know the Light Bobs are coming for them."

"*Sing?*" Cumming shook his head. "It's already hot enough to melt Old Hornie's tail, and the captain wants us to sing!"

"So sing, Cumming" MacKim said.

Captain Cameron's voice sounded again. "Follow my words, boys. Sergeant Ned Botwood of Lascelle's Foot wrote this song. It's in English so some of you may find it hard. If you're not sure, hum!"

MacKim glared at his men, ensuring they were all listening as Cameron broke into song.

'Come, each death-doing dog that dares venture
    his neck,
Come follow the hero that goes to Quebec;

Jump aboard of the transports, and loose every
sail,
Pay your debts at the taverns by giving leg-bail.'

By now, most of the Highlanders spoke at least some English and joined in the song, some reluctantly, others with enthusiasm as they marched and slithered along by the bank of the river.

"The Indians must think we are all crazy," Cumming grumbled as he mumbled the words.

"We are crazy," Chisholm said. "Think about it. Hundreds of Scottish Highlanders, Irishmen, Welshmen, Englishmen and American Colonials, marching beside a river in French Canada, singing a song while hoping not to fight the French or Indians."

"Why are we here?" Cumming asked.

"Because it's our job," Chisholm said. "This is the life we chose, and may God help us."

"Come on, lads! Sing up! Let Johnny François know we're here!" Captain Cameron continued, with his voice ringing free.

'And ye that love fighting shall soon have enough
Wolfe commands us, my boys; we shall give them
Hot Stuff.'

As the Light infantry marched in the sunlight, Cumming asked why they were singing. "You'll know, MacKim, now that you're a corporal!"

"Ask the colonel, for I'm sure I don't know," MacKim said. "Something's in the wind, though. Maybe we're finally going to attack Quebec."

"It's a feint," Chisholm said. "I said a few days ago that Wolfe would reply to the fire rafts. I guess that we're the deception to fool the French. For sure as heaven, if we were going to the attack, we would not be singing like men from bedlam. Anyway, we only have a colonel in charge of us. If we were the main force, it would be a brigadier at least, or Pikestaff himself."

"So where is the main force then, Chisholm?" Cumming asked.

"If I knew that, Cumming, I'd be an officer and sleep on a soft bed." Chisholm swore as he stumbled over a trailing root. "You'll remember that the Grenadier companies were taken away yesterday, so I'd wager all your wages that Pikestaff is leading them somewhere."

"Listen!" MacKim lifted a hand as he heard the booming of artillery. "That's not the normal siege guns." Months of experience in listening to the pounding of Quebec had made MacKim expert in gauging the sound of artillery. "There are far more cannon involved."

"That must be the real assault going in," Chisholm said.

MacKim fought his frustration. He knew that even if he did take part in the final attack on Quebec, it was unlikely he would ever see Hitchins again, yet out here in the woods, he felt very far from his goal. Hitchins may desert again, or a shell may blow him to unrecognisable fragments, or the army could capture him and transport him back to Great Britain as a prisoner. In any of these scenarios, MacKim knew that fate would cheat him of his revenge.

As his frustration mounted, MacKim stamped his feet down harder. He heard the cannon fire increase and imagined that Wolfe was fighting a major battle while they marched up and down. "We're wasting our time here!"

"We're not." Chisholm shook his head. "We're holding back the French from sending reinforcements, tying down their men and keeping them guessing."

"I hope Wolfey has flattened their defences and captured bloody Quebec," Cattanach said. "Then we can go home."

It was not until hours later that MacKim learned that Wolfe had led an attack across the North Channel of the St Lawrence, in which everything possible had gone wrong. When the boats had run aground in shallow water, the Grenadiers had to wade through deep mud to get ashore while the French and Canadian militia fired at them from a redoubt. Forgetting their discipline, the Grenadiers had charged forward without formation, and the French had shot them down by the score. Even so, the Grenadiers had taken the first French position and run onto the second. Only when they had lost hundreds of some of the best and boldest men in the army, did the Grenadiers reluctantly retreat.

Wolfe's second wave, including the bulk of the 78th Highlanders, was ready to continue the attack, but with the casualties piled high and hundreds of French, Canadians and Indians entrenched at the head of a slope made more slippery with blood and drenching rain, even Wolfe decided that success was impossible.

Frustrated and angry, the British had glared at their enemy at the head of the sodden slope as they withdrew.

"That was a fair victory for the Frenchies," Chisholm was recounting details of the battle to the others in the tent, "and well done to them, the rogues." His face darkened. "Then they showed their true colours, and God rot them for the worst parcel of black-hearted villains that the devil ever set on this earth."

"What happened?" MacKim asked.

"As the Grenadiers retreated, including our Highland lads, they left their casualties on the slope." Chisholm shook his head. "That happens in every battle. The normal practice is for the enemy take the wounded prisoner and look after them."

"And?" MacKim was growing impatient.

"As soon as the Grenadiers retreated, a horde of Indians rushed down for scalps. They scalped the dead and killed and mutilated the wounded."

MacKim grunted. "That sort of thing seems to happen after battles as well."

"Civilised armies don't do that," Chisholm said.

"'No, you're right. Civilised men don't torture, mutilate and murder the wounded of the enemy. That is the work of brute barbarians."

"There is a silver lining to the French cloud. A couple of companies of the 78th advanced to fend off the Indians and rescue as many wounded as they could. I heard some French nuns helped as well."

"Well done, the nuns." Cattanach crossed himself.

"One good thing came of it," Chisholm said. "We enhanced our reputation. Fraser's Highlanders were last away. The French were firing volleys and artillery, but Fraser's withdrew in good order." Chisholm raised his head. "Next time," he vowed, "next time, we'll pay them back for the scalping. A reverse is part of war, it's part of the soldier's bargain, but scalping and murdering the wounded..." He shook his head. "These French bastards have gone too far now. They've put iron into our souls."

As news of this latest atrocity spread around the British camps, men muttered in angry groups, vowing vengeance on the French. "We've got to beat the bastards now," Cattanach said. "Murdering rascals."

Nobody mentioned the British shore parties that burned and looted the French settlements along the St Lawrence. MacKim grunted, said nothing and nursed the fires of bitter hatred within him. He thought of Ewan, and of Hitchins, and sharpened his bayonet.

Defeat hung bitter on the British camp. Men polished their muskets and glowered across at the smoking walls of Quebec, inside which the enemy waited. Others muttered dire promises of what they would do when they had the French at their mercy. Only a very few voiced their fears of eventual defeat.

"We'd better leave now," Cumming said. "We can't get them on the flanks, and they threw back our Grenadiers, the best we have. How can we defeat them?"

"It was a reverse." MacKim used his new rank. "It was an ugly reverse but nothing more. Shut your mouth, private, do your duty and allow Pikestaff to do his."

"Yes, Corporal!" Cumming's expression showed his contempt.

"We'll take Quebec," MacKim said. "By the living Christ, we will." The thought of the army sailing away, leaving Hitchins alive in Canada, was something he could not contemplate.

As the French celebrated their victory with a flurry of Bourbon flags, the British prepared for the next encounter. Wolfe had the men further strengthen the defences of the camp beside the Falls, but all the time the days began to shorten. The ferocious Canadian winter loomed before them.

The men murmured amongst themselves, as another rumour spread that Indians had captured three Grenadiers and slowly burned them to death. Rather than spread fear among the soldiers, the story created anger and a terrible desire for revenge. Wolfe was as affected as any of his men and issued a written order:

"The general strictly forbids the inhuman practice of scalping, except when the enemies are Indians, or Canadians dressed like Indians."

"We are falling into the abyss," Chisholm said. "We are losing our civilisation step by certain step. Only blackness remains, and the torments of the pit."

"It matters not, because the campaigning season is fading," Cumming said. "We'll soon be heading back to Louisbourg or Halifax."

"Aye," MacKim said. "Once we've taken Quebec."

I'm not going to Louisbourg. I know where Hitchins is hiding. I've seen his face. I will kill that man.

❧ 22 ❧

FRENCH CANADA, AUGUST 1759

"We're wanted again." Chisholm stood at the entrance to the tent. "Brigadier Murray is leading us on a raid, upriver towards Trois-Rivières this time."

"Why?" Cumming asked. "What good are raids? We're not going to take Quebec. All we're doing is burning houses and losing men to ambushes. We should go back to Louisbourg and try again next year."

"Ask Pikestaff, for I don't know." Chisholm ignored Cumming. "Maybe he hopes to lure Montcalm into a general engagement."

"Montcalm's no fool," MacKim said. "He'll counter with his Indians and Canadians. This expedition will be another waste of time." All the same, he felt a tinge of interest. At least a raid was better than singing through the woods while the Grenadiers threw themselves noisily at French redoubts.

"Wolfe says that the 78th is one of his best regiments," Chisholm said. "We are known for our skill and fighting ability."

"King George might accept us, then," Cumming said. "Highlanders will be seen as loyal British subjects."

MacKim checked his flints. "Maybe." He did not care what King George thought.

Murray's main striking force was Amherst's 15th Regiment, backed by three hundred men of the 60th Royal Americans, the green-jacketed colonial regiment that could compete even with the Rangers as forest fighters. The Light Infantry included the Lights of Fraser's Highlanders, while two hundred Royal Marines added their unique nautical swagger.

"Here we go again, Hugh," Chisholm said.

"Aye, once more." MacKim twisted his face into a smile. *I'm coming for you, Hitchins.*

They marched upstream through the rain, past the battered, defiant city of Quebec across the river before they boarded flat-bottomed boats on the St Lawrence.

"The Frenchies will be watching everything that we do," Cumming said.

"They can hardly miss us." MacKim indicated the fleet of boats filled with red-coated soldiers and nodded towards the north shore of the river. "Here they are now."

As the British rowed and sailed slowly upstream, a body of French infantry kept pace along the shore, with two troops of cavalry riding behind, the jingle of their accoutrements sinister across the shush of the river.

"I've never fought cavalry before," MacKim said.

"You might soon get your chance," Chisholm said. "If we do, make sure your section sticks together. Don't let the Frenchies break our formation, because there is nothing that cavalry like better than cutting up infantry."

MacKim watched the north shore of the river glide past. Rocky, with small cliffs, it did not invite a landing. Eventually, with the soldiers numb with boredom and the noise of the river never-ending, Captain Cameron lifted his voice.

"We're landing. Check your flints are sharp and your powder is dry."

They were about twenty miles above Quebec, with their target, two French floating batteries, moored by the shore.

"Into the boats, lads!" Captain Cameron ordered. "Double!"

"Here we go again," Chisholm said, as they filed into the ship's boats that would transport them from the barges to the shore. And then they did nothing. The boats sat idle in the current, with the banks of the St Lawrence tempting before them and a faint mist drifting between the trees.

"What are we waiting for?" MacKim rapped the butt of his musket on the deck in frustration.

"We're waiting for the tide to ebb, you lubber," a laughing seaman said. "When it goes down, there will be a bit of a beach for you to land on, out of range of the French muskets."

MacKim nodded. It still seemed strange having a tidal river so far from the sea. He looked toward the shore, where the landing place was becoming more visible by the minute, a gap between the rocks and dense woodland. Birds called, their sound sweet in the crisp air, a reminder that nature survived even amid never-ending war.

"Wait for the signal." Captain Cameron gestured to Brigadier Murray, who stood on the quarterdeck of HMS *Sutherland*. A minute later, Murray waved his hat, and the boats pulled for the shore.

"Here we go, lads," Captain Cameron said. "Remember your training, keep together if the cavalry attack, support your companions and may God go with us."

As soon as the boats were clear, HMS *Sutherland* loosed a tremendous broadside which poured dense white smoke over the surface of the river and blasted the floating batteries and the area around the landing place.

"That will keep the French at bay!" Chisholm said with satisfaction. "Thank God for the Navy!"

With the seamen hauling at the oars, the boats surged toward the shore. "Rocks ahead, boys," the sailors warned. "We can't get right up to the beach. You'll have to get into the water and wade."

Although the shore was still three hundred yards away, the keel of MacKim's boat grated over a rock, slid free and thrust into mud.

"That's as far as we go, kilty-cold-bums!" the seamen shouted. "All out!"

MacKim jumped into thigh-deep water and began to wade ashore with his feet sinking into mud. He saw the ghostly white shapes of French infantrymen among the trees and grunted as they opened fire.

"Amateurs. They're well out of range. It will be a lucky shot that hits anything from three hundred yards." He nodded well ahead, where a small splash showed where a spent musket ball landed. "You see? A little thing like that won't hurt."

"Where are the other boats?" Cumming looked around. "We're the only ones in the water!"

Glancing over his shoulder, Chisholm nodded. "They're held up by the reefs, Cumming. They'll be here by-and-by."

"Wade ashore," Captain Cameron ordered. "We can't wait here! Come on, 78th!"

There was more cannon fire from the ships, with the small boats also firing the swivel guns in their bows to support the 78th.

"We're all alone," Cumming repeated.

One of the Highlanders grunted and fell under the French fire. The man's body floated on top of the water with his kilt ballooning around his waist and a thin swirl of blood flowing from his chest.

"Keep moving." Cameron surged three yards in front. "The others will join us soon."

The French fire increased as the Highlanders drew closer to the beach.

"Come on!" MacKim powered forward. He could not see

individual faces through the powder-smoke, only the smear of white uniforms and the dull green foliage.

"Corporal MacKim! Keep formation! We're not the blasted Grenadiers!"

"You heard the officer, lads! Stay together!"

The 78th pushed on into the French musketry and toward the waiting cavalry. Ignoring the shots that pattered around him, Captain Cameron reached dry land. "Come on, 78th!" He peered over his shoulder. "We're first again, Highlanders. What the devil are these others playing at?"

"I think they're shy of the French, sir," Chisholm said.

"Well, we're not. Form into a square and wait for supports. We can't take on the whole damned French army alone." It was unusual for Cameron to sound annoyed.

"Their cavalry should swoop now," Chisholm said, "when there are not many of us. I think they're afraid of the Navy's guns."

"Stand fast, 78th," Cameron said. "Wait for my command."

After a tense half-hour, another boatload of Light Infantry joined them, and then a second, while most of the landing force tested the river depth further out. By the time the British numbers were sufficient to push inland, it was too late; the tide was on the rise, covering the proposed landing beach and increasing the distance to land. The floating batteries remained undamaged, with their crews sneering at the British and replying to the navy.

"That's the retreat." Chisholm was first to hear the roll of the drums. "The brigadier is sounding the retreat."

MacKim glared towards the French. "I haven't even got a shot at them yet."

"We'll be back." Chisholm raised his voice into a roar. "Can you hear me, Frenchmen? We'll be back for you!"

"There'll be another opportunity." Captain Cameron seemed pleased with the enthusiasm of his men. "They won't defeat the 78th."

That was another reverse and another abortive raid. The French are holding us back and the fighting season is nearly over.

"Dry off, eat and rest," Cameron said, as they returned to their parent ship. "I've heard that we're trying again at high water."

"Good!" MacKim nodded, patting the lock of his musket. "I've a message for our French friends," he said, "written with fire and steel."

"Careful now, Hugh," Chisholm said. "I keep telling you; the most eager men are usually the first to fall."

MacKim said nothing. Every night, when he closed his eyes, he could either see Priscilla, or Hitchins' darting eyes at the field of Culloden. This official war with the French was a quarrel between kings; his war was personal.

Leaving the floating batteries, the British inched upstream with the French following on the riverbank and the immensity of the land seemingly set on swallowing them.

"This is indeed a huge country," MacKim mused.

"It's overpowering," Cattanach said. "It never ends."

"A man could lose himself in a country like this," MacKim said. "Just go on forever and forget about all the troubles and disputes back home." *Except that I want to take Priscilla home to meet Mother. That will happen someday.*

"Ready, lads!" Captain Cameron broke MacKim's dreams. "We'll be landing in half an hour. Check your powder and flints."

This time, the British boats were off Pointe-aux-Trembles, where a neat little community sat beside the river, with a prominent church and a windmill with sails that moved slowly in the breeze.

"This is peaceful," Cattanach said. "It's nearly a shame to bring the war to them."

Pointing to the Frenchmen who waited for them, Chisholm shook his head. "Brigadier Murray is crazy if he thinks we'll land there. The defences are far too strong."

MacKim agreed. Muskets poked from the windows of every

house in the village, a solid white block of regular French infantry stood beside the church and troops of dismounted cavalry watched on the shore. "It will be a bloody day."

Once more, the 78th descended into small boats and nosed toward the north bank of the river. Once more, resistance stiffened as the boats neared the shore.

"Look," Cumming said, as more French regulars appeared from the woods. "There are thousands of them."

"Aye." MacKim wished he had room to aim and fire his musket. It stretched his nerves to stand in an open boat, waiting for French musketry.

The second the British were in extreme range, the French opened fire with volley after volley that did terrible execution to the hopeful landing party. A sailor beside MacKim fell silently over his oar as a musket-ball ploughed into his chest. Another yelled as a ball smashed his left arm. More musket balls raised splinters along the gunwales or splashed alongside. Light infantrymen roared as they were hit, or tried to duck, but there was nowhere to hide.

As the tide began to turn, making landing more difficult, Captain Cameron swore. "We're losing men for no purpose here," he said. "Even if we land, we will be shot to pieces before we form up."

"What are your orders, sir?"

"Back to the ship!" Cameron had to shout above the thunder of musketry. "I'm not throwing our lives away."

"Can we fire back, sir?" MacKim asked.

"No. Save your ammunition."

One by one the boats withdrew, to learn later that Brigadier Murray had ordered the retreat. As he stood on the ship's deck, looking over the landing spot where the bodies of brave men still floated on the water and powder smoke drifted through the buildings, MacKim swore in anger and frustration.

"That's yet another reverse. Whoever said war was glorious was a liar. It's pure butchery."

"I know," Chisholm said. "If kings and politicians were to fight each other to resolve their disputes, the war would end at once. Nobody except a fool or a madman would want to take part in this slaughter."

"Except maybe a desperate man," MacKim said.

"Maybe a desperate man," Chisholm agreed.

"Which are you?" MacKim asked. "You're no fool and certainly not mad. Were you desperate when you joined the army? You never talk about your life."

Chisholm was silent as they moved slowly up the river, with the French marching on the shore, sometimes seen, sometimes hidden by the trees but always there, dogged, persistent and dangerous. "I am a fool," he said. "And we'll leave it at that."

Licking their wounds and cursing their luck, the British sailed on. "We have to beat them," Cumming said. Nobody replied; there was no adequate response. At night, they formed a camp on the south shore of the river near the church of St Antoine, threw up the usual entrenchments in case of Indian raids and looked for opportunities to attack the French. Insects came out to irritate them, and the creatures of the dark made their usual unnerving noises.

"Remind me," Cumming asked. "Why are we up here? We are sitting in the woods surrounded by Canadians, French and Indians, being eaten alive by insects. We could do the same at Montmorency. We are not one whit closer to taking Quebec."

"Quit your moaning," Chisholm said. "Grouse, grouse, all you do is grouse. We are here, we are paid to be here, and we volunteered to be in the army." Lying on his back, he stared at the sky above. "Each day of life is a gift, Cumming. Accept it on its own merits, enjoy each breath and look on death as a natural ending."

MacKim looked at Chisholm from the side of his eyes. "I've never heard you talk like that before, James. You are indeed a strange fellow."

"We're all strange fellows, Hugh. No rational man would voluntarily join the army."

"Then, I will ask you again. Why did you join?"

"I was not rational." Digging a small hole for his hip, Chisholm rolled onto his side and was asleep in seconds.

Leaving the bulk of the expedition behind its entrenchments, Brigadier Murray sent a small flotilla further up the St Lawrence to search for any way to annoy the French.

"Murray is trying again." Chisholm sounded weary as he slapped at the persistent mosquitoes.

"Build the fires up," Captain Cameron ordered. "Don't let the French guess what we're doing. This time, we're not broadcasting our intentions."

Leaving the marines in the camp to act as if they were the entire brigade, Murray took the Lights and the 78th.

"We're heading across the river again," Cameron explained, "to the village of Deschambault, and once more, we Light Bobs are in the van."

"Why are we going there, sir?" Sergeant Dingwall asked.

"The French have a magazine in Deschambault," Cameron said. "As long as the Navy controls the St Lawrence, the French in Quebec can't get any gunpowder or military supplies from France, so the more French stores we destroy, the weaker their position becomes."

Possibly because of the increased secrecy, the force crossed the river unseen. Landing without opposition a short distance from the village, they marched through the woods, alert for Indian attack, until they saw the prominent church of St Joseph thrusting above the neat cluster of houses that was Deshambault.

"They've seen us," Chisholm said, as scores of white-coated French regulars hurried out of the church. "De La Sarre's regiment, I think."

"Form a line, lads," Cameron said. "We'll allow them to come to us."

However, rather than fight the approaching British, the

French retreated in good order to the forest without firing a shot.

"Stand and fight," MacKim muttered. "Fight me!"

"Steady, Hugh." Chisholm glanced at him. "Don't invite death. He'll come when he's ready."

Captain Cameron strode ahead. "Lights, take stations in the forest in case the French return."

"With me, lads." MacKim hurried into the woodland, with Chisholm on his right, Cumming on his left and Cattanach immediately behind. Once inside the trees, he readied his musket, stilled his racing heart and searched for Canadians and Indians. He saw nothing unusual at first, only the branches of trees and the green of leaves, until a flash of blue caught his attention. Narrowing his eyes, MacKim concentrated on the colour, knowing it was out of place. The French infantry wore white uniforms, while neither Indian warriors nor Canadians would sport anything so distinctive.

Catching Chisholm's eyes, MacKim nodded toward the splash of colour. He slid forward, knowing that Chisholm was covering him, watching for any threatening movement. He saw the blue quiver, levelled his musket and froze as he made out the shape.

"Come out of that," he whispered. "Slowly."

The woman stood and stepped forward with a faint smile on her broad face.

"Good God! What the devil are you doing here?" MacKim asked

Tayanita looked at him, her eyes alive. "Hiding," she said.

"Hiding?" MacKim stared at her. "You could get yourself killed!"

"That is why I am hiding," Tayanita explained patiently. "So I don't get myself killed."

"How did you get here?"

"I walked." Tayanita looked at Chisholm. "Does that man understand French?"

"Not a word," MacKim said.

"Does he know who I am?"

MacKim shook his head. "Yes, he does."

"What are you talking about?" Chisholm asked. "Is that not the woman we had as a prisoner?"

"Her name is Tayanita," MacKim said.

Chisholm stepped back, levelling his bayonet as if to fend off an attack.

"It's all right, James. She's no more savage than we are," MacKim said.

"What's this?" Cumming ran up with his musket levelled. "I'll shoot the murderous bitch."

MacKim pushed the barrel of his musket upwards. "Keep watch, Private. The French are still close by."

"What?"

"Move!" MacKim did not enjoy using his rank. "Guard our right flank. Cattanach, take the left."

"He was going to shoot me," Tayanita said.

"Yes. You've given me a dilemma." MacKim scratched his head. "Who are you hiding from?"

"You, the French, the Canadians, the Ottowas, the Abenaki." Tayanita smiled.

"Everybody."

"I thought you were going back west?" MacKim said.

"I am," Tayanita said. "But back west is a long way for a lone woman."

MacKim swore, and then sighed. "What do you need?"

"I need you Europeans to stop fighting each other," Tayanita said. "There are soldiers and war parties everywhere."

"I can't do anything about that," MacKim said.

"I need a musket." Tayanita smiled coyly. "Hunting with a knife is not easy."

"We don't carry spares," MacKim said. "If we shoot a Frenchman, you can take his musket."

The explosion took them both by surprise. Everybody

ducked or jumped behind a tree as wreckage rose high from the village, to descend in a slow patter. Choking smoke surged around the houses.

"That's the French gunpowder blown up then," Chisholm said. "I see your little friend has gone."

Chisholm was correct. Tayanita had gone, and so had Cumming's musket.

"Something hit me on the head," Cumming said. "When I recovered, my firelock had vanished."

"Probably a piece of wood from the powder store," MacKim said. "You'll have dropped your musket as you fell."

Tayanita is armed now. That's the last we'll see of her. A pity. I rather liked the little rogue.

When the drums of the 78th began to tap, MacKim led his section back to the boats. He smiled as he looked back at the forest; that was two women he had met in North America now, and both had caused him trouble.

✺ 23 ✺

FRENCH CANADA, SEPTEMBER
1759

"We're off again." As always, Chisholm was first with the news.

MacKim looked up. "Where to this time?"

"According to the rumours," Chisholm said, "this is the big one, the final attack to take Quebec."

MacKim grunted. After a summer of abortive expeditions and reverses, he no longer believed regimental hearsay. However, Captain Cameron soon confirmed Chisholm's information. "The general has issued a general order, which I will read out."

The Lights gathered in a semi-circle to listen to Cameron quoting Wolfe's words.

"Ready, my men?" Cameron grinned at them all. "General Wolfe says that 'a vigorous blow struck by the army at this juncture may determine the fall of Canada.' The general adds that 'We will land where the French seem least to expect us and march directly to the enemy and drive them from any little post they may occupy'."

Cameron grinned at his Lights. "We all know that the French can be quite stubborn in any little posts they may occupy, but Fraser's knows how to remove them."

As Cameron had intended, the Lights cheered his words.

"Now, the general says he will endeavour to bring the French and Canadians to a battle. This is our chance to defeat the monsieurs once and for all!"

MacKim felt a thrill run through him. If Pikestaff defeated the French in a major battle, Quebec would surely fall.

Cameron finished with his characteristic grin. "So check your flints, boys, count your cartridges and make sure there is no oil in your touch holes. You'll have two days' supply of ammunition, food," he paused, "and rum."

Some of the men gave another cheer at that. MacKim frowned. Seventy rounds plus the musket and other kit was a heavy load for a light infantryman to carry into action.

"Don't worry about the weight." Cameron could have read MacKim's thoughts. "You won't be carrying blankets and tents. They'll follow later."

"We'll be in the first wave again." Chisholm oiled the lock of his musket. "Say any last prayers, lads, if we're due for a real battle. I was at Fontenoy, remember and it was hell."

"We know," Cumming said. "You've told us a hundred times."

"No heroics, lads," Chisholm warned. "Death is waiting out there. Don't invite him into coming too early."

For once, MacKim barely thought of Hitchins as he checked his musket and sharpened his bayonet. Feeling the tension knot his stomach, he led his section into the flat-bottomed barge. It was just after nine at night, with the sound of musketry down-river from either a British diversion or a skirmish with the Indians, he did not know which. Surrounded by forty-nine Highland veterans, MacKim felt the mixed excitement and apprehension of men who knew what horrors they might face.

"God be with us all," Chisholm said, as tobacco-chewing seamen rowed their barge into the channel between the bulk of HMS *Sutherland* and the south shore of the St Lawrence. The single lantern that gleamed white from the maintop of *Sutherland* created a contrast between the ship's spider-web of spars and rigging and the dark forest. MacKim stared into the darkness, wondering how many Indians were there and if Tayanita had escaped westward to her people.

"You will keep complete silence in the barge," Captain Cameron ordered. "We will do nothing that might alert the French."

MacKim hated the waiting. Despite the cool of the night he felt sweat trickling down his spine. He stopped Cumming's nervous whistling with a sharp dig in the ribs and listened to the ripple of the river. Chisholm chewed the stem of his battered pipe, saying nothing. All around them were other barges, each filled with fifty equally apprehensive men listening to the surge of the river, a remembrance of other landings, of failures and bloodshed. Somebody snored softly as sleep overcame him, and woke with a start when a leaping fish plopped back into the water. MacKim ignored the stutter of artillery from Point Levis; that noise was so much part of life he no longer heard it.

It was two in the morning before a petty officer hoisted a second light on *Sutherland,* the signal for the boats to begin their journey. The midshipman who sat in the stern of MacKim's barge gave a soft order, and the seamen dipped their muffled oars into the St Lawrence. The operation had begun. MacKim saw Chisholm's lips move in silent prayer.

"It's a grand night," Cumming whispered. "The moon will be high over Ben Wyvis now, and the cattle will be coming home from the shielings."

"Quiet!" Cameron hissed.

Mention of Scotland had stirred old emotions in MacKim. It was years since he had felt homesick but he did at that moment, as the flotilla of boats carrying the seventeen hundred men of the first wave slithered onwards to what everybody expected to be the deciding battle with the French.

I wish I were back home now, he thought, and once again smiled at the image of walking up Glen Cailleach to his mother's welcome, his oath completed and Priscilla at his side.

Chisholm grunted, nudged him and handed over a plug of tobacco.

Nodding his thanks, MacKim placed the tobacco in his mouth. The regular motion of chewing helped steady his nerves as the tide and current carried the boats with more speed than he had expected. When a flurry of wind pushed away the sheltering clouds, a bright quarter moon glossed an ethereal beauty to a scene of war.

MacKim started when the French words cracked across the river.

"Qui va la?" The challenge took the infantry by surprise.

"La France!" shouted Captain Simon Fraser from the boat immediately in front of MacKim's. *"Vive le Roi."*

"A quelle regiment?" the French sentry replied.

MacKim tightened his grip on his musket, wondering if they were again going to experience the hellish ordeal of landing under fire. With the cliffs before them, he did not relish the prospect.

"De la Reine," Captain Fraser replied.

"Pourquoi ne parlez-vois pas plus haut?" (Why do you not speak up?)

"That's a right chatty sentry," Cumming said. "Can we not just shoot him and be done with it?"

"Shut your teeth," MacKim growled, "or I'll shoot you and be done with it."

Captain Fraser gave a little click of his tongue. *"Tais-toi! Nous serions entendus par les Britanniques."* (Shut up! We would be heard by the British.)

"Prepare yourselves, lads," Dingwall said until another voice called from the dark.

"Laisse le passer. Ce sont nos gens avec les provisions." (Let them pass. These are our people with the provisions.)

The French sentry relapsed into boredom, and the fleet slithered past.

"They think we're a French supply flotilla," MacKim translated roughly. "Try and act like Frenchmen, lads."

"How do Frenchmen act?" Cattanach asked.

"They keep quiet," Dingwall snarled, in an undertone. "I won't say that again, you gallows-bait scoundrels!"

After two hours of travelling down the river, MacKim saw dawn beginning to grey the sky.

"We're at *Anse-au-Foulon,*" Cameron said quietly, with the name meaning little to most of the men. "We'll be landing soon."

The boats now altered course, heading for a small cove underneath the Heights of Abraham, just outside Quebec. MacKim could nearly taste the tension in the air, as if death was whetting his scythe, waiting for the harvest.

"It's four in the morning," Captain Cameron said softly. "The French will be fast asleep, or dozing at their posts."

When the boats were about a hundred yards from the cove, spurts of flame split the night. "That'll be the French garrison on Anse au Foulon." Cameron said calmly, as the sounds echoed from the cliffs above.

"That's the game begun," Chisholm said. "Their pawns attacking our pawns as the kings sit in state."

So close to his neighbours that he could not move, MacKim could only wait and hope. Taking a deep breath, he realised he was no longer nervous. As Chisholm had said, the game had begun, and now he was in the hands of God. Pawns could not alter the course of a battle.

When a French five-gun battery opened up on the British boats, MacKim felt only curiosity. None of the fire came close to MacKim.

"You can talk now, boys," Captain Cameron yelled. "The French seem to know we are here." He pointed to the small cove, where a path gave access up the face of the Heights. "There's our landing place!"

As Cameron spoke, the current and tide swept the boats further down, away from the cove.

"Jesus! We've passed it!" Cameron shouted. "Get us to the shore, midshipman! Get us anywhere that we can land."

"Aye, aye, sir!" The midshipman in the stern ducked as a cannonball raised a fountain of cold water six feet from the boat. He shoved the tiller round hard, shouting at the seamen to put their backs into it, and they eased into a tiny stretch of mud under the cliffs.

"Disembark!" Cameron sounded tense. "Get up those Heights, lads, and as quietly as you can."

Other boats followed their lead, crowding the slim strip of mud as the Lights leapt out and began to scramble up the cliff. MacKim saw a tall man standing in a boat just offshore, waving them on.

"Who's that?"

"That's Colonel Howe," Chisholm said. "He's a good man."

"Come on, lads! Up the slope." Cameron pressed to the front, with Captain Simon Fraser a step behind. MacKim leapt ashore, landed in ankle-deep mud and pushed up a near-vertical slope. Grabbing at shrubs to haul himself up, MacKim looked to the right and left where the sheer cliffs soared towards the Heights of Abraham.

"God help us if the French find us now," Cumming said. "All they'd have to do is roll rocks on us, and they'll sweep us into the river."

"Shut your mouth and climb!" MacKim said. "The French are concentrating on the main landing."

"Come on, lads," Cameron encouraged. "We're the Light Infantry. We can do anything."

"*Qui va la?*" The challenge sounded from above.

"Have these buggers not realised what's happening yet?" Cattanach asked.

Slightly behind MacKim, Captain Donald Macdonald answered the Frenchman, telling the sentry that Montcalm has sent them to 'relieve the outpost.' MacKim grinned without humour. Macdonald had only been telling the truth, for the

Lights intended to relieve the French outpost of their duty permanently.

With his musket on his back and his cartridge box hampering him as it rattled between his legs, MacKim scrambled upwards, sliding on the damp rocks, gasping as his handholds slipped. The crackle of musketry at the cove proved that the main body had reached the intended destination, and the French were resisting.

"Keep going! Come on, Lights! Come on the 78th!" Captain Cameron was everywhere, encouraging the men, pulling up those who could not find a handhold, giving orders.

"We're coming, sir," Cumming said. "We won't let you down!"

MacKim did not see Howe overtake him, but the colonel and Captain Cameron were racing to the head of the path. "I told you Howe was a good man." Chisholm's face twisted into a hideous grin. "Come on, Hugh!"

When they reached the summit of the cliff, the 78th cheered, some shouting Gaelic slogans, others merely repeating "78th! 78th!"

"That's the first British cheer that Quebec has ever heard," Chisholm said. "It won't be the last. Now that we're here, the French will have the devil of a job to shift us."

MacKim scanned his immediate surroundings. He had imagined the Plains of Abraham to be level and smooth, while instead, it was undulating, with isolated trees, copses, stretches of dense forest, and even a few farmhouses huddled within a network of small fields. Between the Lights and the intended landing area, the tents of a French camp gleamed white, with a few startled sentries gazing at these unexpected invaders. Other Frenchmen manned the redoubts that faced in the opposite direction, guarding the path by which the main assault would come.

"We're behind the French defences," Chisholm said. "Most of the buggers don't even know we're here. Can they not hear the noise?"

"Take that redoubt," Cameron ordered, and the Lights formed a line, fixed bayonets and advanced at a stumbling run.

Apart from the few French who were attempting to defend the path, most of the defenders were still in their camp, some only just awake as the British arrived. MacKim saw one Frenchman's expression alter from tired disbelief to panic when the kilted Highlanders erupted from an unexpected direction. The man shouted something, dropped his musket and fled, with most of his companions joining him. Within moments, French regulars and casually-clad Canadians were running into the woods and fields. The whole affair did not last three minutes, with minimal casualties on either side.

"We have the redoubt!" Cameron sounded surprised.

"God willing, the rest of the day will be that easy." Chisholm unfastened his unused bayonet and slid it into the scabbard.

"I did not have to fight," MacKim said.

"I killed three of them," Cumming boasted.

"We know you did, Cumming." MacKim said. "We all know you're a champion, and all without firing a shot or bloodying your bayonet. Not many men could do that."

With the French defence brushed aside, the two British forces merged, forming up without any more interference; the first redcoats ever to grace the Heights of Abraham.

"The French will have to move quickly now," Chisholm said. "Our strength on the Heights is growing by the minute." He indicated the steady stream of men toiling up from the cove.

"So I see." MacKim ensured that Hitchins was not among the few French casualties in the camp, and took his place in the ranks. *Now, maybe I can finish this business. I've been lucky so far; I only hope to end my task. Priscilla is waiting.*

It was full morning before the British were fully formed up, with the boats bringing wave after wave of reinforcements who hurried up the track.

"Now let the French come. They have to fight in the open for a change, rather than skulking behind trees and redoubts, the cowardly dogs!" Cumming stamped his feet. "Come on, you rascals!"

"Aye, I've had enough of fighting men who are too scared to fight face to face." Cattanach touched the lock of his musket. "I want to see my enemy when I kill him."

"Oh, the French can fight in the open," Chisholm said. "I saw them at Fontenoy, remember?"

"We remember," Cumming said. "You seldom let us forget."

"The French at Samos are still firing." MacKim indicated an artillery battery a few hundred yards upstream, on their side of the river.

"They're wasting their powder," Chisholm said. "They can't hit us up here, and the Navy can take care of itself."

"Now, all we need is Montcalm to face us." Cattanach raised his voice. "Come on, Frenchmen! The 78th is waiting for you!"

MacKim watched as a messenger approached Colonel Howe, and minutes later the Light Infantry was on the move, trotting towards the Samos battery.

"Come on, lads! We've to silence those guns!" Cameron led from the front as always, his lithe figure eager, his laugh encouraging the men.

"What would Pikestaff do without us?" Chisholm grunted, as they approached a wooden bridge leading to the battery. A wreath of white smoke gushed from the guns as they fired again, with the artillerymen scurrying, loading, sponging and firing like madmen.

"Halt now, lads." Cameron stopped to inspect the enemy, with the Lights waiting expectantly.

"They've no infantry to defend the guns." MacKim scanned the battery. "They're wide open to the rear, but they've seen us coming." He pointed. "They're training a cannon on the bridge, sir."

"So they have, by George," Cameron said. "Tree all!"

When the cannon fired, the Lights dived for cover. Grapeshot pattered around the bridge, splintering the parapet and raising fountains in the water below. Not a single man was hit.

"Now!" Cameron drew his broadsword. "Forward before they can reload!"

Yelling, with naked bayonets, the Lights charged. Rather than stand and fight a horde of Highlanders, the French artillerymen sensibly retreated to the woods in the rear.

"They're running!" MacKim panted as he stopped in the battery.

"Spike the guns," Colonel Howe ordered, "and blow up the powder so the battery's useless. You, Corporal," he pointed to MacKim, "take your section into the woods and ensure the French don't return."

"Yes, sir."

MacKim saw only a slight flicker as the artillerymen slid further into the woods. He knew his men were by now expert woodsmen, able to cope with any number of regular gunners or infantry among the trees. *I haven't fired a shot yet. Will this expedition end the war? Will Quebec fall today? Will I find Hitchins?*

The artillerymen did not try to attack the Lights so, after twenty minutes, Cameron called MacKim's section back. With the battery destroyed and their flank secure, the Lights returned to the main body, now nearly four and a half thousand strong, and watched a team of sailors manhandle two six-pounder cannon up the track.

"Good for the Navy," Chisholm said.

"Two guns aren't much." Cumming had lost his bluster as he looked nervously forward. "The French will have more."

"Maybe they will," Chisholm said. "And maybe they won't."

"We might find out soon," MacKim said. "Here they come now."

❧ 24 ❧

QUEBEC, SEPTEMBER 1759

MacKim felt his tension rise as a company of French Light Infantry appeared on a ridge between the British and the still invisible walls of Quebec. Weak sunlight picked out the white uniforms and glittered from the burnished barrels of French muskets. "Isn't it strange to think that these men are just like us, wondering why they are fighting, hoping to survive the day, hungry, scared and prepared to do their duty."

Chisholm glanced at MacKim. "You're growing up, boy."

"They're French," Cumming said. "They're the enemy. They're the men that burned the Grenadiers alive, and scalped the wounded at Montmorency."

"That's the Guyenne regiment," Chisholm said. "They did not burn anybody alive and I doubt they scalped anyone, either."

"How do you know who they are?" Cumming asked.

Chisholm smiled. "Never you mind, Cumming. You keep your flint sharpened and your tongue still."

"Listen," MacKim said. "The French are sounding the bells."

The sound of church bells invoked a host of memories to the waiting British. To some, they were a reminder of home, while others were contemptuous of anything that hinted at Catholicism. To MacKim, the bells were a symbol that the French were awake and alarmed. "They know the Highlanders are coming to get them."

"The French have to fight now," Chisholm said. "We've landed outside their city, where their defences are weakest. Montcalm has to face us in the open, or we'll batter a breach and storm the place."

"Good." MacKim stared at the Guyenne regiment. *I wonder if Hitchins is somewhere among these men, watching me. I wonder if he remembers Culloden.* That far-off conflict seemed less important now, as the world had moved on and battles were for the control of entire continents rather than a sordid squabble between two rival claimants for a tarnished crown.

After the months of feints, raids and abortive operations, MacKim thought it seemed vaguely surreal and even rushed as the British marched forward with their shoes crunching on the undulating ground and the men silent save for an occasional grumble. A stiff breeze caught the colours, making them flap and snap above the red-coated ranks, each flag a symbol of honour, a reminder of bloody history and a rallying post in attack or reverse.

"Well, there's no help for it now," Chisholm said. "We can't retreat down that cliff so we must win or die here."

MacKim nodded. It was a strange place to die, so far from home, fighting in the quarrel of a king he had never met and who would never know of his existence, and wearing the uniform of the army that had murdered his brother. "We're making history," he said, with a flash of insight, "yet I don't care. I want to get some sleep and something to eat."

"Food, sleep, drink and women," Chisholm said. "The perpetual wants of a soldier. It's probably been the same for centuries. The Romans who crucified Christ were probably more concerned about their next meal than the fact they were executing the son of God."

"What's that got to do with anything?" Cumming scowled at

Chisholm. "You talk a lot of nonsense, Chisholm. What have the Romans got to do with the French and where is Quebec, anyway? I thought we were attacking it today."

"Quebec's on our right," Chisholm said, "beyond that ridge." He nodded to the rising ground known as Buttes-à-Neveu.

"Light infantry to the front!" The expected order came. MacKim trotted forward with the rest. *Now I am in the most forward unit of the British Army. I'm coming for you, Hitchins!*

The ground stretched in front of them, dotted with bushes and an occasional building. Now and then a puff of smoke and the crack of a musket came from behind a bush or from a half-hidden ridge, but the Light Infantry were veterans of a score of such encounters. They moved effortlessly, hugging the dead ground, trotting from cover to cover, meeting fire with fire and slowly driving back the Canadian skirmishers.

"There are more of them now," Cumming said, as he lay on the ground, working his ramrod frantically as MacKim and Chisholm covered him.

"Aye, they're getting thicker on the ground," MacKim agreed. "Like fleas on a shaggy dog."

"We must be nearing the main French army." Chisholm rolled onto his front, checked for marksmen and ran forward to the next cover.

"If the French fight." Cumming replaced his ramrod under the barrel and checked his flint.

"They'll fight," Chisholm assured him.

The Lights moved on again, stopped for a moment to watch a platoon of Grenadiers storm an isolated farmhouse, and continued, pressing back the enemy as the sun slid upwards in the uncaring sky.

Behind the thin line of Lights, Wolfe manoeuvred his army forward, with the sweet music of the fifes joining the stirring batter of the drums. *This performance is very musical,* MacKim thought, as he heard the great Highland pipes wailing in the wind. *We are dying to music, dancing to the devil's tunes.*

"These woods are alive with French." Cumming indicted the forested land on the north, from where puffs of smoke indicated the presence of the enemy.

"That will be the Indians and Canadians." Chisholm glanced over his shoulder to where the British slowly marched in a broad column, following the cloud of Light Infantrymen. The fifes trilled happily, the colours flowed overhead while the scarlet uniforms shone brightly under the autumn sun. Despite his growing cynicism, MacKim recognised a strange martial beauty that twisted something inside him. "Now, there's a sight I'll long remember," he said.

"That's the glory that the army uses to bring in recruits," Chisholm said. "Not long from now, we'll be back to blood and guts and slaughter."

Here and there, a man fell when the Canadian or Indian sharpshooters found their mark. MacKim and the Lights targeted the puffs of smoke, firing, scrabbling for fresh cartridges and reloading with controlled haste. With no way of knowing how effective his shooting was, MacKim only hoped he was helping repress the enemy's fire. *I wish I had a rifle rather than a musket. These Canadians outrange us.*

General Wolfe shouted an order and the column immediately halted. The music continued as thousands of men stood still for a moment while the world held its breath. Wolfe gave another command; the drums rapped their message and the column altered shape to a long scarlet line, facing the French. The whole manoeuvre took only minutes, the result of hundreds of hours of practice on the parade grounds. It was beautiful to see such precision, but bitter that it was all in aid of the massed killing that was to come.

"That's us in battle formation," Chisholm said. "It's a direct challenge to the French. Fight me or run."

"Gin ye daur," Cattanach said, "if you dare," and laughed at his imagined cleverness.

For a moment, MacKim was ten years old again, standing on

Drummossie Moor watching the scarlet ranks. However, rather than facing half their number of starving Highlanders, the British waited for a larger army that included trained French regulars backed by expert Canadian and Indian marksmen. He took a deep breath. *I am Hugh MacKim of Glen Cailleach and the 78th Foot. Come on, you Frenchies!*

The walls of Quebec were a mile in front, with a scatter of houses to the left. *Hitchins is somewhere out there. Kill him, and I am free for the first time since 1746.* "Come on, Frenchies! Fight! Oh God, stand and fight!"

Chisholm glanced at him. "It's all right, Hugh. Take a deep breath. Don't invite death. Let him choose his time."

"Our boys are over on the left." Cumming indicated the Highlanders, with Anstruthers 58th foot on their left flank, while the 47th, 43rd, 28th and the Louisbourg Grenadiers stretched to their right. The second line, the 60th Royal Americans and 15th Foot, was at right angles, facing the woods to the north, with the 35th facing the south in case the French should try to outflank them. The sound of barked orders and the rattle of drums dominated the Heights of Abraham as the British spread like a scarlet plague.

"Here comes Captain Cameron," Chisholm said. "We're moving again."

"Come on, boys!" Cameron disregarded French sharp-shooters as he shouted to the Lights. "We're to guard the rear of the army in case the Frenchies come that way."

MacKim swore. *I want to find Hitchins.*

"This would barely be a skirmish in Europe," Chisholm said, as they doubled around the silent British line. "I doubt that we have four and a half thousand men on the field. We had over fifty thousand at Fontenoy and a hundred guns."

MacKim said nothing. He was only interested in four men; himself, Chisholm, Cumming and Hitchins. He had no desire to guard the rear of the army when his enemies were in front.

"It's a big enough army for me," Cumming said.

"It's the same number as the Jacobites had at Drummossie Moor," MacKim broke his silence, "and that battle settled the dynastic dispute. Maybe this one will end the war, and we can leave this country." *Do I want to leave this country, with Priscilla here?*

"Listen!" Cattanach held up a hand. "There's the pipes again! We're going into battle." He stood straighter. "We should be with the regiment, not dodging savages and Canadians back here."

MacKim took a deep breath. He agreed. The pipes stirred the blood, far more than the rattle of drums or the shrill notes of the fife. It was uniquely martial music that reminded him of the slithering mists and heart-wrenching beauty of home.

"Come on, you French bastards!" Cumming whispered. "Come on and face Fraser's Highlanders."

After spending so many months hiding and dodging among the woods, it felt proper to have the pipes again, to fight in the open as men should, as soldiers did, rather than skulking, ambushing and running away like cowards.

"The French are coming out," Chisholm said. "All the pawns are in array. Now let's see if they can capture the king."

With no sign of any French in the British rear, MacKim had space to watch the formal battle unfold. Unit after French unit emerged from city and camp, the white uniforms pretty in the autumn sun, with the darker clothes of the Canadians a reminder that Montcalm had a mixture of regulars and local units.

"How many of them are there, for God's sake?" Cumming asked. "There are thousands and thousands."

Chisholm frowned as his experienced eye moved from one flank of the French to the other. "About the same as us," he said, "give or take a few hundred, which means we'll win."

Cattanach spat a stream of tobacco juice. "I'm not concerned about the French regulars. They will fight fair, and we'll smash them. It's these damned cowards that hide in the trees and snipe then run away that I hate."

MacKim gave the conventional reply. "Cowardly bastards," he agreed. *But they're not cowards. They use different tactics, that's all.*

The British waited underneath their colours, Grenadiers in tall mitre caps, line infantry in tricornes adorning weather-beaten faces and faded uniforms. In front of the rigid lines, the officers stood, heads up, facing the French. MacKim looked to the 78th at the left centre of the British line, where command had devolved to Captain John Campbell, as all the senior officers had been wounded in various encounters. MacKim could taste the tension, bitter in his mouth. He heard the irregular popping where Canadian and Indians exchanged fire with the British Lights. It still felt unreal, as if he were part of an elaborate charade. Surely the fate of kingdoms and continents could not be decided by this colourful game, this movement of elaborately uniformed men over a relatively small piece of ground?

"This is the worst part," Cumming said. "The waiting."

"No.' Chisholm shook his head. "The worst part is when the artillery starts up, and we can't do a damned thing except stand and allow the French to shoot at us."

"Pikestaff's saying something," Cumming said.

Wolfe stood on a small knoll beside the Louisbourg Grenadiers with his hands moving as he spoke, but the distance was too far for MacKim to hear anything. "What's happening?" he asked as, unit by unit, the British army lay on the ground.

"I've never seen that before," Chisholm said.

"We're praying!" Cattanach said. "We're praying for divine help."

"No. It's because of the sniping," MacKim said. "Men are harder to hit when they lie down."

"Why don't the French attack so we can get on with this battle?" Cumming fidgeted with the lock of his musket. "We're doing no good at all here. Why does Pikestaff not attack and destroy them?"

"Pikestaff knows what he's doing," Chisholm said.

"You lads!" Sergeant Dingwall was panting as he ran to the

Lights. "Captain Campbell wants a platoon of Light Bobs to protect our front."

"We'll come!" Ensign MacDonnell had grown up from the terrified youth at Louisbourg. "Come on, MacKim. Bring your boys. It might stop your incessant chattering. You're like a bunch of washerwomen, gabbing away all the time. Come on. Sergeant Dingwall, you come too."

MacKim ran forward, crouching and jinking to spoil the aim of any enemy marksman.

"At last we're useful," Chisholm said, as Dingwall led them into the disputed land beyond the British line. Once again, MacKim contemplated the undulating Plains of Abraham. Moving from dead ground to dead ground, MacKim saw powder smoke jetting from one farmhouse.

"That's our target, boys," he said. "We'll push the Canadians out of there and use it as a strongpoint to harass the French."

MacKim's section moved forward in the now-familiar style, with two men covering as two advanced, crossing the ground in a series of short rushes. As they drew closer to the farmhouse, the occupants loosed a volley that raised the dust around MacKim. He dived into a fold of ground. "Jesus! How many Canadians are in there?"

"Too many for our little section to handle," Chisholm said. "There must be a dozen at least."

"Sit tight!" MacKim ducked as a bullet hummed past his head, and another burrowed into the ground in front of him.

"Help is coming," Chisholm said, as Ensign MacDonnell led his platoon against the farmhouse.

Waiting until MacDonnell was within twenty yards, MacKim rose and charged forward, weaving as he closed with the house. "Come on, men!" The defenders fired a ragged volley, and then the Highlanders were hammering at the door with musket butts and firing through the windows. The Canadians slipped away at the back.

"They're running!" Chisholm said. "Fire at them!"

"We'll have to hold this position," Ensign MacDonnell shouted. "If the French put artillery in this house, they could rake our army from the flank."

MacKim peered out of the window. "The French know that, too, sir. They're sending out their infantry."

A French regimental column assumed formation and advanced on the farmhouse, their legs twinkling and sunlight glittering on shouldered muskets.

"Well, Cumming, you wanted to fight the French in the open and here's your chance." Chisholm said. "Here they come."

"Every man find a position!" Ensign MacDonnell ordered. "Wait until they are in range before you fire!"

MacKim nodded. That was good advice that the Lights did not need. The French advanced bravely, breaking from column to line while still a hundred yards away from the farmhouse.

"Wait," MacDonnell said. "Wait."

Eighty yards and the French slowed, with the officers peering at the farm. Some of the men stumbled on the uneven ground. Seventy yards and some of the infantry slowed down while others began to hurry forward to close the distance quicker.

"Bloody amateurs," Chisholm mouthed, sighting along the barrel of his musket.

"Wait," MacDonnell said. "Wait for my word."

Sixty yards. One Frenchman, unable to wait longer, fired his musket, with others following his example. Little spurts of dust and stonework showed where the balls hit the farmhouse walls. One shot smashed into the shutters of the window beside MacKim. He did not flinch as a wooden splinter raked down his cheekbone and blood trickled to his chin.

Fifty yards. The French were now within effective range of Bess. MacKim fixed his sights on one squat officer who advanced with more purpose than the others.

Forty yards. Thirty. Twenty-five. The French outflanked the farmhouse, their faces clear, some impassive, others strained; waiting for the response they knew was inevitable.

"Fire!" MacDonnell said. "Shoot them flat."

The Highlanders fired. At that range, firing from secure positions and onto an enemy in the open, the effects were devastating. MacKim saw the squat officer jerk backwards as two balls hit him simultaneously. "Got you, Marcel!" and then he reloaded, fast and efficient after months of experience. The Lights fired a second time before the others were ready, relishing these easy targets.

With many men already down, the French hesitated. Peering through the thick smoke, MacKim aimed at another officer, fired and stooped to reload before he saw the results of his shot.

"They've broken," Chisholm said calmly.

"Cease fire," Ensign MacDonnell said. "Save your ammunition."

When a slight breeze shifted the smoke, MacKim saw that Chisholm was correct. The French were withdrawing in good order, occasionally stopping to turn and shoot. They left a score of men on the ground, some lying still, others kicking and moaning.

"Any casualties?" MacDonnell asked.

There were none. Not a single French shot had struck home.

"We did well." MacDonnell was rightly pleased with himself. He was less cheerful five minutes later when a French cannonball hammered against the stone wall.

"Keep your heads down, lads," MacKim said. "We're helping to win this war. If the French are firing at us, they're leaving the battle line alone."

"And that's much more vulnerable." MacDonnell stood up to stare out of the window. "We'll hold this position until Captain Campbell sends further orders."

"Yes, sir," Chisholm said. "There's Montcalm, sir." He pointed out of his window. "The fellow on the black horse."

MacKim saw the French general in his blue coat with the sun glinting on the cuirass around his neck. He looked very lonely, even forlorn and nothing like the commander of the most powerful French army in North America.

"He's forming column," Chisholm said. "Montcalm is going to attack Wolfe's line."

After all the months of skirmishing, of bloody encounters in the woods, the two armies were finally facing each other on an open field.

"At last," Chisholm touched his scarred face, "an honest battle. God help us all."

The French marched forward under their colours, with white coats above grey-white breeches. In front, blue-coated drummers encouraged them, with the infantry roaring "*Vive le Roi!*" as they marched.

"They look determined." MacKim aimed his musket. After a morning of watching British soldiers fall under Canadian sniping, he hoped to pick off a few of the French if they came sufficiently close. *I wonder if Hitchins is there and if so, what he is thinking as he advances on his own people. Does he have regrets? Come to me, Hitchins, so that I can kill you.*

"They're not as good as they were at Fontenoy," Chisholm said. "Look at the gaps between the regiments. The leading unit is moving faster than the one behind. Now wait for our artillery to carve them up."

The densely-packed column presented a perfect target for the two British six-pounders. Firing solid shot that ploughed into the advancing men, the guns caused mayhem. MacKim saw French soldiers falling left and right, with a terrible mist of blood rising above the brave white uniforms.

"Go on, the guns!" Cumming cheered.

"Now it's the French turn to be fired on with no possibility of replying," Chisholm said. "Poor buggers."

Stationed in between the French regulars, men of the Canadian militia began to return fire, throwing themselves to the ground to reload, as was their practice, and disrupting the column further. MacKim could see the French officers trying to keep the column together, lifting the Canadians bodily and shouting, although the noise of cannon and musketry was too loud to distinguish any words.

"What a blasted shambles," Chisholm said. "We'll lick these devils with ease. Wait –they're going to fire." The column halted and those of the French who could bring their muskets to bear steadied for a volley.

"They're too far away." MacKim rested his musket on the window sill. "They must be a hundred and fifty yards away from our line, three times effective range."

The French fired, with few of their balls reaching the British line. A handful of the British staggered. One officer calmly removed a spent ball from his hat, held it between his finger and thumb and contemptuously flicked it back in the direction of the French.

"Our boys are not firing back," Cumming said.

MacKim sighted along the barrel of his musket. "Hold fire, lads, until the volley is most effective, then blast them back to Quebec."

The French column advanced again, with the men still shouting "*Vive le Roi*" and the Canadians firing and dropping to the ground to reload. The British battalion commanders waited until they were around eighty yards distant, then calmly stepped sideways and behind the colours. There was something impressive about the silence from Wolfe's men, a warning that when they did fire, the effect would be terrible.

"Nearly fifty yards," Chisholm said. "We'll open fire soon."

"Wait," Ensign MacDonnell said.

At forty yards, the officers shouted, "Make ready!" and the second line of British infantrymen stepped into the gaps left between each front rank man. The infantrymen presented their muskets. Now, an unbroken line of scarlet coated musket men faced forward. The French column seemed to shiver in anticipation, with the men in the leading ranks hesitating as those behind them pushed them toward the line of black musket barrels.

"Fire!"

Officers repeated the word along the length of the British line. Every musket held two balls to double the effect, and the French were so close and so densely packed that the British soldiers could not miss. White powder smoke jetted, to limit the view of every man, but there was no doubt that the French column was hard hit.

"Reload!" the British officers ordered, and hundreds of men ripped open paper cartridges with their teeth, poured powder down hundreds of musket barrels and followed with lead balls.

"Aim!"

"Fire!"

The next volley smashed into the battered French. Men fell in dozens as cannon fire also hammered the column, which had now slowed to a crawl. A few Frenchmen returned fire, some turned to run, while more lay dead, or screaming in agony with terrible wounds.

"Load!"

"Fire!"

A third and then a fourth volley battered the survivors, tearing open flesh, shattering bone, killing, maiming, breaking bodies and minds. Within a few moments, what had been an army of brave men was shattered into a panicking mob. MacKim was not sure what happened next. Either a strong wind blew away the powder smoke, or the British stopped firing, but for one moment, he had a clear view of the French.

"They're running," MacKim said. "We've beaten them."

"We have." Chisholm did not sound surprised.

"Fire!" Ensign MacDonnell said. "Pick your targets and fire."

MacKim aimed at a lone officer who stood amidst the shattered chaos of his command. He pressed the trigger and was strangely glad when he missed.

"It's a trap." Cumming stared at the shattered remnants of

the French. "They're trying to lure us into an ambush as their Indians do."

"Fix bayonets!" Officer after officer repeated the command the length of the British line. MacKim heard the sinister clicks and saw the sun glint on hundreds of the seventeen-inch long bayonets.

"Charge your bayonets!"

MacKim grunted at the old familiar orders, hammered into the redcoats on hundreds of hours of drill in Great Britain and North America and now repeated on the battlefield. The men responded automatically, presenting their bayonets to create a hedge of sharp steel toward the retreating French. Only one regiment differed from the rest; rather than present their bayonets, the men of Fraser's 78th Highlanders dropped their muskets, drew their broadswords and charged.

"Oh, dear God in heaven." MacKim stared for a second as the Highlanders rushed at the French, yelling Gaelic slogans that had been heard above the leaden skies of Culloden, at the butchery of Inverlochy and probably at Red Harlaw over three centuries earlier. Above the roar of the slogans came the high wail of the pipes.

"Come on, boys!" With the pipe music in his ears, MacKim leapt through the bullet-scarred window to join the charge. As the Lights did not carry a claymore, MacKim wielded his musket and bayonet.

The Highlanders powered forward, yelling, slashing at any Frenchmen who ran or who showed resistance. After months of creeping warfare, of being sniped at by hidden marksmen, of worrying about ambushes and torture, now they had their chance to fight back, and they exploited it to the full.

Arms were lopped off, heads flew, and Frenchmen fell, sliced open before the swing of the terrible Highland blade. If any Frenchman surrendered, he was spared at once as the Highlanders raced to the forefront of the British army, chasing what was now a panicking rabble. Some of the Canadian militia fired back, with snipers in the woodlands still shooting, causing casualties among the Highlanders. Stooping, MacKim lifted the sword from a fallen Highlander, discarded his musket and joined the charge.

"Hitchins!" He yelled the name. "Hitchins! If you are here, I want you, Hitchins!"

As the French regulars fled, the resistance of the Canadians stiffened. They retreated to the woods and thickets of trees, turned and fired at the advancing British. With Brigadier Murray conspicuous in front, Fraser's Highlanders found themselves once again fighting against a hidden enemy.

"Stand and fight, you cowardly dogs!" Dingwall roared in frustration as the advance stalled. With casualties mounting, the Highlanders fell back, slashing at the bushes in frustration.

"Here comes help," MacKim said, as the 58th Foot and a couple of companies of the 60th Royal Americans joined them. Dropping his borrowed sword, MacKim lifted a musket from a wounded man and plunged into the suburbs of Quebec. Taking cover beside a group of green-uniformed Royal Americans, he fired into the trees.

"Come on, lads!"

The British advanced again, pushing the French and Canadians before them, slower now, more cautious, adapting their tactics to suit the conditions.

Every so often, MacKim shouted the name: "Hitchins! Are you there?" He stared ahead as Chisholm joined him. "Look at that!" The close pursuit had utterly broken the French army. No longer in any formation, a mingled mob of fugitives crammed onto the bridges across the St Charles river and the open countryside beyond, while another section rushed for the precarious refuge of Quebec.

Chisholm grinned. "This is what victory feels like, Hugh! Forget Hitchins. He'll either be dead or will have disappeared somewhere."

Ignoring a fresh outburst of firing in the rear as a couple of

British battalions chased away belated French reinforcements, MacKim shook his head. "No," he said. "I have a task to fulfil."

"Your brother's long dead," Chisholm said. "Let the dead look after the dead. You have seen enough out here to know terrible things happen in wars – all wars. Let the past go and live your life now."

"I have a duty," MacKim tried to explain again. "I swore an oath on the Bible. I cannot rest until I've completed my work." He looked up at the walls of Quebec, where white faces peered over at the chaos outside.

"What are you going to do, check each dead Frenchman and every prisoner?"

"If I have to," MacKim said.

The battle was won and lost. A threatened French counter-attack in the rear came to nothing; the British had defeated Montcalm's French army and held the field. Now, all that remained was to capture Quebec and savour the victory.

"Dear God, we've done it," Chisholm said. "We've defeated the French in open battle, and I'm still alive." He touched his mutilated face. "Oh, God, why did you not let me die?"

"Sergeant Dingwall!" Captain Cameron looked harassed. "I want you to round up prisoners. Take a section of Lights, scour the fields and trees for any Frenchmen who might try to escape, and check on any of our wounded."

"Yes, sir," Dingwall said. "Come on, lads, and keep alert for these Canadian scoundrels."

Replacing the flint of his musket, MacKim moved on. Some-where in this field, or in Quebec itself, he would find Hitchins. Today, tomorrow, this year, he would be finished with his quest, and he could live a normal life.

But what is a normal life? For the past fourteen years, I have lived with this hunt for revenge. It has been central to everything I have done; it has driven me forward, given me meaning. Without it, what am I?

MacKim realised that he did not know. His task had taken over his life, so he did not know who, or what, he was.

Priscilla. Her name and face sprung into his mind with such clarity, he wondered if she was there in person. For a moment, he could almost smell her scent, see her serene eyes and hear the chuckle of her laughter. *I want Priscilla. But what about Jacob? He's a good man, a decent man. Yes, but Priscilla does not love him. She loves me. Perhaps Jacob died in the hospital?* MacKim stopped at the thought. *I should have checked. Many men recover from wounds only to die of fever. I have not heard from Jacob. If he is dead, Priscilla will be free and waiting for me. Once I've got rid of Hitchins, I'll go to her.* Once again, he had that vision of walking up Glen Cailleach to his smiling mother. *We'll go home, where there are no Indians, no Frenchmen and no war.*

The crack of the musket broke MacKim's train of thought. He dropped into a fold of ground as Chisholm replied so rapidly that the double bang nearly sounded like a single sound.

"Over there." Chisholm was at his side, lying on his back and reloading, Canadian-style.

MacKim saw the drifting smoke. "How many?"

"Two."

"Come on then, James."

As they moved from cover to cover, MacKim saw a flicker of movement in the copse, dropped and fired at the same time. He heard the shout as his shot took effect, rolled into some dead ground and began to reload feverishly.

"I hit one."

Chisholm was two yards away, sheltering behind a fallen log, his eyes searching the woodland. "I see him. The other man fled."

"Cover me." MacKim dashed forward in a half-crouch, his musket at the trail, his eyes peering ahead, jinking from side to side to spoil the aim of any attacker. The Canadian he had shot lay on his back, eyes wide with pain.

"You should have surrendered." MacKim glanced at the wound. His shot had taken the man high in the chest, above any vital organ. "You'll still live if you get medical aid."

The man stared at him, not comprehending.

Cursing his stupidity, MacKim changed his language to French. "Do you know of a man named Hitchins? He's a British deserter in the French service." When the man did not reply, MacKim shook him. "Have you heard of a man named Hitchins?"

The Canadian shook his head. "*Non.*"

"He is in the Bearn regiment. Where is the Bearn regiment?"

The Canadian gasped in pain. Blood seeped from his wound. "They were in the column."

The column had taken the brunt of the British fire. If Hitchins had been in the leading four or five ranks of his regiment, it was very likely that he lay on the battlefield, wounded or dead.

"Come on. We'll get you to a surgeon." Throwing away the wounded man's musket, MacKim helped him to his feet. "You'll be quicker walking than waiting for the drummers."

The Bearn Regiment lay where the British musketry had slaughtered it, man after man lying in a crumpled heap, some piled on top of each other. Battle-hardened, MacKim felt little as he inspected each mutilated corpse and turned over the writhing wounded to search for Hitchins. While the dead and severely injured were of no interest to him, he asked the walking wounded if they knew Hitchins. A few recognised the name, and one limping man provided information.

Speaking in the French of the south, he nodded to the walls of Quebec. "He will be in there," he said. "Your English friend was a most reluctant soldier."

"*Merci.*" MacKim helped the Frenchman towards a drummer for his painful journey to the surgeons. "Take care, *mon ami.*" MacKim felt no animosity toward these French regulars; they were professional soldiers in the service of their country, as he was.

"Hugh." The voice was soft.

MacKim looked around, his hands curling around the stock

of his musket. "Who said that?" In a battlefield filled with the moans and screams of terribly wounded men, he found it hard to trace one voice.

"I did." Tayanita emerged from the shelter of a tangled bush.

"Tayanita!" MacKim stared at her. "What the devil are you doing in this bedlam?"

Tayanita indicated the chaos. "Your devil is certainly here, Hugh, but he did not bring me."

MacKim nodded. "The devil is the deity of battlefields and war; of that, there is no doubt." It felt surreal to stand amid such slaughter and suffering, talking to this strange woman. "We seem to meet in such terrible places."

Tayanita sighed. "Your people term us savages." She indicated the hundreds of dead and broken men. "If this is your civilisation, I prefer my savagery."

"I cannot fault you there," MacKim said.

"Come away with me, Hugh. Leave this monstrosity behind."

Come away with me? What a novel idea. MacKim closed his eyes. "I have a mission to fulfil. I have a sacred duty to perform."

"Your tribe demands its blood price?" Tayanita looked around with a look of disgust. "Surely there is enough blood here for every tribe."

"I swore an oath." MacKim saw a body of redcoats trudging towards him. They trundled a hand barrow, covered with canvas on which a wounded man would lie. "You had better hide, Tayanita. If our men find you here, God only knows what they'll do."

"Your God has his eyes closed today," Tayanita said. "They will not find me. Your British soldiers could not find me if I sat on their shoulder and sang in their ear."

"Even so —" MacKim realised he was talking to smoke. Tayanita was nowhere to be seen. For a moment, he felt an overwhelming sense of loss, and then he shook his head. If Tayanita wished to find him again, she would do so. She had that ability, even in the midst of a battle.

"Has anybody seen Hitchins?" MacKim continued his search, asking man after man.

"The Englishman?" a wounded sergeant said. "He ran. He was the first to run."

Two people had now said the same thing. MacKim looked toward the walls of Quebec. He had been wrong in thinking that a final battle would settle his quest. Hitchins was still alive and within the city walls. *Damn the man!*

"I'm coming for you, Hitchins!" MacKim roared. "I will find you!"

He heard the echoes of his voice across the battlefield. Men stopped to stare at him, then quickly turned away. After witnessing the charge of sword-wielding Highlanders, they had no desire to argue with one of these wild men. MacKim gave a sour grin; a reputation had been born today.

As he looked toward Quebec, MacKim fought a surge of depression. *What's it all about, Tayanita? Why are we killing each other so one rapacious king can claim ownership of a continent that another avaricious king wants? What's the point of all this blood?*

25

CANADA, AUTUMN 1759

"We lost Pikestaff." Chisholm sucked on the stem of his pipe. "The whole army is in mourning for him."

"We've lost hundreds of good men," MacKim said. "They'll all be missed. I'm not wearing black for a general I never met. We lost eighteen killed and one hundred and forty-eight wounded from Fraser's yesterday alone, and only God knows how many of the wounded will pull through."

"You've turned into a cynical man, MacKim," Chisholm said.

"Aye," MacKim agreed.

"Now we've defeated their army, we must march into Quebec." Cumming was sharpening his bayonet, testing the edge and sharpening again. He looked up with a wide smile. "We're going to take Quebec." His laugh was slightly disconcerting, his eyes unfocussed.

"Maybe." Chisholm indicated the Plains of Abraham, where the British were busy building redoubts, digging trenches and burying the dead. "Murray, or Townshend, or whoever is presently in charge, seems to think the Frenchies will attack us here. There are thousands of them still at large outside the walls, as well as the savages."

"Let them come." Cumming inspected the edge of his bayonet. "They can break themselves to pieces charging against our musketry."

"We've already allowed the French women and children out of Quebec," Chisholm said. "Now I hear we've granted the garrison the honours of war. That French fellow Ramezay has agreed to surrender if we allow the Canadian militia to return to their homes and the French regulars to sail back to France."

That news hit MacKim like the blow of a tomahawk. He looked up. "We're going to allow all the French regulars back to France? All of them?"

"All of them within the walls of Quebec." Chisholm's gaze did not stray from MacKim's face. "You look concerned, Hugh."

MacKim glanced around. With a dozen soldiers within earshot, it was better not to mention Hitchins. "I'm concerned that we are letting the French off lightly."

How can I reach Hitchins before he sails for France? I have to get into the city, past our sentries and the French without getting caught, or shot. Once Hitchins is in a ship for France, I'll never find him.

Captain Cameron interrupted them. "Brigadier Townshend wants us to patrol between our camp and Quebec, to stop the Canadians and Indians from harassing our sentries. I don't expect any trouble so I'll send a token man. I know you lads have had a busy few months, so I'm looking for a volunteer."

Thank you, God. "I'll go, sir." MacKim looked up. "I've not done with these French devils yet."

"You'll make sergeant one day, Corporal," Cameron approved. "If you survive. As soon as you like, MacKim."

"Thank you, sir."

"I'll come too," Chisholm said, as Cameron loped away.

"No you won't," Sergeant Dingwall interrupted. "The officer asked for a volunteer, not volunteers. You're on your own, MacKim, and tonight's password is success, I believe."

"Yes, Sergeant."

"Oh, MacKim," Cameron reappeared, "I almost forgot. The password for tonight is victory."

"Victory. Thank you, sir." MacKim saluted.

"I've told you before not to volunteer for anything!" Chisholm hissed, once they were alone. "What's in your mind?"

"I'm going into Quebec," MacKim told him.

"Don't be a bloody fool!" Chisholm stared at him. "The French will kill you."

"Only if they catch me." MacKim completed the obligatory checks on his equipment. "After dodging Canadians and Indians in the forest, I think I can get past a few tired French sentries. With the surrender arranged, they won't be expecting any trouble."

"Why the devil are you going into Quebec?" Chisholm asked. "No, don't tell me, you're still after that Hitchins fellow."

"That's right." Grabbing a handful of dirt, MacKim rubbed it into his face, concentrating on the cheekbones and chin.

"Can't you forget your bloody oath?" Chisholm took hold of MacKim's arm. "Come on now, Hugh, drop this foolish idea. You've survived two sieges and a battle. Why get killed now? Your luck won't last forever."

"I swore an oath," MacKim said.

"Bugger your bloody oath!" Chisholm dropped his grip. "You're on your own this time, Corporal MacKim, and if the French don't catch you, Townshend will have you hanged for desertion if you go into Quebec."

"I swore an oath," MacKim repeated.

"Forget your oath, man! That was years and years ago. Nobody can expect you to keep an oath for so long!"

"The family will." MacKim nearly smiled. "I appreciate your sentiments, but I can't break my oath." He straightened up. "Hitchins is the last of my brother's murderers, James. Once he is dead, I can rest easy."

"You're a fool, MacKim." Despite his protestations, Chisholm remained with MacKim as he moved past the smoking campfires to the limits of the British lines. Somebody was singing softly, the words sad on the drift of the wind. "I should come with you."

"Dingwall's watching us," MacKim said. "You get back to camp, James. I might be a while."

"I'll chance Dingwall."

"Get back. That's an order, Chisholm."

"To the devil with your orders, MacKim."

"Go, James, please."

"I'm coming with you." Chisholm lifted his chin in defiance.

"No, James." MacKim shook his head. "One man might slide pass a dozing sentry, but two would double the risk."

Grunting, Chisholm stepped back. "You're a bloody fool, Hugh."

"Chisholm! I want you!" Dingwall roared. Taking advantage of the distraction, MacKim slipped into the darkness.

۞

IT WAS ONLY A SHORT DISTANCE BETWEEN THE BRITISH entrenchments and the walls of Quebec. As MacKim had suspected, the French sentries were lax, smoking long pipes, sipping from bottles and only occasionally peering towards the British campfires. Flurries of rain blighted the night, creating an excuse for the sentries to seek cover and concealing MacKim. The walls were not as high as he had feared and not as formidable as the defences along the length of the river, or the grim fortifications of Louisbourg. In one place, British artillery had dislodged a section of masonry, scattering rubble along the base of the wall.

That's my way into the city. MacKim noticed the tricorne hat of a single French sentry. *When the next squall comes along, I'll scale the wall. That sentry will move to somewhere less exposed.*

The wind rose again and rain, interspersed with sleet, hammered down. As MacKim had anticipated, the nearest sentry slunk away to seek shelter. Hiding his musket beside a prominent rock, MacKim hurried forward, praying that the storm lasted. The rubble provided an easy passage for the first third of the height, and after that MacKim scrabbled up the wall, remembering the skills he had as a child when he and Ewan climbed cliffs for birds' eggs. The memory of Ewan heightened MacKim's resolve to find Hitchins and finally put his quest to rest.

Slipping over the parapet, he remained still for a moment, quieting the pounding of his heart as he examined his surroundings. Behind the wall, a flight of stone stairs descended to the city, dark in the night. Somewhere down there, Hitchins lay, probably asleep, expecting to escape to France.

Where will the barracks be? I'll follow the soldiers. When they go off duty, they'll retire to the barracks.

After weeks of bombardment, the city seemed to be composed more of ruins than of buildings. MacKim negotiated the stairs, knowing he was instantly recognisable in his kilt. "If they see me, they'll kill me, or think I'm a deserter."

Grumbling voices echoed in the night, combined with the tramp of heavy boots. MacKim eased into the angle of two buildings, remaining still as a squad of soldiers trudged past. Heads down, they dragged their feet, their grey-white uniforms gleaming through the dark. One man lagged behind the others, limping a little.

"Wait for me, lads," the laggard begged, as his companions hurried out of the rain.

"Monsieur," MacKim called softly. "Monsieur."

The soldier stopped. "Who's there?"

"It is I," MacKim said. "Over here."

The Frenchman peered into the dark. "Come out!"

MacKim kept silent. When the laggard stepped closer to investigate, MacKim cracked him over the head with a stone, hitting him until the man slumped to the ground. "I am sorry, my friend, I hope you are not dead."

Stripping his victim, MacKim hastily changed, stuffing his kilt and scarlet tunic underneath a pile of rubble. The Frenchman's uniform was tight on his chest but longer in the leg. MacKim lifted the man's musket, fitted the bayonet and nodded. On an impulse, he thrust his tomahawk through his belt. *I must look like a gypsy beggar.*

Feeling slightly less conspicuous without his kilt, MacKim followed the sound of voices. He had no concrete plan in his head, only a vague idea that he must find Hitchins. After that, nothing else mattered. Life could take whatever course it chose. When an image of Priscilla came to him, he pushed it aside. *You are Jacob's wife.*

The city seemed hollow, like a place without a soul. After weeks of siege, and emptied of its women and children, Quebec was waiting for disaster. Whatever happened in the future, the city would never be the same again. It would not be the unconquerable heart of French Canada, the hub of French North America, the gem of King Louis, but would be forever altered with the memory of defeat, or victory.

MacKim merged with the shadows as a body of French soldiers passed, some marching smartly, others bow-shouldered, a few nursing wounds. MacKim examined every face without success. He wished now that he had questioned the man from whom he had taken the uniform. He had rushed, without considering his actions.

A lone man lurched past, his stumbling steps indicative of drunkenness. MacKim waited until he was close and stepped forward.

"The Bearn Regiment?" MacKim hoped his bad French accent would be mistaken for a backwoods Canadian. "Where is the Bearn Regiment?"

"Are you lost?" The drunkard stared at him through red-rimmed eyes.

"It's the ruined buildings," MacKim deliberately slurred his words, "and the rum." He decided to take a chance. "I have a message for the Englishman, Hitchins."

"Oh, the turncoat." The drunkard did not seem surprised. "You're in luck, monsieur. He was on duty with me. He's down that way. If you hurry, you'll catch him." The drunkard smiled, produced a leather bottle from inside his jacket and drank copiously. "*Vive le Roi!*"

"*Vive le Roi.*" Twisting through the narrow streets, MacKim saw a group of men ahead, walking towards him. Even in the rain and half-light, MacKim knew that the largest one was Hitchins. He could sense the evil in the man. Sliding into the doorway of a ruined house, MacKim waited. A soldier walked on each side of Hitchins, one tall and slender, the other with a barrel chest and his face tattooed with gunpowder in the fashion of the Canadians.

Three to one, but I have the advantage of surprise.

"Monsieur," MacKim whispered from the shadow of the house. "Come here."

All three men turned to face him. "Who's that?" The tattooed man spoke with a hoarse voice. MacKim noticed the old scar on his throat and wondered if it had been a British bullet or the tomahawk of an Indian that had damaged his vocal cords.

"It's me." MacKim guessed that the Canadian was the most dangerous of the three. *Get rid of him first, then the slender one.* MacKim stared at Hitchins, remembering that day on the moor at Culloden. The face was so familiar, despite the bitter lines of age and hardship. Hitchins' eyes were never still. They roved from side to side as if seeking redemption for a lifetime of sin.

"Who?" The Canadian stepped forward with his musket held ready. "Come out of there!"

Wordless, MacKim lunged forward. The point of his bayonet took the Canadian in the chest and slid in easily. Twisting the blade, MacKim sliced it out at an angle, creating a wide wound from which blood spurted. The Canadian died instantly, with only a small grunt of surprise.

The slender man reacted faster than MacKim had expected. Rather than backing away, he grabbed for MacKim's musket. Dropping the weapon, MacKim lifted the tomahawk from his belt and crashed it on the Frenchman's head. The force of the blow split the man's skull open, so he fell at once.

"What the hell are you doing?" Reverting to his native English, Hitchins had withdrawn two paces and levelled his musket. "We're Frenchmen like you," he said, this time in French. "*Vive le Roi!*"

"*Vive le Roi,*" MacKim said as he disengaged the tomahawk. "You are correct, Monsieur Hitchins, I am as French as you are."

"You're English!"

"No," MacKim shook his head, "I'm Scottish." Knocking aside Hitchins' musket with the back of his tomahawk, MacKim followed through with a straight elbow to the jaw that sent Hitchins to the ground.

"What's to do?" Hitchins looked up, more in astonishment than fear.

"Keep quiet," MacKim said, "or I'll burn you to death. Nothing would give me greater pleasure, I assure you." Placing the bloodied blade of the tomahawk at Hitchins' throat, MacKim crouched at his side. "You are Nathanial Hitchins are you not, now of the Bearn Regiment, formerly of Webb's Foot?"

"Who are you? How do you know my name?" Hitchins tried to pull back from the blade at his throat.

"I am Hugh MacKim of Fraser's 78th Highlanders, formerly Hugh MacKim of the Fraser clan that fought at Culloden Moor." MacKim waited for a moment. "I see the name means nothing to you."

Hitchins shook his head. "No, nothing at all."

"You were at Culloden." MacKim pressed the blade of his tomahawk deeper, cutting the flesh of Hitchins' throat. "Do you remember that day?"

"Yes."

MacKim saw the dawning fear in Hitchins' eye. "Do you remember the boy you tortured to death?"

"That was Bland." Hitchins shook his head in evident fear. "He set a flame to the boy."

"I remember," MacKim said. "You helped, watched and laughed. Do you remember the child your companion held and forced to watch?"

Hitchins shook his head. "No."

"You were there," MacKim reminded him. "I was the child. You did nothing, while Hayes held me and Bland tortured my brother to death."

Hitchins was shaking in fear. "I wanted to help, but I couldn't. It was Bland. He made us do it."

"Bland is dead. He died of fever. Osborne is dead, the Indians killed him. Hayes is dead, I killed him myself, and that leaves you. Can you think of any reason why I should leave you alive?"

"Bland was to blame," Hitchins said. "He made us do it."

"That may be so. That is not sufficient reason to leave you alive." MacKim increased the pressure of his tomahawk, digging the blade deeper into Hitchins' throat.

"I can tell you something that you don't know!" Hitchins' words came out as a strangled scream as his blood dripped from the tomahawk blade.

"Tell me." MacKim relaxed the pressure slightly.

"If I do, will you let me live?"

"I don't think so," MacKim said. "If you don't tell me, I'll cut out your tongue and burn you to death slowly as the savages do."

"Please! Bland is still alive!" Hitchins said, his voice rising in terror. "He's not dead!"

Despite himself, MacKim relaxed the pressure of his tomahawk. "Alive? Tell me more, Hitchins."

"Yes. Bland is still alive. He caught fever but recovered."

MacKim felt the hatred build up inside him. Of the four murderers, he wanted Bland the most. "Where is he now?"

"He's still in the army, unless he's died since." Hitchins' voice rose as MacKim increased the pressure of his tomahawk. "He got badly burned and joined another regiment."

"Which one?" MacKim tried to remember Bland's face. The corporal had kept his Grenadier's mitre hat tilted over his face forward and had stayed further back, so MacKim wondered if he could recognise him even if he met him.

"Your one," Hitchins said. "He joined Fraser's Highlanders."

MacKim shuddered. "Bland was English." He tried to think of a badly burned Englishman in the 78th. There were none.

"No." Hitchins shook his head violently. "He was as Highland as you are. Please."

"I don't know a Bland in the regiment," MacKim said.

"He would return to his own name," Hitchins said. "He took a different name when he joined an English regiment."

"What was his name? If he is still alive, I will find him."

"I don't know," Hitchins said. "I know he was all scarred and he's in Fraser's." He gave a twisted smile as if to ingratiate himself. "I've seen you with him more than once."

All scarred and often with me. "Chisholm," MacKim said as he cut Hitchins' throat. "James Chisholm." He stood up. *So that was why Chisholm befriended me, he knew who I was. And that was why Chisholm has been trying to dissuade me from my revenge.*

All the clues were there. MacKim remembered some of Chisholm's earlier words: "Well, don't even consider promotion. I was a corporal once." *He told me he'd been a corporal, and a Grenadier.*

"Yes, I was a Grenadier for a couple of years. I found them an arrogant, big-headed bunch," Chisholm had said. *How could I have trusted him? No wonder Chisholm is always guarded about his past.*

Feeling the sickness of betrayal, MacKim watched dispassionately as Hitchins choked to death on his own blood.

26

QUEBEC, SEPTEMBER 1759

*C*hisholm: the veteran who has befriended me from my first day
in the army. James Chisholm, the colleague who taught me
many of my skills and the friend who stood by me and saved
my life on more than one occasion. Is he Corporal Bland?

Stepping over the body of Hitchins, MacKim retraced his
steps, collecting his uniform on the way. Nobody spoke to him or
tried to stop him, while the frequent squally showers helped
cover him as he climbed back over the wall.

I can't believe that Chisholm is Bland. MacKim changed in the
shelter of the fallen rubble, retrieved his musket and made his
cautious way back to camp. *I'll have to check before I do anything. I
can't just take the word of Hitchins.*

"Password!" The British sentries proved to be more alert
than the French had been.

"Success," MacKim said, and then quickly altered it to
"Victory."

"Pass, friend."

As if in a dream, MacKim reported to Captain Cameron and
returned to his tent.

Chisholm lay awake on his cot. "You gave up your mad
attempt then, Corporal?"

"No." MacKim threw himself onto his cot. "I did not."

Chisholm pulled himself to a sitting position. "What happened?"

"I killed him."

"Holy Mother!" Chisholm stared at him. "You mean you got into Quebec, and found Hitchins?"

"Yes," MacKim said.

"You'd be a good man to tell a secret to and know that it's safe," Chisholm said. "What happened?"

MacKim glanced around the tent, where Cumming and three other men were also lying, smoking or working on their equipment. "I won't tell you here. Hitchins did say that Bland was still alive."

"Bland is alive?" Chisholm looked shocked. "You told me that he died of fever."

"Not according to Hitchins." MacKim fought the various emotions that ran through him. Was Chisholm Bland? Or had Hitchins been lying? If Chisholm was Bland, should he kill him and fulfil his oath and walk away, or say nothing and treat Chisholm like the loyal friend he had proved to be in so many different occasions?

"Did Hitchins say anything else?" Chisholm sounded strained.

"He told me quite a lot," MacKim said. "Things that I have to think about."

"It may be better if you share your thoughts," Chisholm said.

"Tell us, MacKim." Cumming sat up on his cot. "What happened? Come on, man, the whole company knows about your oath now. You can't keep a secret in the 78th!"

"I will tell you," MacKim promised. "Once I have straightened them out in my head."

He lay down in his cot with his mind in turmoil. *If Chisholm is Bland and suspects that I know, then I am not safe.* MacKim glanced across, where Chisholm was studying him intently. "I wonder if the Indians will attack us tonight?"

"The French have surrendered," Chisholm said. "Why would they attack now?"

"I don't know how Indians think." Unsheathing his bayonet, MacKim slid it under his pillow. "I'll be prepared if they come."

One or two of the others scoffed, while Cumming quickly copied MacKim. Chisholm shook his head. "It's not the Indians you're nervous of, MacKim. What has Hitchins been telling you, man?"

"He reminded me to watch my back and trust nobody."

Placing his hands behind his head, MacKim stared at the stained canvas a few inches above his head. He lay awake until fatigue overcame him, when nightmares of Hitchins' mobile eyes, combined with Osborne's screams, haunted him. *Oh, dear God, I've given my oath. I must kill Chisholm. I cannot do anything else. If I shoot him when next we're on patrol, I'm free to find Priscilla. Maybe Jacob is dead and Priscilla is waiting.*

MacKim awoke in a cold sweat, to find Chisholm smiling down at him.

"You're a lucky man, Corporal."

MacKim struggled up. "What's the matter, Chisholm?"

"There is a letter for you, courtesy of the Royal Navy."

"A letter?" MacKim chased the sleep from his head. "I don't know anybody to send me a letter."

It was so unusual for an ordinary soldier to get a letter that a crowd gathered around MacKim to view this curiosity. "Open it, then."

A simple wafer sealed the letter, and his name was wrongly spelt on the front: *Corporal Hew Macim, 78th Hilanders. British army.*

Only one person outside the regiment knows I am a corporal. That letter must be from Priscilla.

"Open it!"

"I'll open it later." MacKim stilled the trembling of his hands.

"Open it now!"

"All right."

"Read it out!" Starved of news from outside the regiment, the soldiers crowded around MacKim to devour everything he said.

The writing was large and ill-formed, which surprised MacKim, as he thought that Priscilla was well educated. He scanned the words with his anticipatory smile slowly fading. *My frend Hew Macim*, it began. *I canott thank you enuff for saving my life and lookeing after Prisila when I was in the hospital. Now we are bac home and the rangirs say I am to stay home until I am full better. God bless you hew. God bless you.*
Jacob Wooler.

"Read it!" The men continued.

MacKim read out the words, fighting the tears that came to his eyes. He knew he should be pleased that Wooler was recovering, yet with every word, he thought of Priscilla.

Damn the man; I should have left him to the Ottowas. Now Priscilla is lost to me.

Only Chisholm understood. "You saved that man's life," he said.

"Yes. We did."

"That's something to be proud of, Hugh. That's something in your favour when you stand in front of God's Judgement Seat."

"Yes." MacKim found it hard even to say that single word.

Chisholm patted his shoulder. "I think you should let the past lie still now, Hugh. Priscilla is not for you."

"No." MacKim heard how flat his voice was. "Priscilla is not for me. I still have other things to settle."

"No, Hugh, let it lie."

When MacKim lifted his face, his eyes were unrelenting. "No, James. I will not."

"What are you men doing?" Sergeant Dingwall's harsh voice interrupted them. "Get ready! We're patrolling to ensure the road to Quebec is clear, with no nasty ambushes waiting for the column. Come on, you lazy rogues."

The men rushed out of the tent, with MacKim and Chisholm last to leave.

Stooping, Chisholm retrieved MacKim's bayonet.

He's going to kill me here and now! "What are you doing with that?" MacKim reached for his tomahawk.

Chisholm handed the bayonet over. "Dingwall will get you in trouble if you forget this, Hugh."

"Thank you." MacKim grabbed it quickly.

"What did you think I was doing?"

"I didn't know." MacKim forced a smile. "Come on, James! The nice sergeant is waiting."

He felt as if his world had collapsed; first, his friendship with Chisholm had proved a sham, and now Priscilla was unavailable. He had nothing left, except to fulfil his oath and kill his best friend.

Dingwall eyed his patrol. "We're more used to working in forests now, lads, but you Lights can operate in any terrain. I know there's a truce until all the little Frenchies have sailed home and I know the French will keep their word, but I don't trust the Canadians or the savages. If they see a long column of redcoats marching like wooden soldiers, they might be tempted to lift a few scalps. Well, we'll help them fight the temptation by guarding the flanks. If you so much as have a glimpse of a savage or a Canadian, shoot the rogue."

MacKim felt surprisingly vulnerable when he trotted into the Plains of Abraham. Most of the debris and all the casualties of the late battle had gone. Only the memories remained, and the bullet-scarred houses and trees. *I can't trust Chisholm any more. I have to keep him in view.*

The weather had worsened, with a high wind tormenting the ground with increasingly frequent showers of hail.

"Hard to fire in this," Cumming grumbled. "The rain will get up the barrel of the muskets and dampen the flint and powder."

"Good," MacKim said. "That might keep the Indians quiet."

Dividing into pairs, the Lights spread out, covering each other, ready to fire on sight, wary of every movement. MacKim tried to watch Chisholm at all times, trying not to step in front of his musket.

"Did you see something move there?" Chisholm nodded to a group of trees, shaded by the slanting rain.

MacKim shook his head. *Here we go. He'll lure me away from the others, shoot me and blame the Canadians.*

"I'm sure something moved. Cover me." Chisholm jinked ahead, moving at a low crouch with his musket at the trail.

MacKim aimed, tempted to shoot Chisholm there and then. *No; Hitchins must have been lying. It can't be Chisholm. We've fought together for too long.* With an effort, he shifted aim back to the copse of trees, squinting in his attempt to peer through the driving rain.

Is that branch moving? Or was it only rainwater dripping from above? MacKim swore. He was sure he saw somebody. If he fired and missed, then he would have alerted the enemy to his presence, and he would have to reload, during which time Chisholm was vulnerable.

Good! Let the Canadians kill him, then I'll be free, and I won't have killed the best friend I've ever known.

The branch moved again, swaying.

Aiming and firing in the same movement, MacKim rolled onto his back and began to reload. The cartridge proved obstinate, with the paper refusing to tear. He heard the bark of a musket as he fumbled, dropped black powder on the ground and thereby reducing the force of his next shot. The ramrod shook in his hand as he shoved it down the barrel before sprinkling powder in the pan and rolling back to his front to cover Chisholm, just as the shot cracked the silence. Chisholm yelled once and crumpled to the ground.

In the eighteen seconds he had taken to reload, the situation had altered. Chisholm was down, dead or wounded, lying on his face with his musket at his side while a shadowy figure was just visible within the trees.

MacKim swore, aimed at the figure and quickly fired, cursing when the hammer fell without any spark. *Damn! Damn! My powder is damp! If I reload, I'll waste time, and that man could finish off Chisholm, unless he's already dead.*

Leave Chisholm to the Indians! He might be Bland.

Swearing, MacKim dashed forward, trying to fit his bayonet at he ran. With no pretence at concealment, he waited for the blast of the musket and the stunning force of the lead ball. He had seen the effects too often to have any illusions. The ball would tear into him, flattening on contact with bone to create a hideous wound. He would be knocked backwards, at first too shocked to scream and then the pain would begin. He would lie there, helpless, as the Indian or Canadian came towards him with his scalping knife in hand. Then would come the tearing agony in his scalp and, if he was lucky, a merciful knife across his throat rather than a trip to the torture fire.

There was no musket blast, no lead ball crashing into his cringing flesh. Unharmed, MacKim reached the fringes of the wood and dived down beside Chisholm.

"James!" MacKim stared into the trees. Between the wind, the foliage and the rain, his vision was limited. He could see no sign of anybody, Indian or Canadian. Chisholm lay still with the slow blood seeping from his head. Remembering that Chisholm had loaded and not fired, MacKim exchanged muskets.

The shot was close and MacKim's swerve was instinctive, yet the ball ripped through the outside of his left thigh. He staggered and fell, cursing, feeling the blood coursing down his leg. Fighting the pain, MacKim lifted his musket, prepared to fire at whoever emerged from the trees.

A man appeared from the slanting sleet. Tall, broad and wearing a faded scarlet jacket, he lifted a hand toward MacKim.

"Sergeant Dingwall!" MacKim lowered the musket. "Thank God! Be careful, Sergeant, the Canadians are around."

Dingwall crouched at MacKim's side, his face full of concern. "Will you live?"

"Yes, Sergeant. It's only a graze."

"I heard a whisper that you visited Quebec yesterday."

"I was on patrol, Sergeant. Be careful. The Canadians are watching."

"I know that, MacKim. I heard that you went inside the walls and spoke to a deserter."

MacKim frowned. "Who told you that, Sergeant?"

"Never mind who told me!" Dingwall glanced over his shoulder as if watching for the enemy. "You met Nathanial Hitchins!"

MacKim wished he had not spoken so much the previous evening.

"What did he tell you, MacKim?" Dingwall held his musket in both hands, his seamed, bronzed face close to MacKim. Something about his stance triggered a memory within MacKim. He remembered seeing the great scar on Dingwall's chest when he had checked for wounds when the spent musket ball hit him. *The injury, the rank and the size! Oh, dear God in heaven!*

"It was you," MacKim said. "You were the corporal at Culloden. You murdered my brother!" *He is the scarred Corporal Bland. Thank God it's not Chisholm.* MacKim reached for his musket, only for Dingwall to kick it away.

"That's right, MacKim. I killed your brother for the treacherous Jacobite dog that he was, and do you know something?" Dingwall pressed his face closer to MacKim. "I enjoyed every moment."

"You bastard, Dingwall!" MacKim struggled to sit up until Dingwall placed his nailed boot on his chest and pushed him back down.

"Lie there. What did you do with Hitchins?"

"He's dead, Dingwall, or Bland, or whatever your name is." MacKim winced as Dingwall pushed down harder. "I killed him like I killed Hayes and saw Osborne dead as well. Only you remain, Bland, and I'll kill you as well."

Dingwall's laugh took MacKim back to Culloden and the smell of burning flesh. "I rather fancy that it is I who will do the

killing, MacKim. I'll finish off the entire MacKim brood."
Removing his boot, Dingwall stepped back, dropped his empty
musket and lifted the weapon MacKim had dropped. "I'll shoot
you, MacKim. I'll shoot you in the stomach, so you suffer for
hours."

"You bastard, Dingwall!" Twisting to one side, MacKim
threw his tomahawk. He watched the weapon as if in slow
motion, as the blade missed the sergeant's head by a finger's-
width, with the handle catching him on the temple. It was only a
glancing blow, but enough to made Dingwall stagger and drop
the musket. Ignoring the pain in his leg, MacKim pulled himself
upright, grabbed the musket and pulled the trigger.

Once again, the weapon misfired with a puff of smoke and
nothing else. By that time, Dingwall had lifted the musket he
had dropped.

"Now we both have empty muskets and bayonets, MacKim. I
bayoneted three rebels at Culloden, I thrust my blade in deep
and danced in their blood." Dingwall circled, with his bayonet
pointing at MacKim.

"You're worse than any of the Indians." MacKim held the
bayonet at the ready, expecting Dingwall to lunge forward. He
remembered his mother's words. "*We can excuse the English-speakers; they are brought up in ignorance. When one of our own turns against
us, they are worse than the devil.*"

"You're a traitor to the King," Dingwall said.

"I've fought and bled for King George," MacKim reminded
him.

"You only joined the army to murder four men," Dingwall
said. "I've watched you, MacKim, and I've had you watched. I
know about your murder list. You're no soldier. You're only a
killer."

Is he trying to taunt me? Does he expect me to attack him?

"Why do you think I recommended you for the Lights,
MacKim?" Dingwall was sneering as he circled MacKim, his
eyes narrow and bayonet ready. "Did you think it was because

you were a good soldier? No! It was so you could get killed. You were my Uriah the Hittite, sent to the forefront of the battle."

"It didn't work, Dingwall," MacKim said. "All you did was increase my skills." He felt his wounded leg stiffening. *I'll have to finish this quickly before my leg is useless.*

"I tried to shoot you already, MacKim, when you were on patrol," Dingwall said. "And now here you are, with me, crippled and alone."

MacKim remembered the time outside Montmorency when a redcoat had fired at him. That had been Dingwall. "You're all tongue, Dingwall. Come on then!" MacKim feinted and withdrew.

"I gave you a wrong password last night," Dingwall said. "I knew you were up to something." He stood still. "But it seems I'll have to kill you myself."

"You have a longer tongue than a blade." MacKim circled, limping, favouring his injured leg.

Dingwall remained static. "I'll wound you, MacKim. I'll rip you so you lie on the ground, and I'll set you alight as I did to your brother. You'll die screaming."

At the mention of Ewan, MacKim lunged forward, twisting the bayonet as he thrust at Dingwall's belly. He heard himself shouting, the sound formless, without meaning, a call of hate from deep within him.

Vastly experienced, Dingwall parried MacKim's bayonet and held him, face to face and chest to chest. The blow to his head took MacKim by surprise. He staggered as somebody came from behind him.

"Do you want me to kill him, Sergeant?" Cumming was grinning as MacKim tried to regain his balance.

"No." Dingwall pushed MacKim to the ground. "I'll do that."

Dazed, MacKim looked up. "Cumming, what are you doing?"

"Helping the sergeant." Cumming's grin widened. "I always help the sergeant. I told him about you going into Quebec."

"There's promotion in it for you, Cumming," Dingwall said. "There'll be a vacancy for a corporal in a few moments."

"Dingwall's a murderer, Cumming," MacKim said.

"So are you," Dingwall reminded him. "Osborne, Hayes and Hitchins, remember?"

So this is it. I failed. Bland will kill me as he killed Ewan.

Lifting his bayonetted musket, Dingwall positioned himself above MacKim's stomach. "I'd like to burn you, MacKim, but this will have to do."

The tomahawk whirled from the depths of the trees. MacKim saw the flicker of metal an instant before it buried in Cumming's back.

"Indians!" Dingwall lowered his bayonet and ducked behind a tree. "MacKim, guard my back. We'll finish this later."

MacKim rolled sideways, lifted Cumming's musket and forced himself upright. After one step, his injured leg gave way, and he yelled, fell to the ground and crawled forward. Skidding behind a rock, he searched the woodland for any sign of the enemy. Dingwall had dropped his empty musket and held a short-barrelled pistol in his hand, peering through the trees.

"I see him," Dingwall whispered. "Over there."

MacKim saw the figure standing static among the trees. He was short for an Indian and very familiar. *Tayanita.*

Dingwall levelled his pistol, thumbed back the hammer and aimed.

MacKim fired. The musket kicked back against his shoulder as the muzzle flare momentarily dazzled him. He saw the ball strike an inch above Dingwall's head, sufficiently close to make the sergeant flinch and prematurely press the trigger of his pistol. MacKim did not see where the ball went. He did see Tayanita run forward with a large knife in her hand. Swearing, MacKim rose, fell as his injured leg refused to take his weight, rose again and hopped forward to where Tayanita faced Dingwall.

Lithe and agile, Tayanita ducked low and sliced upwards with her knife, but Dingwall was a veteran of many years in inter-regimental fights and savage campaigning. He caught Tayanita's wrist, twisted and threw her against the trunk of the nearest tree. Tayanita landed with a heavy thump, remained static for a second and slashed sideways. Again Dingwall blocked, this time twisting Tayanita's wrist backwards until she dropped the knife.

That was when MacKim arrived. Fighting the pain in his leg and using the musket as a club, he smashed the butt against the back of Dingwall's head. Rather than fall, the sergeant slammed his elbow backwards, catching MacKim under the jaw. MacKim staggered, retained his hold of the musket and swung again, missing as Dingwall swooped low.

"I've fought French whores who were tougher than you, MacKim!" Dingwall scooped up Tayanita's knife and slashed at MacKim's wounded leg. The renewed pain forced MacKim back a pace, swearing and limping heavily. Dingwall followed up, kicking with his nailed boots. MacKim fell, holding up his musket in defence.

Grabbing Tayanita by the hair, Dingwall lifted her bodily, threw her face down to the ground beside MacKim and planted his right boot on her back. "Do you remember what I did to your brother, MacKim?" He towered over MacKim. "I'll do the same to you, then break in this savage and hand her to the Grenadiers as a whore."

As if in a dream, MacKim heard the rat-a-tat-tat of drums from the far-away British camp as the army prepared for the occupation of Quebec. That seemed like a different world as he fought his private war. Dingwall seemed to have checkmated him, as Chisholm would have said.

MacKim rapidly assessed his situation. He was twice wounded and bleeding, while Tayanita lay glowering in hatred with Dingwall grinding his nailed boot into her back. *Ignore the pain. Dingwall murdered my brother and altered the course of my life. I won't allow him to murder Tayanita as well.*

Bending forward quickly, MacKim sunk his teeth into the

calf of Dingwall's leg. He knew he only had a second before Dingwall jerked away, so he released his jaws as soon as he tasted blood.

The unexpected pain distracted Dingwall just long enough for MacKim to swing the barrel of his musket hard between Dingwall's legs. As the sergeant stiffened and doubled over, MacKim twisted free, balanced on his one good leg and scrabbled for Tayanita's fallen knife.

"Hugh!" Tayanita had rolled away. Lifting the knife in her left hand, she advanced slowly towards Dingwall.

"Give me the knife, Tayanita." MacKim held out his hand. "I have an oath to keep."

Tayanita looked at him for a long moment, her eyes dark as Dingwall crouched, moaning and nursing himself. With a brief nod, she reversed the blade and presented the handle.

"You haven't the guts." Dingwall tried to straighten up, his eyes dark with agony.

"You murdered my brother," MacKim said quietly. "A life for a life."

He expected Dingwall's lunge and countered with a sidestep. Dingwall seemed to move in slow motion, swinging for MacKim's head with a massive fist before he scrabbled for the discarded musket. Ducking the punch, MacKim plunged the knife into Dingwall's neck and sliced sideways.

The sergeant crumpled, dead before he hit the ground.

"He died too quickly," Tayanita said.

"I have no love for torture." MacKim suddenly felt hollow. His mission was complete; his oath fulfilled. He had no more reason for existing. He had lost Priscilla, Chisholm was dead and fighting the king's war held no appeal at all.

"There are reasons for it," Tayanita said. Kneeling, she scalped Dingwall with a few expert slices, ripping off the bloody trophy with frightening skill. "Come away with me, Hugh MacKim. You don't belong here."

"I'll have to see James decently buried," MacKim said.

"Your friend is not dead," Tayanita said.

Chisholm leaned against a tree, congealed blood disguising his hideously scarred face. "What will you do now, Hugh?"

"James!" Despite his wounds and the twisted body of Dingwall on the ground, MacKim could not restrain his grin. "I thought you were dead."

"Not yet." Chisholm glanced at Dingwall. "Was that Bland then?"

"Yes. That was Bland."

Chisholm nodded. "Answer my question, Hugh. What will you do now?" His face twisted into a smile. "I can't see you hankering for promotion to sergeant."

"He will come with me." Tayanita hung Dingwall's scalp from her waist as if it was a fashion accessory. "I've known that since we first met."

"I will go with Tayanita," MacKim agreed without hesitation, although he felt as if he were betraying Chisholm. "I joined the army to avenge my brother. I've done that. I've no interest in killing strangers to help decide which king claims what piece of land that neither have any right to."

"You'll be a deserter," Chisholm warned. "You could be hanged."

MacKim nodded to the west. "They're welcome to try and find me. It's a big country." He glanced at Tayanita, who was listening to them without comprehension. "James, come with us. Please."

Chisholm touched a hand to his scarred face. "I'm a soldier, Hugh. It's the only life I know, and Harriette expects me back."

"Harriette?"

"I'll be husband number four, Hugh. She doesn't care about my face."

MacKim took a deep breath. "I'm glad you won't be alone."

"You're never alone in a Highland regiment." Chisholm indicated Tayanita, who was tapping her feet on the ground. "Your woman is growing impatient."

"We'll get upriver before the regiment notices I'm missing. With luck, people will think the Indians got me."

"They did get you." Chisholm held out his hand. "Good luck, Hugh."

"Thank you." Their handshake was firm. "Good luck to you, too, James." MacKim hesitated. "When Hitchins said he had seen me in the company of Bland, I thought it was you."

"I guessed that," Chisholm said.

"You have my apologies, James."

"No need for that," Chisholm said. "You'd better be on your way. This place will be busy with soldiers soon and all the pomp and parade of victory."

"Come on, Hugh," Tayanita urged. "Before the redcoats come."

MacKim's task was done, his oath fulfilled. Now, the vast lands of the west beckoned, a new start in a new world. He watched Tayanita for a second and followed her into the trees.

HISTORICAL NOTE

Simon Fraser, Master of Lovat, raised the old 78th Highlanders in 1757, during the Seven Years War with France (also known as the French and Indian War.) Simon Fraser, who later rose to General rank, was the son of the unlucky Lord Lovat, who took part in the 1745 Jacobite rising and who the Hanoverian government executed, while confiscating his lands. Around 600 men joined the 78th from what had been the clan lands, and about 800 from the neighbouring territories.

The old 78th were originally raised as the 63rd Foot or the Second Highland Battalion of Foot. They fought at Louisbourg in 1758, Montmorency and Quebec in 1759, wintered through the siege of Quebec in 1759 and 1760, fought at the Battle of Ste Foy in 1760, were present at the capture of Montreal in 1760 and were disbanded in Canada in 1763. They were not related to the later 78th Highlanders, the Ross-shire Buffs, raised in 1793 during a later French war, and which became the Seaforth Highlanders.

Dear reader,

We hope you enjoyed reading *Blood Oath*. Please take a moment to leave a review in Amazon, even if it's a short one. Your opinion is important to us.

Discover more books by Malcolm Archibald at https://www. nextchapter.pub/authors/malcolm-archibald

Want to know when one of our books is free or discounted for Kindle? Join the newsletter at http://eepurl.com/bqqB3H

Best regards,

Malcolm Archibald and the Next Chapter Team